All About Laura

Susannah Bates was born in Suffolk in 1970. While reading English at Durham University, she co-wrote her first play, *Smoke*, for the Edinburgh Fringe where it was nominated for the Guardian Student Theatre Award. She then went on to study law in London and qualified as a solicitor in 1997. She practised law in the City until she gave up to become a full-time writer. *Charmed Lives*, her first novel, was published in 2001.

Acclaim for Susannah Bates:

'Penny Vincenzi fans will devour this – unputdownable' Louise Bagshawe

'This is the kind of book that will keep you page-turning for hours! It's well-plotted, compelling and not at all predictable' *Woman's Realm*

'Susannah Bates weaves together an engaging tale of lust, money and finding love in unexpected places' *New Woman*

'If you loved *Four Weddings and a Funeral*, this novel about a circle of glamorous friends, their tragedies and loves is definitely for you' *Woman & Home*

Also by Susannah Bates

Charmed Lives

All About Laura

Susannah Bates

ARROW

Published by Arrow Books in 2002

1 3 5 7 9 10 8 6 4 2

Copyright © Susannah Bates 2002

First published in the United Kingdom in 2002 by Century

Addresses for companies within The Random House Group Limited can be found at:
www.randomhouse.co.uk/offices.htm

The Random House Group Limited supports The Forest Stewardship
Council (FSC®), the leading international forest certification organisation.
Our books carrying the FSC label are printed on FSC® certified paper.
FSC is the only forest certification scheme endorsed by the leading
environmental organisations, including Greenpeace. Our
paper procurement policy can be found at
www.randomhouse.co.uk/environment

Printed and bound in Great Britain by Clays Ltd, St Ives PLC

The Random House Group Limited Reg. No. 954009

www.randomhouse.co.uk

A CIP catalogue record for this book
is available from the British Library

ISBN 0 09 941505 4

Typeset by SX Composing DTP, Rayleigh, Essex

for my parents

Acknowledgements

Thanks to the following for the help they gave me during the research and writing of this book: Grainne Ashton; Oliver Bates; Annabel Bates; Ron Beard; Simon Berry; Charlotte Bicknell; Charlotte Bush; Jo Craig; Anna Dalton-Knott; Charlotte Eagar; Sue and Chris Hewitt; Yvonne Holland; Sandra Horley; Luciana Lussu; Shane Khan; Marcus Martineau; Daisy Meyrick; Katie McKay; Annabel Sebag Montefiore; Victoria Sebag Montefiore; Eloise Napier; Alex Oddy; Kate Shaw; John Stockdale; Katharine Thornton; Clare de Vries; Algy and Pasha.

In particular, I should like to thank my agent, Clare Alexander, and my editor, Kate Elton – for the way they have worked with me to bring out the best in my writing. I should like to thank my parents for their endless support and encouragement and, of course, Robin – for his patience, his enthusiasm, and for keeping me calm.

Part One

1

In the next street, a clock was striking the hour. David Nicholson stood at his easel, eyes on the canvas as he listened to the chimes.

Four – five – six –

David waited, and the silence told him what he needed to know. He had an hour.

Wiping each brush in turn with a piece of rag he'd torn from an old sheet – it didn't disintegrate in his hands like kitchen paper – David decided that the picture was finished. Even by Enderby's standards. He wasn't going to do any more, and he could use the time to start cleaning up. Fine, it was only a studio, it didn't need to be spotless, but nor could he work properly in air that was clogged by dust, paint, and the toxic smell of turps.

He'd been making yellow ochre that morning, taking scoops of powdery pigment, finer than flour, from one of the heavy glass vessels that sat on the shelf above his worktop and then crushing it into the pool of cold-pressed linseed oil on the marble surface. He'd worked meticulously but hadn't been able to stop random particles of colour slipping away from the surface of marble, swept off and up by invisible ripples in the air. Antique pinpricks of gold, ageing the light and settling on upper edges all over the room: the horizontal ridges in the skirting boards, backs of chairs, rims on taps, the upper line of his raised forearm, the tiny hairs on the back of his hand.

It was only after he'd finished and was filling the empty tubes, scraping and shovelling fresh paint into each one, taking care to loosen the lids for the air to flow out as the paint went in, that David felt the ache in his arm. Artists these days bought their oil paints ready-made, and in truth the difference in quality was so slight that David had begun to wonder why it was that he bothered to make his own, except that he liked to control his materials. And despite aching muscles and stiffened fingers, he liked the rhythmic grinding process. It could trick the mind up a level, to a place where his instincts could breathe, where concentration was at its purest.

Not that that had happened today.

David stood back from his easel to examine the canvas he'd been working on. Alice Enderby's father had insisted David fill in the dress. 'It's not finished,' he'd said, staring at an area of canvas just below the centre and then pointing at it. 'Look.' Enderby hadn't seen that blocking the colour like that would kill any movement. He'd wanted the gold lamé properly done, as if he thought David was being lazy, or stingy with his paints.

Still holding a couple of brushes, David went to one of the windows and opened it. It was an upper window operated by a Victorian pulley system and it rattled swiftly out. Looking at the portrait from a

4

distance, David gave the larger brush an absent-minded wipe. Alice's dress was now solid, with everything explained and nothing suggested. Enderby would have the picture he'd commissioned and he was welcome to it. For two thousand pounds, David could hardly complain.

He went over to another part of the room and examined the picture again, this time through a disembodied wing mirror he'd yanked off his first car before selling it for scrap. It helped him to see his paintings fresh, and the shrinking glass drew his eye to any fault with balance or perspective. A diminished studio flashed into its frame for a second – slanting windows, a diagonal line of ceiling – before David found the easel, and the rectangular image of Alice. He centred her within the rectangle of the wing mirror.

It was fine. A tall picture. A tall girl with pale skin in a short gold dress, standing there in her high heels. Like a prostitute, really.

A solid prostitute.

David put the mirror down. He went over to the sitting-room area of his studio, threw himself into the armchair by the fireplace and shut his eyes. He was uncomfortable with the thought that he might have tried harder, that today was not the day to be doing this. He'd been distracted, thinking too much about Alice's behaviour at yesterday's sitting when he should have been channelling his concentration in a real attempt to finish the picture without letting it go hard.

What he needed, he knew, was the dress in front of him, here and now, with Alice in it and the floor beyond. He needed those all-important details: that long slim shadow of her arm against the gold body, a whisky-dark line that described the form of breast, ribs and belly as much as the form of the arm, a line that shrank and intensified at her wrist; or the dotted quality of light on the lamé, how it altered as the material pulled at her hip. Lost details that made her real.

Still slumped in the armchair, David opened his eyes. He looked across the room, over the edge of a sofa, the surface of a table, on through to his work area, the canvas drawing his eye like a magnet and then repelling it just as powerfully back into his paint-spattered lap. There were things he'd fudged. And although they were only apparent to him, David knew that it would have been a better picture – more confident, more precise – if he'd put aside yesterday's difficulties and insisted that Alice come for a final sitting.

But while he wanted her there in the flesh, David didn't want the person inside. He didn't want the trouble. Alice having school had given him the excuse he needed to indulge personal disinclination over artistic standards, and he'd fallen back on memory. Faulty memory. It was hard to concentrate on the precision of Alice's skirt – slippery and asymmetrical, wrapped around her narrow hips, set against the impression of rug (he was damned if he was going to fill that in too) that flattened the floor all the way to the wall and the door half open beyond. Hard to do that properly when rather less static memories of Alice kept jolting the image about.

Harder still to block out what was really there,

outside and around. He'd had to pull down the calico blinds to shut out a real and seductive Indian summer sun that crept through the gaps, spreading abstract stripes of light across the studio space.

David looked at the mass of empty jam jars he used for his turps, thrown carelessly into the sink along with a collection of brushes, bits of rag and a couple of mugs of cold coffee. It was going to take him at least an hour to sort that out. Then there was all that dust and powder everywhere and, of course, there was himself. He needed to get out of these jeans – so stiff with paint that he'd long stopped bothering to wash them – wash away the smell of turps, shave, then put on his dinner jacket and that stifling black bow tie. Pouring the remains of heavy-grey turpentine from the jam jars into the square base of his sink, sluicing it away with water, rinsing the jars and putting them upside down on the draining board, David decided that he couldn't think of anything he'd rather do less than go to Mel's office party.

He began cleaning his brushes, starting with the smallest, rattling each one separately in a fresh jar of turps, fiddling with the sable bristles so that every last speck of paint was gone, then wiping them with rag and putting them away in the terracotta vase to his right, heads up. Then, reaching high, he lifted the canvas away from the easel – Alice Enderby flat and hanging to one side as he carried her to the wall and placed her face in.

He was washing his hands again when the doorbell rang. Half expecting the cab, maybe even Mel, David picked up the intercom receiver – covered in old fingerprints of grey dry paint – and held it to his ear.

Alice.

'David . . .' she sounded out of breath, 'David, I'm early, I know, but – but could you let me in?'

Wondering what she meant by 'early', David buzzed Alice in, opened the studio door and waited there, picking the dirt out of his fingernails.

Troubled by the thought that perhaps he was to blame – it had been important to get her to talk so, yes, maybe he had been flirting, but nothing serious, nothing that would make her think he'd welcome that kind of advance – David prayed she wouldn't try it again. He'd made it clear to her yesterday, hadn't he? Surely she'd understood, but he couldn't assume anything with Alice. He didn't know how the mind of a seventeen-year-old girl worked. And as she turned the corner of the staircase, her footsteps getting louder, David braced himself. Until he noticed the milk-mild expression.

He opened the door a little wider, 'Come in', and followed Alice into the room.

She was dressed in her self-imposed uniform of denim jacket, a short stretch black miniskirt with spilt cappuccino marks on the side, black opaque tights, and dark chunky shoes. She had a black nylon school bag slung over her shoulder, and she was wearing make-up. She kissed him on the cheek. Rather too close to his mouth, but at least it wasn't *on* the mouth.

'Hello.'

'Hello.'

He watched her stare at the empty easel.

'Where is it then?'

'It's here,' he said, pointing to the tilted back of the canvas. 'Done.' He pulled back the canvas for Alice to

8

see. 'Just a bit more to the skirt of your dress, and the background, see?'

Alice came close and stood bent to one side, so that she could see herself straight. To her, it looked exactly the same.

'Now listen,' David concentrated on propping the canvas back against the wall, 'I'm sorry about yesterday. I really am. I must have given you the wrong idea and I can't tell you how bad I feel. But you do understand, don't you? I'm engaged. And that means I can't – I can't . . .' He straightened the canvas, and looked at her. 'Do you see what I'm saying?'

Alice leant against the wall and grinned at him.

'It's not funny.'

'Da-vid,' she unzipped her bag, 'relax. I'm not here to seduce you. I'm here to see Ned.'

'Edmund?'

'Ned. Edmund. Whatever. He's taking me out to dinner. We agreed to meet here at seven thirty, so I suppose I am a bit early, but you don't mind, do you?'

His mind tumbling, David looked at Alice rootling in her bag. Edmund was his older brother, older by five years, which made him almost twice Alice's age. David did a quick calculation: seventeen into thirty-five . . . *over* twice her age.

Edmund and Alice had met a few days ago. It had been Ned's first day in England after over two years' sabbatical, writing a book on defamation law in New York, and he was staying in David's spare room until he found a flat of his own.

The plane had arrived early at Heathrow. Edmund grabbed a cigarette in the small, squalid, designated

9

smoking area in baggage reclaim while he waited for his flight number to come up on the monitors. He sat heavily on one of the hard carpet-covered seats. A well-dressed Indian about half Edmund's weight shifted to make more room on his left while a pair of girls took up the rest of the bench on his right, both wrapped in shawls, both smoking, and complaining about the cold.

He thought of what he had to do that day: get to David's flat, have a bath (but there'd be no time to unpack), go straight to the office for a meeting with the other partner in his department. Edmund hadn't been there properly for two years, which meant that he and Martin Teviot would have to go through every bloody detail down to who had what files, what the billing targets were, who was whose secretary – blah, blah, blah – and Martin was so fucking anal.

Still in yesterday's suit, with his shirt collar open and his tie pulled down like a schoolboy's, Edmund whirled his empty trolley past a tired, sunburnt family. Three blond children sitting bleary-eyed on their suitcases while the father heaved bag after bag off the carousel and the mother redid her lipstick. Pulling his own luggage – two trunks and a computer – off the carousel, Edmund trolleyed it through customs and into one of the waiting cabs. He gave the driver David's address, got in heavily, and closed his eyes until the cab got in to London.

David had been in the middle of Alice's mouth, which was full-lipped but contained within a width no broader than that of her nose. It was this, he'd realised, that made her face look long, and he was getting quite excited by the way the likeness was coming. The light was perfect. He just wanted to catch the balance of browns, yellows and pinks that made up the shape of her lower lip – and then the doorbell had rung.

'Don't move,' he'd said, putting down his brushes.

David hated being interrupted while he was working. He found it hard to switch his mind from intense concentration to mild friendliness. And so, still thinking about the fleshy colours – how he'd use them to describe the fine variety of bone and flesh and fat and cartilage that formed the area from Alice's lower lip down to the centre of her chin – he answered the bell with a cool, 'Yes?'

'It's me!'

David smiled. 'Hello, stranger,' he said, and pressed the entry button. 'Come on up. First floor.'

'I've got quite a few cases, Davey. Would you mind giving me a hand?'

Leaving Alice in her pose, David put the door on the catch and went down to help his brother. They brought the luggage up together.

'Thanks.' Edmund kicked the second trunk in with his foot and threw his wallet on the chair by the door. 'What a fucking nightmare.'

And there was Alice, stone-still on the little dais in the middle of the room, dressed in gold. David hadn't seen Edmund in almost a year, but he knew that expression.

'Hel-lo . . .' said the transatlantic tones. 'Who's this?'

David picked up his brushes and, turning to the canvas with a fresh eye, noticed at once what he needed to do with the lower lip. 'This,' he said, 'is

Alice. But she can't talk to you. She can't move. I'm doing her mouth.'

Edmund stood watching for a moment. The studio was silent. Alice kept her mouth in position, but her curious eyes crept round in Edmund's direction until they met his. From inside his crumpled jet-lagged face, Edmund smiled.

'Alice, *please* . . .'

'It's my fault, David. I'll go and sort myself out – have a bath if that's all right. Good to meet you, Alice.'

'And you.'

'*Alice*.'

'You don't mind, do you . . .?'

David watched Alice sit on one of his sofas, take a cigarette from her bag and put it to her baby painted mouth. Hadn't Ned seen how young she was?

'Just the two of you?'

'Think so.'

David couldn't help himself. 'Why?'

'Why's he taking me? Or why am I going?'

'Both.'

Alice dragged on her cigarette as she considered her response, and exhaled quickly. 'I don't think that's any of your business.'

'Then why did you ask me if I minded?'

'Do you?'

'Yes.'

Alice smiled.

'No, Alice, I mind – but not in the way you think. Not because I'm jealous. I mind because he's more than twice your age. Your parents are trusting me to take care of you when you come here for your sittings. God knows what they'd do if they found out that my own brother was coming on to you.'

'But he wasn't.'

'Then what –'

'It was the other way round.'

'You mean you –'

'I rang him.' Alice sat back. She pulled her legs up on to the sofa and continued looking at David. 'You think I'm a child.'

'You *are* a child.'

'You think I should be a good girl. Go back to school, pass my exams, and not get into trouble. You think that it's way too soon for me to be thinking about men, which is laughable in the context of the sex-on-legs picture you've just done of me.'

'I think you should stick to boys your own age.'

Alice hunched into the back of the sofa, knees to chest as if she was cold, and brought the cigarette away from between her lips. David couldn't see her face properly, just the smoke rising in shadowy curls above her head. He knew he should be getting ready. The cab would be here for him in ten minutes.

'Is it because you think older men know what to do?' he went on. 'Do you think that we'd be somehow,' he paused, '*better* than someone your own age?'

'If you like.'

'What I'd like is for you to tell me the truth.'

'Then yeah.'

'Yeah what?'

'What you said. You know. You're older, you'd know how to – oh, fuck it, David. It doesn't matter. I'm going to lose my virginity this year one way or another. I'll just get someone else to oblige.'

'I see,' said David, trying not to appear shocked.

'Of course, I'd prefer it to be you. You're better-looking, and you're an artist, which is kind of cool. And we've got this intense thing going on: just you and me alone like this.'

David shook his head.

'But you're not interested, or too cowardly, too . . . engaged. So it's going to be Edmund. And he's not bad, really. I quite like that accent, and that big teddy-bear face.'

David thought of his brother's way with women: the way he always got what he wanted, the way it never seemed to be enough. 'Ned's no teddy bear,' he said. 'He's been with more women than I care to –'

'Excellent.'

'He's not a libel lawyer for nothing, you know. He'll have you for breakfast.'

Alice smirked.

'But you're *seventeen*.'

'So you keep saying. You know, David, for an artist you're being very uptight.' David looked away, half inclined to agree with her. On the other hand, he still felt responsible. Something wasn't right about this, and if he sounded a little prudish and parental, then . . . well, it was better than turning a blind eye. Surely. 'I'm over the age of consent,' she went on. 'I want to have sex. And I'm hoping your brother will indulge me. All right? And if you don't like it – tough.'

As she spoke, the doorbell rang. David picked up the intercom receiver. 'I'll be five minutes. . . . I know, I'm sorry. . . . Just five minutes? Thanks.' He put the receiver down. That was his cab, and he still had to change into his dinner jacket.

As he reached the iron spiral staircase in the corner, Alice lit another cigarette. David heard the careless scratch of her match. With one foot on the bottom step and a hand on the rail, he turned. 'This is crazy. You hardly know me, far less Ned.'

'That's kind of the point,' Alice replied, smiling as she watched him clatter and spiral up, first his head, then his torso, abdomen, legs, and finally his feet disappearing from view as he reached the floor above.

Mel Ashton looked at her ring, at the way it flashed and dazzled in the overhead glare of the hotel lobby as she waited for David to arrive. He was late.

Smiling at the sparkles, Mel thought of the way she'd been in the years before David. Lord, she'd have been pissed off. She'd have been fiddling around with her mobile, taking it out of her bag, checking it, wondering if she should switch it off altogether just to make him sweat, worrying that perhaps she should call him just in case he was in trouble, and then, when whoever it was arrived, she'd suddenly pretend not to mind. Probably pretend she'd only just arrived herself. She'd be all easy and sweet on the surface, while underneath she went on cursing him and wondering if this meant he wasn't serious.

Thank God those days were over. Thank God for David, for being engaged, for feeling safe. She trusted him. And in any case, there was something more important for Mel to think about right now, something that drowned out the issue of whether

David was on time, something she had to tell him tonight.

Examining the ring more closely, Mel felt a little nervous. If anyone deserved to be indignant round here, it was David. He wouldn't be expecting it. Not so soon, at any rate. He might be cross with her for not consulting him first, but it was too late really for qualms like that. And thinking through the things she'd say – the way she'd break it to him – Mel was glad that he was late. She was glad of this time to collect her thoughts, to sober up a little, glad of the privacy.

The doors turned, a warm gust cut through the air conditioning, and Mel looked up. She glanced across the hotel lobby. Someone was coming in and she thought for a moment that it might be David. David, with his low-key style – the long fringe, the old shoes, those careless clothes of his that stopped him from looking too beautiful – drifting through the doors. Drifting towards her with that preoccupied air, as if he never quite stopped thinking about his paintings, or the way things looked. An air that drew attention by its very indifference.

But it wasn't David. It was someone much shorter, a businessman with a businesslike expression, striding towards the lift.

Wiping her ring with the end of her shawl, Mel looked back at the stone, at the specks of light sparkling over its surfaces, and at the underwater-gleam of pink that sliced into its heart. To begin with, she wasn't sure she liked it. She wouldn't have chosen a ruby. Left to her own devices, Mel would have found something less dramatic, less extravagant, and she was surprised by David's choice. He was usually so careful with money, so against anything flash. She thought he'd have found something cheaper, a bit bohemian, something light and pretty with a twist. But David had told her he wanted to do it properly. His idea of an engagement ring wasn't so much a personal statement of taste, but a symbol. A lightweight ring was wrong. This was marriage. This was for keeps. This was serious . . . and Mel was touched by his attitude. She liked having a reminder of it, forever heavy on her finger.

So there it was. A ruby. A big dark ruby on a pale finger. A bit much, perhaps, for everyday hands, and after they got married she'd probably reserve it for special occasions, but until then Mel would parade her ruby. Who cared if it caught against things, got in the way, or made it difficult to wash up? She loved to spend her spare moments – like now – looking into its depths, and thinking of David and their future.

2

Asking the driver to take him to Park Lane, David sat back in his white shirt and black tie, dinner jacket on his lap. It was still too warm to wear it. The cab had no air conditioning but at least it was clean; the upholstery had an air of recent valeting and he could see where the nozzle of a Hoover had scraped at the carpet. A cardboard fir tree dangled from the rear-view mirror.

David was tall. He sat diagonally across the seats, one arm along the back, the other at the window, pristine elbow poking into afternoon traffic. Jets of air – Mediterranean soft – blustered at his face as the cab moved forward, but David didn't notice. He was thinking, still, of Alice. And of Edmund dating women half his age.

David had always expected his brother to be the one to get married first. Ned was older. And while he'd had his fair share of flings and affairs, Ned had always been able to sustain his official relationships for a respectable length of time. David was supposed to be the one with the problems.

'You're too fussy,' Ned had said to him. 'You aim too high, and that's before we get close to the real prob –'

'Too fussy?'

'Laura Taylor was completely out of your league. And she was seeing someone else. And as for that actress with the leather trousers . . . what was she called?'

'Laura.'

Edmund had laughed. 'Yes, David. But *which* Laura – or doesn't it matter?'

David had said nothing. At the other end of the line, Edmund had lit a cigarette. David had heard the click of his lighter, the smoke in his throat.

'You know what you should do? You should find a girl – any girl – just so long as she's *not* called Laura. Sleep with her. Go out with her. Be good to her. And get over this fixation.'

'It's not a –'

'It *is* a fixation, and it's ruining your life.'

And while David would never admit it directly, the truth – and he knew it – was that he did have a fixation. Ned didn't know the whole story. He didn't know how it had started and David wasn't about to tell him. David hadn't chosen to be like this and, to begin with, he'd thought it was coincidence too. But Edmund had spotted the pattern and, in doing so, had forced his brother to face up to it. Because when David looked back over the women that had mattered in his life, the ones he really fell for, it did seem a little odd that all of them should have been called Laura. Right back to the very first . . .

Of course, he hadn't really known her. She'd been one of the models in his life drawing class, and he only ever knew of her as Laura. Laura without a

19

surname. Laura whose body he knew better than he did his own: the colours of her flesh, the shape and weight of her buttocks – how they changed if she leant differently – the fine ridges of her ribs, the small square toenails. Laura about whom he had a hundred questions, but to whom he never spoke.

David had been shy in those days, and anyway, it simply wasn't on to start chatting up the models. It was fine to gaze, watch, notice, measure. From where he sat, David could hold up his pencil and measure how many times her head fitted into her body to get the proportions right. He could even sit quite close, get an unusual perspective, all in the name of art. But speaking, laughing – relating . . . that was out. Particularly with this one.

Because Laura wasn't like the other models, with their stretched faces, their full, fleshy thighs that were so satisfying to paint, their long drooping breasts, sallow skin, or the unusual look in their eyes that suggested that some of them weren't quite normal. Those models fitted with the studio, they were objects to draw, like the gnarled bits of dried wood on the shelf by the desk, or the monstrous spider plants that were yellowing and drying on the table by the window.

If Laura belonged in a studio at all, then it was that of the magazine photographer. She was smooth, slender, sleek, but with a full-lipped, full-on sexuality that she half understood and couldn't extinguish. She tried. She put on boredom, indifference, even resentment, but the contradiction between this attitude and the messages from her skin just revved the sexuality still further. She ended up assuming an attitude of detachment, as if she wasn't inside her body at all. But even that didn't really work. She wasn't ordinary enough. Her nudity wasn't about exposing what was uncomfortable or difficult or uniquely flawed about being human. It was the other variety, the glossy airbrushed species that lurked under beds of men across the city.

During the first few weeks, David had wondered why she didn't try more lucrative forms of modelling until he realised that she wasn't tall enough. She might have done glamour, he supposed, but perhaps she found that sleazy. Perhaps there was something less demeaning about posing for artists. Perhaps she was an artist herself, making ends meet with a bit of modelling on the side.

And yet, for all her beauty, not one of the students in David's class could capture it. There wasn't a single drawing that did her justice, and most of them ended up looking sentimental. There was nothing raw about the way she looked, no edge to give their pictures strength. At the end of the session, when the tutor asked them to prop their work up against the wall so that he could make his assessment, and they could see what the others had done, it was clear to them all that the rows of Lauras were quite embarrassingly bad.

David wasn't the only man in his class to notice her. There was Bob, who talked about her incessantly in the pub afterwards.

'How old do you think she is, Dave?'

'Do you think she *likes* doing it?'

'What do you think she does in her spare time?'

And then there was the other David, and Will Grieves, who'd since been successful, gone on to win awards. They'd dared one another to ask her out. Will had – almost – but he hadn't spoken very loudly, and Laura had decided not hear him, and then Will had looked round, caught the other David's eye, and chickened out. It was crossing a sacred barrier, and even Will Grieves had enough respect for it not to go on.

Laura had not stayed long at the art school. The tutor told them one day that she wasn't coming any more, and David didn't even have the courage to ask where it was she'd gone. But he went on thinking about her. He took the pictures he'd done of her and tried to use them to create one final large oil painting of Laura sitting on the studio floor, leaning back on her arms, her legs stuck out in front of her in an attitude of physical confidence that would allow him to dwell on her body – but with her head bent, to make the pose less confrontational, and more in keeping with what had been so elusive about her. Like the others, it was useless, but David kept it along with the rest of them in a large folder that sat at the back of his own studio, under the stairs. In the early years he'd look at them almost every day, but it was rare that he took them out now. He was over her.

But he wasn't over the name. David couldn't understand why it had meant so much to him. Was it because he'd never heard her speak? Was it because he didn't know her surname? Was there something in the name itself – something that seemed to capture everything he liked best about women – that drew him towards it? Or was it simply chance that all the women he'd really desired were called Laura?

After art school, there had been Laura Taylor: one

of Edmund's friends, five years older than David and simply not interested. David had a crush on her for months before he met, and this time managed to go out with, Laura Weir. Laura Weir was a watered-down version of the real Laura but with shorter hair that sprung in wisps around her face. She'd gone out with David for two years, during which time the hair had grown into a sleeker shape – one that David had preferred – but then she'd dumped him for a man in his forties.

There was Laura Thornton: the girl he'd met on holiday in Spain, the one he liked to remember in her faded blue bikini, with toffee-blonde hair, all salty and tangled. But that affair had ended with the holiday. David had been upset. He'd written to her and rung her, but it wasn't going to happen. Laura had moved on, and eventually he'd accepted that he was going to have to do the same.

And finally: that embarrassing episode with Laura Lisle the art critic, who'd thought it downright weird when David confessed the real reason he'd taken her out to dinner.

David hated his brother telling him what to do; hated it even more when Ned was right. But when, at an exhibition of his work the following week, he noticed an attractive woman standing very close to a sketch he'd done of Ned – frowning at it as if Ned had offended her as well – he remembered the challenge and decided to take it up, if only to prove Ned wrong.

'Hello.'

'Hello,' said the woman, still looking at the sketch. She was very tall, almost as tall as David, with rectangular glasses and unbrushed hair – black, rough, long – getting caught in the strap of her bag. He watched her take off the glasses, stand back from the picture, and squint at it again with an air of critical authority.

'What do you think?' he said.

'Not bad. I like the hands, but it doesn't look finished. It –'

'It isn't finished,' said David.

The woman put her glasses back on to her nose and turned to look at him. Feeling rather too much like an exhibit, David switched back to Ned on the wall: imperfect, but accurate somehow, and bold.

'But that particular sitter wouldn't sit,' he explained. 'Not still, at any rate. I kept having to alter the line there,' he pointed, 'but the looseness works, I think. He's a slap-dash kind of man.'

The woman smiled. 'OK,' she said slowly, 'let's get this right: *you* kept having to alter the line so you, I take it, are the artist?'

'That's right, and you?'

'Oh, I'm just a friend,' she said. 'A friend of –'

'Mine!' David turned to see Nathan Hunt, the gallery owner, with two glasses of wine. Nathan gave a glass to the woman and winked at David. 'Mel's a friend of mine.'

Mel. Perfect.

Nathan put an arm round her. 'Mel, this is David. David – Mel, my adored flatmate, and my friend, but only if she buys something. I'm trying to get her drunk enough to spend some of her considerable earnings –'

'Oh, come on, Nathan. I'm hardly –'

'Some of her *considerable* earnings – she's a lawyer,

by the way – on a Nicholson. I was thinking about those interiors at the back. What about the *Windows at Pouilly*? Would look great above the fireplace . . .'

Nathan was good at his job. Noticing the direction of Mel's attention, noticing that she'd not quite moved on from the sketch of Ned, he changed tack. 'Or a portrait, Mel. Why not? Portrait of a lawyer.'

'He's a lawyer?'

'You could start a collection. Get David to do one of you as well, and –'

Mel glanced at Nathan, amusement in her eyes. 'A collection of portraits of lawyers? Are you mad?'

Liking Mel more every second, David followed them to the back of the gallery, to where his Pouilly paintings were hanging. It wasn't just the name. He liked her intelligence, and her manner. He liked her height and the arc of her hairline – oval and high, high enough to see (in profile) the pale curve of her skull. Behind the sharp glasses and the touch of modern make-up, her face retained the strange simplicity of a Renaissance Madonna. He felt he could stare at it for hours. He'd like to draw it. He'd like to touch it.

But watching the way Nathan steered her, the way he touched her arm and smiled at her, David wondered suddenly if there was something more than friendship there, and felt a flash of frustration. Not a good career move, to tread on the toes of Nathan Hunt. Just his luck to fancy the one non-Laura he couldn't have.

The Hunt Gallery was still relatively new, but it was doing well. It was exactly right for David's style of painting, and Nathan's ability to sell David's work was

outstanding. What's more, Nathan had been prepared to stick his neck out, buy David's work directly
from him and then sell it on. Nathan was successful.
He was skilled, and easy to deal with. He had a good
eye, and a feel for administration that meant he could
run the gallery as a business.

But, so far as David could tell in such matters,
Nathan was not attractive. He was small, and conscious of it. And however often he cracked jokes, told
stories, or rearranged his hair – or maybe because of
those things – Nathan had no presence. He'd be right
beside you before you knew he was there. He was, in
short, no competition when it came to women.
Understanding that it would be all too easy to take
advantage of this, David felt that the last thing he
wanted to do was to put his relationship with Nathan
in jeopardy. It was better to back off. Better not to try.

But nor could he let it rest. So he stood in the
gallery that night, chatting to punters and watching
red stickers go up, but always conscious of Mel there
in the background. And, as the party drew to a close,
as people started to get their coats and leave, David's
curiosity, and a mild sense of challenge, got the better
of him.

'Hey, Nathan,' he said, catching the smaller man's
arm as he put yet another little red sticker on the
frame of one of David's paintings, 'any luck with that
flatmate of yours?'

Nathan grinned and shook his head. 'Christ, that
girl's tight with her money. Born lawyer. Told me
she'd consider it, but only if I lowered her rent.'

'So no deal?'

'No deal – not that it matters. We've sold over fifty

per cent, and I've got at least another three people interested. That couple over there, see? By the big one. And –'

'Actually, Nathan, I was just wondering – something else – could I have a word?'

'Sure,' said Nathan, indicating his office.

They went in and shut the door.

Nathan knew Mel liked him, maybe even loved him, but she didn't fancy him. He was, as she'd so often said, like a brother to her. He'd noticed at once the way she'd looked at David, the way she reacted to him. He'd seen the effortless way that David had, in seconds, slipped into a part of Mel's mind that was for ever closed to Nathan. He couldn't stand in her way. Thinking these thoughts while David spoke, Nathan opened and closed one of the drawers in his desk. And then, looking up, he smiled. 'Go for it, mate,' he said. 'No, really. Reckon you might have a chance. And there's no one else on the scene right now. No. I'm sure of it.'

Now, one year later – and much to the amusement of Edmund, who'd yet to meet her but was still convinced he'd adore 'anyone capable of fixing a mess like you, Davey, that's wonderful news!' – David and Mel were engaged. Ned was right. It was wonderful news. With Mel's unwitting help, David had been able to move on. He was no longer obsessed, no longer gripped by a name from the past. He was embarrassed he'd ever let it get so bad, embarrassed to have been affected by it for so long, and glad to be shot of it. With her rational mind and sense of humour, Mel put things into perspective for him.

Because of her, he was free. Cured. Just like everybody else.

And she was a lawyer. To David, whose late father had been a lawyer, and whose brother was now a successful libel solicitor, there was something dependable about the legal profession. While he would never have gone into law himself, and while he actively enjoyed rubbishing lawyers in front of Ned, David was secretly impressed by the combination of brains, diligence and savvy needed to do that kind of work.

If it hadn't been for his father's job, he and Ned would never have had the education, the opportunities, that made such a difference to their lives. Admittedly, they'd taken those opportunities in different directions, and David – who wasn't interested in the fast cars or expensive weekends that littered the life of his brother – had chosen the different luxury of an artist's lifestyle and a studio of his own. It was all he wanted. But he envied the security that Ned now had for himself, and would be able to pass on to some family in the future. Ned's inheritance had not been spent on a studio or living expenses. Ned could use his earned income for that. Ned could afford to rent flash apartments and eat out while his inherited money was wisely invested to accumulate and re-accumulate income in some healthy City account.

David hadn't been foolish with his money. He wasn't poor. For an artist, he was doing well. But he still didn't like to think too much about how much Ned was worth right now. Ned was getting rich. Ned's children would be able to go to any school Ned chose. And while Ned mixed with the kind of people that bored David to distraction – the kind that went shooting, or racing, or off to St Moritz for the Cresta – Ned would always have a job, always be able to make enough money.

And so, in a different way, would Mel. Mel had the dependability of Ned's career with none of the extravagance, and David appreciated it. Mel was younger than Ned, and not so qualified. She wasn't a partner, she didn't yet have the income. But even if she did have Ned's kind of money, Mel wouldn't be interested in spending it on gloss. She didn't care for the toys and games of the rich. While Ned was proud to be a lawyer – proud of the status, pleased with the money – Mel was genuinely indifferent, troubled even, by these things.

Occasionally, David would hear her on the telephone – fed up to be called at home – talking in that corporate jargon he found every bit as sexy as a foreign language. But later, when he asked her to tell him about it, a weary look would come into her eyes . . .

'You don't want to know about that, do you?'

When he told her what a great job she had, Mel would look a little surprised.

'Really?' she'd say. 'Tied to a desk all day, grappling with unreasonable client demands, and petty office politics . . . and all those *mind-numbing* documents. Have you any idea how dull they are? Here. Look at this one . . .'

He didn't believe she really disliked her job. It was tough and complex, but Mel could do it. What's more, she did it well. She was simply being modest. And thinking back to the man he was before he met her – obsessive, susceptible – David heaved a sigh of relief. Those days were over. He didn't want a goddess any more. Just a woman. A woman like Mel, with a downbeat attitude, easy humour and a sound career. The old inclinations were over, and one thing David knew for sure was that he could do without the flickering attention of girls like Alice Enderby.

3

The minicab got to Park Lane at quarter-past. Suddenly scruffy beside the car showrooms of Mayfair, it slowed down and dropped him at the door.

Mel was waiting at the desk. David could see her from outside: alone in the bright light of the hotel foyer while a couple of receptionists sat beyond, talking to each other, leaning in and laughing. She'd had her hair cut a few weeks earlier and while everybody else had said how much it suited her, David was trying to get used to it. He'd never told her – he certainly couldn't now – but he liked the long hair. Black strands over the pillows, or slunk around her shoulder in an ebony twist. He understood completely that, as a professional, maybe she needed it cut. But the lovely arc of her hairline was lost now beneath perky black dashes – upended, uneven – and David was unnerved by how much that mattered to him.

He pushed through the revolving doors, but still she didn't see him. Her head was bent in half-hearted contemplation of the floor, neck exposed, rising from the folds of an antique shawl: sheen long faded, embroidery frayed. He crossed the marble under heavy lighting: hot-bright, encrusted, set in the ceiling with hard opulence. And as he got close, she looked up.

Occasionally, David wore suits, but Mel had never seen him in black tie. Lifted by an apologetic smile, his good looks blazed unchecked, and her gut reaction was one of weakness, followed by astonishment that this man was actually going to marry her.

David tugged at his collar and gave her a casual kiss. 'Darling, I'm so sorry . . .'

Fighting the inclination to make the kiss less casual – there wasn't time – Mel shook her cropped head and put a finger over his mouth. 'Don't,' she said. 'I'm glad you're late. I'm glad we're alone. I've got something to tell you.'

David searched her expression and found it happy – demob happy. Naughty. It reminded him of Alice. And instead of letting her mood carry him up with her, he felt a resisting fear.

'What is it?'

'Buy me a drink and I'll tell you.' Mel started across the foyer towards a bar that was filling with hotel residents – dark men in pale suits – and available women. Reaching the door, she looked back over her shoulder. 'Better make it champagne!'

And, smiling a barrier over his anxiety, David followed her to the back of the bar. Mel tossed her bag and a letter on to the empty table and discarded herself into one of the chairs in a flip-twist movement of her long body. Then she began unwrapping the shawl, its yellowing tassels catching the edge of her chair, and went on, 'Actually, I've had enough champagne for one day. I'm going to have gin. You?'

'Mel.'

'Whisky?'

Not waiting for him to reply, she turned from him to the waiter. 'Gin and tonic, please, and a glass of malt and water, half-half, no ice.'

Deciding that Mel's shawl would look better on a piano, David sank slowly into the other chair. 'You're not pregnant, are you?'

'No, darling.'

'Then what?'

'I've handed in my notice.'

David checked her face again. He wanted to be sure that she was telling him the truth, sure that she was actually doing it, that this was for real. But it wasn't necessary. He could breathe her excitement. He could tell how set she was, how sure, by a quickening in her voice. Her eyes merely confirmed it.

'I've had enough,' she continued. 'I know you think it's a great career. It *is* a great career. But it's not making me happy. I need a change.'

He looked around the room: at the false panelled walls, the well-stocked bar, the neutral tones and well-kept lack of personality. His eye moved on, rested for a second on the available women, and then returned to Mel.

'. . . I need time,' she was saying. 'I need to choose my job. I want it to be my choice. For myself. To please myself – you understand? Not because my father –'

'I know Greg pushed you into law, but that doesn't automatically mean it's wrong. Surely you can see –'

'Not because my father, or my future husband, thinks that I should.'

Recognising the tone in her voice, the same broad tone of certainty he'd hear from politicians on shaky ground, David decided not to push it. He hated confronting her, hated questioning her judgement, hated having to defend himself against the articulate barrage she'd fire back – and, invariably, the more fragile her argument, the fiercer the fire. It was humiliating not to be able to match her point for point, and simpler not to try.

Letting it drop, David leant aside to let the waiter put their drinks on the soft paper mats with the hotel's logo embossed into them. He passed Mel her glass of gin and tonic – a fizzing cylinder with ice cubes that jostled with the slice of lemon, melted against the pockets of air that collected at the sides of the glass and bubbled up to the top – and took up his own quiet tumbler of whisky.

'So when are you leaving?'

'Christmas.'

'And then?'

Mel smiled. 'Who knows? Thought I might take a few months off. I could start sorting out your studio if you like – I'll temp if I have to – and then it's April, and the wedding . . . in fact, I don't think I'm even going to think about a proper job until after we get back.'

'What about money?'

'We'll get by.'

'We?'

'I've got a bit saved, and there's that money I inherited from Mum's parents – set aside by Dad for

34

when I wanted to buy a flat. And you're not doing so badly . . . don't look at me like that, David! I'm not expecting you to *keep* me.'

He gave her a diffident smile, but Mel wanted more. She wanted him to share her excitement.

'I will get a job, darling,' she said with a smile that tried to lift the reservation from his. 'I promise. But first I need a break.'

They finished their drinks and went in to the party. David had never liked office parties, and Mel handing in her notice made it infinitely worse. Before, there had been a reason. Before, he'd been happy to do whatever was necessary to help her get on. Now it was dead. He was placed next to someone from her firm's accounts department, someone who'd never met Mel and who wanted to talk about the holiday she'd just had in Spain, and a shy male trainee. David picked at his bread roll. His trousers were scratchy. His collar felt tight.

At the other side of the table, directly opposite, was Mel. David watched her with detachment. He'd never seen her so animated. She hardly touched the salmon mousse, and gave up on the chicken alto-gether. As the waitresses brought on the cheesecake, she leant across the table, arm out, to make some laughing point to a senior-looking man in glasses. He was laughing back at her. She could have been about sixteen. And with that short hair, that pink face, that mouth a great wide smile, David hardly recognised her.

He played with his cheesecake, forking it around, and his mind began to wander – away from Mel, out of the ballroom, back through the foyer and into the night. It drifted on. Back, on, and into his past. He thought of the sketches on the racks, the ones he'd long stopped looking at, and wondered vaguely if they were still there.

Mel knew that she was drinking too much. She didn't usually get drunk, she certainly didn't have a problem, but tonight was different. For the first time in years, Mel Ashton didn't need to be responsible. Who cared if she didn't look professional? Who cared if she lost control? She looked happily round the table, saw David toying grimly with his cheesecake, and realised, suddenly, that he did. He cared.

'You OK?' she mouthed.

David nodded.

'You sure?' Not waiting for him to reply, Mel got up from her seat. She walked round to him, and squatted by his chair. 'Would you like to go home?' she said. 'We can leave now, if you want.'

David looked at her.

'We can leave now, and be home by,' she checked her watch, 'by eleven. Or we can stay and dance. Or we could find a bar. Would you prefer that?'

They went back up to the bar they'd been in before. It was emptier now, and quieter. They ordered more drinks: another glass of whisky for David, and –

'Think I'd better have Coke,' said Mel.

'Really?'

She nodded.

'You don't want a Cosmopolitan or,' David picked up the cocktail menu, 'or what about a White Russian?'

'Or a Green Lawyer?' she said, laughing. 'No, thanks, darling. I'll stick to Coke. You don't really want me drunk and disorderly, do you?'

He smiled back – a good, real smile. 'Don't know about that . . .'

She sat beside him on one of the sofas, leaning against him, shoulder to shoulder, with comfortable affection. David shut his eyes. He could smell her scent and, slowly, he inhaled the associations it carried. An organised woman, maternal, effective. It was the cool calm smell he'd get in the mornings as he watched her prepare to go to work. She'd be sitting at her dressing table in her dark suit, touching her face with minimal make-up, brushing her nose with powder, and then he'd hear the soft *squirt-squirt* of her scent. And while she collected her handbag and briefcase, while she pulled on her coat, the smell would spread, suffusing the room with crisp class.

'Bye, darling,' she'd say, leaning over him, fresh and lovely, off to a world of grown-ups and responsibility. David would reach up his arms. He'd pull her in for a final kiss and, laughing, Mel would let him.

'I must go.'

'Just one more kiss.'

'David.'

'Mm – you smell lovely . . .'

Full of sudden-remembered love, David turned and kissed her, there in the open bar. Did it without thinking. And, shifting her body round, Mel kissed him back.

Kissing in the hotel bar was forbidden – it already had a dodgy reputation – but the barman decided to make an exception. He brought them their drinks and, returning to the bar, he stood with his back to them, wiping glasses. And in the low-lit enclave of the hotel sofa, with their drinks untouched beside them, Mel and David continued kissing each other and touching, with the slow attention of a couple in love.

Later, in the cab home, with Mel squashed happily in his arms, David stroked a hand through the smooth short strands of her hair, and chose not to think of her resignation, or her decision not to speak to him about it first. Why let it spoil the moment?

He thought instead of taking her to bed. They hadn't been like this – not so easy, so simply physical – in a while. David wasn't sure what had happened. Wedding plans, perhaps. Or it might have been that haircut. Or maybe it was the portrait of Alice, sapping his energy? But whatever it was, it was still a relief for him to find that it wasn't permanent. Nothing had faded. The desire was strong as ever.

Mel shifted sleepily and, adjusting her position so that it was still comfortable for him, David told himself how lucky he was to have her. It wasn't just the stability she'd brought to his life. And it wasn't just the sex. There were other things, too. Like the way they could be close, really close – just now, for instance, the way they could kiss and laugh, the sudden intimacy of it – yet give each other space.

David liked his space. He liked the way Mel left early for work, and came home late. He also liked the fact that, in spite of being engaged, Mel was still officially living with Nathan. She had a room at Nathan's flat. Her address was Nathan's address. And while she spent almost every night at David's studio, the emphasis was different and, to David, it mattered. Sure, when they married their living arrangements would change. She'd move in with him, but she'd still have her own life, just as he had his. Room to breathe was healthy. Healthy and mature.

Mel opened her eyes. 'Darling?' she said.

David stopped stroking. 'Yes?'

'I was just thinking . . . about tomorrow . . .'

'Yes?' said David, wondering what was coming. They were supposed to be visiting Mel's parents in Yorkshire that weekend, to discuss preliminary wedding plans. The date had been set aside months ago, but David wasn't looking forward to it. He found Mel's mother suffocating. There was a layer of anxiety beneath her home cooking – her excessive hospitality – that oppressed him. And as for her father . . .

To begin with, David and Greg had got on. Greg was jokey, easy-going. He'd taken David to the pub and gone out of his way to say how pleased he was to be gaining a son; how the place had always been dominated by women, how pleased he was to have someone on 'his side'. Initially David had been flattered, but he was now beginning to see through the smiles and confidences of his future father-in-law.

He didn't like the controlled atmosphere in that house. Everything they did – where they went for walks, when they got up, where they sat after dinner, what they watched on television – it always had to be Greg's idea. And that included wedding details. Whatever David had suggested, Greg would criticise or complain about the expense. If he hadn't felt so deeply sorry for Mel, for having such a ghastly man as a father, David wouldn't have agreed to go at all.

'Would you mind very much if I went alone? I just thought: I'm going to have to tell them about handing in my notice. And,' Mel sighed, 'well, what with Dad's views on the subject . . .'

'You'd prefer to handle it by yourself?'

'I don't want to mess you around, sweetheart. But I do think it might be best if I –'

'You're not messing me around,' he said, stroking her again.

'Won't you get bored?'

'Not with Ned around.'

'Oh Ned,' she said, sleepily. 'Of course. I'd forgotten about him.'

Holding her in his arms while the cab swung at a corner, David looked out at the London night. He was, as Nathan kept reminding him, a lucky man. He was lucky to have Mel. Suddenly, he felt ashamed of his thoughts at dinner, ashamed that he'd given even one second's faithless thought to those sketches on his racks: the ones of Laura, third rack from the top, at the far end of the line – wrinkling, yellowing, gathering dust. Some would be smudged, others fading, edges curling. They'd carry the suffocating smell of old paper, and it was time for David to throw them away.

He'd pick a time when Mel wasn't there, when she was working, or asleep, maybe even later on tonight, and take down the drawings. Take them all down, every last one, and throw the damn things out.

4

Edmund had been amused by Alice's call. It had come right in the middle of a conversation with Martin Teviot about a new client. Martin had had to wait while Edmund took out his diary, told Alice he was free that evening – why didn't they meet at the studio at seven thirty? – and wrote her in. He raised his head as he closed the diary and looked again at Martin.

'Where were we?'

'The thing is, Edmund, she wants you. You, and nobody else.'

Edmund took the file. It was brand new, and slim. There was just one sheet of paper inside: Martin's attendance note of a telephone conversation that morning, already signed off with the number of time units he'd spent on the file. Edmund skimmed its contents. Annabel Glass, a smart acquaintance of his who'd written a novel, had heard that he was back in London, and she was looking for legal advice on the question of how defamatory it was. Shaking his head, Edmund reached the bottom of Martin's attendance note and dropped it back on the file. He knew all about Annabel Glass and her ridiculous novel. He'd met her at a dinner party before leaving for the States, and she'd told him about it, at length.

In fact, he'd met her before, aged nineteen, in a King's Road nightclub. Annabel had been a couple of years older than Ned. He'd been mesmerised by her and so, it seemed, had everyone else. Stunning, aristocratic, way out of his league, he'd thought, as some forgettable man briefly introduced them and took her off to dance.

And now here she was in her late thirties: fading, single, desperate. Her sister, Miranda, had invited Ned to dinner and – really, he should have guessed she was up to something from the fact that he'd been invited so far in advance – everyone there was neatly married. Everyone except him and . . .

Edmund had taken one look at Annabel, seen the monumental effort she'd gone to to achieve a look that had once been natural, and wished he'd never accepted. Under the scrutiny of the other guests, he listened politely to the plot-line of her book and fidgeted his way through dinner. He left before coffee, with talk of an early morning meeting.

But the trouble with Ned was that his invented excuses were always much too convincing. He looked much too sorry – much too regretful to be leaving – and Annabel (who was still, mentally, ten years younger) smiled secretly to herself and wondered how long it would take him to call. When he didn't, she rang Miranda, got his number, and decided to help him out.

With success at university and success at work, Edmund's confidence had increased, and so had his ability to pull women. With this confidence, however, came cynicism and suspicion. Behind the bank balance and success, Ned was the same man he'd always been. Yet the tables had turned. Suddenly, those same girls that had once lit his eye with longing – the gorgeous ones who'd not given him a second glance – were now falling over themselves to get him to their dinner parties. On one level he quite enjoyed it, but it affected his respect for the very women he fancied and, because of that, he'd not been able to settle.

But while he was used to escaping women bent on marriage, Ned wasn't used to Annabel's brand of persistence. She'd called him in New York, sent him emails, updated him with the progress of her book, told him when it was listed on the Amazon website and then, finally, she'd asked him to have a look at it.

'I don't expect it's your kind of book, Ned, but I thought I could get them to send a proof copy over for you to –'

'That's so kind. But why don't I wait until it's out properly? Then I can buy it in the shops.'

'I'd really like you to read it,' she'd said.

Ned had prevaricated and circled until she told him she wanted his professional opinion.

'My *what*?'

'I'm worried it might be defamatory, Ned, darling. I need you to check it.'

'I can't do that. I'm not the right person for the job. It's not my area. I'm really not . . . Don't your publishers have a special legal department for that sort of thing?'

'Couldn't you just check it out for me?' she'd pleaded. 'As a friend?'

Edmund couldn't stomach the thought of trawling through a trivial novel by Annabel Glass. He'd never be able to charge her the proper amount. He had better things to do with his time and he didn't like the undertones.

'I'm sorry, Annabel. I'd love to help you out, I really would, but as you know I'm in the States right now. I'm not sure when I'm coming back, and I really do think you're better off getting the publishers to deal with it.'

'But I –'

'Annabel. No.'

He thought he'd thrown her. Communication had dwindled. He even heard that she'd met someone else, someone rather suitable. But that had been months ago, and he could tell – just from reading Martin's attendance note – that whatever relationship Annabel had been in was now over. She'd turned to her little address book, her list of single men, and Edmund was back in the firing line.

'Well?' said Martin.

'Why couldn't she get her publishers to do it?'

'They have. But she still wants you, Ned – your view. She's willing to pay for it.'

'Oh God.'

'I told her you'd ring today, or tomorrow.'

Edmund shoved the file back across his desk towards Martin, and into Martin's lap. 'Forget it,' he said.

'Edmund . . .'

'No.'

Martin sighed. 'You saw what happened with Ridgewell. And Jim North's case against the *Sunday*

News went to Oliphant's. We need the business.'

'Not her kind of business. If you want to do it, Martin, fine. You call her. But I've got better things to do with my time than pussyfoot around with silly women writers. No.'

Martin knew Edmund's 'No's' of old. He hadn't forced it. Instead, he nodded, muttered 'Fair enough . . .' picked up the file and left the room, silently closing the door.

Back in his own office, Martin looked at the file in his hands. Files meant money, and he hated the idea of refusing even one. Putting it to one side, he decided it was worth waiting a few more days before getting back to Miss Glass. Ned was angry now. But over the weekend, he might change his mind, and Martin was prepared to wait.

Edmund was still wound up about it when he let himself into the studio at seven fifteen. He knew he should have swallowed his pride and taken her case on. He should have listened properly to Martin; the poor guy was only doing his job.

Throwing his briefcase on the sofa, he wondered what time Alice would turn up and got quite a shock to see her already there, standing halfway up the spiral staircase, looking at one of David's paintings on the upper wall.

'Hi,' she said, turning to him.

She'd made an effort. Her hair was clean, there was quite a bit of make-up and Edmund saw at a glance that, without it, Alice wouldn't really have been pretty. Her figure was good, but the blonde hair was artificial and the face was too narrow, the eyes too close together. He saw now why, in the portrait,

45

David had made Alice hold her head at an angle, so that the narrowness was softened. But it said a lot about the girl's character that she didn't look mean, just quirky-sexy.

Alice had brought with her in her bag, and was now wearing, a creased plum-coloured satin shift dress that came down to just below her bottom. Edmund resisted the temptation to walk towards her, round the spiral steps of iron, right underneath the one she was standing on, and look up. Instead, he pulled off his tie and asked how she'd broken in.

Alice was coming back down the steps very carefully in a pair of heels she'd lifted from her sister's wardrobe, trying to concentrate on not slipping, and not spilling the full glass of white wine in her hand. She got to the bottom and smiled.

'David let me in,' she said. 'Told me to help myself from the bottle in the fridge – is that OK?'

'Of course. Is it any good?'

Alice took a sip through her smile and looked at him over the rim of the glass.

Edmund had had a long day. He looked back at Alice – clever, alert – and decided to go with it. Tonight was going to be fun. He'd take her somewhere outrageous, spoil her rotten, spoil himself, and forget about the office. Telling her to go on helping herself to wine, Edmund went up to his room to change.

Later – after a starter of hot foie gras, followed by the largest swordfish steak she'd ever seen, and at least two bottles of wine – Alice was looking at herself in the mirror while she waited for the loo to be free. She leant forward over the basin to examine herself more carefully under the halogen spotlight but the mirror was brown-tinted, and she still looked perfect. Maybe a bit more lipstick.

She was enjoying herself, far more than she'd expected. Edmund was making her laugh so much she'd almost forgotten why she'd suggested dinner in the first place. And after a shaky start, when he discovered she was still at school, he'd made her feel fantastic. He'd been impressed by the school she was at, but then so was everybody. It was one of London's top schools, it took girls only in the sixth form, and it was notoriously difficult to get into. He'd let her talk about her interest in music, and sort of implied she was beautiful when they'd discussed a career for her as a singer. But Alice wasn't sure she wanted to be a singer, so then he'd given her all kinds of other ideas about what she might do with her life. He'd offered to give her some work experience in his office, so that she could see if she wanted to become a lawyer.

'Not that that'll affect what you read at university. If anything, I'd say *don't* do law. It's not as much fun as the arts and if you're doing it for the rest of your life, you should use university as a time to broaden your mind with something else.'

'Did you do that?'

Ned shook his head.

'Well, it doesn't seem to have done you too much damage,' said Alice, looking straight at him.

Edmund had laughed and filled her glass. 'Have you thought about acting?' he'd said.

Zipping open the black sequinned handbag her godmother had given her for her birthday, Alice heard the loo flush and a door open. She leant forward again, lipstick in hand, noticing the way her satin dress slipped – not quite revealing a nipple. She could repeat that movement for Edmund when she got back to the table, she thought, controlling her mouth to apply the lipstick.

'Excuse me.'

Alice turned – top lip done – half smiling her apology for blocking the basin. 'Oh I'm sorry,' she said.

'Thanks.'

Alice stood away, the lipstick still rolled out, while the other woman washed her hands.

Alice was not the kind of girl to notice other women. If she did, then it was usually because there was something about the woman – blonder hair, longer legs, taller thinner figure – something that Alice could identify easily and instantly as superior, as a threat. Alice had a brain that assessed the surface element in people very quickly. She'd developed a system of hierarchies to help her categorise whoever it was by looks, brains, talent, wealth, and she'd yet to meet a girl who exceeded her in all four areas. It was superficial, she knew, but it gave her fragile teenage ego the boost it craved and she now did it by habit. It wasn't that she necessarily valued these things above other human qualities, but nor was she immune to their appeal.

Aware that she was being watched, the woman looked at Alice through the mirror and Alice quickly looked away. She concentrated on the liquid soap as it fell into the palm of the woman's left hand, in creamy mother-of-pearl swirls from the chrome pump attached to the wall, and wondered what it was that had drawn her attention. What was it about this woman that was threatening Alice into her assessment routine?

Figure – smaller.

Hair – darker.

Legs – couldn't see. The clothes were unusual: white, loose, three-quarter-length trousers that flopped expensively above tanned ankles and feet clad in green leather flip-flops, and a tailored shirt, cut from purple silk that shone part-pink, part-emerald. They hinted at a good score on the brains/wealth scale, but there was nothing so out of the ordinary about them as to justify the head-turning effect she'd just achieved. Was it the face? Surreptitiously, Alice watched the woman examine herself in the mirror.

The thing she noticed first was the woman's skin. It was tanned, natural, and smoothed to a tone so even, so perfect, that it might have been bland were it not for the brave shape of the bones beneath its surface; bones so pronounced it was as if she had not seven layers to her skin, but only one. And then there was the hair. Alice wondered how long it took to get hair to look like that, with those screen-goddess waves that shone like polished rosewood. They rolled back from a brow that was broken – slightly left of centre – with a scar-like widow's peak.

The woman took her wet fingers from under a flow of water that automatically stopped. She lifted a starched napkin-towel from the side of the basin, held it for a second between her hands while she checked her own reflection once more – and then, in

49

one movement, dropped the towel in the basket and left.

Alice looked at herself in the mirror again, but the things that had pleased her before – the blonde highlights, the model body – seemed obvious somehow, and flat.

Slipping back into her seat, she looked at Edmund, who seemed to be looking back at her from somewhere deep inside his head. He smiled his way out, but the flesh around his eyes looked tired. She was about to tell him about the woman she'd seen – about her reaction, and what did Edmund think? – when he spoke first.

'I've just bumped into an old friend,' he said. 'Joss Savil. Sitting over there in the corner, see? Opposite the woman . . .'

Alice knew before he said it. She knew with the certainty of someone used to things going their way. Of course Edmund would know her. Of course all that business downstairs had a point. The woman had not felt like a stranger and now, of course, she wasn't going to be.

'. . . in the purple shirt – see? And white trousers.'

'Yes! Yes, I saw her downstairs just now. She –'

'Must be the wife.'

'The wife?'

Edmund looked across the room. A waiter blocked his view for a second and then she was there, leaning over the table, body liquid gold where the shirt undid, hair touched by candlelight, eyes slanting as she smiled and said something to her husband.

Edmund shook his head. 'Poor old Joss,' he said. 'He'll never keep her. Not in a million years.'

Alice looked over and examined what she could see of Joss Savil. He was sitting at an angle to the table, facing his wife with his back to the room, and the first thing she noticed was his size. He wasn't exactly fat, but he was huge. His chair strained like a bucket full of water. Each nail, each carefully crafted section, each joint was tested to its limit. His great long legs – clothed in light-weight tailor-made trousers – were crossed, and a nonchalant foot rested against the chair of the neighbouring man. Rough, dark curls brushed the back of his neck as he threw back his head and laughed. Alice could hear the laugh all the way across the restaurant.

'What does he do?'

'Used to work in the City,' said Edmund, 'stock-broker or something, but then his father died and he inherited a heap of money and an estate in the Scottish borders. I think he tried to go on working there for a bit, but it got absurd. You know, they were paying him as much in a year as he was making from his own investments in a month.' Edmund looked at Alice looking at Joss Savil. 'A stockbroker makes about –'

'I know,' said Alice. 'Dad's one.'

'Well, multiply what your father makes by twelve,' said Edmund. 'And then multiply that by ten, then double it, and you'll have some idea about how much Josslyn Savil must be worth.'

He refilled her glass. 'Of course, the poor man's ugly as sin. Sweet, but hideous. And knows it. Took him years to get a girlfriend. I'm talking decades. I can still remember people trying to set him up, but he'd stubbornly refuse to consider any but the most

51

beautiful women – way out of his league, obviously not interested – and then he'd put them on pedestals, get hopelessly complicated, and fuck up. So, of course, when he found that girl, nothing would convince him to let her go. Nothing. They got married this summer, in London. I couldn't get over for the wedding, so I've never met her, and maybe I'm out of line but everyone says she only married him for his money. And now I see her, I can't help thinking . . . I mean, no woman that beautiful would settle for a man that –'

'Perhaps she's in love with him,' said Alice.

'No.'

'How come you're so sure? You haven't even met her.'

Edmund smiled and nodded. 'Fair enough,' he said. 'But we can, if you like. He suggested we join them for coffee.'

They went over after pudding. As they got closer, Joss turned and then stood up. He pushed aside his curls and smiled a charming, misshapen smile.

'Ned! Here, come and sit here. And – Alice, is it? Hello, there. I'm Joss.'

The nose was large, the skin was sallow, and the eyes drooped at the corners, making him look half asleep. But his expression was mild and capable. He had an attractive stoop that gave him an authoritative air of concern for whoever it was he was talking to.

'Is this chair okay for you, Alice? Or would you prefer to be next to Edmund? And you must let me get you a drink . . .'

He spoke right into her eyes. He wasn't pretty, but Alice could see exactly what his wife saw in him.

Accepting a glass of champagne, Alice sat where he suggested.

'This is so kind of you,' he went on, as the waiters brought up chairs and made room for two more. 'So kind, to interrupt your dinner – I hope it's not too tiresome of us. It's just I haven't seen Ned for months, and I did so want him, and you, of course, to meet Laura.'

The woman turned at the mention of her name, and there was an embarrassed flicker of acknowledgement in the smile she gave – as if she was trying to tell Alice that she wouldn't have dreamt of not speaking to her in the loo downstairs if she'd known they were about to meet.

'Laura, this is Alice.'

'Hi, Alice,' she said, with a slight American accent, and held out her hand. Alice took the hand and shook it. The fingers were cool, so soothingly soft that Alice felt it would improve her own messy ones with their bitten-down nails just to be held.

'Hi.'

They ordered coffee, a bottle of Sauternes, a couple of glasses of cognac and a cigar for Edmund, who didn't really want it. He put it to one side and gave himself another look at Joss's wife: talking to Alice about where she'd found the material for her shirt – some place in Indonesia – while Alice fingered the sleeve with suppliant respect. He registered the East Coast accent. It was so faint, he had to listen for a while to be sure that it was there at all.

He was experiencing that strangely certain, one-sided familiarity with someone whose picture in the press could make him feel as if he knew them, yet

53

someone to whom he was just a stranger – and felt the disadvantage to be his. Edmund had a weakness for newspapers' diaries and gossip columns. Photographs of Josslyn Savil and his then future wife had occupied these particular sections of print at the time of his engagement, and Edmund – who went on buying English papers even when he was out of the country – had seen them all. Maybe it only happened with beautiful people, he thought, but it was really quite odd to have Laura Savil sitting next to him and behaving as if they'd never met. It almost felt rude.

He looked up and noticed Joss, smiling proudly. 'Pretty, isn't she?'

Edmund nodded and they both looked back at her – still talking to Alice about Indonesian fabric.

'I want her portrait done,' Joss went on. 'She's resisting, of course. Thinks there's something rather vain about it, and doesn't want to spend hours and hours with a total stranger, but that's ridiculous, don't you think?'

'Yes,' said Edmund.

'You're good at persuading, Ned. Do it for a living! Tell me – how can I get her to change her mind?'

Edmund took up the cigar. 'I can find out from my brother, if you like. He might have a few ideas.'

'Your brother?'

'He paints.'

Joss handed him one of the restaurant's small matchboxes. 'Any good?'

Edmund considered this. 'No idea. But I suppose . . . well, yes. I mean, he doesn't make a bowl of fruit look like a field of cows. And he doesn't insist on pickling his subjects in formaldehyde. He's modern, but you can tell what his pictures are meant to be, which helps. I still think he charges a ridiculous amount, but if people are prepared to pay it, then why shouldn't he? He's been doing Alice just this week, so you can ask her.'

'Ask me what?'

'Your portrait,' Edmund told her, as he lit the cigar. 'Joss is thinking of getting Laura painted, and I was thinking –'

'Oh, Joss. Please,' said Laura. 'You're not still going on about that, are you? I can't make him drop it,' she added to Edmund. 'On and on . . .'

'Why are you against it?'

Laura sighed and smiled. Then she looked around the room and sighed again. 'Oh, I don't know,' she said. 'I don't like the idea of posing, I guess.'

'Do you dislike being photographed as well?'

'At least that's over quickly. Portraits – paintings, that is – they can take months, can't they?'

'Not with David,' said Alice. 'He did me in days!'

'Who's David?' said Laura.

They talked on. But Edmund could see that the keener Joss became, the quieter Laura was. He was on the point of deciding that perhaps it was kinder to discourage Joss, when he thought of what this might do for his brother's career. David was doing well, but he'd never painted anyone famous. And while Laura wasn't exactly famous, it was a step in the right direction – and Ned couldn't quite resist the idea of presenting his brother with yet another Laura, a beautiful one at that. He imagined David would smile at his former self and the two of them would laugh.

David needed a bit more teasing, and this was too perfect to pass up.

By the time the bill arrived and the restaurant was closing up, he'd taken down Joss's London number, and told him he'd get David to ring them in the morning.

5

'So,' said Joss, as the four of them revolved out of the restaurant doors and into the night, 'what shall we do now?'

It was warm for late September. People were walking past them with the slow pace of holiday-makers. A couple of waiters were bringing in the chairs and tables of another restaurant at the far end of the street. A group of girls in T-shirts and jeans and open-toed shoes laughed their way past, and on round the corner.

Alice was standing with a coat slung, mafia style, over her left shoulder. She had her eyes shut, feeling the warmth on her skin. Laura stood next to her, holding a slim evening bag of microscopic pearls, and looking at the pavement.

Edmund glanced at his watch. 'Nowhere open,' he said. 'Nowhere good. Not at two in the morning.'

'We could still go to Tsar's. Ant said he'd be there tonight with Tania, and Rory –'

'You're a member of the Tsar Bar?' said Alice.

Joss nodded, loose hair sliding over his forehead. He looked amused – taking the question to express surprise that a man as inelegant as him would be offered membership – and agreed. 'Not really my scene, I know. We don't go there much. But I can have three guests, so shall we . . .?'

'Oh yes, let's – please, let's! Edmund?'

A cab was coming towards them. In the slow-speed photograph of Alice's intoxicated mind, its orange light dragged a comet-tail line. They all got in, opened the windows, and then they were speeding west, up Piccadilly, towards Hyde Park Corner. They passed a freeze-frame snap of Bond Street to the right – the distinctive Tiffany Clock sticking out over the pavement for a second, the glow of Asprey's beyond – and then lost it to yet more shops and houses flashing past, the streetlamps, the spots of light from the Ritz, each trailing a visual echo, and fading into the warm dark night.

Alice dragged her attention back into the cab and looked down the length of her own legs to her feet, at her sister's sparkling shoes. She had the oddly liberating sense that somebody else was in control. Somebody else was being responsible, dealing with bills and fares and checking the time. All she had to do was go along with it, enjoy it.

Alice and Laura were on the back seat, and the men had their backs to the driver. Joss was sitting opposite Alice, but he'd turned to listen to Edmund, who was explaining the details of some case.

'. . . the plaintiff's reputation at the time of trial isn't relevant, Joss. It's the time of publication that counts. And in Ridgewell's case, the man's public image *at the time of publication* . . . I mean, that *Weekend News* article was years ago. Years and years. I remember I was staying with Sara and Jamie, and Sara was amazed.

Ridgewell was spotless then. If Vixen Jones and all that S and M stuff had come out first, then Perrin's article wouldn't have made any difference, Ridgewell's name would already have been mud. But it didn't, and the court has to ignore . . .'

The cab took a corner. Joss's knees swung round, touching hers, and Alice looked up. But his gaze was fixed on Laura, in the opposite corner. Alice looked too, at Laura's extraordinary face, with its fabulous mouth, and the twist of hair at the scar-like part of her hairline. Laura's eyes were on Joss. An adult charge shot both ways across the cab, down the diagonal, and reduced Ned's voice to a murmur. Alice knew the glance was private. She shouldn't have seen it. Yet, like a sudden light in some stranger's bedroom on the opposite side of the street before the sweep of a curtain, it was impossible to ignore.

Ned's wrong, she thought. Blind and wrong if he thinks they're not in love.

Joss's friends were sitting near the back.

Alice followed Laura, the loose white trousers gliding through the angular leather and diamanté of the other women in the bar, the frail silk of her shirt narrowing discreetly to a point at the back of her waist. Laura walked with concealed control, her whippet-strong Achilles tendons responding to the floor and lifting her forward. Alice watched the buffed brown skin at her heels, gently flipped by the flat green calfskin of her sandals as she trod carelessly through the puddles of alcohol, and scatterings of ash that lay in the path to their table.

'You're here!'

'Everyone – they're here! Laura, darling, how was Greece? . . . God, how lovely. No wonder you're so brown.'

'What took you so long?'

Laura's hand was clasped in Joss's great fist, a trace of silver at her wrist, as she let herself be greeted.

'Ned –' Joss stood back for him – 'Alice: this is Anthony. Anthony Emerys. And then there's Tania – Tan, sweetheart . . .' They waited for him to lean over the glasses and bottles on the table and kiss her. 'Tania Ford, Amanda Granville, Ulrich Rheinhardt, Rory Clifford . . .'

Joss listed the faces: heads all at different heights, different angles – some forward, in acknowledge-ment of the introduction, some still in conversation, unaware or rude. One of the girls was sitting on a man's lap, leaning back to talk to another girl who was examining her fingernails and gesticulating in short brushlike movements.

Alice smiled as she listened and nodded. But she felt the pace of drink – the champagne, the burgundy, and all that chateaux nectar – whirling in her brain, taking with it the seven or eight faces round the table, along with their names, names that merged, their syllables bubbling into one multibarrelled andro-genous Euro-aristo nursery-word. She felt as if she'd walked into the pages of a social magazine.

Laura, she noticed, had retrieved her hand from Joss, and was caught in conversation with a slim Chinese man, who was wearing glasses and listening to her with formal elegance. It was a brand of formality that released the reverse in Laura. She took off his glasses, put them on the end of her own nose and peered provocatively at him over their titanium rims. 'How do I look?'

Not wanting to be caught staring, Alice looked away. She ran her eyes past Joss, laughing loudly at something Tania had said, and bang into Edmund's: tired, older. Then he seemed to pull himself out from somewhere. He smiled the way he'd smiled at her that first day, when she hadn't been allowed to smile back. 'Let me get you something to drink,' he said. 'Champagne?'

Alice nodded.

'Laura – champagne? Joss? Right. I'll get a bottle, then.'

But they didn't stay long at the bar. The others had been there since eleven and they were tiring of the thud of its music, the density of its bodies. Here was a room full of micro-performances that none but the performer was bothering to watch. There weren't enough mirrors, and restlessness was kicking in.

Edmund's bottle of champagne had scarcely enough time to settle in its bucket before Joss was suggesting they go back with him and Laura to Chelsea. It wasn't clear who was included in this invitation, but they all accepted with the satisfied smiles and nods of having half expected it all along.

'Will you come too?' said Laura to Edmund. She was still wearing the titanium glasses.

Edmund hesitated. 'I really should get Alice home to bed. Her parents will be wondering what on earth she's doing, out on the tiles at three in the morning.'

'They're away,' lied Alice.

'Are they?'

'Please come,' Laura went on, taking off the glasses

61

to add a dash of sincerity. 'It won't be so much fun without you.'

Both women looked hopefully at Edmund.

He put down his glass. 'We'll never find cabs at this time of night, you know. We'll stand for hours and hours on Park Lane – your feet'll die in those things, Alice. And it'll be daylight by the time we –'

'We've got a car.'

'Who's driving? We're all wasted.'

'Anthony. Says he's fine. And Rory's so grand these days, he's got a driver. We can always call a cab from home, if you insist. But you might find you like it . . .'

Joss and Laura's house was at the bottom end of a narrow lane in the heart of Chelsea – in the warren of streets that connect the King's Road to the river. It was brick-fronted, Georgian, and positioned at random between a more conventional row of terraced houses on one side, and a pub on the other. It was set back from the road behind a wall with a high wrought-iron gate, and they waited there – their voices tinkling into a pre-dawn blue, those women without coats or wraps rubbing at their arms for warmth – while Joss pressed in the security number.

As she passed through, Alice looked up to a point where, above the gate, suspended from the arching iron of its frame, the mellow orb of an original gaslamp dangled in the early morning mist. She stopped with her neck bent back as far as it would go, and stared up at it. The cold had sobered her up, but the evening was still unfolding like a dream and the lamp – just hanging there like that inside its glowing orbit – had, for Alice, a fascinating weightlessness. Edmund had to fetch her.

'Come inside,' he said.

Trailing beneath the light, up a path of worn stone slabs lined with great rows of overgrown lavender bushes that tickled at her legs and exhaled the smell of empty drawers and bath-time, Alice followed Edmund into the house.

It was dark in the hall, just the gate light from behind throwing down their shadows on the stone floor, and a light coming down from the top of an oak staircase. It smelt of lilies. Alice could just make out their pale trumpet shapes in a spray arrangement in the far corner. She stepped across a scattering of envelopes that one of the other guests had knocked from a pile of letters on a table by the door and bent to pick them up.

'Oh, leave those,' said Joss, striding through a door that led to the kitchen with a tray, a lit cigarette in one hand. On the tray was an ice bucket, some bottles of tonic water, and two magnums of champagne. It didn't look very stable, and Edmund took the magnums off.

'Thanks.' Joss rearranged his grip on the tray and started to climb the stairs. They creaked with each step. 'We're up here. Just dump your stuff on that bench thing and come up.'

The drawing room took up the whole of the first floor. Six pairs of windows – three on the street side, three on the garden – would have made the room white-bright by day, but now the curtains had been drawn and the effect was enclosed and dark, wintry-warm.

Someone – Rory – was playing the piano, thumping out blues with stiff unpractised fingers, and stamping at the pedal. The rest of them had flopped, lain, sat, curled, propped, rested their bodies on and around the arrangements of antique sofas, stools and chairs. Some were listening to the music, but most were talking over it. Laura had just finished lighting candles, and was shaking the flame from a match. Alice watched her, watched the uncertain ripple of grey, rising and disintegrating as the match was thrown into a hand-painted ashtray.

Edmund followed Joss across the room to the drinks cupboard. It was a small room concealed behind a door that had been covered with the same material as the walls, and seemed so full of various gins, vodkas, whiskies and liqueurs that champagne was hardly necessary. He found a space, put the magnums down and began opening one of them.

'Got any glasses?'

Joss pointed to the back of the cupboard.

Reaching up, Edmund brought a few down, released the champagne cork and began to pour. 'That's for you,' he said, handing it to Alice.

Alice took her glass over to the piano. Partly to watch it being played, but mainly to play it herself whenever Rory decided to stop. She knew she could play better than him and the exhibitionist in her was tired of being ignored.

Laura was there with him, sitting on a stool at his other side, marvelling at how fast his fingers moved.

'Isn't he great, Alice? Look at his hands.'

Hearing her, Rory threw all his energies into accelerating the speed, fudging notes and banging out the bass.

Alice wasn't impressed. She wandered round the

piano to look at the photographs – in particular, a black and white one of what looked like Joss's parents getting married, gliding out of church down a tunnel of regimental swords. And another one, also black and white, of Laura in her wedding dress, sitting on an unmade bed with her veil back, smoking a pre-church cigarette, a rebellious half-smile giving life to the finished face.

'Ah,' Laura went round to join Alice and picked up the picture, 'look at that. My last cigarette. Joss said he'd only marry me if I gave up. God, how I miss them.'

'But Joss smokes.'

'I know – the old hypocrite.'

They looked over to where Joss was standing by the fireplace, a cigarette between his fingers, flicking ash into the fire and laughing with the same noisy joy that Alice had noticed in the restaurant. Anthony was laughing too.

Rory stopped playing the piano. 'What's the joke?'

'Oh God. Come over and listen, Rory, you simply must hear this. Ant, tell him again, will you?'

Alice grabbed her chance. Putting her glass to one side, she settled on the piano stool – still warm from Rory's exertions – and flicked through the sheet music propped against the stand: a predictable collection of Mozart, Andrew Lloyd Webber, the Beatles, a yellowing Rachmaninov Prelude and there, right at the bottom, Debussy's Arabesques. Alice opened it, found the one she knew – the first one – and began to play.

A near-slip at the start told Alice at once exactly how drunk she was, and she was glad she'd not been

65

too ambitious. She didn't really need the music for this one. Almost knew it by heart. The notes trickled from her fingers and, one by one, the others stopped talking and listened.

They were all looking at her when she stopped, even Rory. Edmund and Joss had walked close while she'd been playing. Edmund was resting forward in the 'S' of the instrument, and Joss was at her side, watching her fingers.

'Go on,' he said.

Alice bit her lip, brought her left hand low and, stretching it, sprang into the opening bass octaves of the 'Maple Leaf Rag' – a light, bouncing bom *bom* – not too fast. Not – too – fast. She tried to rein in her fingers, but they raced on – bom *bom* – bom *bom*.

'How old did you say she was?'

'Still at school.'

'Shit.'

' . . . bom *bom* . . .'

Gradually, the rest of the party turned back to their conversations as Alice played out her repertoire – varying dreamy nocturnes with popular classics, stuff they could sing to, stuff they couldn't, but nothing too heavy. After about an hour she stopped. Edmund was still there in the 'S', listening. 'Go on,' he said again, but Alice had reached the end. She closed the lid and looked out beyond Edmund's shoulder to where the party was still swinging, bubbling, chattering and smoking there amongst the sofas, but something of its magic had gone. It took Alice a moment to realise what it was.

She double-checked and then she looked at Edmund. 'Where are they?'

'Disappeared about ten minutes ago.'

'Disappeared?'

'I think they've gone to bed.'

'Did I drive them off?'

'No,' he smiled. 'Not at all. They were loving it, especially Joss, but they've slipped away. Shall we go too?'

They walked together down to the Embankment, where Edmund knew there'd be cabs. 'Let's cross here and get one going in the right direction,' he said, hurrying Alice – in her fragile shoes – to the other side, but failing to attract the attention of the first cab that passed.

'She is in love with him, you know,' said Alice, reaching the pavement. She bent back her left knee, and then her right, taking off the shoes as she walked beside him. Edmund felt her lowering, and looked from the stockinged feet – careless on the cold dry stone – up into her face.

'You've shrunk.'

'Don't change the subject.'

'What subject?'

'Laura – in love with Joss. Who, by the way, isn't nearly as ugly as you think he is.' Alice noticed Edmund's expression. 'And even if you don't agree with that, you have to have seen the way she was gazing at him. She gave up smoking for him. She crept off early to bed with him. She loves him.'

Hailing the next cab with more success, Edmund opened the door for Alice and asked her to give the driver her address. Alice was about to oblige when she remembered her night's mission and stopped short at the cab door. Her address? She wasn't going home yet, no way, not with Edmund so clearly smitten, not with her ambitions so nearly realised.

'What is it?'

'My . . .' She turned to Edmund, who was standing very close behind her, ready to follow her into the cab.

'Your . . .?'

'My bag.' Alice saw him looking at the little black sequinned square in her hand. 'I mean, my school bag. I left it back at the studio. It's got my stuff.'

'Do you need it tomorrow? It's Saturday.'

'We have morning school.'

Edmund gave the driver David's studio address, got in behind Alice, and they crossed the river in silence. A thin sheen sat on the water, seemingly still, then narrowing with the sudden curve of its tide, fast down the riverbank towards the Houses of Parliament and on past the docklands, out to sea. The streets were empty, pavements quiet after the drama of Friday night. They passed a young man walking with morning energy in the opposite direction. It was Saturday for him, and he had things to do.

Edmund was tired. He calculated that by the time he'd collected the bag from the studio, and then taken Alice to Kensington, and then come all the way back again to Battersea, it would be another hour before he got to bed. At least it was Saturday. He could sleep until lunch, take it easy, and then go to the office on Sunday – mainly to sort out his desk. Why was there always so much admin to do? He really needed two secretaries . . .

Alice could see Edmund's face in the reflection on the glass barrier in front of them. He was sitting slouched with his legs stretched out directly in front of him, crossed at the ankles. He was looking down, fiddling with his watch and frowning. She turned and looked at him straight but he didn't look back.

What was going on? Here they were, coming back to his place at five in the morning, so why wasn't he . . . ?

Was he worried she'd say no?

Was he worried about her age, wondering how to go about it?

Oh well, thought Alice, sliding up the leather seat. She was just going to have to do it for him.

'*Whaa-oh!*' Edmund turned in sharp response to the sensation of Alice's leg slipping against his as she heaved herself on to his lap, facing him. '*Alice.*'

She came closer, shifting up on to him, getting her knees good and comfortable on the broad cab seat. Her slim thighs pushed over him, opening, rubbing, shifting, forcing the short skirt up, and further up, and –

Oh God. He was getting an erection. He was getting an erection, an erection with a teenager.

'Alice.' He pushed her roughly away. 'Get. Off.'

But she was much lighter than he'd anticipated and fell back into her corner, thumping the side of the cab.

'Oi, you two . . .'

'Sorry.' Edmund leant forward to shut the partition and then looked round to where Alice was nursing her leg.

'You OK?'

'Yeah.' Her tights had laddered, but she was fine.

Edmund waited for a moment, staring at her, and then, his eyes still on her, he eased himself into his corner. 'What on earth was that about?'

'Wasn't it obvious?'

Edmund scratched at one of his eyebrows. 'Yes. Yes, I suppose it was obvious. I just . . .'

He trailed off, and neither of them spoke. The cab shot effortlessly south along streets usually jammed with cars – round corners, through green lights, over empty zebra crossings, into the heart of Battersea. Edmund felt he had to say something, but he didn't know where to start. What possible thing had he said or done to provoke her? Sure, he fancied her. But there was all the difference in the world – wasn't there? – between finding someone attractive, and acting on it.

Alice was equally baffled. Why else was he here with her now? He'd been staring at her all that time she was playing the piano. Staring. All evening. She was positive he fancied her. And here they were now, alone. What had she missed?

'But I thought . . .' she began, but suddenly it seemed too much, even for her, to admit what she'd thought. Alice looked away, out of the window on her side of the cab.

'You thought I wanted you,' said Edmund. He looked at the shape of her neck squashed against the black leather seat. 'Oh, Alice –'

'Forget it.'

'I –'

'Just forget it, will you? I made a mistake. I was wrong.'

'No,' he said. 'You weren't.'

70

She turned to him.

'You weren't wrong,' he went on. 'I did – *do* – want you. But it can't . . .'

'Can't what?'

'Alice, you're only seventeen. You –'

'So what? It's not against the law. I know what I'm doing.'

'I'm sure you know exactly what you're doing, but I happen to think that you are too young. Too young *for me*.'

Considering this, Alice looked down, and then back at Edmund with clear young eyes. He hoped with sudden panic that he wasn't making a mistake. She was right, after all. It wasn't against the law. And in spite of the sophisticated approaches he got from women his own age, it wasn't every day that girls cried out for sex with him.

Women over thirty – the women he knew, at any rate – had a way of twisting desire into predictable courtly patterns. It was always their fantasy, their rules, and it was always the same. And thinking of all the times he'd longed for something fresh, thinking of how often he'd submitted to the weary ritual of persuading women to sleep with him – frequently outmanoeuvred into the role of sexual seducer when it should have been the other way round – Edmund wondered if he was just being perverse.

'You're smiling,' said Alice.

'I –'

'You're laughing at me.'

'No. No, on the contrary, I was just thinking how lucky I am to have you wanting me like this.'

'But you won't take me.'

'No – I mean yes – I mean . . .' he groaned. 'I would if I could, Alice. I just . . .'

'Just what, Edmund? What's the problem?'

The cab pulled up at the studio. Telling Alice to stay there, he'd get the bag himself, Edmund ran up. Seconds later, he was down again. Handing her the bag, he decided it was better she go home by herself. He couldn't, wouldn't take advantage. Not on the first date. But nor could he let it go. He shut the cab door and, leaning in at the window, he told her that he'd ring, that they'd take it slowly, and then if she still wanted him, after getting to know him a bit better, then perhaps . . . who knew? But they were both tired. They'd talk about it tomorrow.

'Tomorrow?' Alice shifted up the seat – nothing tired about her expression, nor the way she was fingering his hand, his wrist. 'But, Ned, it is tomorrow.' She smiled, pointing at the hands on his watch. 'See?'

Ned was glad that the cab door was shut.

'Alice,' he said, laughing, 'stop it.'

Pulling away, he handed the driver a couple of notes – more than enough to get her back – gave him Alice's address, and waved them off.

That was the best way to deal with it, he decided, watching the cab move away. Amazed at himself, his self-control, Edmund went back upstairs. Perhaps at last, like David, he too was growing up.

Still marvelling at his restraint, Edmund let himself back into the studio. A lamp had been left on in the corner of the room and, looking round, he noticed Alice's picture. But the angle of light was wrong. He could see more of the canvas – the crinkles and bumps of its surface – than he could of Alice herself. Edmund walked towards it and was in the middle of the room when he heard a slipping noise coming from the area around David's racks of paintings.

He turned, but couldn't see much. Just thin strips of light, thrown by racks on to racks on to racks, and then on to the far wall – and one of them was moving. There was more slipping, scuffling, and then a voice said, 'Shit.'

'David?'

'Ned, is that you? Ned? Ned?'

'Hang on.' Edmund switched the main lights on, and there was a sudden crash and a shout of pain as one of the upper racks fell to the floor. Unframed sketches shot out across the boards, into the light, gathering dirt on their corners as they stopped at Edmund's feet, then David, in pyjama bottoms, hopping over the sheets of paper, not caring if he creased them. He was clinging tightly to his other foot.

'Everything all right?'

'Fucking *fucking* loose racks.' David hopped to the edge of the sofa and sat on it. Still holding the injured foot, he squeezed it hard between both hands, not daring to look at the injury. 'Christ, that was painful. Right over my toes – look,' he took his hands away, 'look, Ned – I'm bleeding.'

But as Edmund bent to look, a voice came from behind him – slow, warm, and full of sleep. 'David, darling, what are you –'

He turned to see a girl standing at the top of the spiral staircase, dressed in a grey T-shirt.

73

'I'm fine,' said David. 'Fine. Go back to bed, just stubbed my toe.'

The girl yawned, and then laughed as she realised what he'd said. 'Stubbed your toe?'

'What's so funny?'

'Darling, it sounded more like you'd lost your leg. You were *howling* – it woke me up.'

'Actually, Mel, it was extremely painful. Look. I'm bleeding.'

'Oh, David.' Still laughing, Mel came down the stairs. It was only when she got to the bottom that she realised they weren't alone.

Ned was looking at her, taking in the tousled hair – short spikes pointing in different directions and a squashed bird's-nest effect at the back where she'd been lying on it. Down one side of her face were long red lines from the creases in the sheets. Wiping her eyes, she looked at him with blurry surprise – and then she smiled.

Ned had seen photographs of Mel on the mantelpiece, her black coat by the door. He'd heard her voice on the answerphone – low, authoritative – and smelt her scent in the bathroom. But he'd yet to meet her. Office demands and evening commitments had kept them apart. Now, suddenly, here she was.

He'd expected a tidy lawyer: suited, controlled, concealed. Instead, he'd caught her inside out. He'd stumbled on the unwashed sleepy bed-girl, and no woman, not even the ones he'd slept with, had ever let him see her in such a mess. After the highly maintained girls of New York, after Laura Savil, even Alice – whose youth required less effort – Edmund wasn't used to women looking like this. There was a postcoital air about her, faint charcoal smudges where mascara hadn't quite come off, that made it hard for Edmund to meet Mel's eye. It was worse, somehow, than if he'd caught her naked.

'Mel – Ned. Ned – Mel. Now please can someone help me?'

Mel turned from Ned to David's swollen toe.

'Oh, darling,' she said. 'Darling, sorry. Of course.' Kneeling, she took it in her hands. 'Let's have a look . . . oh yes, it is quite nasty, isn't it? Not bleeding too much, but . . . what happens if I press there?'

David gave a sharp wince.

'Sorry, darling . . . and there?'

'Aiee!'

'Ok. I'll just check you haven't broken anything – can you wiggle that one? And that one? Great. You'll lose the nail, I think – on one, if not both – and there'll be some bruising. *Poor* you. Just hold it there.' Mel stood up. 'We'll need to clean it up and put on a couple of plasters, and then get you upstairs. Can you manage to reach the kitchen?'

Ned remained in the studio, listening to the fuss – to David lapping it up. Torn between feelings of irritation ('David's not a little boy any more, don't encourage him') and envy (when had someone last – ever – fussed over Ned like this?), he began picking up the sheets of paper that had fallen from the racks. Different sizes, different colours, different media, but all of naked women. Pictures he had not seen before.

There was a charcoal sketch of a young girl's back, sitting on the floor. David had worked hard at the spine line under the skin, the shadow from each bump describing an overall curve, a finely structured path beneath the blank space of flesh – curling up, lost in the detail of hair and tendons at the base of her neck while, at the opposite corner of the page, it faded to nothing at the small of her back.

'Ai!'

'Just another second while I get you to the chair, and . . . there.'

Ned picked up another: the same girl, in the same position, but viewed from further away, part profile, hinting at the shape of her front, but more of her arms, and her hand – palm flat on the ground, flesh folding at her wrist – taking the strain. The head was turned away. And another: this time in direct profile.

It was an exercise in studying all viewpoints, and – with each study – David was moving gradually round to the front. Edmund could see that he'd not had much time with this one. He was concentrating mainly on making sense of the way she was sitting, legs twisting away, hips sunk at an angle. But breasts, shoulders and chin had been suggested only in the briefest of sweeps, a couple of thrusts up the page. He picked up another and another – different poses now, different lights – but all, very clearly, the same girl.

Putting them in a neat pile on David's worktop, Ned went into the kitchen, where Mel had got out the first-aid kit and a bottle of Dettol. She was dabbing cotton wool into the saucer of diluted Dettol while David sat on the table, his foot in her lap. Ned hadn't smelt Dettol in years.

'That rack fell right across my toes. Slipped from its notch and – wham!'

Mel put the cotton wool down and reached for the

tube of Savlon. 'You were lucky not to break any bones,' she said. 'Similar thing happened to my mother last year with some gardening tool. Can't think what the old bat was doing, gardening in bare feet, but she broke two toes. Can you believe it? Had to go to casualty.'

They all watched Mel's fingers dot white antiseptic cream over David's injury.

'I broke my toe once . . .' said Ned.

Mel peeled the backing off a plaster. 'Now,' she said, 'hold still.'

' . . . it was agony.'

'Not too tight,' said David.

'OK – OK – how's that?'

David wiggled the toe, looked from it to Mel and reached for her hand. 'Thank you.'

Mel ruffled his hair. Edmund couldn't see David's expression, but he could see Mel's. The sheet-lines on her face were fading, her hair looked a little less mad than it had, and it was harder to see the smudges round her eyes when she smiled. Ned was torn. Part of him longed to be looked at like that, longed for a soothing hand, and part of him wanted to stuff his fingers down his throat.

'David.'

'Mm?'

'David, listen. Before I forget, I bumped into Joss Savil tonight.'

'Who?'

'Joss. Joss Savil. Savil as in Savil Lehrer? The bank? I was at school with him, remember?'

David said nothing.

'His father was Richard Savil, and his mother was a

77

Clyde. His marriage was in the papers, David. Surely you saw that.'

'Can't say that I –'

'Well, anyway. Alice and I ran into him earlier. Him and his new wife, Laura, who's stunning, David, really stunning, and he wants her portrait done. So,' Ned laughed, 'so against my better judgement, I put in a good word for you and he's expecting a call in the morning. Reckon you should call him first thing in case she . . . What? What is it? What's wrong?'

David seemed, for a moment, to forget that Mel was there at all. 'I wish you wouldn't do this,' he said. 'I *wish* you'd mind your own business, and leave me to mine. Just because you're staying here, you don't have the right to interfere in my work.'

'Hang on, David. I was only –'

'I don't want to waste my time on society portraits. And I'm not desperate for help. All right?'

Edmund looked at Mel, staring down at her own bare toes on the tiles, and then he shrugged. 'All right,' he said. 'All right, forget it. I'm sorry. Laura wasn't particularly keen on the idea in any case.'

6

For all her rebellious instincts, bunking off was never an option for Alice, who, half an hour after she'd crawled into bed, was crawling out again and putting on her clothes for Saturday school.

Alice's school was, originally, a boys' public school and had only recently started taking girls in the sixth form. Unlike the boys, who wore regulation black suits, ties and white shirts, the girls did not yet have a uniform of their own. Jeans and trainers were out, but so long as the girls wore dark colours, and so long as skirts came to no more than two inches above the knee, then that was the limit to their dress requirements.

Officially, the girls gloried in this edge to their freedom. It made them seem more mature than the boys – even more than they already were. They could hang out in cafés and bars on weekday afternoons, and not be recognised as school pupils. But the truth was that, while the typical boy would haul on his suit each morning with happy indifference, the girl had to get up half an hour early and scrutinise her wardrobe for the most trendy, most flattering clothes she could get away with – and preferably ones that were still clean. It was so much harder to dress when everything she chose gave off another message about the kind of person she was. Or about who she wanted, or dared to be. Alice stood at her wardrobe, a mahogany antique with a crammed hanging area on one side and a column of drawers, spilling out clothes on the other, and saw nothing she liked.

'Mum!' she shouted, jumping down the stairs to her parents' room on the third floor of their house. 'Mum, where are my trousers?'

She opened the door to a room full of morning light and the warm smell of sleep. Alice's mother was at her dressing table, her father was in the bathroom, and harpischord music floated from the speakers at either side of the unmade bed.

'Oh, darling,' Camilla Enderby turned on the stool and looked at her daughter with a guilty expression. 'Darling, I'm sorry. They're still at the cleaners.'

Alice stomped up the stairs, followed by her mother.

'What about the pair of navy trousers you got from that shop in the Fulham Road? You haven't worn them in ages, and I'm sure they're clean.'

'They're middle-aged.'

Camilla followed her daughter into the room and opened the curtains. 'Or there's that skirt Isobel brought back from Italy.'

Alice's older sister was spending the year in Florence studying history of art and improving her dress sense. She'd given Alice the skirt for her seventeenth birthday and at the time Alice hadn't particularly liked it. She hadn't then known that skirts like that would be hitting the September issues of every fashion magazine, but now she realised that it was cool.

'Oh yes.' She yanked aside the hangers, found the one with Izzy's skirt and took it out. 'Excellent.'

It was blue – dark enough to pass for navy. It was quite short, but that was OK. Today was Saturday, and she only had morning school. The chances of being made to go home and change were minimal, and it was definitely the right image.

It was only when she got to Kensington High Street tube station that Alice began to feel ill. Not violently ill, but weak. Light-headed. She shut her eyes, sniffed in hard and began to sort through her memories of the previous night. She couldn't wait to tell Emily about it. Emily had lost her virginity that summer on holiday with her family in Spain, and this was one of the main reasons that Alice was now so desperate to lose hers. But she wanted to – to do it – give it – with – to – someone who'd give her something in return, something more than merely being relieved of the burden of innocence. Alice wanted to be good in bed, like she was good at passing exams, good at music, and good at getting what she wanted. And right now she wanted a man who knew what he was doing, a man who'd be able to teach her things.

Taking the first tube that came, Alice changed at South Kensington on to the Piccadilly line. She was glad it was Saturday. The carriage was free from commuters. Perhaps she and Edmund could have lunch after school and then perhaps they could get the whole thing over and done with this afternoon!

Suppressing an excited smile – feeling it observed by the unshaved man sitting opposite – Alice imagined having done it. At last. She imagined how it would be: after lunch, perhaps, going back to David's studio . . . or a hotel, or whatever. Edmund's problem. She imagined them kissing and fondling, and clothes coming off, and then, glossing over intercourse itself, she imagined lying there with her hair tangled in postcoital abandon over the pillow. Just the before and after.

She got off the tube and lolloped in her short Italian skirt and her chunky shoes – shoes that gave a puppyish impression of enormous paws and more room to grow – through the school gates with a mass of other pupils, through first one cloister, then another, and straight into the chapel, which was open to the public, and which the school still used for assembly.

Emily was already there in the area of chairs allocated to the Upper Sixth, turning in her chair and talking in whispers to Steve Wilson and Tim Montford, both leaning forward to listen to her. Alice had fancied Tim last year. She'd liked his pretty face with its continual expression of mild surprise. She'd liked the way he walked – sort of shufflingly cool. They'd snogged at Steve's party a couple of months ago, but then it had been the school holidays and both of them had gone away. Getting back to school at the beginning of this term, Alice had taken one look at Tim, compared him to David Nicholson – who'd just started her portrait – and decided that Tim was a baby.

The three of them looked up as she approached.

'Nice,' said Emily, reaching out to touch the material. 'Nice skirt.'

Steve looked at Tim and said, 'What skirt?' loudly.

Alice grinned at Steve as she sat down, and smiled briefly at Tim. 'Hi.' Then she turned her back on them and took Emily's hand. 'I've got so much to tell you, Em . . .'

'Where's Alice's skirt? Anyone seen Alice's skirt? Tim?'

Alice ignored him. 'You know that guy I was telling you about?' she said to Emily.

'The artist?'

'No, Emmy. The artist's brother. Edmund – remember?'

'You'll get sent home like that.'

Emily rolled her eyes and smiled again at Alice. 'Go on.'

But as Emily spoke, her voice was drowned by a general heaving and the entire school got to its feet. The organ music swelled as the deputy headmaster and the chaplain swept in from the side and up the aisle at the front. They stood in silence while the deputy headmaster climbed the steps of the pulpit, flicked at the microphone and arranged his papers.

'Be seated.'

Alice sat back down on a pile of hymn books that could only have been put there by Steve. She had to twist round, take them out, and put them on the floor while the deputy headmaster made the day's announcements, and the boys in the row behind laughed openly at her.

'Oh, grow up,' she hissed, and turned her back.

Mel stood in the bathroom, looking at her face. She was amused by the way a hangover could make her look slightly prettier than normal. Her lips were redder, her eyes brighter, and she didn't even have a headache – just a frail sense that it would arrive at some point later in the day. Perhaps I'm still drunk, she thought, stepping into the empty bathtub and turning the water-flow to shower.

Wondering for a second if she should be driving – maybe it would be better to wait a couple of hours, crawl back to bed with David, and sleep it off – Mel knew that, however tempting, it wasn't really an option. She was expected to be with her parents in time for lunch, and it simply wasn't worth her while to be late. Not worth her while to risk an accident, either, but she couldn't start off on the wrong foot, not with the things she had to tell them.

Standing under the flow of water, enjoying its weight at the top of her spine, Mel thought back to the day before, to the moment of handing in her resignation. It hadn't given her quite as much pleasure as she'd expected. Philippa, her boss, had looked genuinely upset and genuinely worried about redirecting Mel's files. What were they going to do without her? Did she really have to leave? What kind of incentives could they offer? But Mel had been firm. Her mind was made up, she said. She'd stay the requisite three months, if that was what Philippa wanted, and leave at Christmas.

'And it's not as if I'm going to a rival firm,' she added, feeling as though she was leaving a lover, a lover who couldn't understand that she was going because she simply wasn't happy, and not because she had a better offer.

'I know,' said Philippa, staring miserably at the

envelope that Mel had given her, containing the formal letter.

Mel felt terrible. She liked Philippa. She didn't want to let her down.

But before she had a chance to say anything, Philippa had flung the letter into her tray of correspondence.

'Oh – fuck it,' she said, slipping into City language that sat at odds with her headmistressy look, and grinning. 'I'm just jealous. Let's leave this shit and go and get some lunch. I know it's only eleven thirty, but it's Friday, and I need a drink.'

Trying to remember exactly what they'd drunk – after that first bottle of champagne – Mel rinsed her hair, turned off the shower, and got out. There was definitely some red wine, and something small and nasty with their coffee, and then more champagne. And then that gin and tonic with David, and God knows what she must have had for dinner. Mel leant forward, making sure that the water-flow had been firmly redirected to the taps, otherwise the shower-head would drip. She felt slightly dizzy.

Drying her hair with a towel, Mel went back to the bedroom. David had moved over into her part of the bed, lying in a broken diagonal with his face obscured by pillows and hair. Mel stopped rubbing and looked at him there – at the childish vulnerability and complete absence of self-consciousness – and felt glad he wasn't coming with her. It wasn't going to be pleasant telling Greg, and she'd rather handle it alone. For his own good, as well as her pride, Mel wanted to protect David from whatever ugliness lay in store.

David lay in bed pretending to sleep while Mel got

up. He'd drifted off while she was in the bathroom, but had woken again when she'd sat on the bed to put on her shoes. His toe was still sore and he'd have liked to squeeze it, but something held him back. Lying there quietly – breathing slowly – he heard the click of her handbag, and the distinctive double-beep from her mobile as she switched it on. He heard the rustling of her papers: the scribbled notes, magazine cuttings, and old service sheets that she was planning to take to her parents for the weekend. And then . . . there it was: the soft *squirt-squirt* of her scent.

Keeping his eyes closed and his breathing regular as Mel came close to kiss him – he could smell the mint of the toothpaste she used – David felt guilty. He wasn't entirely sure why he was doing this: why it was necessary to pretend to be asleep, why he wanted to avoid the conversation they'd be having if he were awake.

He heard her going down the spiral staircase – waited for the heavier clunk of the outside door – and then he too got up. Pulling on his dressing gown, David limped down into the studio.

He thought of what Edmund had said last night, how he'd dropped it in so casually: *Him and his new wife, Laura* . . .

Damn you, Ned. How am I expected to get over this when you won't help me? I don't want to meet another Laura. I can't. I won't. I . . .

But other inclinations were at work. And it wasn't long before David had twisted his mind into the sophisticated premise that in fact it would be good for him to meet another Laura. This was an opportunity for him to prove that he was well and truly free. He couldn't hide himself from Lauras for ever. That was as good as admitting he still had a problem. That would be absurd. No, he'd meet this Laura – whoever she was – and exorcise the ghost. It was absolutely the right thing for him to be doing. In some ways, it was perfect timing. Then he could marry Mel with a clear conscience.

Standing at the bottom of the stairs, David ran his eye over the studio with rather too much excitement for someone about to do their duty. He was thinking about what he needed to do to the room before this Laura – and her husband – arrived. He needed to get his best pictures stacked casually against the wall so that they looked like a random selection. He'd keep Alice's picture on the easel. It wasn't framed yet, but it was a good likeness, as they knew her it made sense for them to see it well displayed. And he needed to clean the place.

Deciding there was no point washing himself or shaving until he'd finished cleaning the studio, David changed straight into his painting clothes, heaved the bucket of Mr Muscle, Windolene and Jif from under the basin, dug out a scrubbing brush and a couple of clean dry cloths, rolled up his sleeves and got to work.

He started with the bathroom, clearing the mess of bottles and soap from the tiled area around the taps – slimy half-empty plastic bottles, long dusty dark blue vials, slim remains of dry, cracked soap, a couple of mini hotel bath and shower gels they'd taken from that place they'd stayed at in Shropshire – and threw them into the sink. He got out the yellow bottle of Jif, squirted it at random all over the bath, found a scratchy cloth and then – with the clinical lemon-smell rising through his nostrils, right up into his head – he began to scrub, using the shower-mixer on the end of its silvery snake-like tail to dilute and wash away the ring of dirt.

David had worked for six months as a barman after leaving art school, and he knew how to clean things properly. After rinsing the bath, he took a dry cloth and wiped the enamel dry. Wiped until it gleamed. He took each bottle – the dumpy, squashy white ones with price tags softened by slimy drips of 'New Salon Formula', the smart long-necked Ylang Ylang and Bergamot aromatherapy ones his mother had given to Mel, the childish bright blue squeezy ones that sat on their lids – and wiped them too. Then he turned to the basin and began the same process with that – shoving toothpaste tubes, toothbrushes, Mel's contact lens equipment and so on into their respective washbags – and picked up the bottle of Jif.

By eleven thirty, while Edmund was still asleep, David had done the bathroom and the kitchen. He stood looking at the studio, and decided that perhaps now would be a good time for him to ring the Savils, to find out if they were serious, if they really wanted to come over today and, if so, what time? Of course, the room needed a thorough clean anyway, but there was no immediate need to do it if they weren't coming.

He went into Edmund's room and Edmund, who was a light sleeper, immediately opened his eyes.

'Have you got that guy – Savil's – number?'

'You've changed your mind?'

'Not exactly. But it would be rude, don't you think, for me not at least to ring, now that you've gone and stirred him up?'

'So it's my fault?'

'No, no. I just thought . . .' David sighed. 'Do you have the number or not?'

Smiling, Edmund lay in bed and pointed at the far corner of the room. 'It's in my jacket – the one on that chair – that's it – should be in the inside pocket – no, other side.' He waited for David to make sense of the folds of material. 'I think it's on the inside of a pack of matches.'

David took out the packet and opened it. Someone had written a number in bold felt-tip, crossing the sevens.

'He's really expecting me to call?' he said.

'Yes. And his name's Joss.'

David went straight down and dialled the number. A woman with a foreign accent answered.

'I was calling to speak to Joss Savil.'

'Mr Savil is not here. Who is speaking?'

'My name's David Nicholson. He doesn't know me, but I'm Edmund Nicholson's brother and I was just calling about a portrait I understand they might be –'

'You want to speak to Mrs Savil?'

David had to wait some minutes for Laura Savil to come to the telephone. When she did, the voice was so soft he had to press the receiver close to his ear.

'Hello,' she said. It was a low voice. Low and calm – '. . . Laura Savil speaking' – and American.

David took a deep breath. 'My name's David Nicholson,' he said again. 'I'm the brother of Edmund – Ned – who I think was with you last night.'

'Of course I remember. You're the artist, right?'

'Yes, that's right and I . . . well, Ned said that your

husband was thinking of – of getting you painted, and he said you were expecting me to call today. But I quite understand if you – if it isn't such a good idea in the clear light of morning. Or if you've got someone else. I mean . . . well, anyway, I was just calling –'

'Oh, we haven't got anyone else,' said the voice. It curled up at the end in a smile. 'And it's so kind of you to call us so soon. Shall I get my husband to ring you when he gets in?'

Finishing the call, David put down the receiver and heard Ned splashing in the bathroom. Washing away his Friday night, brushing his teeth, leaving lumps of toothpaste in the bowl of the basin, spilling dirty water against the mirror, depositing all his scum, his exfoliated skin, his specks of stubble on the freshly polished white enamel. And then, no doubt, he'd move on to the kitchen and spoil that too over a greedy fry-up breakfast.

David opened the fridge and moved the eggs, bread and bacon into the fruit and veg drawer at the bottom. Ned would never look there. If he wanted a cooked breakfast, he could bloody well go out for it. And it was easier to make him do it like this than to try to explain why he didn't want Ned messing it all up. Ned would simply laugh at him.

Joss Savil called at twelve. He spoke first to David – they arranged to meet at the studio for a drink that evening – and then to Edmund.

'Thanks for that, Ned.'

'Not at all. I should be thanking you. For letting me and Alice gate-crash your party last night.'

'Alice! That was it. Laura thought it was Anna, but

90

I knew she was wrong. Alice. Wow. Why don't we mix with girls like that any more, Ned? What's happened to us?'

'Us?'

'She's seventeen. *Seventeen!* Must hang on to every word you say.'

'Not exactly.'

'I don't even meet seventeen-year-olds any more – apart from Helena, and cousins don't count. How do you do it? What's your secret?'

Edmund was still in his dressing gown, a soft, white robe he'd been given by the hotel his firm had chosen for their last annual conference. He sat on the sofa with the telephone in his hand and crossed his legs – bare, brown and hairy down to feet that were suddenly smooth. He looked at his feet, his ankles, the slit of leg up to above his knee where the towelling had fallen open.

'It's the body, Joss. Can't you tell? Girls go nympho. Can't keep their hands to themselves. I have to push them away.' Edmund heard Joss laughing and smiled as he remembered last night. 'So you're coming over at six?'

'That's right.'

'Well, I'll see you then.'

'With Alice?'

'We'll see.'

Alice had break between eleven and eleven twenty on Saturday mornings. She was sitting on the grey lino floor by the lockers in the girls' loos, smoking, half listening to what the others had been doing last night, half observing her own reflection in the long mirror on the far wall. The light was ugly and, although the pink paint on the wall behind her had been freshly done over the summer, she could still see the chipped bits and the old graffiti beneath.

'Of course he fancies you,' said Emily, giving Sam – a voluptuous, dark-skinned girl with naturally ringleted hair and traces of acne on her cheeks – a half-smoked cigarette to light hers from. They'd been at Harry Brewer's party last night, at his parents' house in Putney – a vast semidetached with a garden that stretched into helpful darkness. Harry Brewer was a friend of Sam's brother's; he'd been in the year above them, and was now about to go to university. Sam had snogged him.

Lighting her own cigarette, Sam stretched her legs forward, crossing them at the ankles so that Alice could see the soles of her Doc Martens.

'Thing is,' she said, 'I do quite fancy him. I don't want him going to Oxford and leaving me here, not now that this has happened.'

'Well, there's not much you can do,' said Emily, taking her cigarette back.

'I can go to sixth form college.'

'In Oxford?'

Sam nodded.

'You're not serious?'

'No. You're right. I'm not,' Sam grinned, and leant round to look at herself in the long mirror, blocking Alice's view of herself. 'But wish I was. I hate this dump. I hate fucking Saturday school. I hate – Whose is that?'

From inside Alice's black nylon bag came ripples of electric Bach. Alice felt for her mobile and pulled it out – Bach getting louder, faster, angrier, uglier, and then silenced by her finger on the green button. The others stopped talking and watched.

'Yeah?'

'Alice, it's Edmund. Can you talk?'

'Oh, hi, Edmund.' Alice tried to give the others a cool, controlling smile which frothed over at the sight of Sam's and Emily's expressions.

'Who's *Edmund*?' whispered Sam.

'Bloke she had dinner with last night. Forty, or something.'

'*Forty*? Fuck . . .'

'Maybe it was thirty-five, but still. Older than Stevens. Older than Smith-Jardine, come to think of it.'

Giggles.

'Can you imagine snogging Smith-Jardine?'

'With that beard.'

'All the bits in it . . .'

Alice got up and went into the basin area.

'What time do they let you out?' said Edmund.

'One.'

'Want to have lunch?'

'All right.'

Edmund laughed slightly. 'Well, you don't have to have lunch with me, Alice, if you'd rather not.'

'No – no, I will . . . I'd love to!'

'That's better. Shall I meet you outside school? Or can you get a cab to Notting Hill?'

Alice hesitated.

'Don't worry, I'll collect you. You're just off St Martin's Lane, aren't you?'

'Yeah. On the right, past the Coliseum, you need

93

to look for the brown school sign – there's a funny one-way system that brings you round.'

'It's a silver Saab with a soft, black roof. I'll be there for you at one.'

To Alice's relief, the roof was still up and Edmund was waiting inside the car when she, Emily and Sam walked through the school gates as the chapel clock struck one.

'That's it,' she said, pointing at the car under the plane trees on the other side of the square. 'See you guys on Monday.'

'You're not coming to the pub?'

'She's got better things to do – right?' said Emily.

'Right.'

'Good luck!'

They stood watching as Alice went to the car, opened the door, and disappeared into its silvery body.

Inside the car, she kissed Edmund hello and then pulled back to look. She hadn't seen him dressed casually before. She took in the jeans, and the open-necked shirt – revealing a hairy chest. Alice wasn't sure about hairy chests. She didn't know any and, while she thought she wanted a Real Man, this evidence of lion-like male virility was rather too much for her. He looked wrong. You're a city lawyer, she thought, refusing him another life. You're a powerful, urban man with important things on your mind. Please don't dress like a cross between a student and a cowboy. Don't pretend to be something you're not. It only makes you look sad.

Edmund felt the scrutiny. 'You OK?' he said.

'Starving.'

'It's the hangover, sweetheart. But they do great

Bloody Marys where we're going, and huge portions, so put on your seat belt and prepare to be spoilt.'

Alice pulled the seat belt round as he started the engine and the car filled with the intelligent, discursive voices of a radio programme. It was air-conditioned there in the car, and a slight brown tint to the glass lent a sudden distance to the sight of her friends standing at the gates, identical bags slung over their shoulders, the sunlight on Sam's brushed ringlets, Emily's head bent, looking at a slip of paper with prep instructions on it.

Edmund turned the volume down and switched the programme round to Capital Radio. He steered slowly past all the uniforms, the pale blue ties, the black scuffed jackets, the teenage hairstyles, the weekend expressions, past Emily and Sam and a growing gang of friends congregating by the gate.

He took her to a restaurant recently opened by a friend of his at the smarter end of Westbourne Grove. They sat at a table by windows that ran the complete height of the room – windows that had, today, been folded and stacked back so that the restaurant spilled easily into the early autumn street. Broad awnings meant that the table was in shadow, but the temperature was perfect.

And at three thirty they were still there. Relaxing into the drink – the Bloody Marys, the ice-cool, too-cool bottle of white Burgundy, and then the extra half-bottle because it was so good, and because Edmund's friend had said they could have it on the house – Alice began to fancy him again. She was getting used to the jeans. Even the hairy chest was less intimidating, and she had begun to wonder what it felt like. Half listening to him, she soaked up the afternoon, the warmth in the air, the sound of distant shoppers, the murmurings of other couples in the restaurant, the sleepy sexiness.

Edmund was telling her about an apartment he had to see that afternoon – he was meeting the estate agent at four o'clock. Not far from the restaurant. He took the particulars out of a folder and showed them to Alice. Alice looked at them, but she wasn't really interested.

'Do you like it?'

'Yeah.' She handed the papers back to him. 'When are we going to have sex?'

Edmund leant towards her. 'When you're ready.'

'I am ready.'

'OK, then you're just going to have to wait until I'm ready.'

'Oh *God*,' Alice yawned and looked at her watch. She was smiling when she looked back at him.

Looking into her eyes all the time, Edmund sat back in his chair again, folded his arms and said nothing. He felt his heart beating. He was just starting to wonder if this was a sex-charged moment, or a playground staring match – or both – when he felt the slight ridge of her anklebone shift softly against his calf.

He went on looking at her, at the underwater effect produced by sunlight through the green awnings. Her hair – released now from its ponytail – fell to one side, crinkling in shades of green where the clip had held it. Her pale skin, warmed by the wine, still had an ice-mint surface. A black T-shirt stretched over what he could see of her body above the line of the table. She was sitting back too. Arms firm and straight, hands clutching the sides of her chair as she felt for him with her leg.

She came with him to the apartment. It was all on one floor, all white and freshly painted. They could smell it. Everything was new – all the fittings – and there was no furniture. Only bleached floorboards. Expensive lighting. Chrome kitchen. And three separate terraces: one off the kitchen, one off the bedroom, and one off the sitting room. There were bookshelves, and huge cupboards to be filled, and a smart clean smooth-stone gas fire in the middle of the sitting room, with a chimney going straight up. You could sit either side of it, and look through it.

Alice went out on to the main terrace – into the bright light, with Izzy's skirt catching the breeze. She stood tall, facing out: brief black top, fluttering skirt, bare legs, firm shoes. There were flat, striped, cushion-covered bench-seats around three of the four sides. She knelt on one of them, bare knees on hot canvas, and looked over the plants, around the edge, and down into the pulse of Portobello Market, while Edmund stood in the cool interior, watching her, the estate agent's patter in his ears.

7

Mel was driving north, alone. She was sad that David wasn't with her. After three hours of motorway she missed him, and it would have been nice to have someone to share the driving. But, even so, Mel knew it was better to do this by herself. For all she knew, her father might start blaming David for her decision to quit, and she didn't like to think too much about where that would lead, because one thing Mel knew for sure was that her father would not be pleased. She felt a little sick as she turned off the motorway, up towards the house.

In spite of a good education and good grades, Greg Ashton's career had not gone well. He'd gone to university, read engineering. On leaving, he'd been offered a job in industry involving a two-year training scheme, and then various managerial roles of increasing importance. It was supposed to be fast-track, and Greg had high hopes. He was bright enough to get to the top, but brainpower wasn't enough. Within a couple of years, it was clear to his employers that Greg lacked the right personal qualities: the confidence, the authority, and the trick of office politics. He wore his ambition too openly.

But it wasn't until he was forty that Greg realised he wouldn't make it. The people he was looking to, people he'd slaved for – the ones who'd taken the prime years of his working life – were going to let him down. Angry, humiliated, and true to character, Greg had stormed out. He'd got together with his friend Mark Purefoy, a dissatisfied solicitor with more charm than sense and the two men had set up a business in London on their own, but it hadn't worked. And when that business had folded, along with his friendship with Mark, Greg just wanted out.

'We're moving to Yorkshire,' he announced to his wife one evening.

'What?'

'Yorkshire.' Tossing the estate agent's particulars in Clare's direction, Greg opened the fridge. 'Found a house. Got a job in Leeds. Marketing.'

'Marketing?'

'Well, I'm sorry if that isn't posh enough for you, Clare, but I can't swan off the way Purefoy did.' Greg took out a bottle of tonic, unscrewed it with a twist and poured it over a generous glass of gin.

Clare was cooking dinner. She turned down the heat under the potatoes, picked the particulars off the floor and glanced at the front. The house in the picture looked more like a farm. It was square and grey, and surrounded by bright yellow oil seed rape. Perhaps it was the perspective of the photograph, but the fields seemed to stretch for ever. Vast squares of hard yellow, fading to a murky haze. Apart from a few outbuildings, with rusting roofs and crumbling walls, the house stood alone – and there were no trees.

'Looks nice,' she said, cautiously checking the price

and then the map to see why it was so cheap.

Mel often missed the turning. It was badly signed and straight off the motorway. It needed a sharp shift of gear and a robust undercarriage to cope with the sudden rubble and clay that led to Wheaton Farm. In spite of her father's attempts to make it look otherwise – he'd erected private property signs, and installed a pair of extra gates that he was now fighting the farmer about – this ill-kept lane was not their drive. It was part of a whole network of lanes that lay over the fields in their area. Lanes that Clare would walk along or, more accurately, be pulled along by Bess, the great strong dog that Greg had found when Clare told him she got scared up there alone.

Mel was early and the gates were shut. She stopped the car and got out, into mild sunshine and a wind that pulled at her hair. In the next field, a tractor reached the dry beech hedge, turned, and set off in the other direction, the earth folding in brown waves behind it. Mel lifted the hook and pulled the main gate back far enough for the car to get through. Beyond the hedge, the tractor churned on up, away, and the rough chug of the engine was supplanted by low, insistent motorway. She got back in, drove through and up to the house, past Bess tugging at her chain and barking.

The kitchen window overlooked the entrance to the house. Through it, Mel could see her mother filling a glass jug with water from the tap. As Mel drew close, Clare looked up and out. Suddenly she was smiling, turning off the tap and waving with her free hand. Leaving the jug on the side, she went round and out through the latched door.

It had taken much longer than expected for Clare to recover from the gardening accident to her toes – she still couldn't run properly – but the limp had gone and she walked towards Mel with her arms outstretched.

'Darling, you're early!'

Clare was small and Mel, whose height came from her father, had to bend right down to kiss her. Their cheeks pressed close, tight enough for neither of them to kiss the air. Mel felt the love in that pressure. She'd have liked to stroll out with her mother, look at how the garden was doing and talk in the sun. But the issue of her job pressed too, and Mel knew she had to tell them straight away.

'I've got some news,' she said. 'Where's Dad?'

Greg was inside, sitting in the best chair – his chair – in a dark cool room that smelt of cigarettes. The sofa to his right was covered in thin fabric that had once been in a room with more light. Its floral pattern had faded to white, and the cushions sagged. Greg was reading the papers, restlessly turning the pages, and listening. He heard it all – Mel's car, Bess's barking, female voices – and now he was waiting for them to come to him.

'Hi, Dad.'

'Melanie.'

Greg was rather less open than his wife. He didn't rush at Mel, didn't shower her with compliments, but it was clear that he too adored his daughter. He put the paper down, looked up at her standing in the doorway, and then he got up out of the chair and kissed her.

'How are you?'

'Mel's got some news, darling. She –'

Greg looked at Mel. 'About your work?' he said, curly grey eyebrows pushing his forehead into folds.

Mel nodded.

Quietening his excitement, telling himself that she couldn't be made a partner *yet* – it had taken Purefoy at least ten years – Greg held the door for his daughter.

'Well, come on in, love. Come and tell us.'

She was too young, surely. But there would be signs. Greg wasn't quite sure what those signs would be, but imagined that postings abroad would come into it, or six-month placements with client companies, pay rises, new responsibilities – signs that his daughter had been singled out for fast-track success. Wondering which of these it was, Greg strode back to his chair, he sat in it and waved a hand at the sofa.

'Sit down, sit down!'

Mel sat.

Clare remained in the doorway. She and Greg looked at their daughter with smiling expectancy.

Mel sighed. 'OK,' she said, more to herself than to them. 'OK. It's like this. I've been working hard. Too hard –'

'Too hard?'

'All hours, Dad. For months now, and –'

'All hours is good,' said Greg, scratching his tight grey curls. 'Hard work and lots of it. Can't afford to be slacking, love. Not at this stage in your career.'

Mel examined her hands, and twisted the engagement ring round so that the stone was on the inside.

'Drink?' said Clare.

'And, of course, you've got to make sure it's the *right* kind of work. Can't afford to waste time on all those lectures and courses you seem to –'

'But that's part of the process.'

'Yes, yes. But you've got to bring *value* to the business, love. Show them you're –'

'Dad.'

'Show them what you're made of. Show them you can do it.'

'Glass of wine? Or something soft?'

'Oh, *woman* . . .'

'I'd love some wine, Mum. White, if you've got it. But why don't I –'

'No,' said Greg. He put a hand on Mel's arm. 'Your mother can get it. No, you sit right there and tell me about where this hard work of yours has taken you.'

So she did. Clenching her fingers over the ring, digging the stone into the pad of her palm, Mel told her father she'd handed in her notice. She was leaving in December. No, she wasn't going to another firm. She was quitting altogether. And no, she didn't want to try any other kind of law.

. . . that wasn't the point. No. She just didn't want to be a lawyer any more. Actually, she'd never wanted to be a lawyer. . . . Yes, really. . . . No, that had been his decision. And now she, Mel, was going to take some time out and think about what she wanted to do with her life.

The ruby dug deep.

. . . It had nothing to do with David. . . . David liked her being a lawyer. . . . No, he did. . . . *What?*

. . . Well, if Greg really felt that way then they'd just have to get married in London instead. OK. Fine.

103

. . . Well, that was his call. But this was too important. This was her life, for God's sake. Not his.

. . . She didn't mind being poor for a while. And, anyway, there was a bit of money, wasn't there? What about the cash she'd inherited from Mum's parents? The cash he'd – Actually, Dad, it's not your money. But if you – Oh, all right it might be your money technically, but in equity it's clear – . . . I think I'm rather better-qualified than you to – . . . No, don't lie, Dad. I saw Granny's Letter of Wishes, and I know she – . . . Jesus. I can't believe you're – . . . All right, take it. *Take it.* I don't need it. I'll live with David.

. . . Really, Mum? . . . Yes – yes, you're probably right. Although I don't think he is tired. He's just a bloody-minded . . . Yes, I know. Can't discuss anything sensibly right now. Can't even – . . . OK, I'll call you when I get there.

She set off back to London, flying down, in and out of potholes on the lane, breaking hard at the turning – dangerous, sharp – and out, accelerating through the gears, into motorway traffic. She burnt. How could he speak to her like that? How could he?

Greg was aggressive. Mel knew that. He picked fights. He'd lose his temper with other motorists, neighbouring farmers, telesales people, or the man in the village shop. He could even – which, to Mel, was unforgivable – lose his temper with Clare. But until today, he'd never raised his voice at Mel. Until today, she'd never known what it was like to be on the receiving end of anger quite like that. Anger that was *practised*, somehow. Easily released, well-directed, hard, vicious rage.

Mel had known that her father would be upset

by her news. She'd expected it. What she hadn't expected, however, was quite such a sudden about-face. Greg had got to his feet, eyes so blind and big with rage, so close that she could see the whites all the way round. Suddenly, it wasn't about her job. It wasn't even about David and the wedding, or the money she'd been left. It was all about control. He'd left the room with a wham-slam of the door, heels hard on the kitchen tiles as Clare opened the door again.

'Darling?'

Wham-slam went the outside door, latch rattling as it bounced back and forth and rested open. Mel had tried to follow.

'Better leave him,' Clare had said.

So they'd stood at the window, and watched him let Bess off her chain. Still holding the chain, he'd climbed with it over the far gate, and walked off up the rubble lane, swinging the heavy links. Very slowly, saying nothing, Clare and Mel had left the room. It wasn't until they were out in the sun that Mel felt able to talk.

'What the hell was that about?'

Clare smiled. 'He's tired, darling. He –'

'Tired?' said Mel, opening the car door. *'Tired*?'

'He just needs to walk it off. He'll be fine when he gets in.'

'But, Mum, all I did was hand in my notice. I – How dare he talk to me like that?'

'He doesn't mean it. He's just sad that you're giving up. And so am I, darling. All that hard work down the drain. Are you sure you –'

'I'm positive,' said Mel, getting into the car.

'He's just tired.'

How many times had she heard that? Sitting at the kitchen table aged five, dressed in her pyjamas, eating baked beans on toast as her father came in from work, his voice impatient in the next room. Poor Daddy – so tired. Or in traffic, quiet in the back seat while he ranted at Clare for failure to read the map properly, and find him a route that wasn't stiff with cars. Or sullen demands for a cleaner towel, a pen that works *for fuck's sake*. Or just a bit of peace and quiet, woman – is that too much to ask? And every time, Clare had waited until she was alone with Mel before explaining that poor Greg was just feeling terribly, terribly tired.

Mel loved her father, but she was frequently embarrassed by the way he behaved. Most people didn't tolerate it. But then, most people didn't have to. They simply cut him off, didn't speak to him, refused his calls, or got their lawyers to handle him. There were certain restaurants in Leeds that wouldn't let him in. And Greg – genuinely baffled that so many people could be so rude, so mean, so entirely irrational – would shrug his shoulders and walk away. There were always other restaurants he could go to.

And, although Greg tried harder with Clare – he couldn't walk away from her so easily – his efforts never extended to stopping the anger in the first place. True, Mel didn't see it happen very often, but she knew he'd still shout at her, still treat her with an appalling lack of respect. The only difference was that, when the storm passed, Greg would hang out rainbows. He'd try to cancel out the bad with a few swift acts of love. And, invariably, Clare would accept the gesture and forgive him.

Oh, but his capacity for love is just as strong, she'd say to Mel. He's a passionate man. He had his bad moments – didn't everybody? – but those moments were more than compensated for by good times.

Pulling into the next petrol station, Mel stopped the car. It was hot in there – hot, airless and sickly – but she remained at the wheel with her eyes shut. She was still smarting from his words, still shocked to find herself on the receiving end of such appalling treatment. But that was nothing compared with a thought that, only now, was rising to the surface . . . a thought of Clare: Clare's attitude, her smile, her absolute lack of surprise. Clare, standing in the sunshine, waving Mel off as if what had happened was nothing new.

And perhaps it wasn't. Perhaps this wasn't one of Greg's 'bad moments'. Maybe he didn't have bad moments. Maybe this was his regular behaviour. And maybe what Mel had seen, since she'd left home, were simply the 'good moments' – bright spots of pretence over a dark stream of anger.

8

David was ready when the doorbell rang. More than ready. He'd been ready for half an hour, and was at the stage of rearranging his photograph frames and ashtrays.

A sweet smell of polish overpowered the usual fumes of paint and white spirit. He'd done the floor, the skirting boards, the rungs on the chairs, the easel. The sketches from last night had been put back on to the racks – a temporary measure, but he'd deal with them when he had more time, and when he was definitely alone. He'd wiped his jars of pigment. He'd plumped up the cushions on the chairs and the sofa, the way his mother's cleaner did. He'd put drink and glasses on the coffee table. He'd opened the windows – windows that, he had to admit, needed professional attention (they looked filthy now, next to everything else) – and a warm breeze was clearing the air.

'Hi! Come up. First floor.'

'Thanks,' said a man's voice, and David pressed the entry button.

He was glad to greet them by himself. Without Ned: smug, social, and in the way. Or Mel: observant in the background. But turning the door-catch, preparing his face for a smile and an easy-going, 'Come in! Come in! I'm David,' hand-shaking perhaps, and then, 'What would you like to drink?' David found his plans wiped blank by the woman waiting for him behind the door.

Laura.

Not any Laura. Not Laura because of Laura. But *Laura*.

'Hello.' She gave him a stranger's smile – sophisticated, dressed. 'I'm Laura, and this is my husband.'

'Joss,' said Joss, holding out his hand. 'Joss Savil.'

Then silence. A slip of silence. And into that split-second freeze-frame, with vibrations of their voices dying on the stairs, David brought a decade of his life. He couldn't see her quickly enough. His eyes grabbed at her, at the tamed roll of hair at her neck, at the polished skin – flat on the sharpened plane of her cheekbone, sliced by light from a window on the landing – and at the fall of light clothes, semi-opaque, over a body known.

Laura. American, and he'd never realised.

His smile lurched dangerously. It faltered at her eyes, swung into Joss's, and then reconnected with the present.

'Come in! Come in! I'm David.'

Hand-shaking. Shaking hands.

'What would you like to drink?'

They wanted wine. Wine. Wine. He smelt them – flower-fresh, polite – as they went past, into the studio. He closed the door behind them.

Wine.

'What a fabulous room, Joss. Look at the height – and the staircase!'

'And the paintings, darling. That's why we're here.'

'Oh look! It's Alice . . .'

They stood in silence, looking at Alice on the easel, while David pulled a cork out of the bottle, poured out three large glasses and took two over. He saw Laura's back view. Her slim brown calves beneath a wrap-around skirt that stopped at her knees. Tailor-pointed, low shoes in the same faded red fine-weave canvas as the bag in her hands – both behind her back, fingers twisting at the handle. He stopped in the middle of the room, a glass in each hand.

'You're very talented,' said Joss, coming up. He took both glasses from David, and held one out to his wife.

'It's absolutely her,' Laura went on, one hand waving at the painting, the other still clasped to her bag. 'You've got the way she doesn't seem to give a damn, that sassy attitude she has, and the vulner-ability . . .'

'Darling,' said Joss gently. 'Take your glass.'

Praying that she didn't recognise him – more for her sake than his – David looked at Laura, who slid her red canvas bag into the crook of her brown bare arm, took a sip of wine and looked back. He watched her slanting eyes sweep from his to the floor and then back again.

'Have we met before?' she asked.

Not knowing quite what he was going to say, David opened his mouth.

But the sound of a key in the door, laughter, and the sudden explosion of Ned and Alice – and all the thrill, the heat, the sexual time bomb of their afternoon – filled the gap. It filled the studio.

'Hey!'

Edmund went straight over to Joss, shook his hand warmly, and then kissed Laura firmly and affectionately on the cheek. Alice smirked at David. And David finished his glass of wine in two sharp gulps.

'Hello, Alice. Having fun?'

With her nylon bag still slung over her shoulder, Alice came up, leant round and kissed him – alcohol from her breath wrapping the air around them as she came close – and laughed. 'Yeah. You?'

'You met Joss and Laura last night, didn't you?'

'Hi, Laura. Hi, Joss,' Alice took a heavy step in his direction for a kiss. 'What a great evening! What a great house! I loved that piano.'

'I loved that playing.'

The noise level rose with the greetings, turning the studio into a drawing room. David couldn't fight it. He was past thinking about anything right now, except Laura. He went into the kitchen to get more glasses, another bottle from the fridge, and privacy. Mechanically, he opened the glass cupboard.

That this was happening at all was extraordinary. But to have it happen here – right here in his studio – and to have to play it out in front of Ned, and Alice, and Laura's husband . . . David took the glasses with an unsteady hand, and went to the fridge. He just had to get through this evening. Just get through it.

Bottle in one hand, glasses in the other, he paused by the sink and looked out at the street below. The level of the kitchen window, the irregular styles of building in the street, meant that he could see right down its length. The boys from number 20 were kicking a football backwards and forwards. The window was open, and David could hear the ball picking up a rhythm, slide-scraping over the tarmac, then thudding at their feet, and then a lifting silence to the next shallow bounce.

In the silence, he heard the others.

'What I like best are the legs,' Alice was saying.

Joss's laughter. 'Me too.'

'No, silly! No, I mean, look – look how he's flattered me. And the hair, too. It looks natural, for God's sake!'

'You mean it's not?'

Then softer, further away, Laura to Ned: 'Are there any others we can see, do you think?'

'Yes, I'm sure – there's a pile over there, and there were some rather lovely drawings he was looking at last night, somewhere in these racks . . .'

David rushed back in with the glasses. 'Ned, here.' He gave Ned the corkscrew and the second bottle while he poured the remains of the first into a glass for Alice and brought Laura's attention away from the racks. 'I'm afraid I don't have many original portraits here for you to see. Most of them go straight to the people who commissioned them.'

'Of course.'

'But I do have a few old ones, like that watercolour up there on the far wall, see?'

'How lovely.'

'Of my mother.'

Laura went towards the picture: Virginia Nicholson's dark head bent over a great long book that might have been a photograph album, open on her lap, its line cutting a bold diagonal across the seated body. Laura looked up at it, then back at David, and then at Ned, searching for the family likeness, and finding it in David. 'She's like David, right?'

'Maybe to look at,' said Ned. 'But what about those drawings, Davey? You know, the ones you were looking at the other day.'

Pushing the full glass into Alice's hand, David came back to Laura. 'And there are a few more,' he said. 'Over here, see?' He guided her away from Ned, over to the pile he'd selected, propped against the wall under the staircase, next to his marble worktop.

'Oh, look at your jars. How neat. You make your own paints?'

'Some of them. Now look: this was a judge I did last month, and here's a family group, and here's another man in uniform . . .' David spread the canvases, some in heavy gilded frames, some bare, out along the wall beneath the window. 'But I'm afraid there are no single women, in oil that is, except Alice.'

'Single women?'

'Women by themselves. In the picture, I mean.'

'Oh, I see.'

'But I have got a portfolio of photographs of my work. Would you like to see that?'

Laura nodded. 'I'd love to,' and then, looking at him again, she frowned. 'You know, David, I must say I'm sure that we –'

She was about to ask again if he thought they'd met before. He could feel it, feel the scrutiny, when Mel walked in, expressionless.

She was wired. Spring-tight tense. Her jaw was fixed, her teeth gripped. The drive had been tearless, hard and fast. The car engine, its hot roar, had rammed and penetrated her head and the after-effects were still there, narrowing now to a pinpoint ache.

A party. A little party of people she'd never met. Mel looked at Alice and Laura, and felt the stench of her day – its petrol pumps, sandwich wrappings and clogged motorway loos – in her clothes, on her skin, through her hair. She smiled because she had to, and made for the spiral staircase.

'Hi,' she said to the room. 'I'll just go up and –'

David caught her hand. 'Come on, darling.'

But Mel didn't want to 'come on'. She didn't want to meet these people. Not right now. Perhaps she was being irrational, he wasn't telepathic, but couldn't he see how shattered she was? Couldn't he tell, just by looking at her, that she really wasn't up to being social? Wasn't the day's nightmare etched across her face? It wasn't often she needed his support. It wasn't often she felt this weak. It was because of her, because she'd known it would be bad, that David hadn't come with her today. She'd done him a favour, let him off. Couldn't he, just this once, return it?

David, however, was thinking only of Laura – of how he could keep a lid on this increasingly strange situation. And so long as everybody behaved properly and stuck to the rules, then he could cope. He just couldn't handle any more surprises. It was bad enough that Mel was here. Wasn't she supposed to be in Yorkshire tonight? He was sure it was a whole weekend. Quite sure. Yet she was back. Back prematurely, behaving unpredictably, and with an unfamiliar look in her eye. David, uneasy, fastened his grip on the framework of convention, and fastened on Mel too. Now that she was here, he didn't want her disappearing upstairs out of sight. He wanted control, and Mel was too tired to resist.

'Come on, darling.' He led her into the room. 'This is Laura. Laura Savil – Mel Ashton, my fiancée . . . and Laura's husband, Joss . . . And Alice, who,' party laughter, 'who I *hope* you recognise from –'

'From her picture. Of course.'

' – and Ned.'

Ned was shocked by Mel's appearance. Beside Laura's tan and Alice's flush, her skin had the extreme pallor of someone about to be sick. Beneath the sharp dark fringe, her eyes strained with each introduction. Ned thought for a moment that she might crack, and then quite suddenly she seemed to recover. She greeted Ned with a professional smile, held out her hand and asked him how he was.

Ned gave it an automatic shake. 'I'm fine,' he said. 'How are you?'

'Desperate for a shower,' she took the glass that David was offering, and held it out while he poured in the wine, 'and desperate for a drink. Thanks, darling. Can I do anything?'

David gave her a grateful smile. Then he looked at Joss and Laura, who'd gone back to the row of pictures propped against the wall, and shook his head. 'No,' he said. 'No, just –'

'Just occupy me and Alice,' said Ned, for him. 'Keep us out of trouble, while he gets down to business.'

'Talking of trouble,' said Alice, opening her bag – taking out a cheap plastic lighter and searching on down past a mass of school-related papers, grubby make-up containers and a hardback copy of *The Three Edwards* she'd stolen from the school library – 'Talking of trouble, where are my fags? I'm sure I had another pack in here somewhere.'

'Take mine,' said Ned. 'There's a pile of duty-free by my bed.'

'Your bed?'

'Up the stairs. Second on the left – and don't nick the lot. Just one pack . . . Alice?'

'Yadda yadda,' said Alice, racing up the stairs.

Ned turned to Mel.

She was watching David, looking at his hands on the great gilt frames – the easy way he raised one of the smaller portraits, holding it so that the light was a little better, explaining about the differences between head-and-shoulders 'mugshots' and rather fuller portraits, and how that would affect the size that Joss and Laura chose.

'Long day?' said Ned.

'That obvious?'

He grabbed the bottle of wine and topped up Mel's glass. 'Only to someone who's had more than his fair share of long days,' he said. 'That's the trouble with our kind of work. And when it eats into a warm weekend, it's a bloody imposition.'

Mel liked the way he'd decided to skip the what-do-you-do exchanges – of course they'd know about each other, both lawyers, it would be silly to pretend otherwise – and then she remembered that this wasn't quite the case. As of yesterday, she was leaving law. She didn't need to work weekends. There was no 'our kind of work'. Not any more.

'Except I wasn't working,' she told him, smiling.

'Probably should have been. There's a mass of paper on my desk, and God knows what in store for me next week, but –'

'Bad girl.'

Mel laughed. 'Yes, maybe,' she said. 'But as I've handed in my notice, it's not exactly –'

'Your notice?'

Mel drank from her glass, and nodded.

'Interesting,' said Ned. 'So you're leaving – Blythe Mattheson, is it? Or –'

'W. J. Oliphant.'

'Sorry – WJO – for where? Who gave you the better offer?'

'Nobody did,' said Mel, enjoying herself. 'I'm quitting. For good. The whole damn thing. Bye-bye. *Adíos*. No more law.' She lifted her glass. 'Hooray!'

Ned stared at her. 'Why?'

'I don't want to do it any more.'

'Why?'

'I feel trapped.'

'But you could take a sabbatical.'

'Like you?'

'Or change firms.'

'Why bother?' said Mel. 'We're all the same these days, don't you think? Blythe's, Oliphant's, Maclaughlin's . . . you muddled them up yourself. Same aims. Same sweatshop culture. International law factories. Not much point going to the trouble of changing, when the only difference is the colour of our files.'

'It's not like that at Fenwick & Moore.'

Mel laughed. 'Rubbish!' she said. 'You're just as bad as us! I read that piece in the *Gazette* by your

117

senior partner, banging on about globalisation and providing a comprehensive international advice and keeping up with London US firms.'

'Sodding US firms,' said Ned, grinning. 'Trouble is, they pay so well. I was head-hunted the other day. Offered double my existing salary to switch, which is tempting until you realise that not only will they extract every ounce of flesh, but they'll know exactly how.' He refilled her glass and went on, 'But you don't have to quit law altogether, you know, to get away from that. You could try something gentler. What about legal information? Or in-house work? Or a different department? Which one are you in at the moment?'

Alice returned with the cigarettes, and was listening, smoking, watching – waiting for her moment to join in. But it was hard. She'd never heard of Blythe Mattheson, or WJO. She wasn't quite sure what globalise meant, or how the 'legal information' differed from regular work as a lawyer. She had nothing to contribute. One of the things that Alice enjoyed about Ned was the way he talked to her as an equal. All last night, and again today, he'd enabled her to forget the age gap and bask in his attention. She, Alice, had felt all-interesting, all-important. Listening to him now, however – hearing the way he raised his conversation to Mel's, to a different world – Alice felt the limits of her own.

Smoking in the girls' bogs, lesson notes and prep. Exam-fever, UCAS forms and street-cred style. It didn't really compare to the big world. To corporate law, and interest rates, and secret files. Expense accounts, offices, and international calls.

Alice knew there were masses of women in the City, lots of women just like Mel, but until today she'd never met one. The working women she knew were either friends of her mother (and they were the kind of women who ran interior design businesses, or did low-key PA work) or the teachers at her school. And Mel, like the teachers, wasn't immediately noticeable. Her clothes said nothing. There was no special air about her, no style, nothing on the surface to grab the attention. But as she listened, Alice began to take an interest. Mel knew things. Her voice was neither refined, nor rough. It had – to Alice's ear – authority. Her conviction was absolute. And Alice fell to wondering how long it would take for her to get like that? How long before she too could match a man like Edmund. She wanted to be as conversant with macho Cityspeak. She wanted that kind of power. And suspecting that it came from Mel's training as a lawyer, thinking that it was Mel's best asset, Alice – like Edmund – couldn't understand why Mel would now want to give it up.

'Commercial.'

'There you are,' said Ned. 'Change. Try litigation. Or what about property? Or employment? You don't need to stop altogether.'

'Yes I do.'

'But –'

Mel's smile faded. 'I just do. All right? . . . Can I?'

'Oh, I'm sorry,' said Alice, holding out the cigarette packet. 'Help yourself.'

Edmund watched Mel extract one and light it. Curiosity no longer idle, he looked at the dirt on her fingers – dirt from the dust on the boot of the car –

and, unsmiling, ran his mind over what he'd seen of her last night, the way she'd mollycoddled David.

'What are you going to do instead?' said Alice.

'I don't know. I was thinking of –'

'Perhaps Mel thinks she doesn't need to do anything,' said Ned. 'Not now that she's getting married. It's *adiós* to the office and *holá* to the nursery.'

'That's not what I'm –'

'I don't know why we bother. And sometimes I don't know why you women bother, either. We train you up, we spend hours and hours making you into first-class lawyers, you work like dogs and then – *just* at the point you start to enjoy yourselves, just at the point when we start to get a return on all that time and effort and money – you go and quit. You give it all up and have babies.'

Alice's eyes shot round to Mel, who took one last smooth drag from her cigarette and stubbed it out.

'I think it's best if I pretend I didn't hear that,' she said, the smile a little forced. 'Don't you?'

Conscious that he'd overstepped the mark, and wishing he'd held his tongue, Ned gave an uneasy smile. But before he could reply, Mel had turned to Alice and was asking her what plans she had for her own future career.

Alice had no idea. The tests she'd done with the school careers officer had told her she was ideally suited to work as a librarian. A *librarian*. Alice had never been so insulted. She wanted to be a singer, she said, or an actress, or . . . or maybe something rather more serious, something more like law?

David was on the sofa next to Laura, showing her

photographs of his work. His world had shrunk to that island of upholstery. Sitting beside her, following but not seeing the photographs of his work – reduced from large bold canvas to glossy card-sized squares – David breathed her in. The smell of Victorian roses flowering out of her hair, the leg against his on the sofa, the quiet American voice. All parts of Laura he'd never known, parts that gave dimension and made her real. Because, until now, he'd never touched her, smelt her, heard her voice. He'd only seen her, in the clinical light of the art school studio. His sense of her as a living organism with blood in her veins, air in her lungs, thoughts in her head, had a corresponding effect on David's sense of himself. He felt alive.

Joss and Laura had planned to leave at eight to be at a dinner party back in their part of town before eight thirty. In the end, they left at nine – laughing into the night, full of praise for David's work, his studio, his wine – having commissioned a life-size portrait of Laura. David would be going round to Cheyne Lane on Monday to do preliminary sketches, to see if the London house would make a good setting, and to decide what Laura might wear. The main picture was set to be done in the spring. Both dates were in their diaries.

9

Edmund picked up a couple of empty glasses and took them into the kitchen where David was pouring a glass of wine back into the bottle.

'What are we going to do about dinner?'

David didn't answer – he was too busy concentrating on not spilling any – and Edmund watched him, amused. The wine wasn't that good, but it was as instinctive for David to save it as it would have been for Edmund to throw it away. He waited until David had finished, until he was putting the bottle in the fridge, and then tried again.

'David,' he said, 'shall we go out?'

David, still bent over the fridge, looked in at its contents. There were two dozen eggs in that fruit and veg drawer, a half-finished packet of bacon, three tomatoes, and an old lump of cheddar in a plastic cover that curled away where it had been cut.

'No need,' he said. 'We can have omelettes.'

'David . . .'

'Yes?'

Ned was laughing. 'It's Saturday night. Let's go somewhere fun. There must be hundreds of places near here.'

Mel came in with a tray of empty bottles, full ashtrays and dirtied glasses. 'Come on, darling,' she said to David. 'We can run to a pizza.'

'Pizza?' said Alice, following her, trying to stub a cigarette out in one of the ashtrays as it moved. 'I say we go somewhere expensive.'

David took out the eggs and the lump of cheese, and put them on the side. 'Great,' he said. 'You and Ned do that. Mel and I'll stay here. There's the second part of that documentary we saw last week on –'

Alice inspected the cheese. 'But there's mould on this,' she said, giggling. 'Look.'

'There's supposed to be mould on it.'

'Not with maggots.'

Edmund picked it up and tossed it into the bin; it hit the side with a rustle and a thud. 'Come on,' he said. 'We're all going out.'

They walked to the local pizza restaurant. A wind was rising. It blew at Edmund's face as he walked with Alice, her hand in the crook of his arm. David and Mel were in front. They weren't holding hands, he noticed. They were striding into the wind, pacing together, almost the same height even though Mel's shoes were flat – flat, unlovely trainers that put a bounce in her step and let her walk with androgenous ease. Yes, thought Edmund. It did make sense. The trainers, the short hair, the thoughtless jeans. She could get away with it because she was tall, but it was still Economy. Not minimalist perfection. Just Economy – and it was really no wonder that David had chosen her in the end.

Because for all his talent, his eye, his ability with paint, David's tastes and habits weren't really what people expected from an artist. He liked keeping things clean and orderly. He didn't get drunk, he didn't suffer from depression, he liked saving money. He could have been a bank clerk. Edmund knew him so well, he didn't find it surprising. He could see that the uncompromising fussiness that David showed with the state of his bathroom was the same fussiness he had with the things he created. David wanted a calm, well-run home – controlled, inexpensive – not ramshackle bohemia. And Mel looked like she was the kind of woman who'd be able to provide that for him.

Last night – the crazy hair, the sleepy woman, still half drunk from her office party – it was, he realised, uncharacteristic. Today, Mel had pulled her outer self together. Ned had seen the deliberate shift from visible exhaustion to controlled professional, and he was disappointed. He liked women with their characters, their feelings and their passions on the surface. He wasn't interested in the person she wanted to be. He wanted the person herself. So he was disappointed, but not surprised. This was much more David's woman – less Ned's. And, smiling, Ned reminded himself that this was only right.

Mel stood beside David as they waited for a table to be set up. She wanted to tell him about her day, about the things that had happened, the way she felt. She needed to let it out, make sense of it by talking, yet something held her back. It wasn't just that they were with other people. It was more a sense of David's pre-occupation, a sense that any interest he expressed would only be polite.

Mel was always thinking about her father: the way he behaved, the things he said, the influence he'd had on her career. But whenever she spoke to David about it, he didn't really understand, and perhaps she was expecting too much from a child of healthy, loving parents. He'd listen for a while, then he'd sigh, say something he thought would be enough – 'The guy's a control-freak,' was typical – and change the subject. It was almost like he was embarrassed. Embarrassed to see the untidy, knotted underside of Mel's family life. Embarrassed not to have the answers. And Mel would be miserable. While she knew she'd solicited it, she still hated that casual damning of her father. It wasn't David's place to be rude about him, yet what else could he do?

Over the last few months, she'd stopped talking to him about it, stopped exposing him to it. It wasn't really his fault. She couldn't blame him for it, but the truth was that David didn't understand. He'd never understand. There was a limit to his interest. And Mel didn't want to face that lack of sensitivity again. It would be foolish and masochistic of her to tell him what had happened. For David to know it and ignore it – or do the minimum – was far harder for her to bear than him not knowing at all.

So, willing her mind away from the events of her day, Mel said nothing. Leaning against a pillar, she watched Edmund talking to a waiter. Beyond him, Alice bent to examine herself in the glass. She pulled her pale hair round her neck, twisted it, and glanced surreptitiously at David, who was standing with his arms folded, looking at his feet.

Mel wondered what he was thinking about. His paintings, perhaps? Or maybe he was battling with his dislike of restaurants. He thought they were a waste of money and, generally speaking, Mel was inclined to agree with him. But these days, they never ate out and, standing there, Mel realised how much she enjoyed the indulgence, how much she'd missed the bustle and ritual of restaurant culture. Even if it was only pizza.

The first time that David had suggested they drop the restaurant, cook something together at his place and then watch a video, Mel had thought that there could be nothing more romantic. The very ordinariness of it appealed to her. That David should want to be like that with her suggested that he wanted her in his life. But now that they'd been together for almost a year, she wondered if evenings in were really as intimate as they seemed. With both of them looking at a screen, not at each other – following the twists and turns of television lives while their own sat on pause – Mel felt that, if anything, it was the reverse. David didn't do it deliberately, of course. He'd always worried about money. Even now that he was getting quite successful, David felt that his job would never earn him enough. An irregular income meant that he still budgeted according to a worst-case scenario, and that meant cutting out on extravagances. And because Mel knew how much David minded about this, and because her income had been – until now – guaranteed, it had always seemed a bit tactless to suggest going out. But she liked it when they did, especially when they were alone.

'OK, darling,' said Edmund, tugging Alice's twist of hair and pointing to the table in the corner. 'We're on.'

Mel and Alice sat with their backs to the wall – the men opposite – on tiddly black chairs that weren't quite stable. They shuffled into position. Edmund took his menu from the waiter, stuck his legs out confidently under the table and lit a cigarette. He was hungry. He'd had far too much to drink that day, and he needed to eat. It was all right for Alice – she'd have a small headache tomorrow and be fine by lunchtime – but he, Ned, would be suffering after-effects as far ahead as Monday. He ordered garlic bread, lots of water, and a bottle of house red.

When the wine arrived, Alice raised her glass, drawing their attention. 'I think,' she said, 'I think – to your engagement!' Her words weren't entirely clear. 'To David and Mel!'

They all clinked their glasses – cheap glasses of Valpolicella, splashing over their wrists, dark red spots on the paper cloth. They clinked on round and drank.

'So,' said Ned, into the silence. 'When's the wedding?'

'April.'

'Long way off.'

Mel smiled. 'Not when you think of all the things we have to organise – church, flowers, caterers, dress, music . . . Which reminds me, darling,' she turned to David. 'Darling?'

'Mm?'

'I was thinking about your guest list, and mine . . .' Mel took a breath, 'just wondering if it didn't make more sense for everyone if we did it in London after all. Yorkshire's such a long way for everyone to go. And we could hire a venue instead – hotel or something – or there's that place in Barnes where we could get them to do the lot. Probably work out cheaper, and we wouldn't have nearly so many things to worry about . . .'

Ned looked at Alice, who looked up from her menu, straight back at him, and pulled a face.

'There's no swordfish steak, and there's no foie gras,' she said, tossing the menu to one side. 'What *am* I going to eat?'

Ned laughed. 'You'll get what you're given.'

'You sound like my mother.'

'You sound like mine.'

Alice grinned. 'I think I'm going to like your mother,' she said, sinking from her chair, disappearing from view.

'Alice?' He felt her wriggling under the table.

'Hang on, Ned, I . . .'

'Alice, what *are* you –'

'There,' she said, arriving on the other side between Ned and David, and standing up. 'Now where are the bogs? I'm desperate.'

'Over there,' said David, shifting his chair so that she could get past, and pointing. 'See? Beyond the bar.'

'What shall we order for you?' shouted Edmund, after her.

Alice turned. 'I'll get what I'm given,' she said coyly. 'Isn't that what you said?'

She set off through the tables – through a frenzy of Latin music – with the nylon bag slung over her arm, playing with her hair. The skirt was eye-catchingly short. And Edmund, along with half the restaurant, followed her with his eyes. It wasn't until she disappeared behind the bar that he realised that he too was being watched.

'What?' he said. 'What's so funny?'

'Nothing.'

'Then why are you laughing?'

'We're not, Ned. Really, we're not. We just . . .'

'Just what?'

Mel leant back for the waiter to refill her glass. 'Well, I think she's great,' she said. 'She's pretty and sexy and bright and funny . . . So what if she's half your age?'

'There's nothing between us,' said Edmund.

Mel gave him her sweetest smile.

'Really,' he went on. 'Nothing. Tell her, David.'

David spluttered into his Valpolicella. 'I don't know,' he said. 'How should I know what you and Alice have been up to?'

'But you know I only took her to dinner last night, David. You know I sent her home in a cab. I –'

'So there's nothing going on?' said David.

Edmund hesitated. 'Nothing like that. Nothing.'

'Believe that, and you'll believe anything,' murmured Mel, smiling, filling David's glass.

Ned turned to her. 'You think I've had sex with Alice,' he said.

'I didn't say –'

'You think I'm the kind of person who'd take advantage of an innocent –'

'Well, I wouldn't exactly describe Alice as innocent. But –'

'You think I'm taking advantage of her,' he repeated.

'Oh Ned,' said Mel, unable to resist it, 'Alice strikes me as being much too intelligent to let anyone take advantage of her.'

'But I'm not even –'

'Close? Oh dear. Poor Ned. How very frustrating for you.'

'But –'

But Alice was back, swinging her way towards them.

Later, with their orders taken and a second bottle of wine on the way, Ned thought of what Mel had said. Opposite him, Alice was eating her slice of garlic bread. She was holding it gently in nail-bitten fingertips as she tried, with her wrist, to wipe away the melted butter that glistened round her mouth and slithered over her chin. Edmund watched her and wondered what was stopping him. Why shouldn't he? If people had already assumed the worst, then he may as well have done it.

It was late when they left the restaurant.

Mel had started to worry about David. He'd been quiet that night. He'd insisted on paying for her (but only because Ned was paying for Alice, only because he was too proud) and in spite of the commission from the Savils, in spite of the money it would bring in, he'd still think he couldn't afford it.

'You OK?'

'I'm fine.'

'You're quiet.'

'I'm tired . . .'

She dropped back with him, leaving Ned and Alice to walk on, arm in arm, and took his hand. 'But you're not cross, are you? I know you're trying to save money, but I –'

David smiled. 'Don't be silly,' he said. 'I'm not that stingy.'

'Yes, darling. I know. I just –'

'It's fine,' he said.

David let her hold his hand – it was easier than

pulling back. He'd rather share his hand with her than his thoughts. Every recent glimpse of Laura – the glass-fine wrist as she turned the pages of his portfolio, the smooth curve of her leg, the brush of her lips as she kissed him goodbye – filled his mind. With the real world so hopelessly out of line with his inner life, David felt the lonely disconnection pressing in on him, and longed for solitude.

Later, inside, while David switched on the lamps and ignited the gas in the grate, Edmund poured them all a glass of cognac from the bottle of duty-free he'd bought at JFK. Alice sat on the floor by the fireplace, light from the flames flickering down her side as she lit a cigarette. Edmund sat in the armchair next to her. He reached for a strand of her hair and wound it around his index finger.

'So when's the portrait set for, David? Soon?'

'Won't that clash with the wedding?'

David looked quickly at Mel. 'March is okay, isn't it? Or will you need me to help with the –'

'It's fine,' said Mel.

'The spring.'

'And where?' Ned went on. 'Where will you do it? London or Merwick?'

'Merwick?' said David.

'That's his place in Scotland,' said Alice.

'New York, London, Scotland . . .' said Mel. 'How many houses does the guy –'

'Only *just* Scotland.' Edmund unwound Alice's hair from his finger and watched it fall to her shoulder. 'Just a few miles from the border.' He looked at David. 'I'd check when the shooting season ends, if I were you. Don't want to be stuck in the middle of nowhere for weeks and weeks, living off an endless diet of turnips and stringy pheasants, putting up with dinner conversation that revolves around what the bag was, or how the latest pro-hunting lobby efforts are going, picking lead shot out of every mouthful.'

David laughed. 'It won't be that bad. Can't see a woman like Laura putting up with that kind of thing for longer than a weekend, can you?'

Edmund tried to imagine Laura's hair squashed under soaked tweed, the slanting northern rain in her eyes, while her ankles strained across uneven plough – great chunks of mud dragging at her steps. He tried to imagine her taking a pheasant – feathers everywhere, blood dripping from its beak – from the gentle mouth of one of Joss's dogs and carrying it correctly, by the neck, back to the old game cart.

After David and Mel went to bed, Alice heaved herself up off the floor and into Edmund's lap.

'Hello,' he said, not moving, and taking another strand of her hair.

'Hello,' she murmured, twisting so that they were face to face. Her legs sprawled out over his and dangled to the floor.

She was dark against the light from the fire. He couldn't see her expression as her face came towards him, only the backlit outline of hair, the dark narrow shoulders, a dark narrow ribcage, and the casual swell of her hips. Closing his eyes, he let her kiss him – a good, smooth, cognac-lubricated kiss. Warm and young and easy. He felt her shifting over him with light pressing hands: in his hair, at the back of his neck, touching at his collarbone and round to his top button.

10

David woke, thirsty, to the sound of church bells and looked at his alarm clock: 7.45. Heavy with sleep, he stared at the clock face with the sense that something had happened, something big, and then his eyes closed.

Laura.

In his dreams, in his studio, his arms.

Married.

David sat up. Mel was silent, curled with her back to him, sleeping. He swung his legs round the side of the bed, stood up, and went to the bathroom – opening the door to find Alice in there, in Ned's dressing gown, brushing her teeth with Ned's little Virgin Atlantic Upper Class toothbrush. She turned round, still brushing, foam spilling from her mouth as she smiled.

'Hi.'

And spat.

'Hello, Alice.'

He waited for her to rinse her mouth and wipe it with a towel – his towel. Still smiling, she took the towel from her mouth. 'Sleep well?'

'Yes, Alice. Did you?'

'Yeah – eventually.' She turned back to the basin, to

her reflection in the mirror, and started whistling. *Half a pound of tupp-enn-y rice. Half a pound of trea-cle . . .*

With the door open behind him, David leant in the frame and put his hands into the pockets of his dressing gown. Alice stopped whistling, bent her head, and turned on the taps again.

'Won't be long,' she said.

David watched as she put her hands under the flow of water and splashed it up into her face. Then, with her eyes still shut, water trickling over the lids, she turned and felt for the towel. He handed it to her.

'Just gotta pee and then I'm out of here.' Face dried, she looked up from the towel. 'OK?'

He nodded.

'Well, shut the door then.'

David shut the door. It had to happen at some point. It was surprising, in some ways, that it hadn't happened sooner – a girl as curious, as confident, as pretty as that. And she could, he supposed, have done worse than Edmund. For all his womanising, his playing around, Ned wasn't stupid, and he wasn't a bastard. In fact, after all the things that she'd said – about losing her virginity, and how she didn't care much who it was – Alice was hardly the one that needed protecting.

He leant against the wall outside the bathroom, closed his eyes, and heard Alice's whistling.

Pop! goes the weasel – he heard, out of tune.

Then again, a bit better.

And then perfect.

Alice got the bus. Her parents thought they knew where she was (staying over with Emily), she didn't have to be home until lunch, and she felt like some time to herself. Standing in the dusty sunshine at the top of Battersea Bridge Road, waiting for the bus to take her to the top end of the King's Road, where she'd get off and walk up Sloane Avenue, through South Kensington, and on to her parents, Alice ran her mind back.

So. It was done. And had it been as she'd expected? Yes and no. It had been less intense. Less romantic. Not romantic at all, in fact. No movie sex. No eroticism shot against the light. But funny – really funny. She couldn't remember now the things he'd said, but she remembered laughing until it hurt. And of course it was much funnier because, with David and Mel next door, they'd had to be quiet – and that always set her off.

Smiling at the bus timetable, Alice remembered Ned getting out of his trousers with exaggerated slapstick stumbling, then tossing up his boxer shorts adeptly with his foot, catching them with his left hand and flinging them stylishly into the corner of the room. Alice had tried to copy him with her knickers, and ended up flat on her face.

'Ow!'

'Alice, ssh!' He was there with her, shaking with laughter as he helped her up. 'You moron. You'll wake the whole street.'

'Ow . . .' She got to her knees, rubbing them, laughing too. 'How do you do that?'

'*Shhh!*'

'How?' she whispered, as he kissed her. 'Show me. You made it look so easy.'

'You do it like this . . .' Taking Alice's flimsy

knickers he did it again, this time girlishly. They'd landed on the lampshade.

It was only when they'd finished, when Ned came back from the bathroom, that it got serious. He climbed into bed and lay on his side, protecting her back with his own body as an outer layer. Reaching over, he circled her waist with his arm and brought her close.

'I wish you'd told me,' he said.

It was dark now. With nothing to look at, Alice became conscious of the way he smelt. In his skin, on his sheets. Beneath the overtones of toothpaste and soap, the cognac, maybe even dinner there somewhere. Beneath the starch from his shirts, beneath traces of leather from the collar of his jacket, his shoes, was the warm confidence of clean male sweat, and Alice loved it. She buried her head in the pillow and inhaled.

Edmund put his cheek against the back of her head. He kissed her hair, and she felt him against her, the unfamiliar line of the front of his body shaping, slotting, fitting around her shoulders, her back, her bottom, her legs, down to the cold part at the bottom of the bed, as if designed.

'I wish you'd told me.'

'Told you what?'

'Alice.'

'What?'

'Please don't pretend.'

Alice had turned and pressed herself to him. 'I'm not pretending,' she said. 'Just because I'm young, that doesn't mean I'm a . . .'

Edmund smiled as he kissed her head.

'. . . what I mean,' she went on, 'is that I *have* done this kind of thing bef –'

'Alice, darling – don't.'

Alice hailed the bus and got on. She climbed the steps to the top level, which was empty, and went to the front. She felt tired. Her body ached in new areas, ached like it had done when she'd learnt to ride, with sensations more interesting than painful. She felt the pull as she climbed, the strain right there on the inside, tightening sinews at the top of each young thigh. And in the swinging action of her pelvis as she walked up the aisle, jolted from one chrome pole to the next as, with the bell ringing in the distance, the bus moved forwards and on around the next corner. And again, stiff in the small of her back as she sat on the threadbare plush-red seat, crossing her lean smooth legs.

Later, at home, following a quiet Sunday lunch with her parents, Alice practised the piano. Usually, she practised for an hour and a half each day. She'd do half an hour scales and arpeggios in the morning, before breakfast, and maybe a Bach fugue if there was time. Her other pieces – it was Gershwin and Beethoven at the moment – she did before leaving school in the evenings.

The Debussy, Mozart, Rachmaninov – those were her Grade 8 pieces. She'd done them, got the distinction, back in June. It was time to move on. But because she had near-perfect command of the notes of those pieces – didn't need to work at them bar by bar, over and over again, then backwards, or with differing rhythms, then very slow, or very fast, bringing out the bass, or the tenor parts, listening again and again to the harmonies, perfecting the tone, making it sing in beautiful arching phrases, through subtle and continual repositioning of her hands to counterbalance the weight of each thumb – she preferred to enjoy the fruits of her work, rather than face fresh technical challenges. She'd played them the other night at Joss and Laura's house, and she was playing them again now.

Hearing that Rachmaninov melody for the umpteenth time – that mournful chromatic progression stretching up up up that had taken her weeks to master – Roger Enderby threw aside the Sport section of the *Sunday Times* and flipped through the pile by the side of his deck chair for the Business pages. OK, so Alice could now ease it from fingers so technically confident that it seemed to flow straight from her blood. OK, he was proud of her. But the process of getting to that stage had comprehensively ruined this particular prelude for her father. And those lessons she had – he didn't like to think of how much they cost, how it added up – were they worth it, just to feel like this about the end result?

Next to him, on the other deck chair, in the faded sundress she wore when it was hot, stretched Camilla, half asleep. Sunlight covered her skin like a blanket – warming it through, opening the pores – as she listened to her daughter. Roger's papers rustled in leaves and twigs she should be sweeping up. Pigeons cooed in the neighbouring garden. But all her attention was centred on Alice's playing – not on the details of the notes (Camilla didn't know her bass clef from her treble), but on the expression. Like Roger, she'd heard this piece a thousand times, but to her it had never sounded more beautiful.

11

David was covering his painting of Alice with retouching varnish. He'd laid it flat on the floor and was kneeling over, spraying the varnish across the canvas by attaching a mouth atomiser to the bottle, taking a deep breath and blowing carefully through it so that the varnish was sucked up and out in an even sheen.

They were having lunch with his mother that day. Virginia had been expecting only David and Ned, so David had rung her earlier – before she went to church – to say that Mel was coming too. He'd got the predictable response.

'Oh, *wonderful*! I've got the tiara out of the bank now, so she can try it on. I'd forgotten just how heavy it is, but she'll look amazing with that long neck of hers and . . .'

David bent over the canvas and blew the poison gently out. He wanted to get the whole picture covered before they left. He'd done the bottom section of the painting – up to the hem of Alice's skirt – when Edmund emerged and stood in his white towelling dressing gown at the top of the spiral stairs.

'Morning!' he said broadly, as if to the morning itself, and then, 'What are you doing to Alice?'

'I'm varnishing her.' David stood back from the painting, the bottle in his hands, and turned to his brother. 'Sleep well?'

'Very.'

Both were silent, and then David laughed. 'Oh, come on, Ned.'

'What?'

'I saw her in the bathroom this morning, whistling and answering back. Christ, that girl's impertinent.'

Edmund grinned. 'Highly impertinent.'

'She needs to learn some manners.'

'She's perfect.'

Still grinning, Ned thought of the things that Mel had said. He thought of Mel's implication that it was Alice rejecting his advances – not the other way round – and felt a childish satisfaction. Gliding down the stairs, he headed for the kitchen.

'Coffee?'

David put the bottle of retouching varnish to one side and followed his brother into the kitchen. Edmund was opening cupboards, looking for the one David kept his coffee in, looking for the kettle, the fridge.

'I'll do it,' said David.

'And where are my fags?' Picking up a cheap green plastic lighter that Alice had left behind, Edmund wandered back into the studio. 'I'm sure I had a pack left. Unless that minx took . . .'

David made two mugs of coffee and thought, uncomfortably, of the things that Alice had said.

'Milk?' he called out.

'No, thanks,' said Edmund. 'And no sugar.'

'It's instant.'

'Don't mind.' Edmund came back in, still grinning, with a lit cigarette and one of David's ashtrays. 'Jesus, Davey – it's toxic in there. Thought the whole place was going to blow up.'

He put the ashtray on the kitchen table and they sat opposite one another, with their dark glazed mugs in front of them. The mugs were old. Edmund knew them well from the days when he and David would rush in from the garden and drink apple juice from them, Virginia reminding David to hold his in both hands so that he didn't drop it. They'd been cheap, these mugs, and most of them were chipped. Virginia had clearly decided to upgrade and give them to David. She couldn't have given them to Ned – Ned had been in America – but he couldn't help still slightly resenting that David had them. And David had the yellow lampshades from the spare room, and David had that rug they'd kept their Scalextric track on, and the four gilded Louis XIV-style chairs – fake, but not cheap. Edmund would definitely have liked those.

Edmund had always been conscious of a kind of restrained favouritism between David and his mother. It wasn't that David was more loved, but he seemed to need more looking after. Even now that they were adults, Virginia couldn't stop doing things for David – spending an extra hundred pounds on his birthday so that he could have that fold-up easel he needed for painting trips abroad, or driving him to the airport in the days when he didn't have a car – and then having to do something for Edmund to make it fair.

The trouble was that Edmund didn't need so

much. The tools of his trade were provided. The firm paid for his car to the airport. He tended to get all the toys – the latest mobile telephone, palm pilot, speed camera detector – and all the luxuries for himself. And Virginia never really knew exactly what it was he wanted. She'd probably buy him a dining-room table, or a sofa, when he got his new flat, to balance out the various things she'd given David, although it was more likely she'd just give him the money. It wasn't the same, and Edmund noticed. He noticed that what happened spontaneously for David became duty for himself.

On the other hand, he couldn't really blame Virginia, not when he was every bit as guilty. Like her, he'd find himself doing things for David. He'd look into travel insurance offers when David was planning a trip, he never put David on hold when David rang him at work, and he'd always bring a good bottle of wine to David's dinner parties. He'd bought David a modem for his computer so that David could get emails. He'd insisted on reading David's purchase contract thoroughly before he bought the studio. And at Christmas, he'd get every-body else's presents in one morning, and spend the next three days researching state-of-the-art spotlights to find one that covered all angles, with any variation of light quality, and nothing too heavy – for David's portraits and still lifes. He couldn't help himself; even when it clearly wasn't appreciated, like the other night when Ned had told him about Joss looking for someone to paint Laura, and David had got so irritated.

David pulled the large bowl of sugar close to his

mug and began spooning it in. He hoped that Ned's preoccupations had nothing to do with Alice, and felt uncomfortable, knowing what he did about Alice's motives. But what could he do? The last thing Ned would want was brotherly interference. And in any case, was it really so bad? Even if she was using Ned for sex, so what? Ned wasn't exactly innocent. Maybe he was using her too. Maybe he was . . .

David threw aside his teaspoon. 'So you'll see Alice again?' he said.

Ned laughed. 'What do you think?'

'Tonight?'

'Today, if she's on for it and her parents let her. I thought we could have lunch at that pub you like in Richmond. You know, the one with the garden. I just need to ring and find out what time it – what?'

David was shaking his head. 'You can't,' he said. 'We've got lunch with Mum, remember?'

It wasn't far from the church to her apartment, but Virginia Nicholson felt each step. Everything had to be done slowly these days. Resting at the railings, she looked out across the square – Sunday-quiet, the traffic lights turning from red to green and back to red again for an empty road. She could hear the bleeping for the blind people and was glad that hadn't happened to her yet. She wasn't blind, she wasn't deaf, and although the arthritis meant that she should use her stick, she could just about manage without it.

For sixty-eight, she supposed it could be worse. She had some friends who, with HRT and active lifestyles, could have been a generation younger. But she knew others – people younger than her – who'd died from heart failure, and quite a few had cancer. And her poor William, of course. Fifty-four when his was diagnosed. Only fifty-four. Fifty-eight when he died, which was twelve years ago now, but shock at how young he'd been, at how many things he'd miss – David's wedding in particular, and the joy of knowing Mel – still tore at her.

But her own health wasn't bad. The only thing that troubled Virginia was how cold she felt all the time. Like here, now, wrapped in autumn sunshine, soft grey wool and fur but still with fingers and toes of ice. She'd always suffered from bad circulation, even when she was young, but she hadn't been able to rid herself of the notion that this was the beginning of the end, that the chill would creep like frostbite. Starting at her extremities and working in. Her nails would fall off, her skin would turn green, her bones would soften to pulp.

Because of this, Virginia's apartment was heated vigorously all year round. The rooms were large and airy, so most of the heat would collect way above her head in the intricate fronds and petals of plaster at the cornices, around the acanthus leaves at the top of her Corinthian columns, in the central oval of vines and tendrils.

But with patience, and with obsessive attention to closing windows and doors, Virginia had overcome the problem. The flat was warm. And she discovered other tricks: if she left the electric blanket on, there was (contrary to the warnings on the box) no nasty explosion. She could sleep the whole night through. Piping hot baths were always good, and leaving her thermals in the airing cupboard so that they were warm in the morning. And there was that cashmere shawl Mel had given her for Christmas last year. Bright yellow wasn't Virginia's style, and she didn't wear it outside, but it made a difference to have it wrapped around her in the evenings, while she listened to the wireless, or read, or did the crossword.

Virginia didn't have a television, mainly because William had never liked them. There were newspapers for anything important and if they wanted to see a film, they went to the cinema. And although William was gone, Virginia still found herself doing things – or not doing them – because of the patterns she'd acquired with him. Edmund had offered to give her a television when he went to New York, but she'd told him she didn't want it. And anyway, with all those black wires and bulbous lines, it would look horrid. Where would she put it?

'What about your bedroom?'

'My *bedroom*? Why on earth would I want it in there?'

'Well, Mum. You could –'

'I don't know about you, Edmund,' her laughter was supposed to make him think she was joking – she was, but there were undercurrents, '*and I don't want to know,* but personally, I use my bedroom for sleeping.'

Edmund told her she could get it fitted to a nice eighteenth-century-style cabinet and have it in the corner of her drawing room. Virginia had said, 'Yes, yes,' in tones that said, 'No, no' – and he'd left it.

Taking the lift to the first floor, Virginia removed a glove and, cursing herself for putting her keys back in her bag when she'd just gone through the same rigmarole with the outside door, she felt for them again. The lift was old and wooden, with two sets of doors. The lights flickered. It reached Virginia's level with a clunk, she pulled aside the first set of concertinaed metal, pushed the outer door and, keys in hand, stepped carefully over the gap.

She was at the oven – closing her eyes for a moment, enjoying the jet of heat on her face, the furious spitting and crackling, the soft smell of roasting chicken – when the others arrived. Pulling off the tin foil, spooning juice over the bird's backs, she heard David's key in the lock.

'Hi, Mum!'

And then Edmund's deeper voice: 'Christ, it's a furnace in here. Let's get one of these things open.'

Virginia put the chickens back in, shut the oven door, and went to greet them – her hands still in the oven gloves. She hadn't seen Edmund in months. The last time was that trip to New York that had neatly coincided with the trip Sally Bartlett had organised to see the Goya exhibition. But in the end it had been rushed. Sally had needed help with the tickets, the exhibition had odd opening times, and Virginia had really seen more of Sally, more of Goya, than she had of Ned. She knew that she should now run to him, kiss him, tell him how she'd missed him. But his back view there – large, spread-eagled to the window as he hauled it down – was so like William, she had to look away.

'Hello, darling,' she said to Mel, kissing her. 'How was your week?'

Mel smiled and undid her coat. 'Fantastic,' she said.

146

'You did it?'

'I did it! And . . . well, it's going to take a while to talk my parents round but I can't tell you how free I feel, Virginia. You were absolutely right.'

Virginia patted her arm. 'Of course I was right. And now you can really enjoy getting ready for the wedding. I went to the bank on Friday, you know, and got the tiara. Perhaps we can try it on after lunch! It's heavy, I'm afraid. I must have forgotten . . . but now, of course, I do remember it did give me a bit of a headache. So maybe you won't want it, or –'

'Of course I'll want it,' said Mel, glancing over to where Edmund was struggling with the window. 'I'll take painkillers if I have to.'

The window opened and Edmund turned. 'Mum,' he said, smiling. 'How are you?'

'Cold,' said Virginia, offering her cheek.

Edmund kissed it and went back to the window.

'Oh, darling, I didn't mean . . . No, do leave a crack open if you . . . Perfect. Now tell me how you've been. How's work?'

'Work's fine,' said Edmund. 'I left Martin in charge, and he –'

'Martin?' she said, but she wasn't listening. She was pointing David and Mel to a fading navy leather box that sat on the coffee table. 'Martin?'

'Martin Teviot, he's –'

'Of course, darling. Your boss.'

Partner, thought Ned. He's my partner now.

'Well, anyway, he did a good job in my absence. Hardly feels as if I've been away. Of course it's busy, but there's still time to look at flats, and –'

'Great.'

'And I'd love you to see this place I've found up in –'

'Just be careful with it, David. No, it's better to stand behind her. That's right. Oh, Mel.'

Edmund turned to see. David had moved away and Mel was standing at the mirror above the fireplace with the tiara balanced on her head, its elaborate art-deco pattern crowning her, making her taller than ever, straightening her out, somehow. The dash-dash short hair suited it. Virginia and Mel gazed with pleasure at the effect. David looked at the floor, and Edmund looked at David.

Mel picked up another glass and sank it gently into the bubbles.

'We didn't get very far, I'm afraid,' she said, swilling the water in and then watching it darken with wine that had not been drunk. 'And there's a chance we may still have it in London after all.'

She took the glass out, rinsed it, and put it upside down on the rack for Edmund to dry.

'Really?' said Virginia. 'At St Peter's?'

'I don't see why not.'

'But how lovely! Shall I ask the vicar about dates? I know April's busy, what with the run-up to Easter, but I'm sure he could fit you in.'

Edmund took the glass, wiped it with the cloth, and wondered what say, if any, David had in this wedding. The two women had talked about nothing else all lunch. His mother had always wanted a daughter, he knew, but this was ridiculous. It was almost as if it was Virginia marrying Mel, he thought, not David. Putting the glass in the cupboard, he reached for the next.

'With most people living in London,' Mel was saying, 'it seems mad to make them all come up to Leeds, don't you think? And it may be cheaper, you know, in the long run, if we can find somewhere down here that'll do the lot.'

'Oh, oh, oh!' said Virginia suddenly. 'Oh, Mel, I know the perfect place. Sally Bartlett's daughter got married there last year. Down by Putney Bridge, in the gardens, the ones that overlook the river. Bishop's Park, is it called? A great hall-like building – Jacobean, I think.'

'Sounds ideal.'

'Fulham Palace – something like that – and I seem to remember there's a church right next door, so I suppose you could even have the service there if you'd . . .'

On it went, and Edmund stood there, wiping and wondering. He thought, sadly, of the rows of girls that Virginia had met with him. Girls she'd chat to, laugh with, cook for. Girls that, when they left, always said how nice she was, and never understood the subtle distance she kept. But Ned noticed. He saw that while Virginia gave them her undivided attention, she never gave much of herself away. She kept her opinions down. She'd say, 'How interesting,' or, 'Absolutely,' when Ned knew those weren't her real thoughts at all. It was as if the women Ned had chosen weren't worth the exposure – the effort – and the slight, he felt, was on him.

Of course, Ned understood that a future daughter-in-law warranted more attention than some girl that Virginia might never see again. Of course it would be different. But he couldn't help suspecting that

Virginia had been like this from the very start. David's girlfriend. David's wife. His guess was that she didn't really think that he, Ned, would ever marry. So what was the point getting to know the latest one? And, really, who could blame her?

'. . . so if you speak to the man at St Peter's, I can get in touch with whoever it is in Bishop's Park.' Wiping round the baking tray, rinsing it under the tap, Mel put it firmly on the rack. 'Do you think your friend Mrs Bartlett would have his number? Or did her daughter get married in another church?'

Edmund picked the tray up, examined it, and gave it back to her.

'Reject,' he said. 'You need to do the outside.'

Mel took the pan and, laughing, showed it to Virginia. 'Look at that great lump of fat! How could I have missed it?'

But Virginia was looking at Ned. 'Oh, darling,' she said, 'I'm sorry – banging on about wedding plans. Must drive you mad listening to us discussing vicars and venues and so on.'

'I'm fine,' said Ned quickly.

Virginia took his arm. 'But tell me about *you*. How's *your* love life?'

'Mum.'

'Of course you don't have to, darling. I just – just . . . But if it's private then –'

'What?' said David, coming in with a tray piled high. 'What's private?'

'Ned's love life,' said Mel, smiling into the sink.

'Ah . . .'

Virginia saw David's smile, Mel's smile. Even Ned was smiling.

'What?' she said, releasing Ned's arm and focusing, wisely, on Mel, 'Come on, darling. Tell me. Who is she? Why the smiles?'

Mel gave Ned a playful glance. 'What's it worth?'

'More than your –'

And then, with perfect timing, the telephone rang.

'Blast,' said Virginia, and went to the bedroom to answer it. 'Blast, blast, blast.'

Edmund waited until she was gone, until he could hear her voice in the other room, and then he turned to Mel. 'If you say another word, I shall personally –'

'Come on, Ned,' said David. 'It's not Mel's fault that you –'

'I don't care whose fault it is,' said Ned, suddenly serious. 'I don't want Mum to know about Alice and I'd be grateful for a bit of discretion.'

'But why does it matter?' said Mel. 'It's not as if you've got anywhere with her. You said so yourself last night.'

'Ah,' said David.

'What?'

'That was last night.'

Mel stopped washing up. She looked round over her shoulder at Edmund, and found her answer in his face. He looked quite ridiculously pleased with himself.

'I wouldn't worry,' David went on. 'I'm sure it was more a case of Alice taking advantage of Ned than the other way round, but that won't stop Mum from –'

'I think you'll find it was mutual,' said Ned.

And David laughed. 'I think you'll find it wasn't.'

Within seconds, Ned was on to him. Just what did David mean by that? What did he know?

David said he hadn't meant anything. Really. He was just –

'Stop wasting my time.'

'But you won't like it. You'll –'

'David,' said Edmund, wiping his hands. 'You're starting to piss me off.'

So David told him. Turning back to the sink, Mel listened. She heard how Alice had thrown herself at David, and how, when David rejected her, Alice had simply shrugged her shoulders and moved on to a rather less scrupulous accomplice. And after initial indignation at the thought of someone trespassing on her property, Mel felt rather pleased. Not every man would have passed up the offer of a seventeen-year-old virgin, particularly one like Alice. But David had, and it seemed to Mel to reinforce his commitment to her. She didn't like the idea of women throwing themselves at her husband-to-be, but she couldn't exactly stop it from happening, and it was good to know that she could trust him.

But while this story reflected well on David and his relationship with Mel, it wasn't so flattering to Ned. And Mel – filled with sudden pity – couldn't bring herself to look at him. Wishing David would shut up, but not really wanting to get involved, Mel simply went on washing dishes, and listened to Ned deflating behind her: to the calm voice telling David to 'Go on', . . . 'And then what?' . . . culminating in silence.

In the next room, Virginia was laughing. 'But, Sally, darling, what about the cheese? Did that . . .? No!' More laughter.

'Think I'll walk home,' said Edmund.

He walked down towards the river, across a still Sloane Square and along the King's Road for a bit before turning left, down past the old wall of the Physic Garden, and on – in sunlit Sunday quietness.

He wasn't in love with Alice. He'd been flattered and, now he realised where she was coming from, he felt a little foolish. But his world wasn't about to collapse. The humiliation had more to do with David and Mel knowing about it, and probably Virginia too by now. David could never keep secrets from his mother, and how else would he explain Ned's sudden departure? No, Ned's regret was more to do with the fact that he'd gladly taken what his brother had rejected, than it was to do with Alice herself. Silly girl, he thought, remembering her clumsy seduction in the cab. Silly girl.

And then he thought of David and Mel: observing, knowing all along that he was being taken for a ride. It didn't occur to him that Mel had been in the dark as well, that she'd been every bit as shocked as he was by what David had just said. Instead, he found himself resenting her, resenting the way she'd played with him – all those comments in the restaurant last night, goading him on. He'd misread both women. But while he was inclined to forgive Alice (he himself had behaved like that at times, and anyway she was young), Mel's involvement was altogether uglier. David had just kept out of it, which was fair enough, but Mel . . .

Edmund got to the Embankment and turned left, passing a group of girls like Alice – long-haired, confident, rhythmic – all looking up and out, ready to catch his eye. The boys that slouched beside them were looking down, down at feet in designer trainers, skirted by loose-fitting designer jeans, curiously feminine. The group moved past him, trainers shuffling, and Ned walked on in the opposite direction.

Tomorrow, he'd ring Alice. He'd meet her for dinner or a drink, and talk about it with her. He wasn't quite sure what he'd say. He didn't want her to feel sexually rejected, but nor did he want to go on being used. Perhaps now that she'd had sex, now that she'd used him, she'd lose interest and move on. A bit insulting, sure, but that would be least complicated, and then he could move on as well.

Crossing Albert Bridge, he headed south towards the studio, slowing his pace, unwilling to return just yet. He dawdled in a newsagent, deliberating over the Sunday papers when he knew all along which ones he'd get. He took them to a café and sat with them and a strong cup of coffee until it got dark, enjoying the very sections Alice's father found an effort, and then he went home.

Opening the door to the studio, he heard shrieking, laughter and what sounded like the shower.

'Not there! Put your hand *there*, Mel – and *press*!'

'Shit. Shit.'

'Press it!'

'I am!' The thunder of water faded.

'OK, now pass me – No don't. I'll get it. There . . .'

Edmund walked up the spiral staircase and stood at the door to the bathroom, where David was trying to mend a leaking tap assisted by a very wet Mel, who was sitting on the edge of the bath and laughing. He saw her there, and felt for a moment as if the laughter was directed at him.

Then Mel looked round and her laughter subsided. 'Hi,' she said.

David looked round too. 'Hello, Ned. Tap's fucked. We've found a whole damp area of wood at the back here and I'm trying – Mel, keep pressing, will you? – I'm trying to fix the washer.'

'Need a hand?'

'No, don't worry. We're nearly . . . there. Now let go – *let go, Mel* – and I'll just sc-r-ew this in tight, and – there!'

Leaving David to put all the bottles and brushes back – he wanted to do it all properly – the others went down to the kitchen. Mel told Ned about the tap. They'd mended it so that there was no more leaking, but it didn't actually work. They were going to have to get a plumber in, and that meant no baths or showers until it was sorted out. Mel was going back to her own flat that night.

'I should go anyway.' She wrung out the sleeve of her cardigan. 'Haven't seen Nathan in months.'

Taking the cardigan off, hanging it on the back of a chair to dry, she sat at the table and looked at Ned. He was sitting opposite with his head bent, his mind preoccupied. She thought of the things that David had said that afternoon about Alice, and Alice's intentions.

'Ned,' she said.

'Hm?'

'Everything all right?'

Edmund looked at her. 'I don't know how you have the nerve to ask me that,' he said.

Mel stared back.

'Oh, come on, Mel. Don't pretend you don't know what I'm talking about. You must have known, and yet you still went ahead and –'

'Known?' she said. 'Known what? I don't understand.'

Edmund shut his eyes. 'Alice. You must have known about Alice. About what she was up to and what she was thinking, and yet you were happy to let me walk straight on in and –'

Mel stood up. 'Hang on a moment.'

' . . . just walk straight on in and make an utter fool of myself. Worse than that, you encouraged me –'

'Encouraged you?'

' "Poor Ned," you said. "How frustrating for you," you said. Implying –'

'I was *teasing*,' she insisted.

Ned gave a short laugh. 'Teasing?'

'Yes,' said Mel. 'It was a joke.'

'Funny joke.'

'And in any case, I didn't –'

'I'm sorry, Mel, but you did. You goaded me, quite deliberately, into –'

'Will you let me finish?'

Ned stopped and waved his hand with a theatrical loop of the wrist. 'Of course,' he said. 'After you.'

Mel hesitated. While the lawyer in her smarted at the injustice, while words of rebuke and self-defence sprang at her tongue, the bride-to-be shrank with embarrassment. This wasn't some asshole at a City meeting. This wasn't some idiot lawyer at the end of a telephone. This was David's brother. She had to rise above it.

'I – I think perhaps you've misunderstood something,' she said carefully. 'I had no idea about Alice. I didn't know she'd made a pass at David, and I certainly didn't know she was on a mission. Really, Ned, I think you must have got –'

'David didn't tell you?'

'No,' she said.

'But surely he'd have said something. Surely he –'

Mel smiled. 'Strange as it may seem,' she said, 'we don't spend all our time discussing you and your love life.'

'But he must have told you about Alice – about Alice making a pass at *him*.'

Mel shook her head. 'No,' she said. 'No, he didn't.'

Edmund said nothing, but the unspoken question – 'And doesn't that worry you?' – hung in the air. Doesn't it worry you, that he doesn't tell you things like that? Don't you want to know why it happened? What else doesn't he tell you?

Above them, they heard a door close and David's feet on the spiral stairs.

'Mel?' he called out. 'Mel, if you want that lift to Nathan's, we should really get going.'

12

Mel hardly went to Nathan's flat these days. Most of her things were now at David's, and there was no real reason for her to go back, except to keep up the illusion of an independent life and, of course, to see Nathan. It was a basement flat, down a flight of narrow steps lined with boxes of geraniums that had been put there by a previous owner. The flowers were all dead, and most of the leaves were yellow, but the plants refused to die. They clogged the air with the smell of greenhouses – warm, sweet, dusty – particularly on nights like this. Mel opened the little gate and went down the steps with keys in her hand. She could see the television through a gap in the curtains, and she heard its indistinct noise.

Nathan was always watching television. When he was at home, he'd have it on in the background all the time, and that was another reason Mel preferred David's studio. She opened the door, which led straight into the sitting room, expecting to find Nathan in there on the sofa with a packet of crisps, and saw instead a strange girl with plum-coloured hair and black clothes standing in the middle of the room, trying to find the right button on the remote.

The television died, and the girl turned to Mel. 'Sorry about that.' She held out her hand and smiled. 'You're Mel, right?'

'Yes,' said Mel. 'I –'

'Hi. I'm Fenella. I'm a friend of Nathan's.'

Mel often shook hands with people. She did it at work, in meetings, all the time; with men or women, old or young, clever or stupid, successes or failures. And while she liked it in that context, the way it could establish an air of equality and friendship in situations that tended to be far from that, she was less happy about it socially. For her, it still suggested business. But as she shook Fenella's hand – a hand that had been recently moisturised and slipped a bit in her grasp – it felt oddly necessary.

She looked for somewhere to put her briefcase and noticed that the room was different. The chairs had been rearranged so that the sofa had its back to the door, and the armchair was now opposite the television. The light that usually sat on her desk had been moved to a table by the sofa – a table that looked new. There was a large flower arrangement on her desk now, and a bowl of potpourri on the low glass coffee table.

Fenella pushed her hair from her face. 'Can I get you a drink?'

'Love one.'

'Nathan's just gone out for some more red, but there's still a bit left in here. And there's white in the fridge, if you'd prefer.'

'This is fine,' said Mel, putting her briefcase on the floor. She sat in the armchair on cushions that, for once, had been puffed up. 'Thanks.'

'OK then. I'll just get you a glass, and the bottle of white for me.'

'But I can have the white,' said Mel, sitting forward again and noticing suddenly that Fenella had been drinking red. 'Really. I don't mind.'

'I don't mind either.'

Fenella went into the kitchen and Mel, half expecting to be told to make herself at home, looked around the room, wondering what else was different. There were quite a few books she didn't recognise. Smart art books, and heavy exhibition brochures piled on the shelves by the window and arranged in alphabetical order. Mel went over to the CD player, opened the disc slot and found Schoenberg's Violin Concerto in there. Jesus. She took it out, searched for its case and put on some of Nathan's Van Morrison.

Fenella came back in with the bottle of white, and two glasses. She poured out the remains of the red, tipping the Rioja bottle right up on its end to get the last drop out, and then began on the bottle of white, scraping at the green plastic cover with the pointed end of the corkscrew.

'Nathan will be so pleased to see you,' she said. 'He was saying just the other day that it's really like you don't live here at all any more.'

'I hope he's not too upset.'

'Oh no.' Fenella flicked off the green plastic, brought up her elbow, and twisted in the screw. 'Not at all. It gives us more space. In fact, he was rather wondering if you might want to – Ah, here he is!'

There was a rattle of keys and Nathan was in, pulling the keys out with one hand, while the other held a supermarket bag with the dark red end of a bottle visible at the top.

'Hi, Fen. They didn't have the – *Mel*!'

'Hello, stranger,' said Mel, hugging him. 'How are you?'

'Never better,' he grinned. 'And you've met?'

'Yes, darling. We've met.'

Nathan took the bottle out of the bag. He picked the corkscrew up off the glass surface of the coffee table, and smiled at Mel.

'What do you think of the flat?' he said. 'Impressed?'

Mel's bedroom was cold, colder than the rest of the flat. Going in later, half expecting it to have undergone a makeover as well, Mel noticed that Fenella had restricted herself to switching off the radiator. She threw her bags and briefcase on the narrow bed, and sat next to them, accumulated mail in her hand: bills, flyers, a couple of postcards and an invitation to a housewarming party being given by someone from her law school days, someone she thought she'd lost touch with.

Slowly she looked around the room. Her room. Her things – lifeless now, and dusty. She'd got so used to living in David's studio, with David's things, and David's life, it was strange to be back. Strange and sad. She looked at her books on the plain white shelves: a disorderly combination of smart legal textbooks and yellow Enid Blyton; travel guides and *Living with God*, on top of a pile of other religious books given to her on her confirmation; slim American teenage trash slotted in between heavy degree texts.

Thinking of her degree, of how she'd enjoyed it, Mel

wondered if she shouldn't go back and do a masters of some sort. Maybe a Ph.D., but it wouldn't make any money. And, anyway, Mel wasn't an academic. Sure, she'd done well at university, but she needed the stimulus of other people working around her. She needed daily interaction. She needed . . . she needed a better idea of what she was doing. That was the truth. And for the first time since handing in her notice, Mel felt the exposure. Only Virginia had supported her decision to quit. Everybody else – David, Philippa, her parents, Ned – they had all, in their various ways and for their own different reasons, disapproved. And what if they were right? What if there was nothing else? What if she was making a mistake? What if . . .?

Not now, she told herself, heaving her bag on to the floor and pulling out her mobile. I'll think about it later. I've got masses of time, and more important things to think about at the moment. Checking her alarm clock – nine thirty wasn't too late – Mel rang her parents. She'd been putting it off ever since she'd got back from Yorkshire, and the more she thought of her mother alone up there, the more it worried her. She wanted to hear Clare's voice.

But it was Greg who answered.

'Yes,' he said.

'It's me.'

Both were silent, and then Mel said, 'Is Mum there?'

'She's busy.'

'Can I talk to her?'

'I said she's busy.'

'Dad, I want to talk to her. Can you please fetch her for me?'

'Strange as it may sound, Melanie, your mother is not at your beck and call. She does have a life of her own, and right now she's in the bath.'

'You'll tell her that I rang, then?'

'You've got a nerve,' said Greg suddenly. 'You come up here, you announce to us that you're dropping out, you speed off like some harpy without so much as a . . . and then you expect us to behave as if nothing has happened?'

Mel said nothing.

'I thought you might be ringing to apologise, to say that you'd seen sense. But no,' he laughed angrily. 'Oh no, how silly of me! Now –' he swallowed – 'now you listen here. If you're expecting us to accept what you've done after all the years we've given you, the education we've bought you, the sacrifices we've made, well, you can think again. And I don't want to hear another squeak out of you until –'

Mel took her mobile from her ear, held it out and looked at it – her father's voice shrinking to something tinny, trapped inside – but still it wasn't enough. Disconnecting him wasn't really enough either, but it was better than listening. The strange thing was how little she felt, beyond flat demotivation. Her family, her career, her bedroom. Thank God, she thought, for David.

13

David waited until Ned had left for work – gone by seven – and then he got out of bed. He put on his dressing gown, came down the spiral stairs, which were cold under his bare feet, and went into the kitchen. Another glorious September day. Sky so pure it hurt. He ran water from the tap into the kettle, white light refracting through the jet, up into his eyes, his shape cut dark on the shimmering wall behind, and thought of Laura: her voice in the next room, American-warm, classless.

As the kettle boiled he stretched down, unthinking, to the fridge for the milk; then up to the cupboard for Nescafé and sugar; then round to the shelf for his mug, and a teaspoon from the drawer. He did the same thing every day. Only today, this morning, everything shone. The milk was sharp-cold, fresh. The coffee smelt of plantations and dust tracks. And he could see each sugar crystal, brilliant white.

He'd arranged with Laura that he'd be there at ten, that they'd have the morning. This suited him fine. The plumber was coming at one thirty to sort out the taps. But a morning would give him more than enough time for the preliminary sketches of

Laura. He just needed to look at the house and her wardrobe, decide what she was going to wear, and whether the London house would be a suitable location for the picture.

'Make sure you greet me in whatever clothes you think you might like to wear in the picture,' he'd said, as he said to all his sitters. 'It does make a difference.' It tended to interfere with the likeness, somehow, if he was greeted in a tracksuit, and then had to paint the same person in a ball dress. But he'd said it without thinking and he realised later, with a smile, that this rule didn't exactly apply to Laura. He was already used to her naked, and whatever she wore when she greeted him today was unlikely to interfere with that particular first impression.

The only thing that continued to bother him was the thought that he hadn't answered Laura's question. Her, *haven't I seen you somewhere before?* He felt sure that she would ask it again, and wondered what he might say that would divert her.

It didn't take him long to pack up: just his pad of A3 cartridge paper, a few sheets of the expensive rougher-textured watercolour paper he preferred, his charcoal, his chalks, his conté, his pencils – soft pencils that wore down easily and had a greater variety of tone, pencils he sharpened with a knife by scraping away at the wood so that the leads stuck out long, none of them brought to the even point that a sharpener would turn out – and a blackened putty rubber that picked the mark off without wearing away at the page itself. There were no cumbersome stretched canvases, no paintbox, easel, palette. Just sketching materials today. And, with the exception of the paper, they all fitted into the saggy straw basket with the leather handle that Virginia had brought back for him from the Philippines last summer.

He slung it on the passenger seat of his car, put the A3 pad – with the other sheets slotted inside to protect them – on the back seat, and drove across the river. He parked in the next street (Cheyne Lane was lined with yellow) and walked with his straw bag over his shoulder, and the pad of paper under his arm, up to the high iron gate.

Laura answered the bell. She buzzed the gate open, and then opened the front door – bending down for a second to wedge it with a brass doorstop in the shape of an elephant's foot – and came towards him, up the lavender path. Her feet were bare on the flagstones.

'Let me help you.' She took the sketchbook from him. 'Did you have trouble parking? I know it can be bad. Joss is always complaining about the restrictions.'

David followed her into the hall. To his left, a door had been left open and he could see into a dining room. A mass of silver had been laid out on the table, waiting to be polished. Flemish paintings lined the walls, except above the fireplace, where what looked like a very old landscape indeed was fixed into the wall panel itself. Daylight caught the uneven, yellowing texture of its surface.

Laura put down the sketchbook, went round the side of the staircase and opened the door that led down to the kitchen. 'Coffee?' she said, going down.

David followed her.

'Or juice? I know we've got apple, and cranberry, and there's probably orange juice somewhere around

. . . Oh, Grace – this is David. David – Grace.'

An oriental woman in overalls stopped unloading the dishwasher and smiled at David.

Another world. A London house so large that it felt more like a country one. That dining room. Those paintings. That silver. Not that he needed to see them – the security system alone gave some idea about how valuable the house contents would be. And servants. David stood at the kitchen table while Laura poured them both a glass of apple juice, and then one more for Grace, who returned to unloading the dishwasher. He wondered if she thought of him as she thought of Grace: provider of a service, someone to be charming to, but still not quite an equal. Then he reminded himself, rather meanly, that Laura had once taken off her clothes for ten pounds an hour. She was no higher than him, or Grace. Some people would say that she was lower. And anyway, what the hell did it matter? He was here to do a job.

The kitchen was large and well lit, but unpaintable. The hall was too dark. The dining room too formal. They spent some time in the drawing room upstairs. Joss had said he wanted the painting to be full length, but – conscious that this was a portrait, not a study, that it was about Laura's character, not her body – David was trying to find a position that wasn't too strained, that centred on her face. He made her sit on the club fender round the fireplace, sketched for a few minutes, and then decided that she looked like any newly married woman with a posh fireplace.

'Could you try sitting in that?' he said, pointing to the primrose striped silk lyre chair beyond the piano.

Laura sat in it bolt upright, looking straight at him.

David got her to put one elbow over the arm but she seemed uncomfortable, and the design was still wrong. And it was no good sitting her at the piano if she didn't play. He tried her on the staircase, but it was really too dark.

He quite liked the little sitting room beyond the hall, with french windows that led out to the garden. It was full of papers, piles of books and magazines, photographs of Laura at the helm of a boat, of Joss shooting, and a flattering black-and-white Lénare of a woman who must have been Joss's mother, looking strange and pale and Greta Garbo. At first glance, he'd thought the room was too cluttered. But after the unsatisfactory sketch on the stairs, they decided to give it a go.

There was an old sofa at one end. Laura sat on it and curled her bare legs up under her bottom. David sat closer in, on the round low seat in front of her – covered in today's newspapers, scattered over yet more old issues of *Country Life*, and thick Christie's catalogues – and looked up through a frame he made by squaring his hands together. Laura looked back at him through the fingers. He crinkled his eyes and blurred them at her to rid the image of details, to see the overall design.

Then he asked her to swap places so that he was on the sofa, looking at her on the low cluttered seat with the room beyond her. Again, through the fingers. If he moved along to his left, and down a bit, he'd get the french windows in behind her, and a suggestion of garden. He'd get a sense of the room, of Joss and Laura's life going on in there. And if he moved some of that crap off the low round seat – not all of it, but enough to give Laura a bit more room – that was better – get her to sit back a bit on it – so that her body snaked away from him, from the soles of her feet in the foreground, curling up round her knees, then back the other way at her denim hips, then back again in an S up to her shoulders . . . Could she put an arm behind herself and lean on that? Or was it terribly uncomfortable?

'No, I'm fine,' she said.

He pulled his pad towards him, flipped to the next clean page, and began to draw very quickly. He covered the page in sweeping charcoal marks. The line of her far arm, supporting her weight at the side of the seat. The slant of her shoulders going one way, the slant of her jaw another. Detailed darkness under her neck and the sweet nugget-lobe of her ear.

Then – dash, dash – the position of her hips in amongst the magazines. Rapid etching for the shadows in there. Skirt over thighs. In at the knee, and dark. Then steering the edge of his charcoal stick not too carefully round the curved edge of the seat, from the point at her arm where it first appeared, right round – out of the picture altogether for a bit – then catching it again and on to the busier place where one of her ankles cut across it. And the room beyond, the vertical line of the windows, the fireplace, the mirror.

Laura looked down at her hand, and listened to the squeaking of his charcoal.

'Laura, look at me.'

She looked.

'I'm just doing your left eye,' he said. 'I . . .'

David looked back into her eye, very closely now,

examined how it fitted into her face, and balanced with the other eye. He needed to get the triangle of eyes and mouth right in relation to the outer oval of her face, and it was all so familiar. He could almost have done it from memory.

'There.'

He turned from her brow – its scar marked by the merest flick – to the part of her face that was in shadow.

David liked that scar. It was new. In his art school days he probably would have seen it as a flaw, but now he liked the contrast: a woman so lovely, so cushioned from the world: perfect house, perfect clothes, perfect husband, perfect body, and a sharp slice at her brow. It made her beauty serious, less spoilt-looking. He wondered what had caused it. Some accident perhaps, tripping on the stairs, or maybe something smarter. One of her skis catching an edge, tumbling through the snow, forehead touched by the tip of a pole. Or sailing in the Adriatic, a sudden change of wind, the boom swinging round, catching her unawares.

Working at the shape of her nose, David was surprised by how controlled he was. Here they were together, alone – close to the realisation of his most intense fantasy – and he was able to function perfectly normally. Even when Laura began wondering again where it was they'd met before, he didn't falter. He told her, smiling, that if they'd met before then he most certainly would have remembered.

'But –'

'Come on,' he said, laughing. 'I'm an artist, so it's my job to remember faces. I don't forget people. And in your case it would be impossible. I mean, I'm sorry if it embarrasses you, Laura, but you have to admit that no one, no man, could forget a face like yours.'

And Laura was just too used to hearing that sort of thing, too used to her own beauty, to question what he said. She gave him what was obviously her set response in such moments: 'Oh, David,' she said, 'that's real nice of you to say so,' and changed the subject herself.

David had learnt that a large part of painting a commissioned portrait was regular breaks. It wasn't like having a paid model. The paid model wasn't in a position to complain about getting restless, uncomfortable, or bored. If the artist wanted to keep going for an extra twenty minutes without a break, the paid model kept her pose. Not so with a commission, and particularly not with Laura.

So at eleven thirty they had a break. And it was only when they were back down in the kitchen – Laura making him a cup of coffee while chatting on the telephone to some friend about a dinner party she was organising – that David realised how much of his previous self-control had depended on the distraction of his work. Suddenly, he found it hard to do the simplest things. He almost missed the edge of the chair he was planning to sit on as he pulled it out. He had trouble lighting his cigarette. And he'd only had two sips of coffee before it was all over the table, swilling on to his trousers, with the mug smashed into three neat pieces on the tiled floor.

David jerked back, scalded. 'Shit,' he muttered, looking for an ashtray, but it was impossible to guess which of the many cupboards. 'Shit. Shit.' Grace was nowhere to be seen, and Laura was still on the telephone, with her back to him. He stood at the kitchen table, covered in steaming coffee.

'Hey, don't worry,' she was saying. 'You look after yourselves. You guys are having a rough time of it out there and . . . ex-a-ctly. The last thing you need right now is some dumb dinner thing! You think he'll be OK? . . . That's good. Good . . . and what about the baby? . . . Oh, OK. So I guess that means they can't come either, right? . . . No, don't worry about it. Sure, he'll be sad, but he'll understand. We can find someone else . . .'

As she spoke, she turned – and put a hand to her mouth.

'Oh my God!' she said, laughing. 'I've got to go. Something's just – . . . No, don't worry. I'll call you.'

She put the telephone down and looked at the mess.

'So sorry,' said David weakly.

'Oh, forget it. Grace?' she called up the stairs. 'Gracie, would you come down here for a second?'

David stood there dabbing his trousers, with Grace wiping round him, and Laura trying not to laugh. 'You're not burnt, are you?'

'I'm fine. Really, I'm just so sorry I –'

'You want another cup?'

'No! No, I mean, I'm so sorry, Laura. I hope it wasn't valuable or anything.' He watched Grace dispose of the broken pieces, and find him an ashtray. 'I – Can I buy you a replacement?'

He felt an idiot saying it. Even if it was worth fifty pounds, that would be peanuts to people like Laura and Joss. It would be easier for them to order a whole

172

new set than try to look up the right model number for David to go along to whatever shop it was and get another one.

Laura shook her head. 'It's fine,' she said. 'Really.'

'But what can I do? I feel terrible.'

Laura smiled. 'Well, David, I'll tell you what you *can* do,' she said, as they went back to the small sitting room. 'You can come back here for dinner on Friday. And so long as you behave and don't break any glasses, I – No, I'm kidding! These guys have just dropped out, see, and, you know, I can't think of a better replacement. You must bring your fiancée as well, will you do that? And Edmund and Alice? The four of you would be just perfect.'

His trousers cooling and drying, David followed Laura back up the stairs to the sitting room. He was pleased with his first sketch, but keen to try another pose, keen also recover his composure. And if he was expected to stay until one o'clock, it would seem slack – wouldn't it? – to push off before twelve. Pulling the curtain so that its sweep was more generous, and asking Laura to sit in the corner of the sofa, David perched on the stool and began a second sketch. With a few brisk strokes, he'd placed her in the picture. But the second he began on the likeness, the second he met her eye, it started to fall apart. Laura was looking at him. There was lightness in her expression. Lightness, and a certain interest he hadn't noticed before.

David sharpened his pencil into the wastepaper basket, and wondered for a moment why she'd invited them to her dinner party. It was great – flattering and exciting – but still a little strange. OK, so Joss knew Edmund, but not terribly well. And she didn't know David at all. There must have been lots of people she could have invited, but she'd chosen David. Why was that? Might – might it just be because she liked him? Could it be because she . . . David stopped himself. She was married, for God's sake. Sure, she liked him, and she was amused, but she wasn't interested in him. Not like that. This was all in his head, and it had to stop. Now. Before it –

But it was already too late. David now found it impossible to look at Laura without his imagination running riot. He couldn't detach. He couldn't see her as before, in anonymous, depersonalised terms of pattern, line, and form. This wasn't some object to draw. This was Laura. Every time he looked at her, she was looking back at him. And it was suddenly very difficult to believe that this was simply because she had to, because the pose required it.

David lost all sense of time. He forgot about Laura needing breaks. He forgot that the plumber was coming at one thirty. And it was only when Laura said, finally, that she really had to move – she couldn't feel her left leg at all, and she had to be at the gym at two o'clock – that David realised how late it was. Hurriedly, he pulled his things together. He had to hide the second sketch away. It was hopeless, the head was far too big, and the arm looked as if it belonged more to the sofa than to Laura. Explaining that he had enough material to go on, that he'd take his work home with him and come up with a fuller design for them to approve in due course, David bade her a swift goodbye and left.

'Don't forget about Friday!' she called down the lavender path.

Tossing his sketchbook and straw bag in the back, hearing all his things – pencils, charcoals, chalks, penknife – tumbling over the back seat on to the floor, David swore loudly, turned on the engine and reversed out of his slot. He drove home with the car windows wide open, his dark hair blowing about, thinking about the woman on the sofa.

And the further he drove, the more his mind began to clear. His heart returned to its quiet pulse, reason resumed control. It was, he told himself, no different from painting the portrait of someone famous. Of course it was going to be strange. There was bound to be more adrenalin. It was quite understandable. And the sense that Laura found him equally interesting? Well, that was his ego. She didn't find him any more interesting than Grace. She was simply holding a pose.

Then why did she ask you to dinner on Friday?

Because those other people fell out.

But why you, in particular?

Indicating right, he waited for a gap in the traffic and swung the car into his street. Get your facts straight, he told himself. It's not just you. It's you, Mel, Ned and Alice.

David parked and got out. Praying that Jake, the plumber, would be late, he was annoyed to get back to the studio and find his prayers answered. There was no sign of him. No van outside. No scribbled note on the door. And inside, there was a message on the answerphone from Jake's wife, saying he was caught in traffic.

David slung his materials on to the sofa and went to look at the bathroom. In spite of leaving the ventilator on, the room was still damp from yesterday's sprays. The smell of wet carpet depressed him and, going back downstairs, David couldn't help but contrast the tinpot style of his studio with the solid-gold quality of the Savils' house. After the efficiency and perfection of Cheyne Lane – there was no question of something not working there – the studio had an air of underlying neglect he'd not noticed before.

Sure, he was obsessive about keeping it clean, and it looked fine, but underneath the well-swept floors, behind the gleaming fittings, was a system in increasing need of attention, and David knew it. He'd known for some time that the taps were weak. He suspected that there were difficulties with the water pipes themselves. The surveyor's report had mentioned how old they were, and had recommended getting them replaced within a year, and that was almost a decade ago, but David had never got round to it. He hadn't wanted to think about how much it would cost. He'd turned a blind eye and wished the problem away, with the result that things had got worse. Much worse. And, thinking what it would cost to have the whole place overhauled – rewired, repiped, repainted – David knew he'd never be able to afford it.

David was a perfectionist. He knew he couldn't compete, shouldn't try to compete, with people like the Savils. And if he couldn't make his studio as shiny and rock-solid as their house in Cheyne Lane, then . . . then he'd really rather not try at all. He couldn't see that, while having the system comprehensively replaced was ideal, there was still something to be said for attempting what he could afford – and not just patching over the cracks. In his eyes, it was all or nothing.

He was an artist. He'd chosen a career that wasn't centred round money. And if the price he paid for that was a studio in dodgy working order, with a damp smell in the bathroom and pipes on the verge of collapse, then he was happy – proud, even – to live here. That's what he told himself as, listlessly, he tidied his things, picked a pencil off the floor, threw away a magazine, and waited for the plumber to arrive.

David had never really grasped how privileged, and how completely artificial, his position was. He didn't see that it was only because some ancestor of his had been devoted to the acquisition of wealth that the studio belonged to him at all. He didn't need to worry about rent, or food, or clothes, and failed to see that, if it wasn't for that inheritance, he might never have been an artist in the first place. He'd have got hungry. He'd have been driven crazy by the clatter of a council block, disrupting his concentration. He'd have hated living off benefit, hated limiting his materials.

Instead, David thought that what he did was high-minded, non-materialistic. And ever since he'd decided, in his words, to turn his back on riches and concentrate on art, he'd derived real pleasure from his version of economising. Every time he chose the cheaper item, the rougher form of travel, the harder, slower route, he did it with pride, and he'd do it again today.

All the same, he wished that Jake would hurry up.

And when, by four o'clock, Jake still hadn't arrived, when he'd simply made the odd sporadic call from a crackling mobile – 'Sorry, mate. Yeah I know . . . Be with you in ten' – David was in no mood to be polite.

'If you're not here by quarter past,' he said, 'you can forget it. I'll get someone else.'

'What's that? What? Sorry, mate – can't hear you. Hello? Hello?'

David hung up.

Jake arrived on the dot of 4.15, pressing the buzzer repeatedly until David was able to get to the intercom and let him in. Jake wasn't fit. His feet shuffled up the stairs and by the time he got to the top he was completely out of breath.

'All right,' he said, stooping at the rail. 'What can I do?'

'It's my bath taps,' said David wearily. 'I told you that when we –'

'Oh, that's right. Your taps. Washer, wasn't it?'

'I've no idea.'

David led him up the stairs to the bathroom and opened the door. He bent over the bath – turned the taps – and showed Jake what the problem was. Then he showed Jake the damp area behind the taps, and then took him down to the kitchen.

'Oh yes,' said Jake, heaving himself on to the worktop directly beneath the damp patch in the corner, and reaching up. 'Mm.' He took his hand away and looked at it, then held it out for David to see. It glistened, and there were flakes of paint on it. 'Good thing you got me when you did, mate. This ceiling's about to fall in.'

'Really?'

Jake nodded and looked up again. 'Did a job like this just the other week, you're lucky you caught it. Still. Reckon if I get the taps fixed for you then you just need to air it out, leave the windows open if you can. It'll take a few days – weeks maybe – to get it dry.' He went on tickling it, flaking the paint away to an ugly grey beneath. 'Mm.'

'And the taps?'

Jake hopped off the worktop. 'Could do a quick repair job now – got some spare washers on me, somewhere – but they're an old set of taps, aren't they? Yeah, they're worn away, mate. You're better off with new ones really.'

'How much will that cost me?'

'The thing is, with fixing taps, you really need to drain the system. Any idea where the water comes in?'

David wasn't sure.

'Well, I'll have to find that – see if it's possible – otherwise I guess I have to isolate the pipes round the bath, but let's hope it doesn't get to that. Anyway, drain the system, that'll take a couple of hours, insert the taps – or mixer, or whatever it is you –'

'Mixer?'

'Yeah, like what you've now, you know, with a shower bit? Well, that won't take long to fix once the system's drained, unless there's some other problem. So let's say three hours . . . that's a hundred and fifty plus VAT plus whatever you spend on the taps themselves.'

'Or you could mend the ones I've got already?'

Jake smiled. 'Sure. And that'll just be the call-out charge. It's up to you, mate.'

David didn't smile back. He walked out of the kitchen, back into the studio, thinking.

'Well?' said Jake, following, picking his ear. 'What do you want to do?'

'I think perhaps you could just sort out the taps I've already got, I mean, of course I see what you say, and obviously I'll need new taps, or a mixer or whatever, at some point,' David looked at his watch, 'but I really don't have time to get them now, so –'

'Fine by me,' said Jake, heading up the spiral stairs once more.

David followed him. 'Just so long as they don't leak.'

'Oh, they won't leak,' said Jake, opening the bathroom door. 'Not for a while. And in the meantime you can find yourself a nice new set of taps.' He knelt at his tool kit, opened it, and took out two small black flat rubber rings. 'Here we are.' He found various other tools – pliers, screwdrivers – and began to lay them out as well.

'Well, I'll leave you to it then, shall I?'

'Yeah, fine. Any chance of a cuppa?'

14

Mel's office was on the fifth floor of the W. J. Oliphant building. Every morning she'd get the lift. She'd stand there, grim in the silvery cube, resenting the other people squashing in with her – people she recognised from W. J. Oliphant, and people from offices and businesses higher up the building that had nothing to do with WJO – resenting the pushing, the hassle, the bodies. It made her think of cattle in lorries, and gas chambers. Most of all, she hated the repetition. Day after day after day, that silver box going up and down, and up and down, and no way out. Double claustrophobia.

Standing in the lift that Monday morning, however, Mel felt different. Just three months, and then she'd never have to do this again. The thoughts and fears she'd had last night – that she was too exposed, that she was making a mistake – evaporated with the morning. She wasn't stuck any more. The doors were opening.

The fifth floor was devoted entirely to WJO's commercial practice. It was gently partitioned – part open plan, part glass offices, part filing cabinets. These partitions could be altered very easily. Last week, she'd come in and seen a colleague's office transformed overnight into an open-plan section for more secretaries, with that colleague restationed at the other end of the corridor. And it looked as if it had been like that all along. That kind of thing happened all the time, and the result was that the place had the transience of a stage set. Nothing, it seemed, was permanent. No one irreplaceable.

Walking up to her office, Mel wondered what they'd do to it when, at Christmas, she left. Would Joe, the guy she shared it with, be allowed to stay there? Would they move someone else in? Or would the space be requisitioned by filing cabinets? Whatever they did, one thing she knew for sure was that any trace of her having been there would be gone by New Year.

Glad that she was, at last, doing something about it, glad that she was leaving, Mel opened the office door. Joe wasn't in. Switching on the light (the room had no window; neither she nor Joe was senior enough for that) she glanced straight at the in-tray on her desk, checking for new post, new messages, new work. It didn't look too bad: a couple of large bottle-green envelopes from Fenwick & Moore (she recognised the firm's colour) with those draft Acquisition Agreements for United Bathrooms that she'd been hassling them for. That was good. And a Post-it note – bright pink, stuck to the screen of her computer – from Philippa, her boss, asking Mel to come and see her at some point that morning.

'And are you free for lunch?' she'd scrawled at the bottom. 'Want a gossip!'

Mel put the note in her in-tray, turned the

computer on, and then she noticed the red light flashing on her telephone. One message.

'Darling?' Mel's mother took a breath. 'Darling, it's me. I'm sorry we didn't talk last night. I'm afraid there was another incident with Bess. She got me on the leg this time and Dr Evans had just arrived when you rang, so I was a bit stuck. But I have been thinking about you, sweetheart. I do know how hard it must be, the way they make you work, and all those difficult things you have to do. It can't be easy, but all of us go through times where we feel like giving up, and that's the challenge. And the really important thing is to struggle through. It will get better.

'I think it's best if you wait for me to call you, darling – just for the moment. I'm sure that if you leave it for a few weeks, it'll calm down. He won't stay angry for long. It's because he loves you, you know, that he's like this. It shows how much he cares. Give it a couple of weeks, give yourself time to think about it properly, see what you're doing. I'm sure you'll . . . But please don't worry, sweetheart. It'll be all right. I promise. Love you.'

Mel replayed the message.

'. . . Sorry we didn't talk last night. I'm afraid there was another incident . . .'

And again.

'. . . another incident . . .'

'. . . another incident with Bess. She got me on the leg this time and Dr Evans had just arrived when you . . .'

Mel put the receiver down sharply. She was overreacting. All her father had done was shout at her last Saturday, get a little cross, and here she was on Monday morning, her imagination in overdrive. She was still upset by the things he'd said, still shocked, but that was no excuse to start accusing him – even in the privacy of her thoughts – of monstrous things. Be rational, she told herself. Think it through. It was, as her mother said, just another incident, and Clare was always having accidents. This was nothing new. This was just . . .

Oh, stop it, she told herself. Just stop it. And, thinking of all the wonderful things her father had done – the sudden compliments, the presents, the steady encouragement, the affectionate touches – Mel began to calm down. He was passionate, sure. He said some pretty awful things. But he wasn't capable of hitting anyone. He was quick to anger, but just as quick to apologise. And OK, so he hadn't apologised last night, but he was tired and Mum wasn't able to come to the phone. She . . .

Mel stopped short – remembering her father's words.

She does have a life of her own, he'd said, *and right now she's in the bath*.

But that wasn't Clare's story. Clare had just said that there had been an accident with Bess – a doctor there, and everything.

Stomach lurching, Mel picked up the receiver and replayed the message.

It had come at four in the morning.

Mel wondered what to do. It was clear from her mother's message that she didn't want Mel to ring – but nor could Mel leave it. Her father would have left for work by now. It was the perfect time to call.

'Mum?'

'Darling,' Clare's voice was low. 'Darling, I thought I told you it was better not to call right now.'

'Is Dad there?'

'No – no, but what if he –'

'He won't find out.'

'He can, darling. He can get back any time, call 1471 and find out exactly who's rung.'

'Does he do that?'

Clare was silent.

'Mum – I'm worried.'

'Worried? Sweetheart, you know what your father's like. He just wants to know who's called, and what's been going on. I bet you do 1471 too. We all –'

'No, Mum, I'm worried about you. Your safety.'

'Oh, darling!' said Clare, laughing. 'You worry far too much. It was only a scratch. It . . . Listen, I just gave the poor dog a fright. I came into the kitchen without looking – virtually trod on her – and she bit back in reflex. She was defending herself.'

'When I rang, Dad said you were in the bath. He didn't say anything about –'

Clare sighed. 'He just didn't want to worry you. He knew it would fuss you, and it seems he was right. I shouldn't have told you about it. Shouldn't have . . . you must stop fussing about me, you know. Especially when there are more important things for you to be thinking about right now. Like your wedding, and getting your job back.'

Realising that she was getting nowhere, realising that it was going to be much harder than she thought, Mel gave up. She'd have to find other ways of doing it. Explaining that she wouldn't be getting her job back, that she'd meant every word she'd said on

Saturday, Mel ended the conversation with her mother and turned to her files. But she couldn't concentrate, and she was still thinking about it when, at eleven, she went in to see her boss.

Philippa's office was the messiest in the firm. It was so messy, there was no room even for a trainee – not that much training would happen in that chaos. The spare desk was covered in piles of files that would slip off into other piles. Philippa would then come back from meetings and throw yet more files and notes on top. It was a tip, and Mel walked in to the familiar sight of Philippa and her secretary, Gail, rifling through it.

'They must be here,' Philippa was saying crossly. 'He only gave them to me last week.'

Gail threw an old tangerine skin into the bin and started on the next pile. 'You're sure you didn't put them somewhere special? I thought we agreed that you were going to put any original documents on *my* desk.'

'Yes, yes, Gail. I know we did, but I had to rush on to that meeting with – Ah! Do you think they might be with my Morgan Trust prospectus?'

'I'll go and see,' said Gail.

Mel shut the door behind her.

'Oh, Mel,' Philippa sighed heavily as she returned to her chair. 'Mel, Mel, Mel, Mel . . . *why* are you leaving us? *What* are we going to do without you?'

Mel leant against the wall.

'It's not fair,' said Philippa. 'I want to leave too. Why don't we all leave? We could set up a commune in Norway – did I tell you I was there for a conference this weekend? It was great – and forget about all this.

Just look at it!' Philippa swept out her arm over her empire of papers. 'Why do I do it?'

'Because you enjoy it,' said Mel, laughing. 'You really do. And you're good at it.'

'So are you.' Philippa stared at her with benign belligerence, Mel stared back, and then they both laughed.

'Well, are you on for lunch?'

'Sure. But can you wait until one? There's that bathroom agreement I'd like to look at before we go.'

Philippa, who'd been at the first meeting, and who'd had trouble keeping a straight face when the clients had begun talking about their stock, raised her eyebrows.

'Oh yes, of course,' she said. 'U-bends and laser flushes. How's it going?'

Joking with Philippa about it – and then getting her head down and reading the paperwork – Mel cheered up. Her interest returned, and it wasn't until she was in the restaurant, with Philippa pouring her a glass of wine and asking about her weekend, that Mel thought once more of her mother's message. Her expression changed, and Philippa who, in spite of being messy, never missed the things that mattered, noticed.

'What is it?' she said, handing Mel the glass. 'What's up?'

Philippa had always been easy – astonishingly easy, for a boss – to confide in. Mel might not have liked the work at WJO, or the hours, or the way the firm's bureaucracy shifted the office space around. But she couldn't complain about the people she worked with, and she knew that the friendly atmosphere in her department was due, entirely, to the person at the top.

Now that Mel had decided to leave, Philippa felt more like a friend than ever and, taking the glass from her, Mel remembered that Philippa did voluntary legal work for a women's charity. She remembered Philippa trying to encourage all the women in her department to do it too. And she remembered, guiltily, how she'd resented what she'd seen as an attempt to eat away yet more of her free time.

'Do you still do work for Women in Crisis?' she said.

Philippa nodded. 'Not so much now, unfortunately. I don't do the helpline. Running the department . . . you know how it is. But I do go to the meetings, and I'm still involved in recruitment,' she smiled. 'Are you thinking about joining us?'

'No,' said Mel, swilling the dark yellow wine. 'No, it's more your advice I'm after.'

Philippa watched her – watched the wine – and waited.

'I'm sure it's nothing,' Mel went on.

'Rarely is.'

'But I'm worried about my parents – my mother. She . . .'

Again, Philippa had to wait for Mel to find the words. In the end, she prompted. 'She . . .?'

'My father . . .' Mel bent right over her glass.

'You've got to give me more to go on, Mel. What's your father done?'

'I don't know that he's done anything.' Mel raised her head. 'Christ, Philippa, for all I know, he's completely innocent, and this is just me and my twisted mind.'

'But what do you think he *might* have done?' Philippa said. Her voice was cool and calm. 'Come on, Mel. Take a deep breath and tell me your suspicions. Doesn't matter how far-fetched they might seem, just go for it. Nothing is going beyond this table. I promise. But I think it'll do you good to air them, don't you?'

Mel nodded.

'And then we can try to figure out if there's anything to it.'

So Mel told her. She told her about the way he treated her mother, the way he spoke to her, and the way he'd try to make it up later. There were early childhood memories – like the time he'd driven back from a walk on the moors with Mel in the back of the car. They'd been playing the gate game. Every time her mother got out to open a gate he'd pretend to drive off without her. They often did it, and Mel loved it. Only then, one time, he did it for real. He left her to walk the ten miles home, and her mother had got back in tears, drenched, brown hair clinging to the sides of her face, while her father had roared with laughter at what a great joke it all was. Mel remembered being scared of him, even then.

And there were later memories. Smaller things, like her father shrinking her mother's housekeeping allowance to fifteen pounds a week and then complaining about the standard of food she gave him. And bigger things, like him falling out with anyone she made friends with; or the time he'd refused to let her visit Mel in London and then a few weeks later, all apologetic, he'd organised a surprise first-class trip, staying at a smart hotel, as a special treat, to thank her for being such a wonderful wife. And then there were those accidents. Never anything big – tripping on steps, incidents with gardening tools, confrontations with Bess, things like that – but it seemed to be getting worse.

'Have you ever seen your mother have an accident?' said Philippa.

Mel shook her head.

She went on – told everything, with memories coming thick and fast – while Philippa listened, punctuating Mel's flow with the occasional question. Philippa knew better than to offer an opinion. She'd never met Mel's parents. It wasn't her position to pass any kind of judgement. Right now, the important thing was to get Mel asking the right kind of questions. Mel needed to be properly informed.

And, back in the office, Philippa had a book on the subject.

'Not always an easy read, and you might not agree with some of the – Oh, where the hell is it? Gail? Gail, have you seen *The Charm Syndrome* anywhere?'

'On top of your computer,' Gail yelled back.

'Oh, yes.' Philippa grabbed the book – pleased – and handed it to Mel. 'Knew I'd put it somewhere clever. Keep it as long as you like.'

She found Mel the number of Women in Crisis: a charity helpline with a backup network of refuges across the country. 'And don't be afraid to call them. You may have doubts about whether your mother's in trouble, and of course none of us really knows what goes on behind closed doors, but it really won't hurt to talk with someone trained in this. Just to get another perspective.'

Mel resolved to read the book. She wasn't so sure about the helpline – it seemed a bit extreme. The lawyer in her felt it was important, at this stage, to gather evidence. She'd act later, only if and when she was certain. It would be too awful to get it wrong, to accuse her father falsely, and alienate him for ever.

15

Edmund put five small cassettes on his secretary's desk and another one into the palm of her hand.

'I want this attendance note done first, please, Suzanne, and then can you call Oliver to confirm lunch today? Book the table for twelve thirty – I'll meet him there – and then perhaps you can get on with the other tapes, which have to be done today. Please. Before you go home. If you don't think you'll have time then arrange for someone else to help you. All right?'

Suzanne was a married woman in her mid-twenties, plump, with evenly fake-tanned skin, and permed hair that was pulled to the top of her head, held in a topknot like a strawberry stalk, with the rest of it spilling in spirals over her forehead and down her neck – frivolous looks that belied considerable administrative skills. She picked up the cassettes, checked to see that they were all full, and nodded.

'I'll get Kim.'

'Thanks.' Edmund turned and walked back up the corridor, clicking his fingers with the breezy air of someone in control of his life.

Suzanne watched Edmund walk away, his

shirtsleeves rolled to the elbow, and smiled at the unselfconscious finger clicking.

'Lunch where?' she called after him.

Edmund stopped clicking and turned, one hand buried in his hair, the other outstretched towards her as he walked back. 'God, Suze, I don't know – somewhere posh and boring. Try Jasper's. Or there's that new place on Bishopsgate, where the old Midland Bank used to be.'

'Hungry Trader,' said Suzanne.

'Any good?'

'I haven't been there, so I wouldn't –'

'Great. Book a table. Smoking, if they have it, and –'

Suzanne's telephone rang. From the flashing light next to Edmund's extension, they both saw that it was for him, and her tidy fingers picked up the receiver.

'Edmund Nicholson's line? Yes, of course, Mrs – sorry, Miss Glass. I'll just . . .'

She glanced at Ned, who was shaking his head and making cutting actions with his hands.

'No!' he mouthed. 'No! No! No!'

But Suzanne wasn't the kind of secretary who did automatically what her boss wanted. She sat there with the telephone receiver in her hands and gave Ned a weary look. Annabel had rung three times already that morning. Suzanne was getting bored with finding excuses.

'Please. I'll buy you lunch on Friday.'

The weariness turned to reproach.

'Don't look at me like that, Suze. No, don't. It's not fair. You're supposed to be on my side, for God's sake. And if you knew her better, you'd agree with me, I know you would. She's ghastly. She . . .'

But Suzanne wasn't going to budge. He knew that look too well. And in spite of himself, Ned laughed. 'Christ,' he said, heading back to his room. 'The things I do for you lot.'

He picked up the ringing telephone on the desk in the corner. 'All right – thanks.' He sat down as Suzanne connected them.

'Annabel, how are you?'

He sounded as though he really wanted to know, so Annabel told him. 'To be honest,' she said breathily. 'Not great. This book is a terrible strain. I've lost so much sleep, I look like a character off *EastEnders*, and I –'

'I'm quite sure you don't, Annabel.'

'Well, I *feel* like –'

'But I thought you'd be pleased about it, pleased that someone was publishing it. We're all so impressed.'

'You are?'

'Of course we all are – everyone is. It's fantastic.'

'You're just saying that. You haven't read it.'

'But I will. I will.'

'When?'

Edmund put her on the speaker-phone and loosened his tie. 'Soon,' he said. 'Now why don't you tell me what's bothering you?'

'I don't want to be sued.'

'And what makes you think that you will?'

'Because it's full of people I know. I didn't realise it was actually going to be published. I thought it would just . . . I'm worried I'm going to offend people.'

'Who exactly.'

'I don't know . . . My ex employers, I used to be in PR.'

'Do you mention them by name?'

'Of course not, but they'll know it's them.'

'You think they'll want the rest of the world to know it's them as well?'

Annabel said nothing.

'PR is their business, sweetheart. They're not going to name themselves, are they? Now, tell me – who else?'

'My friends. I don't mention them by name either, but I'm still –'

'You haven't got any lawyers in there, have you?'

'Well, no. Apart from the hero and he's – well, he's the hero, so that's all right, isn't it?'

'Your hero's a lawyer?'

'Of course he is, Ned! I told you that yonks ago. That's another reason I want you to read it. I need you to check I've got the details right.'

Edmund picked up the receiver. 'Perhaps we'd better have lunch,' he said.

They arranged to meet the following day. Annabel said she'd bring a proof copy of the book with her for him to read. 'I hope you'll like it,' she said excitedly. 'You're only the third person I've shown it to, you know. After my agent and my editor.'

Edmund imagined her referring to him as 'my lawyer' (my lover, my partner, my husband, my – hero? Oh God . . .) and, heart sinking, told her he was sure he'd like it. He – No, he couldn't wait either, and, yes, he really had to go now. He'd see her tomorrow.

Then he put down the receiver and rang Suzanne. 'Get me the Glass file, will you? I think Martin might have it. Or I suppose Victoria might have sent it down to storage, if she's being extra diligent. And then get the library to send me any press cuttings they can about recent libel proceedings in fiction.'

Then he rang Alice.

Alice was in late medieval history, taking notes, ink flowing along the lines of her A4 page. She got to the bottom, shook it dry, and then Smith-Jardine started talking about the Welsh revolt.

'Oh fuck.'

'Alice.'

'Sorry, sir. Sorry . . . what date was that?'

Smith-Jardine looked up from his file. 'Who can tell Alice what date Llywelyn attacked?'

'Twelve eighty-two.'

'Got that, Alice?'

'Yeah,' said Alice, scratching the number at the top of her fresh page and shaking her pen hard. Her cartridge was almost dry.

'In future – and this applies to all of you, *including you, Radcliffe –*'

'Sorry, sir.'

'If you want to check anything on Edward the First – or Second or Third – you'll find it in Prestwich – and I'd make a note of that, if I were you, Radcliffe. Prestwich. There are at least ten copies in the library.'

'What if it's not in Prestwich, sir?'

'Make it up.' Smiling, Smith-Jardine looked at his watch – five minutes until break – and closed his file.

'Anyone seen the papers this morning?' he said. 'What's the news about Owen's knee?'

Alice's mobile was switched off and it wasn't until break, when she was back with the others, sitting on the floor by the lockers in the girls' loos, that she got Edmund's message.

'Alice, hi,' said the still unfamiliar voice. 'It's Edmund. Listen, I finish here about six or seven and would love to see you – speak to you. Any chance of a drink, or dinner? Or have you made other plans? Or perhaps you're not allowed out during the week? I don't have a clue about these things, I'm afraid, but ring me. I'm in the office all day.'

Alice played it over to herself a couple of times. She liked his voice, and she liked his tone, its ease – like asking a girl on a date really wasn't a big deal for this man – mixed with a certain degree of care.

He left a number, and Alice rang straight back. She suggested they meet for a drink at a pub called The Scarsdale.

'It's just where Pembroke Villas –'

'I know where it is,' said Edmund, his mind thrown back ten years, to when he and a crowd of rowdy friends – all men – had knocked over one of the outside tables, sending beer glasses flying, splintering, crashing. They'd been ordered off the premises, but he doubted that the landlord would recognise him now.

The Scarsdale was close to where Alice lived, which would at least give them more time.

'You can't make dinner?'

'Not really, I have to be home at eight, and unless there's something on at school – a concert or whatever – they're pretty strict.'

'Quite right.'

'But they will be going away,' she added with a smile. 'On Thursday – for a week.'

'A whole week?'

'Yeah – they're going to Italy.'

'Lucky them. Lucky you . . .'

'Lucky *you*, you mean!'

'Lucky us,' said Edmund, perking up a bit. 'Got to go, Alice. There's someone waiting – Yes, come in, Victoria, put it there – I'll see you there at seven.'

'Six.'

'Oh, all right. Six. And don't be late.'

The sun was setting as Alice and Emily left school. They walked beneath the gothic stonework of an arch that separated the college and chapel from the rest of the world – a medieval arch that had seen centuries of London life: from the first stonemasons and monks, to tradesmen, diplomats, aldermen, beggars, carriages, bicycles, Daimlers, motorbike couriers – their modern schoolgirl silhouettes and the flood-lighting oddly compatible with the variety of its history.

They passed the watchman at his box, the oily-black gate spikes, and out into London traffic. They stood at the red pedestrian traffic lights and waited for them to change, for the flow of cars to cease – both of them halfway across the road before the pedestrian beeps started – and the great bells in the chapel tower rang out six o'clock.

'Shit,' said Alice, breaking into a run.

'What time did you say?'

'Six – six – come on, Emily.'

They ran to Leicester Square underground station, barged through tourists coming out on their way to the West End shows, and fed their season tickets through the barriers. They ran down flights of steps, past the blue and white tiles, down and round to the westbound Piccadilly line platform, and up to the electric signal, suspended from the ceiling: 'Heathrow – 1 minute. Next Train Approaching.'

'We'll go direct to Earls Court – get out there,' said Alice, standing back as the train shot past, braking.

It was full, but they managed to squeeze on with the hard confidence of natives. This was their territory, and they knew how to make it work for them. They squeezed – politely now, but just as determinedly – to the middle of the carriage where there was more room. Both warm – out of breath – they stood between the silent rows of seated passengers, with the hems of their skirts at eye level.

'Two – four – six . . .' Allowing two minutes per stop, Alice stretched forward, ran her finger along the Piccadilly line map in front of her, and calculated how long it would take them to get to Earls Court. '. . . twelve – fourteen minutes, and then another five – if we run – to the pub. That's – oh God, Em – it'll be six thirty.'

Emily steadied her feet on the floor as the train pulled off, and bent to examine her reflection in the dark glass. 'Do you care?'

Alice caught her breath. 'He told me not to be late.'

'Come on, Alice. Half an hour's nothing, I made Steve wait a full hour once. And this isn't even deliberate.'

Emily and Steve had an on-off relationship that was going through an off patch. After her experiences in

Spain – experiences she hadn't enjoyed nearly as much as she'd expected to – Emily was keeping her distance. She still fancied Steve. He made her laugh and kept her on her toes, but she wasn't sure she wanted him mauling her the way José had done. Right now, it was easier to cool off and fool around with Alice for a bit.

'But Edmund's not expecting you to be there,' said Alice. 'He'll be so fed up . . .'

Emily looked at her. 'Do you want me to come, or not?'

'No – no, I do.'

Alice had told Emily all about Edmund that morning, first thing, in the common room, before prayers.

'He'll definitely ring today,' Emily had said.

And, sure enough, he had.

The first thing Alice had done, after speaking to Edmund, was to ask Emily what she should do now.

'You want to have sex with him *again*?'

'Yeah. Yeah, I –'

'Be honest, Alice. Did you actually enjoy it?'

'Of course I did. It was great! It was like – well, I don't need to tell *you* now, do I?'

Emily smiled, but she didn't believe her. How could Alice possibly have enjoyed all that licking and thrusting and sweat? Let alone be able to relax while that was going on. How could anybody?

'You really like him?' she said.

'Yes.'

'As much as David?'

Alice bit at one of her fingernails.

Emily thought that it would be best if she came

along, to help Alice decide, and to turn the meeting into a three's-a-crowd scenario should Alice have a change of heart.

Edmund was there at five to six. He'd bought a bottle of white and was sitting outside with it, pouring out his third glass, when Alice turned up – with a friend. He watched them at the railings: side by side, bags slung over their shoulders as they looked for him. Oh God. So much for talking to her about his concerns. So much for asking her if she had wanted him, or whether the other night was really just about losing her virginity. Well, perhaps there was no need to ask. Perhaps his question was already answered.

'Maybe he's inside, Alice. Maybe he's gone home.'

'There he is!' Alice came towards him, through quiet Monday drinkers. 'Ned, I am so sorry – stupid train took for ever – and, oh, this is Emily. Emily – Ned.'

Edmund and Emily smiled at each other.

'Sorry to barge in on your drink,' said Emily, sitting on the chair that Edmund had expected Alice to take, dropping her bag to the floor, and crossing her legs. 'Hope you don't mind.'

'Not at all.' Edmund moved aside for Alice to sit in his chair and pulled up a third. 'Is wine OK for you, or can I –'

'Wine's great,' said Alice.

They watched Edmund go inside for an extra glass and another bottle – it wasn't lost on Alice that if they'd been with Tim and Steve they'd have had to do that for themselves – and then she leant over the table. 'What do you think?'

Emily shrugged. 'He's all right.'

'Well, he's great in bed.'

'You're no judge.'

Alice giggled as she bent her head and opened a fresh pack of cigarettes.

They were both smoking when Edmund returned. 'Here you are.' He filled the three glasses, sat down and looked up at the Marlboro Lights going in and out of lips coated in identical lipstick. What was he doing? He should be in the office, or taking someone like Helen from the office, or Victoria – even Annabel – out to dinner. Not sitting here with a couple of adolescents, thinking about . . .

'I'm not going to be able to stay long, I'm afraid,' he said. 'I've arranged to meet a client for dinner, which means leaving here at,' he looked at his watch, 'well, really at seven, I'm afraid.'

Alice looked at her own watch, then back at Edmund, suspiciously. She could feel him lying his escape. He was slipping away from her, and she was suddenly very certain that she didn't want that to happen.

'Stay until seven thirty,' she said.

'I'm sorry, sweetheart. I can't. Really. Which means we've got to get all this drunk in ten minutes,' he grinned. 'Finish that – good girl – and you, Emily, and let me refill your glass, that's right. Now tell me how long you two have been best friends.'

They talked stiltedly as they finished the bottle of wine, and then Edmund picked up his wallet and keys, and got to his feet.

'Time to go,' he said. 'Great to meet you, Emily. And do let me know if you'd like a day in the office, or whatever, to see what it's like – might put you off for life, but maybe that's a good thing.'

'Thanks,' said Emily, letting him kiss her cheek.

Edmund turned to Alice, but he didn't look quite into her eyes. 'Bye,' he said, kissing her on the cheek as well.

'Bye.'

They watched him leave, taking with him his car keys, his City suit, his important client dinner, his promises of new experiences – sexual and social – and Alice felt the loss.

'Do you think he'll ring me?'

'Don't know,' said Emily, emptying the bottle into her glass. 'Seemed pretty keen to leave, didn't he? Maybe he's decided you're too young. Maybe you *are* too young.'

'I'm not.'

'You'll have trouble keeping him interested.'

'No I won't. He fancies me. You should have heard the things he was saying the other night.'

'Yes, but did he mean them?'

It had taken Jake, the plumber, no time at all to mend the tap. Within half an hour he was gone, clutching his cheque and heading for his van. David stood at the kitchen window and watched the van pull into the road. He was glad that it was only the call-out charge, glad he hadn't been persuaded to spend any more money. Probably didn't need to, anyway. The taps were fine. And even if he did need them replaced at some later point, he wouldn't get Jake to do it. No way.

David spent the rest of the afternoon sorting out

his desk – and not thinking of Laura. Not thinking of her, he paid his bills, balanced his accounts, and decided to stretch a couple of canvases in preparation for a commission he had coming up next week to paint some headmaster in Islington. It was important to give the client a choice of sizes. He'd just finished the first and was sitting in front of *Channel 4 News* with it between his legs, distracted by grisly footage of Palestinian riots, when Mel got back from work.

Looking up as she came in, David was struck by his own response. Instead of the calm that her presence usually provided, the calm he'd come to expect, he felt vaguely uneasy. This was his future. This was his choice, and there was no room for days like today, not any more. No room for that kind of illicit thrill. And while he knew that this was a good thing – he was right to get shot of the past – David felt a moment's guilt, followed by desire to make it up to Mel.

'Darling,' he said, smiling at her.

Mel looked at David there – with the news on and the canvas between his legs – and smiled back. It was a familiar sight. Around him were the tools and materials he needed: his stretchers, his roll of canvas, his scissors, his staple gun. And on the easel was a large sketch of Laura Savil, her body snaking over a low stool that was covered in magazines.

'It's wonderful,' said Mel, taking off her coat.

David put the newly stretched canvas to one side and switched off the television. He kissed her, poured her a glass of wine, and they looked at the sketch of Laura.

Mel drank from her glass and leant against him happily. This was as it should be: the two of them standing there, after a good day's work. Mel was tired and there were things on her mind: her parents, the wedding. And now there was Nathan's dodgy love life. He'd rung Mel that morning to ask her and David to dinner on Friday night, to meet Fenella properly. 'Tell David she's a wonderful cook,' he'd said. 'Make him jealous!'

'Watch it,' Mel replied, laughing, 'I can cook too, you know!' but she was worried about how serious it sounded.

So many things to talk about, but the dominant feeling was one of gladness, that David was here for her, and that he would be for ever. This is what's important, she told herself. This is what we have to make time for. And wishing that they had more moments like this one – just the two of them alone – Mel put her arms around his neck and kissed him.

'I love you.'

'Love you too,' said David, willing it.

She kissed him again, and smiled. 'So how was the plumber?'

Picking up the other square of canvas – cut from the great heavy roll on the floor to fit over the smaller 24 x 28 stretcher size – David told her about the way Jake had tried to get him to replace the taps, and what that would have cost.

'What kind of idiot does he think I am?' he said.

Mel watched as, with a pair of pliers and a staple gun, he sat back on the chair and began to attach the canvas, starting from the middle of each side of the square, and then rolling and shifting it round ninety degrees after each staple was fired in, to ensure that the tension remained evenly spread over all four sides.

'So what did you do?'

'Got him to mend the existing taps,' said David, as rolling the picture round again, he put the pliers carefully in position and closed them over the rough canvas material. He eased it over the stretcher – firm, taut – and fired the staple in.

'They work fine, and I only had to pay the call-out charge.'

'Fantastic.'

'Yes,' said David, firing another staple. 'So it's all fixed. You can have a shower or a bath whenever you like.'

They talked on, their conversation punctuated by shots from the staple gun. And while they talked, they watched the canvas – tightening and flattening, its slackness shrinking to the corners – until Mel told David about Nathan and Fenella, and the invitation to dinner.

David looked up. 'When is it?'

'Friday.'

'Oh God.' David yanked at the next section of canvas and, tensing his jaw, he fired the gun again. 'We can't go,' he said. 'I'm sorry, darling, but we're expected with Laura and Joss. They're having some massive dinner party. Twenty, or something. She wants all of us – you, me, Ned, Alice – and I promised her we'd –'

'But I promised Nathan,' said Mel.

David fired his staple gun again, and again. It was too noisy to talk over. When that was done, he picked up a hammer and hit wedges into each corner to increase the tension on the canvas. Mel stared out ahead of her until he finished – resting his arm on the

206

canvas, the hammer dangling from his hand.

'Come on, darling,' he said. 'You're really saying you'd rather eat scrambled eggs with Nathan and Fenella?'

'He says she's a good cook.'

'You'd rather do that than go to a fabulous full-blown dinner party at the Savils'?' David told her about the house in Cheyne Lane, the dining room, the servants. Incredible, wasn't it? That people still lived like that.

'Sounds amazing,' said Mel. 'It really does.' She looked at David – anxious, determined – and was surprised by how much it mattered to him. Since when had he developed an interest in smart parties? She thought he hated that scene.

But that wasn't really the point, she told herself. The real question here was whether she should insist they go to Nathan's – make a stand – or whether she should give in. Would this set a precedent? She didn't want to be married to someone who'd always expect to get his own way – someone like her father – and part of her felt it was important to establish ground rules now. But the other part of her simply wanted to make David happy. She hated not giving him what he wanted, hated disagreeing with him, hated denying him, and, in the end, that was the part that won through.

She hoped it wasn't too much like a parent spoiling a child. But, in this case, it was surely right that David should go to Joss and Laura's party. They were his clients, and after the number of times he'd accompanied her to office parties and client dinners, it was only fair that she should go with him now to his. It wouldn't be that difficult to get Nathan to change dates.

'But?' said David.

Mel smiled at him. 'But nothing.' She reached for the telephone. 'I'll see if Nathan can make Saturday instead.'

'Oh, darling.'

David getting his own way was the David she'd known at the beginning: the loving, laughing, flirting I'll-do-anything-you-want man that had made her think it was for ever. And it was still for ever. He could still be like this. He could still shine for her – she just had to do the polishing herself.

Now he sat behind her on the sofa, stroking her neck and her wrists, the inside of her elbows, all those places she loved to be touched, while she spoke to Nathan and moved him to Saturday. And, when the conversation went on a bit, when Nathan had to check that it was OK with Fenella, David slid to the floor. He removed the hard smart shoes, and began softening up her toes. Mel's feet were really too ticklish, but the vigour of her reaction – her sparkling eyes, the rapid way she was ending the call – clicked David into automatic pursuit.

'Great, Nathan,' she said, very quickly. 'That's great. I'll call – a! – no,' suppressing her laughter, Mel pushed David away. She squirmed her feet up under her bottom so that he couldn't get to them, but David was determined. He caught her and kissed her neck. 'No, Nathan, it's fine. See you around eight on Saturday. Great. Thanks. Bye!'

Ned got back to an empty room. But the half-drunk glasses of wine, the discarded shoes, and a woman's shirt on the stairs told him where the others were. David's tools and materials were strewn across the floor. Mel's briefcase was open on the sofa, spilling its contents: some draft contract, a mass of office pens and highlighters. Her keys and purse had fallen to the floor.

16

The fine weather continued. There were still no clouds but the air was getting thinner, cooler, and the sheet of Indian summer sky had finally started to fade. It hung high, pale, dry, over a tired city. Edmund and Mel hurried, independently, to work – sunlight in their eyes as they came up out of the same underground station, the same steps, ten minutes between them. Each carried thoughts of meetings, day-plans, calls, things that absolutely had to be done that morning, and things that would wait – thoughts that blinded them to the display of morning light, the particular pink-fresh glow, the shadow of a pigeon in flight, rippling over the heads of the crowds, then flat on the open road, and then – if they'd only look up – a glorious feathery flash to the other side. All things that would stop David in his tracks.

David, however, was still in bed. He lay there dozing, with the curtains fluttering and the breezes on his body, thinking of Laura. He couldn't help it. The effort not to think of her while Mel was around – kissing him and touching him and talking of the wedding – had pushed him to his limit. And with Mel now gone, David gave himself up to remembering each precious second of yesterday's sketching session. It had felt wrong, somehow, to do that with Mel present, but the sense of faithlessness he felt when she was there vanished when he was alone. It was, he told himself, harmless. There was nothing bad in day-dreaming about unobtainable women, and Laura Savil was about as unobtainable as they got. Unobtainably beautiful, unobtainably rich, unobtainably . . . married.

He wondered for a moment why she'd done it. What was so special about Joss Savil? He wasn't powerful, or clever, or particularly funny. He was just rich – but was Laura really so material, so superficial, so utterly empty as to marry a man for his money? David wasn't sure. He tried to think what it would have been like for her in a foreign country, without family or friends, so poor that she was modelling naked to make ends meet. The attentions of a man like Joss would have been heady stuff. Perhaps it was naïve to expect a girl in Laura's circumstances to resist the opportunities he offered.

David turned on his back in the large rumpled bed and stared at the ceiling. Maybe Joss was kind to her, he thought. Maybe that was it. Maybe, beneath the pompous exterior, he was affectionate and caring. But even if that was the case, what about love and desire? What about physical attraction? It would be a big sacrifice, especially for a woman as lovely as Laura. Perfect lifestyle, perfect home, but always something missing.

It wasn't until midday that he finally got up, put on his dressing gown and went downstairs. The studio was a mess. His materials were all over the floor,

Mel's shirt was just hanging there – irritated, he pulled it from the banisters – and her rubbish scattered on the sofa. She'd just grabbed her briefcase, taken the things she needed, and left the rest of her crap for him to clear up. David sighed. Look at this. Yesterday's newspaper, yesterday's receipts.

He was in the kitchen tying up a large black plastic bin bag when the telephone rang.

It was Joss. 'Have I rung at a bad time?'

'No,' said David, recoiling from a smell of rancid rubbish on his hands. 'Not at all.'

'Gather you and Laura had quite a productive time yesterday,' Joss went on. His voice was smooth and mellow. 'She tells me your sketch was rather good.'

'Well, I don't know about that. It –'

'We were rather hoping you'd bring it with you on Friday – if you're coming, that is.'

'Of course we're coming,' said David quickly. 'And I can certainly bring the sketch if you're –'

'Perfect,' said Joss. 'And what about your brother and his lovely little friend? They coming too?'

David told him he'd get Edmund to call back today, and then rang Ned at work.

Edmund was in a meeting. He got the message later that morning – in Suzanne's loopy scrawl: 'Brother rang. Are you and Alice free for dinner, Friday, with Joss and Laura? Call Joss. Says you have the number.'

Ned checked his diary. No, he was doing nothing on Friday. Nothing he couldn't cancel. He wanted to go – it would be good. Joss's parties were always good. The only difficulty was Alice.

He could tell it straight – just say it wasn't working with Alice and ask if he could bring someone else. But while Ned was sure he could find a replacement, nobody obvious sprang to mind. There was also the matter of Joss: Joss's admiration, Joss's envy. And however puerile that was, Edmund found that kind of thing hard to resist. He sat at his desk, the message in his hands and looked at the telephone. He hadn't actually ended it with Alice – nor had she with him – and it would only be for one night. She probably wouldn't be able to make it, anyway.

He dialled her number. Expecting to be put through to the answering service on her mobile, he was surprised to hear her voice.

'Ned! Hi.'

'Aren't you supposed to be in class?'

'I am in class.'

'Then what –'

As she replied, he could hear a rising mass of adolescent voices in the background – mainly male – and quite a lot of laughing.

'We're doing a test, the teacher's gone for a pee or something. How are you?'

'Worried you're going to fail your test. Why don't you call me back when you're less busy?'

'I'm not busy. I've finished. How was dinner?'

'Oh fine,' he said quickly. 'Boring. Listen, Alice, before your teacher gets back and puts you in detention, do you want to come to a dinner party on Friday? With Joss and Laura. It's probably not your scene, but they were hoping you'd come and play the piano again. David and Mel will be there, and –'

'I'd love to,' said Alice, who had her fortnightly

piano lesson that evening, between seven and nine.
'What time?'

'Oh I don't know. Eight, I expect. I'll pick you up.'

'OK.' She could always say she was ill – miss the lesson. She could do with more time to get to grips with that middle section of the Beethoven, in any case. 'What shall I wear?'

'Something sexy.'

'What are you wearing?'

'I'll be in a suit, I expect, but can we talk about this later? I just need to know if you can come.'

'I can,' she said. 'Definitely.'

As Edmund put the telephone down, he was pleased. He wouldn't have to do any explaining to Joss. And after dinner perhaps, or when he dropped Alice home, he could wrap the whole thing up and they could both move on.

Trouble is, he thought, as with false chivalry he ushered Annabel Glass into a City restaurant for lunch that day – move on where?

Was this the only alternative?

Observing her as she considered the menu, Ned had to admit that, while fading, Annabel's looks were still good. He didn't think much of the kind of book she'd written, but he admired the fact that she'd tried. She wasn't stupid, or unkind. And while she was, he suspected, self-centred and vain, so was Alice. So were most women. Most men, for that matter.

Annabel felt the scrutiny, and basked in it. She knew she looked good. Of course she had to work at her appearance, but she had time. She wasn't rushing from nursery school to the supermarket. She wasn't breastfeeding at four in the morning or putting another load in the washer. It was still a world of gyms and restaurants and dry-cleaners, and Annabel wanted a man rich enough to make sure it would always be that way.

She waited until he'd ordered the wine, and then took out a proof copy of her book. 'I know it looks long. But really, Ned, it's not. And it's very easy to read.'

'Great.' His eye skimmed the back. Society girl meets devilish lawyer with surprising heart of gold – and bank balance to match, no doubt. Smiling, he put it to one side.

'All right, I'll have a look at it, but –'

'Oh, Ned, thank you!'

'But I'm doing it as a friend, not as a lawyer. Not through Fenwick & Moore, you understand?'

Annabel nodded.

Ned patted the book. 'I know I do defamation,' he went on, 'but romantic fiction isn't my area. And while, of course, I won't charge you for it . . .'

'Really?'

'. . . nor can you expect my opinion to be anything other than that of a friend. You understand? There may be things I'll miss, things that an expert in this area would pick up, things that your publisher's lawyers are specially trained to spot.'

'So what you're saying –'

'What I'm saying, Annabel, is that you are not my client. If your worst nightmares do come true – if you find yourself defending libel proceedings and it's because of something I failed to see – then you won't be able to seek compensation from me.'

Annabel hadn't seen him serious before. She'd

imagined him at work – imagined him in court, at meetings – but it was different when directed at her. Sexy. And, watching him drop the book into his briefcase, she lit a cigarette and hoped it wasn't too late to alter the scene of Lady Marsden's will.

'That's fine,' she said, offering Ned one – easily, elegantly. Ned took it, and found the lighter already in his hand. 'Now then,' she went on, 'business over, we can get on to the interesting stuff! I want to hear all about New York, and what it's like to be back. Where are you living?'

'With my brother.'

Annabel caught the tone. 'Is that nice?' she said, managing to combine a smile with a little frown of sympathy. 'Or a little bit . . .'

Ned laughed. 'Let's just say I'm looking for some-where to buy.'

Annabel nodded, smiled, and let him continue.

'It's not that we don't get on –'

'Of course not.'

'But now that he's engaged, I think it's best for me to move out. Don't want to cramp their style, and –'

'That's so nice of you.'

Ned smiled. 'Oh, there's a selfish reason too. I'm not sure how often I can come back to discarded clothes on the stairs and talk of wedding plans. There's a limit, you know, to the –'

'Oh quite,' she said. 'So you're looking to buy, and . . . do you know where?'

'Notting Hill.'

'Fantastic! And have you found anywhere?'

'Maybe,' he said.

'Tell me! Oh, how exciting! Have you got the

216

particulars with you? Oh wonderful! Let's see . . .'

Two hours later, and two bottles down, Edmund left the restaurant with a warm glow. He knew what she was doing – could see that she was trying a bit hard – but that didn't make it bad. It was nice to have someone take an interest in the things that interested him, even if they did have an ulterior motive. It was flattering that someone attractive – and Annabel Glass was definitely attractive, so what if she had to make an effort? – yes, it was flattering that a woman like that would have ulterior motives towards him. He liked being in the company of someone who seemed to see him at his best, who thought his job was impressive, who was intrigued by the time he'd spent abroad. He was the hero of her book, for God's sake! How flattering was that?

She made him feel bigger and more important than he was. And really, after Virginia's lack of interest and Alice's games, he could do with a boost to his ego.

Mel, meanwhile, was in the office, flipping through Philippa's book and thinking about her mother.

After the lunch she'd had with Philippa yesterday, she'd read the book, and spoken to someone on the helpline. But while they'd been interesting, and while she'd gone into the question in some depth, the message always seemed to be the same.

In cases of actual violence, they said she should call the police. But what good was that, weeks after the event, when the alleged victim herself denied it? So, instead, Mel was told that she should try to reassure her mother: let Clare know that she cared, that she was there for her. But it was hard to do that when Clare didn't accept that there was a problem in the first place.

'Of course he gets angry,' she'd say, as she'd said before. 'Don't we all? And he loves me, darling. He really does. You don't need to worry. I'm happy! And you should see how sweet he's being at the moment.' Then she would go on to relate some little treat they'd had together – tea at Betty's or seeing a film that Clare particularly enjoyed.

And the longer Mel left it, the more she began to doubt her own suspicions. Perhaps it was just an overreaction to her father yelling at her that day. Maybe she was wrong.

Mel was still sitting there, with the book in her hands, when Gail came in.

'Sorry to bother you, Mel. Just checking which train you want for Friday's trip to Swindon.' She waited while Mel found the right page in her diary. 'The United Bathrooms one? And I need to know if you'd like me to book you a return seat. Philippa says there's no way she's spending Friday night in Swindon – she's getting the ten o'clock – but maybe you'd rather leave it open?'

'Better leave it open,' said Mel, with a sigh. 'I bet that awful Nigel Reardon will turn up, and drag it on into the night.'

It was only when she turned to her personal diary that Mel noticed the clash. Even if she did manage to get an earlier train, she would never get back in time for dinner. She couldn't have gone to Nathan's. And she certainly couldn't go to some formal dinner party given by the Savils.

Reluctantly, and with some fear, she rang David. She told him she was sorry, but she was going to have to pull out.

'Why?'

'I've got a meeting. It's a big one, darling. All day in Swindon – don't know what time it'll finish – and then there's the journey back.'

'You can't take a day off?'

She laughed and shook her head. 'Not really. See, it's not –'

'But, Mel, you're *leaving*.'

'It's just not like that,' she said. 'I wish it was, but these people are still my clients. They rely on me. They . . . How would you feel if your lawyer left you in the lurch for a dinner party?'

'Oh, for God's sake,' said David, 'you don't have to tell them it's a dinner party.'

'But I –'

'Don't you think you might, just for once, put yourself second? It's not as if your career is on the line. I go to your dinners – with your friends – and your office parties. The amount of times I've grovelled to your boss, your secretary, your clients. But do you do the same for me? Have you ever done the same for me?'

'You've never asked.'

'I'm asking now.'

Mel sighed. 'You don't understand,' she said. 'It's different for lawyers. We have a duty to our clients. We can't simply down tools and head off into the sunset the second we get a nice invitation. We –'

'Of course. That's right. Lawyers have a duty, artists are disposable.'

'Don't give me that, David. I'm only telling you what's expected of me. I don't have a choice in this. I can't go to the Savils'. But that's no reason for you not to go by yourself. What's stopping you from doing that?'

Mel knew the answer: because we're engaged, and we do things together. But David had yet to reply when her door opened and Philippa came in, pointing at the time.

Mel stood up. 'I must go. We'll talk later but, honestly, I don't quite see how I can get out of something like this. It's just not –'

'It doesn't matter,' said David suddenly. 'Really. You go to your meeting in Swindon. I'll go to Joss and Laura's by myself. Don't know why I didn't think of it before.'

17

So David went alone. Turning up bang on eight with the sketch rolled and taped in his hand, he was the first to arrive. He was shown into the little sitting room where Joss, dressed in an immaculate suit that turned his huge body into something splendid, was standing very close to the television with his head bent.

'Hang on,' he said, not looking up.

David continued to stand there. He looked at the screen as well – at a mass of Ceefax racing results – and waited with the roll of paper, awkward in his hands, until Joss switched the television off.

Then he put down the remote and gave David a sweet, apologetic smile. 'Hello,' he said, shaking David's hand. 'How are you? I am sorry about that. I –'

'It's fine,' said David, finding it impossible not to smile back. 'Did you win?'

'Came in third – which, in fact, is perfect. Don't want him to overqualify at this stage.'

David gave a stupid nod. He hated giving the impression he understood something he didn't, but it was so much easier to fudge it with a nod than to start asking about things he really wasn't interested in.

'Still. Very rude of me,' Joss went on, looking at his watch. 'And Laura's even worse. Not even out of the bath, I expect.'

Both men smiled again, and Joss continued, 'She thinks you've done a fantastic job, you know. She was so excited about it. I've heard of nothing but how talented you are. All week.'

David gave him the sketch. 'Don't know about talented,' he said. 'Better see for yourself when you've got a –'

He hadn't expected Joss to open it there and then. Taking the cigarette from between his fingers, Joss put it into the side of his mouth. He brushed the fall of ash from the roll of paper and tore off the masking tape, hurriedly unscrolling, holding it out in front of him like a town crier, battling with the curling corners – and said nothing.

'You don't like it.'

'It's great,' said Joss, scrolling it back up, propping it in a corner, and taking the cigarette out of his mouth. 'Great. Now. How about a glass of champagne?'

David longed to say, 'But what about the design, the angle of her head? What about the pose? Is it too much? Do you really like it? Or are you just being polite?' Instead, he took the glass that Joss offered, thanked him, and followed him into the garden.

'Yes,' said Joss thoughtfully. 'Perfect.'

David smiled. 'Well, perfect's a bit of an exagg –'

'And Fred – Fred Gateshead, you know him? The trainer? He'll be chuffed to bits. Means the handicapper won't spoil his chances at Sedgefield.'

They were still talking about Joss's horse when

Laura came downstairs in a large silk dressing gown, splashed with great bright flowers, wrapped almost double round her waist.

'Darling one, could you possibly get my – David!'

'Hello, Laura.' He kissed her.

'You're early!'

'No, my sweet,' Joss patted her bottom. 'You're late.'

Laura grinned. 'Well?' she said to David. 'Did you bring the sketch?'

David indicated the loose scroll, up against the wall, and Laura turned to Joss. 'So what did you think of it, darling? Did you like it?'

'Of course.'

'Don't you love the pose? And I'm so glad I don't have to smile – I was worried you'd make me.' Looking at David, Laura adjusted her dressing gown and smiled a great deal.

David smiled back. 'I'm afraid the nose still isn't quite right.'

'And nor are the clothes,' said Joss suddenly.

David and Laura looked at each other, then both of them back at Joss.

'You think she looks too casual?'

Joss helped himself to another glass of champagne from the tray. 'I'm sorry. But if this picture is going to hang with the others in the dining room at Merwick, then I think my wife should be wearing something a little more – appropriate. Don't you?'

'But, darling, I like the clothes I've –'

'No, Laura. I've got to look at that picture every day,' he turned to David, 'and I don't want my wife looking like some student. I mean, for God's sake, man, she's my wife. She's – she's beautiful. Dignified. Surely you can see –'

'I'm sorry,' said David, surprised at his vehemence. 'I'll change it.'

'That skirt is way too short. The T-shirt's tight. It's all wrong. It makes her look cheap, and . . . I'm sorry, David, but I just don't recognise her. That's not the woman I married. Laura's discreet. She'd never flaunt herself like that. It's why I –'

'Joss, honey,' Laura put a hand on his arm. 'I'm the one to blame here. I chose the clothes.'

Joss shook it off.

Not looking at David, Laura gave a small laugh. 'Well, anyway,' she said. 'Should get moving, I guess. I was just wanting my earrings, honey – those little Chinese ones. Could you get them out of the safe, and bring them up?'

David watched her leave. She passed an arrangement of fresh gardenias in the hallway, the silk hem of her dressing gown trailing in her wake. Looking at all the beautiful things around him – imagining yet more beautiful things upstairs – he wondered if anything more than that was holding the Savils together.

Alice had been looking forward to Friday. She'd cancelled her piano lesson. Her parents were now away, and her only problem was finding something to wear. Something that would make her seem as adult as Joss and Laura's other guests. Something that, more importantly, would convince Edmund that she was. Emily's doubts about the age difference, her doubts about Alice's ability to hold the interest of

224

an older man, had made Alice more determined than ever to prove that she could. It was important she didn't look out of place.

'How about that dress you wore the other night?' Edmund had said, when she'd rung him about it that morning. 'The one you were wearing when I took you to Angelo's.'

'They've seen it before.'

'That doesn't matter, Alice. It's what's inside that –'

'It makes me look young.'

Edmund laughed. 'What's wrong with looking young?'

Silence.

'All right,' he said, laughing. 'Why don't you borrow something from your mother? That ought to make you look grown up.'

Still Alice didn't reply.

Worrying that he'd pushed it, Edmund backed down. 'I'm sorry, sweetheart. I didn't mean –'

'No,' said Alice, smiling. 'No, it's a good idea. I'm just wondering if she'll have taken her nice stuff to Italy. There's a gorgeous top she has. Camel-coloured chiffon with little pearl buttons down the back. I could wear it with my black trousers, and black heels.'

Edmund thought it sounded drab – she'd look like a shop assistant. But when he picked Alice up that night, he realised he'd been wrong. Yes, the shirt was camel-coloured chiffon, it had long sleeves and came primly to her neck. But it wasn't lined, and Alice wasn't wearing a bra. He shut his jaw and kissed her.

'What about the knickers?'

Alice locked the front door, and put the keys into her black sequinned bag. 'What about them?'

'Left behind as well?'

'Well, Ned, that's for me to know –'

'And me to find out?' Grinning, he opened the cab door and watched her climb in – a flash of small round breast shifting under the fabric of her shirt. 'I can't wait.'

Closing the door with a slam, he leant forward and caught the eye – the *well, mate, you're in for quite a night* expression – of the cab driver in the rear-view mirror.

'Cheyne Lane,' he said.

'Cheyne Lane,' echoed the driver, and set off. He was skilled. In a series of smart manoeuvres – whirring through narrow red-brick residential lanes, over the bubbled cobbles of a mews, then sharp left, braking to take the thud of speed bumps, and out into the roar of the main street again – he avoided the Friday-night congestion. Not that either of his passengers noticed.

Alice was too busy chattering and laughing – was it really OK to wear this shirt? Did he think there'd be lots of people there? Anyone famous? – in between surreptitious checks at the reflection of her head in the glass partition, and flips of her shiny hair. And Edmund was concentrating on forcing a quiet distance between them. He listened to her chatter, gave paternal 'wait and see' answers to her questions, and noticed her noticing herself. He looked at the nail-bitten fingers restlessly tapping at the sequins on her bag and found it easier than he'd expected to focus on the immaturity, the lack of self-assurance beneath the cocksure attitude. This was going to be

OK. She was playing with him, sure, but she wasn't serious and he wasn't serious about her. He was going to enjoy tonight, and then he was going to let her go.

Grace let them in.

'They're in the garden, sir – madam. Just go through the door to your right and down the steps.'

'Thanks.'

Edmund waited for Alice to check her face in the mirror above the fireplace in the hall, and then they went on through the little sitting room – full of flowers, magazines all cleared away – past a man with a tray of champagne, and on to a terrace with steps down to a party of about twelve.

It was dark. An indigo sky pressed in, with a bank of orange-grey cloud gathering to the south. Candles dotted out the edges of the garden, burning evenly, unflickering. Voices wilted in the air.

'Ned!' Joss was at the foot of the steps holding a fat bottle of champagne. 'Come down. You know Giles and Chrissie, don't you?'

The smiles said that they didn't.

'Oh. Well. Giles and Christine Verney. Ned Nicholson, and . . .' Joss trailed off as Alice moved into light from the candle between them, '. . . and Alice,' he finished appreciatively.

Glancing at Ned as he kissed her, Joss gave Alice a glass of champagne, and took her arm. 'You look fantastic. I'm going to extract you from Ned for two seconds. You don't mind, do you? There's someone I want you to meet.'

Ned watched them go. He saw Alice turn for a

moment and give him her most provocative smile, before Joss led her off to the other end of the garden.

They had to squeeze their way round groups of conversations but Alice didn't mind. She drank from her glass and looked at the other guests: at the array of clothes and jewellery, the faux indifference to where they were. And there was David – more faded somehow, in this exotic crowd. He was sitting on a stone seat, talking to a slim black woman in a long white dress. There was no sign of Laura.

'Where is she?'

'Upstairs,' said Joss. 'Can you believe it? Still doing her hair, or something. Or maybe it's her nails.' He smiled at her. 'You women.'

It was almost nine o'clock when Laura finally emerged. David heard her voice, the mellow accent undercutting the tones of the English women, and turned to see her in a backless dress of buttermilk yellow, no earrings, and hair rolling back from the scar on her brow.

She was working her way through the garden. 'I'm sorry you had to wait,' she was saying. 'Do you want to come in? Dinner's ready. Hi there, Joel. . . . Just go back up into the hall and through the doors on your right, Grace'll show you. . . . Mark! . . . Thank you. So do you! How was Hong Kong? . . . I know. Not that different from here, really. . . . Isn't it? They say there's a storm coming. . . .'

The dining room at Cheyne Lane was at street level, and positioned directly beneath the drawing room. It was large enough to sit twenty to dinner. A great table stretched the length of the room. There was no cloth and the wood had been polished so hard that the mass of wedding crystal, cut glass, and silver reflected off its surface, doubling the candlelight so that the room itself was glowing.

David bent to look at the *placement*, at the names written out on slips of paper and tucked into a small leather board made especially for the purpose. It was propped against the back of a chair by the door and he was really more interested in the board than he was in where he was sitting. It was modern. He looked at the quality of the leather, at the perfect finish, with its subtle patterns of gold – intricate, crafted, worked into the surface. He noticed the elaborate J and L, entwining at the centre, and felt disgust at the extravagance, the silliness. It would have cost some idiot hundreds and hundreds of pounds.

Laura bent over his shoulder, touching him with one hand while the other pointed. 'You're there, David. See? Next to me.'

Next to me. With the sensation of her fingers on his shoulder staying long after she'd removed them, David moved into the room. Why? Why was he next to her? Unable to stop the internal questions, David stood by his seat, watching the faces of the other guests – softened by drink. Standing there, he watched Laura directing them and wondered, what must it be like? Did she really like this silk-hemmed world? *Placement* boards and silver tureens, with someone like Grace forever cleaning in the next room, a life of stiff invitations, stiff collars, stiff upper lips.

He was still thinking these thoughts when Laura came up, sat down, and began talking to the man on her other side – Giles Verney. She encouraged him to help himself to the crack-thin toast that had been left for them in little racks all round the table – 'And have some pâté.'

Giles did as he was told. 'This looks delicious, Laura. Can't think how you do it.'

'I don't.'

'Well, you know: organising all this must be quite an operation.'

'Just a few telephone calls,' she said. 'When I think of what someone like you – or David for that matter – does during the day, it's nothing.'

Giles and David looked at each other.

'Giles is in Property,' said Laura. 'And David's an artist.'

'Really?'

'He's doing me in the spring.'

Giles put a mouthful of toast and pâté into his mouth and nodded at David. 'Where did you study?'

'Clerkenwell,' said David.

Giles piled more pâté on to a tiny bit of toast. 'Didn't go to Italy or anything, then?'

'No.'

'Pity. Friend of mine – seriously talented – went somewhere in Florence. That place with the funny name.'

As Giles talked on, Laura got up from her chair, murmuring, 'Excuse me.' She left the room, leaning against the door to the hall as she opened it – her brown back smooth and dark against the buttery folds. The departure was so sudden, it stopped Giles mid-sentence.

'Did I say something?'

David frowned. 'Don't think so. We were just talking about painting, weren't we? And art schools . . .' he trailed off, remembering that he'd mentioned his art school, Clerkenwell, by name.

Oh God, he thought, jaw tightening.

Giles shrugged. 'Probably got something to check in the kitchen. Just goes to show, you know. These things are never really just a couple of telephone calls. Poor Chrissie gets completely swamped, and our dinner parties aren't nearly so lavish.' Chuckling, he took up his glass. 'Only last week, she was telling me not to ask people to dinner without checking with her first.'

Must have made the connection. Maybe even recognised him. David sat there, listening to Giles, and wondered what he should do. Go after her? Or would that make it worse?

'I'll just see if she needs a hand,' he said to Giles.

'Oh, she's fine. New to it, of course, but got the whole thing running like –'

'Won't be a second.'

David got up and went through the door into the hall. 'Laura?' There was clatter from the kitchen below, but no mild American voice. She wouldn't be down there. She'd be somewhere private. In her bedroom, maybe. Or out in the garden? David was just going into the library when he heard her on the stairs.

'Laura!'

He ran back. She looked at him, down over the side of the banisters, and he saw it in her expression, in the lack of surprise that he'd followed her, in the way she couldn't look him in the eye. He saw that he was right.

'Oh God, Laura, I –'

'Go back in.'

'But I –'

'Go. We can talk about it later. Just don't say anything. Please. Please go in.'

They went back.

Giles stood up as Laura returned to her seat. 'I'm sorry, Giles,' she said. 'Feeling kind of nauseous. Can't cope with this heat at all. God knows how you men put up with jackets and ties. Talking of which, Giles, you must tell me where you got this one? I love it.'

David waited until the next course, until Giles was talking to the woman on his right. Then he picked up the decanter in front of him to fill Laura's glass, which was already full, so he simply did his own and put it down.

'Laura,' he spoke in a low half-whisper. 'Laura, I'm appalled. I – I suppose I must have hoped that you wouldn't remember. I hoped that I could just do the picture and that would be that. I didn't think, and I . . . I'm so sorry.'

'It's not your fault,' she said. 'I chose to do it. And it wouldn't be so bad if I'd also chosen to tell my husband about it. But I haven't, and –'

'Joss doesn't know?'

Laura leant forward with her elbows on the table and her head light in her hands. She looked at her plate as she spoke. 'He mustn't find out. Ever. If he does, he'll hit the roof.'

'But it's just modelling. Surely he'd understand.'

'It's not *just modelling*, David. It's . . .'

'It wasn't porn you were doing at Clerkenwell. It was art. Anyone can see that.' But Laura's head was bent to the table. She was close to tears. At the other end of the table, he could hear Joss's laughter. Beside him, close to, Laura looked as if she might be sick. 'Laura, listen. I don't have to do this picture. We can call it off, if you –'

'Call it off? Are you mad? What would we tell Joss?'

David said nothing.

'I want you to promise me that you will keep this a secret.'

'Of course I will. But I –'

'Promise,' she said, but word came out thin. She swallowed, and tried again. 'Promise?'

'OK. OK. I promise. Nobody – *nobody* – will know.'

Edmund was sitting at the other end of the room. He had Christine Verney on one side and Joss's friend Tania, who'd been with them that night at the Tsar Bar, on the other. They were having a conversation across him about fake tan.

'You have to get it done professionally. There's a salon at the top of Church Street where they –'

'I know the one,' said Christine, looking up from her white forearm. 'You say it doesn't even smell?'

'Not like that stuff we had in the eighties, and you don't get those nasty orange streaks.'

Edmund looked through the line of their conversation to where Alice was sitting next to Joss. She'd pushed her plate to one side and was leaning over the table with a cigarette in her hands, talking. As she spoke, her mascaraed eyes would dart back and forth like birds – checking the reactions on Joss's face, and then back to a resting point at the end of her smouldering cigarette. Edmund couldn't hear what she was saying, but he could tell – from the balance of interest and amusement in Joss's expression – that she was taking risks.

He watched, and hoped that Alice would know when to stop. He hoped she'd have enough sensitivity to distinguish between different kinds of flirting, to understand where flattery and compliments became actual intention – foreplay. Not that he cared for himself, of course. Alice could toy with whoever she liked, so far as Ned was concerned. But Joss was vulnerable. Joss's lack of self-confidence, his lack of success in the early days, meant that he was easily flattered, and Edmund wasn't sure that he'd have the restraint to pass up on the ego trip that a bout of heavy flirting with a teenager would give him.

He didn't doubt that Joss would stay faithful to his wife. Adored her, couldn't believe his luck . . . the words, in Joss's voice, were clear in Edmund's head. And Laura was certainly the kind of woman to warrant that devotion from her husband. Edmund watched her at the sideboard, checking the food with her back to the room – straight and glowing, completely naked to the waist, where the fine yellow silk of the halter-neck fell round to a single button. The fluid lines, the barest snip of shoulder blades, the fine indentations of her spine against the surface of her skin. Perhaps Joss thought that, by flirting with Alice, he'd keep Laura on her toes. But it was a dangerous game.

'. . . ask Ned.'

'OK. Ned –'

'Ned, can you tell which of us is wearing fake tan?'

Ned smiled, and – saying he had no idea that either of them was – felt suddenly sure that both were covered in the stuff: illusory tans, illusory sun in their hair, illusory beauty. Well-groomed, well-controlled copies. Not unlike Annabel Glass, and utterly lacking.

He ate his last mouthful of pâté, leant back for Grace to take his plate and, looking again at Alice, tried to imagine her at thirty. Would she lose her originality, too? Watching her laugh, raucously, at something Joss said, Edmund felt sure that she wouldn't – couldn't. It wasn't just her age. She'd always be like this. It would sometimes get her into trouble, but that was no bad thing.

Aware that she was being watched, Alice stopped mid-laugh and looked straight at Joss. She gave him a slow smile. And Edmund, who could do nothing, looked down at the rows of knives and forks and spoons at either side of his plate, and the mass of crystal glasses. Course after course, wine after wine, hour after hour for Alice to create as much trouble as she chose.

Alice was laughing inside and out. The tentative flirting she'd begun in the garden was getting fabulously out of control. She'd no idea that Joss would be so responsive, so daring, and Edmund was watching. She'd thought that, at some point, Joss would get grown-up on her and move away. Instead, he'd rearranged Laura's *placement* so that he could sit next to Alice, and now he was looking right into her eyes as he asked what on earth she saw in Edmund.

'I like older men,' said Alice, looking back.

'You do?'

'Yes.' Alice felt strangely liquid inside.

'Why?'

'Well,' she perched her gaze back on the end of her cigarette, 'let's see . . . I like a man who knows what he's doing.'

'Ah.'

'And I like a man who knows how to treat me.'

Joss laughed. 'You like being spoilt.'

Pause. 'Yes.'

'And Edmund spoils you?'

Alice grinned at Joss and cast a quick glance at Ned, who looked back involuntarily and took another sip of wine. 'Not as much as I'd like,' she murmured.

'I see.' Joss refilled her glass. 'And how much is that?'

'Well, he hasn't sent me flowers –'

'No flowers at all?'

'I haven't got any jewellery.'

'What?'

'No fast car.'

'Disgraceful.'

'No holidays.'

'Bin him!'

'But he does take me to fabulous restaurants,' she lowered her voice here, 'and he's very good in bed.'

It was the sight of Joss's large behind, squashing in next to Alice's neat black one on the piano stool, that decided Edmund. It was time to leave. He'd been waiting for her to stop playing for over an hour – he'd no idea her repertoire was so extensive – and when, at Joss's request, she started improvising, Edmund realised it could go on all night. There was 'Zorba the Greek', there was 'American Pie', then the 'Can-Can', and classic stripper music – there for a moment, and then lost as Alice searched, or didn't know it properly – and, between laughs and drinks, there was Joss, la-la-la-ing out the gaps.

Edmund stubbed his cigarette into the hand-painted ashtray and looked around the room. About half the party had already left – mainly those with children. Compared to that impromptu party the other night, it felt more sedate. Joss and Alice were out of touch with the mood of the others, the mood that Laura had gone for. Planned, measured, civilised, and not nearly so much fun. And one of the results was that Alice, for all her camel-coloured chiffon and smart black trousers, felt younger than ever. He wondered what to do about her. It was late. He was too tired, and, in any case, Alice was probably too drunk to have the conversation he'd planned. But he knew he couldn't leave her there.

Laura was sitting by the fireplace, on the club fender, legs crossed, her feet on the inside, with the buttermilk silk in a twist at her knees. She was leaning back against the wall with her arms folded, chatting to Chrissie Verney, who was also on the fender, but with her legs on the outside. Edmund went over, apologised for interrupting and, insisting she remain seated, kissed Laura goodbye.

'Thank you,' he said.

Laura nodded. 'You OK for getting home?'

'We'll be fine,' he smiled. 'Bound to be cabs on the Embankment. Bye, Chrissie . . .'

He went to the piano.

Noticing him approach, noticing his air of farewell, Joss reached for the glass of whisky he'd left on top of the piano and knocked it back in one. 'Uh-oh,' he said.

Alice, who was playing Scott Joplin again, managed to continue playing as she looked up from her fingers – she loved being able to do that – then she missed her position and stopped.

Edmund stood there. 'I'm sorry, guys . . .'

'Oh, *Ned*.'

Edmund shook his head.

'I can make sure she gets back all right,' said Joss helpfully. 'If that's any –'

'No, Joss. It's not. Alice has school tomorrow.'

'On Saturday?'

'Come on, Alice. Did you have a coat?'

And then, to the surprise of both men, Alice freed her bottom from its wedged position between Joss and the curved wooden handle of the stool, and stood up. 'No,' she said. 'Just my bag over there on the stool.' Edmund passed her the square of black sequins. 'And my fags.'

Taking her packet of Marlboro Lights and her grotty little lighter, Alice put them into the bag and zipped it shut. Joss tinkled ignorantly at the upper notes for a second. Then he stopped and heaved himself to his feet. 'Party-pooper,' he said to Ned, wrapping his words in a smile. 'What are we going to do without her?'

'You'll manage.'

Joss smiled down at Alice – smiling back at him, exhilarated. 'I guess we'll have to,' he said.

'Goodbye, Joss. Thank you *so* much.'

'The pleasure,' Joss took her shoulders, and took his time, as he kissed both her cheeks, 'was all mine.'

Alice couldn't resist a glance at Edmund's face. It was mild, tired, and disappointingly benign. 'Come on then,' he said. 'Let's go.'

David decided to leave as well. It was driving him mad – watching Laura, and unable to stop himself from wondering about her marriage. Laura and Joss had barely spoken all night and David was increasingly doubtful. He failed to understand what Laura loved about her husband. Not only was he ugly and unremarkable, he was also unpleasant. How could she love a man who spoke to her like that, a man who'd 'hit the roof' if he heard about her modelling, a man who'd flirt with a schoolgirl right under her nose and humiliate her in front of his friends? It had to be the cash. And the more David thought about it, the more depressed he grew.

He left with Edmund and Alice, expecting to share a cab with them back to the studio, and it was only when they got outside that he realised he was wrong. Edmund and Alice were going back to Alice's parents' house.

'Is that wise?'

'They're away,' said Alice, leaning on Ned's arm and giving him exactly the same smile she'd given Joss earlier. 'Away! Away! Away!'

It was still hot outside, airless and thundery. Edmund could feel the cotton of his shirt, damp against his skin. He walked with Alice – singing noisily – down to the Embankment and a flow of orange cab lights.

David hailed one, and opened the door for them.

'No, you go on,' said Edmund. 'I'll take her home in the next one.'

So David got in by himself and opened the window.

'Bye!' yelled Alice, waving. And then, very slowly, crescendoing into the night, '*Baay – baay! Miss Am-er-i-can Paay! Drove my chevy to the – woah! – levee, but the levee was draay . . .*'

The cab pulled off. David closed the window. Chuckling, he sat back and turned his head. Behind him, their figures – Edmund's still, and Alice's spinning wildly – shrank to doll-specks at the side of the road.

'You're not coming in?'

'No, Alice. I'm not.'

Alice stood at the edge of the pavement, staring bullishly through the open door at Edmund in the cab.

'Why aren't you coming in?'

'Because of what I just said, Alice. Weren't you listening?'

Alice just stood there frowning.

Edmund sighed. He got out, gave the driver ten pounds and waited for his change – all under the spotlight of Alice's gaze. As the cab left, she skipped up the steps to the front door of her parents' house.

'I knew you'd come!' she said, unzipping her bag for the keys. 'I knew you would!'

There was a short stone balustrade at either side of the steps, and Edmund sat on it. 'I'm not coming in,' he said.

'Yes you are!'

'No, Alice. I'm not. I just want to finish our conversation, and then I'm going home.'

Alice sat next to him. She stared at the infinitely fine chain of her evening bag – wound it about her fingers like a cat's cradle – and listened as he told her, again, that it was over. It took him for ever – going on and on about how great she was in bed, that it had nothing to do with him not fancying her or anything. It was really more to do with her not being serious about him . . .

'You're just jealous.'

'No, Alice. I –'

'You're jealous that I was flirting with Joss. You were jealous. Jealous and cross.'

'Sure I was cross. You've no right behaving the way you were.'

'And you've no right telling me.'

'Someone's got to.'

Alice found her keys again, and stood up. 'I'll flirt with who I like, Ned.'

'Not where other people's marriages are concerned you don't.'

She put the key in the lock and twisted it – the insistent tone of the burglar alarm timer getting louder and louder as she pressed in the numbers – and then it was quiet. She went in and, still holding the edge of the door, looked back at Edmund with a heartless smile that made him wish he'd said nothing.

'Good night, Ned.'

'Alice,' he said. 'I mean it. Leave Joss alone.'

She closed the door.

18

During the night the weather broke – with a gunshot crack of thunder and a sudden flood of rain.

David slept badly – slipping around in his head, with a grey dawn growing at the curtains. There was Mel, back from Swindon, deeply asleep when he'd got in. She was curled before him now in a different position with the sheets disturbed, caught down in the dip at her hip. And there was Laura. Images of her lapped at his mind, lapped at the line of Mel's body. Laura's wrists, as she turned the pages of his portfolio; her waist double-wrapped in the bright dressing gown; and her feet – light down the lavender path. He heard again the broken catches of her talk – *David, please. Go back in . . . And what would we tell Joss? . . . secret. Promise me?* – and felt the stick of charcoal in his blackened fingers – rough and rapid – scraping the shape of her body into the grainy paper they'd used at Clerkenwell.

He tried to make sense of it. Laura hadn't told Joss she'd modelled. She didn't want him to know, and David had to admit that it was fair enough. Most people didn't understand life class modelling. They thought there was something sleazy about it and perhaps it was wise of Laura not to tell him. Particularly after the things that Joss had said about her, about the way he saw her – dignified, discreet.

Then he thought of that marriage. He thought of the deal: financial security in exchange for conjugal love, with all kinds of conditions attached including, no doubt, enduring beauty and dignity on the part of the bride. He thought of Laura – in breach of the dignity condition, and scared of what that might mean. One slip, one injudicious word from David, and she could lose the lot or, at the very least, the right to Joss's respect. There'd be more humiliating evenings, evenings far worse than the one she'd had last night.

For all its shiny charm, that marriage of theirs was rotten. He was sure of it. Brown patches were starting to break the surface. David thought of the way Laura had looked at him the day he'd sketched her at Cheyne Lane. He thought of her fingers on his shoulder last night. He thought of her desperation over dinner and the unhappy expression on her face when later, in the drawing room, she'd half listened to Chrissie Verney while Joss and Alice sat at the piano and laughed. Laura wasn't happy and David felt for her, but there was something more than pity in his heart. Something discordant. A guilty kind of hope.

He looked again at Mel – constant, sleeping beside him in light that had paled by a fraction – and felt his conscience stir, along with the reflex to defend himself from whatever imaginary accusations floated in the air. He'd done nothing wrong. Nothing had changed between him and Mel. Nothing tangible. These were merely thoughts. There was no need for

243

him to feel guilty. And anyway, Mel was fine. Look at her dozing there, contented. Mel didn't need protecting. Laura was the one with real fears, real threats to her happiness. Laura was the one in trouble. She had a marriage she wanted to save, and the right thing to do – he knew – would be to cancel the portrait altogether.

Laura hadn't been keen to do that last night because she was sure that Joss would smell trouble. But it didn't have to be like that. David could do it all – pull out, cancel dates, and so on – directly through Joss, who wouldn't suspect a thing. It wouldn't be hard to find a plausible, unrelated, reason. Any reason. He could use Joss's complaints about the sketch, somehow, or say he got his dates muddled up. Not difficult.

Except . . . except after years of longing, after finding her at last, even though she was married, could David really walk away? Could he be that altruistic?

He got up, went down to the kitchen and made himself a cup of coffee. He took the kettle from its stand and stood at the window, filling it, as he looked out at the street below, wet and windswept, shrinking in the cold.

Ring today, he told himself. Do it while you still can. Call the whole thing off.

He got Joss. 'David! How are you? Get back all right?'

David said that they'd been fine, and thanked Joss for the evening.

'It was fun, wasn't it? You must come again. Persuade that girl of yours –'

'Mel.'

'Mel. That's right! Get her to come too.'

'Maybe,' said David, irritated. More irritated than he'd expected to be. He thought of the way Joss had behaved yesterday: the things he'd said about David's sketch, the lack of apology, the forced bonhomie, the bold assumption that of course David wouldn't mind the odd tantrum, the odd insult or, if he did mind, then he'd want the commission enough to put up with it . . . It reminded him why he hated men like Joss. He'd like to tell Joss that he had no desire whatsoever to come to any more of his stupid parties with his stupid *placements*. But this wasn't the time for that.

'But the main reason I'm calling,' he went on, 'is – well, I'm afraid it's about the portrait.'

'Of course. Great. I was going to call you myself, in fact. We need to go through exactly when you're –'

'I can't do it.'

Silence.

'Joss?'

'Listen, David, if this is about last night, I take it back. Had a million things on my mind and really wasn't thinking straight – should never have said those things. But we looked at it again this morning, and I love it now. It's a great little sketch. And I was going to call you about it today because we do need to sort out exactly when you –'

'I'm sorry, Joss,' said David, enjoying himself, 'but I really can't do it.'

'I don't mind what she's wearing, you know. I didn't realise how well regarded you are, David. It wasn't until Alice explained. I never would have

dreamt of interfering if I'd known. Please, David,'
Joss's voice dropped an octave. It was serious. Man-
to-man. 'You're the only person she'll agree to be
painted by. It took me hours to persuade her to see
your work, and now I've gone and ruined it all by
making some stupid remark about clothes.'

'Laura still wants to be painted by me?'

'Of course she does,' said Joss, laughing. 'She
thinks you're a genius! Said so again this morning.
It's like she's got a crush on you or something.'

And David crumbled. It was too much. It wasn't as
if he was doing anything wrong, he told himself. Not
if Laura actually wanted to be painted. She was fine
about it. Joss was fine about it. He, David, was fine
about it. And Mel?

David sighed. He wasn't perfect. He couldn't help
it if his thoughts sometimes ran away with him. But
thoughts were all it was. Nothing more. He'd
probably have the same thoughts even if he did
refuse to paint Laura, so why not do the damn thing?
In any case, it would create a bigger issue to pull out
now. Mel might start asking questions, might get
paranoid for no good reason. One could argue that it
was best for her too if he simply went ahead.

'And if you want to paint her in a T-shirt and that
old denim skirt, then – well, so far as I'm concerned,
it's better than no picture at all.'

'OK,' said David, smiling. 'I'll do it.'

'Fantastic! But there is one other thing. We were
just wondering – I know it's a bore, but would you
mind terribly if we brought it forward?'

'Forward?'

'To some time in November?'

David lifted his diary from the shelf and turned to a blank November. 'When exactly were you thinking?'

'Sooner the better.'

'You really can't do April?'

'Er, no,' said Joss, laughing. 'Not really. And certainly not if you want her in that denim skirt. It wouldn't look quite right in the final stages of pregnancy . . .'

David shut his eyes. 'Congratulations.'

'Early days, of course. Only two months gone. But we thought it would be best to rearrange dates, and try to get it done before she gets any bigger.'

'Of course. How is she?'

'Fine. Still doing far too much – poor darling felt ghastly last night. And she hid it so well, didn't she! But we'll soon quieten her down. Get her up to Merwick and away from late nights and shopping, which I'm afraid means you'd need to do the picture there and not in London, but that would be OK, wouldn't it?'

'Sure,' said David, not listening. 'How wonderful for you.'

'Isn't it? I'm not sure I go for some of those American-sounding names she's been coming up with, but anyway. We were hoping perhaps that first week in November. I know that's only a month away, but if we leave it much longer she'll start showing.'

David said he was free.

'Great. Then why don't you come for the weekend before? The fourth and fifth. We're having a shooting party. And a firework party,' he chuckled, 'if I can get my act together. I'll get Ned, and some cousins of mine, and –'

'I don't shoot.'

'That doesn't matter. Come for the fireworks, and bring your girl too if you like. Then stay on for the week. Will that give you enough time?'

'I expect so. I –'

'Great! Great. Well, you're both in. So it's Saturday the fourth of November to – to whenever you reckon you're finished. How does that sound?'

'Sounds fine,' said David, looking out of the window. It was dark, really dark. He looked at the black rooftops, at the yellow squares of light in people's windows, at the heavy rain and, far away – over the City – a sharp scribble of lightning.

'. . . *per christum dominum nostrum, Amen.*'

'Amen,' said Alice, slipping back up into her seat. She felt like shit. Everything was uncomfortable. Knees tickled by the stitches of her hassock, spine dug at by the hard wooden back of her chair, and a steaming, scalding headache, as if the alcohol she'd been drinking last night had burnt an ugly zigzag through the tissue of her brain.

She stood with the hymn book in her hands, her mouth firmly shut and her face getting paler and paler while the men-boys around her growled out, '*Immortal, invisible. . .*'

'You OK?' hissed Emily.

Alice nodded.

'. . . *in light in-ac-cess-i-ble, Hid from our eyes.*'

White and silent amongst tuneless treadmill syllables, Alice sent her mind back to Edmund, sent it looking for the sadness she should be feeling, and found nothing but a hangover. A hangover, and a few pinpricks of shame.

Alice raised her eyes to the great marble robes of some small Victorian dignitary. It was only a bit of harmless flirting. She'd done it to make Ned jealous, and it had worked. Ned could claim the moral high ground all he liked, but Alice knew better. The truth was that he hadn't liked her flirting with Joss. OK, so maybe she shouldn't have picked on someone else's husband, but she didn't have much choice, and Joss was such a willing accomplice.

And, anyway, fuck it. She'd had fun. Joss was great. He'd made her feel fabulous, funny, talented. He made her happy to be younger than the others, rather than embarrassed about it. He wasn't critical. She could say anything, admit anything, and still feel admired. Yes. She liked Joss Savil a lot.

And she liked him a whole lot more when, at break, a special delivery for Miss Alice Enderby arrived at the school gates. It was an unusual arrangement of orchids and lilies – an arrangement so vast that the school bursar, who took the delivery, had to get the headmaster's secretary to help him carry it across the yard, in the rain, to the sixth form common room. It didn't have a card.

The school's wastepaper bins were dark green, bucket-like and perfect. Alice collected several. She filled them with water and flowers, dotted them round the common room: on the broad window ledges, on top of the piano, the desks, the lockers . . . and still there were flowers left over.

When school finished, she wandered through the gates in the pouring rain with what was left of the flowers in her arms. Emily held the umbrella for both of them.

'Who are they from?' she said. 'Is it Edmund?'

Alice smiled through the leaves and wrappings.

They'd waited at the traffic lights and were walking over the road, Alice shifting the weight in her arms so that it was comfortable, when they heard the horn. No tooting or whistling, no cheap beep-beep, no ordinary noise. This sound was long and resonant. It had authority, and – mid-crossing – both girls turned.

Parked right outside the chapel, in the place set aside for Daimlers and dignitaries, was a smart flat sports car. It gave one final leisured honk and a door opened. Joss got out, the rain darkening his linen suit. Alice looked at his size – the big hand pushing at his curls, big arm thrown up in a single wave – and hesitated.

'Leave Joss alone,' Ned had said.

Alice remembered sitting on the steps outside her parents' house, winding the bag strap through her fingers.

'I'll flirt with who I like.'

'Not where other people's marriages are concerned you don't.'

Still standing on the tarmac, Joss leant into the car and honked again. He was getting wet.

'Alice! Come on . . .'

Laughing suddenly, Alice gave Emily a wild grin and darted back across the road.

'See ya!' she yelled – wrappings flying, flowerheads snapping. Emily stood on the other side of the road, watching Alice and the flowers swallowed up in Joss's dark Ferrari.

He took her to a place in Knightsbridge, down a back street, in a basement. It was large and busy, with split levels at odd angles, and bright clear lights.

'Sir?'

'It's Joss. I have a reservation for two.'

'Joss . . .' said the waiter, searching the book, and then he looked up smiling. 'This way.'

They walked past the bar to a table round at the side, up some steps, in the corner. It was a table set for four, with one chair right in the corner – and this was the one Joss sat in. The table was too large for Alice to sit opposite, so she sat next to him and unfolded her napkin with raised eyebrows.

You're up to no good, she thought. No good at all.

Alice was not easily shocked. She was used to being the naughty one, and part of her couldn't help respecting Joss for being even naughtier. But it was naughtiness taken to new realms, and Alice wasn't sure she was up for it. There was a difference between naughty and bad, between gossip and bitching, between secrets and betrayal. She wouldn't do it if someone were to get hurt.

But there was nothing wrong in having a bit of fun, especially if that fun was limited to ticking Joss off. And a man twice her age . . . she couldn't quite resist it.

'So where's your wife?' she said, in 'nice weather' tones.

'What?'

'Your wife.'

'Laura's having lunch with a friend,' said Joss, pointing the waiter to a bottle on the list before turning back to Alice and smiling. 'As am I.'

'Yeah, right,' said Alice, laughing.

'You don't think I'm your friend?'

'Come on, Joss. I think we both know you're looking for a bit more than friendship, here.'

Joss paused. He waited for the waiter to finish pouring the wine, looked at the table for a moment, and then back at Alice. Right into her eyes. 'But, Alice,' he said, as the waiter descended the steps, 'I'm married.'

Alice snorted. 'I know you're bloody married,' she said. 'And, frankly, Joss, I'm shocked.'

'Why are you shocked, Alice?'

'Because you're coming on to me.'

Joss smiled and shook his head. 'Sorry to disappoint you,' he said. 'But no. No, I'm not.'

'Then what –'

'I'm just taking an interest in you, in your career. I want to talk to you about possible places for playing the piano, including this one, as it happens. I'm taking you out to lunch, and then I'm taking you home.'

'But . . .'

'But what?'

'But the flowers! What about the flowers?'

'What flowers?'

Alice examined Joss's face very closely. He was smiling. She found it very hard not to smile too. And then she was laughing – the laugh of disbelief, the laugh of a shared joke – and he was laughing back. Laughing because he was winning, because he was better at it than her, because she was right and she had no way of proving it.

'You fancy me,' she said.

But Joss merely went on laughing, and blithely shook his head. 'No I don't.'

'You do. You do. You're –'

'I'm married, Alice. Laura is, I think even objectively, the most beautiful of women. And while I think you're very pretty, and very sweet . . .'

Alice winced.

'. . . I'm really not interested in whatever else you may have in mind.'

'But I don't have *anything* in mind,' said Alice. 'You're the one with – with things in mind.'

'What things, exactly?'

Alice fixed him with her eye, unsmiling now. She was determined not to laugh – it would discredit her position – but found that the alternative was worse. It was too charged, too exciting, too dark.

So she looked away, and knew that he had won.

19

Once Virginia Nicholson knew that Mel was planning to have the wedding in London, she wasted no time in finding possible venues, and she and Mel arranged to see two that Saturday: the one in Bishop's Park that Virginia had liked, and a military club that David's father had belonged to. Mel had spoken to her parents about it earlier in the week, and they'd planned to come along as well, to help with the final decision.

Mel still had doubts about her parents, but those doubts had started to fade. She'd hardly spoken to her father, but she'd heard from her mother that he was being wonderful. He was appreciating everything she did in the house, and there had been no more accidents. Clare seemed happier than ever. Mel wasn't sure how long this honeymoon period would last. But with encouragement from Virginia (who knew nothing of Mel's fears and who'd looked genuinely shocked when Mel suggested leaving them out of the loop) Mel decided that she would shelve Philippa's book, shelve her anxieties, and involve her parents in plans for the wedding – a wedding that Greg was now keen to pay for.

'Of course I'm bloody paying,' he'd said, when Mel

had rung. 'Not having some female I've never met footing the bill for my own daughter's wedding.'

He was also, to Mel's dismay, adamant that the wedding would be in Yorkshire. It was the proper place, he said. He could oversee matters – make sure it was done properly. Clare could do the flowers herself. Greg had a friend whose wife did catering. And he'd already looked into steel bands . . . Greg loved steel bands. He and Clare had even had one at their wedding. There was one in Leeds that was very reasonably priced, and although the manager had been a little difficult, Greg was sure it wouldn't be a problem. The only thing Mel needed to think about was the dress. She could have anything she liked so long as it covered her up properly. Greg wasn't religious, but he really couldn't bear it when women showed too much flesh in church.

Mel didn't like the sound of that at all. Instinct told her that however enthusiastic he was now, her father wasn't reliable. She foresaw all kinds of difficulties and fallouts in the run-up. It was safer, and infinitely less stressful, to do it herself in London.

And, much to Mel's surprise, Clare had sided with her.

'Darling,' she'd said to Greg, on the other line (she and Greg often spoke to Mel like that – one of them in the bedroom and the other in the kitchen), 'don't you think that we should let Mel decide? After all, it is her wedding.'

Greg had sighed heavily.

'And do you really want all that worry and trouble, the house turned upside down, and all those people wandering around?'

'I'm paying for the damn thing.'

'Please, darling,' said Clare, her voice catching. '*Please*? For Mel?'

Amazingly, she'd won. Greg agreed to the wedding in London, he still wanted to pay, and they were due to come down that weekend to help choose the venue. They hadn't met Virginia yet, and while Mel wasn't exactly looking forward to it, she knew it was important.

But in the end, Greg and Clare had pulled out. Clare had rung Mel that Friday. And Mel – who was on the train to Swindon, bent over her bathrooms contract and making notes – didn't bother replying to her ringing mobile. Whoever it was could leave a message. There was too much for her to do. She hated mobiles on trains. It was only when she finished working that Mel pulled out the mobile and listened to the message.

Clare's injury – the one from where she'd been bitten by Bess the night that Mel had rung from Nathan's flat – had taken much longer to heal than they'd expected. She was still having difficulty walking.

'And really, sweetheart. You should see me. There's still that ridiculous mark on my nose, and I haven't been to the hairdressers in months. I so want to make a good impression on David's mother – she sounds so nice – and, right now, I'd only be ashamed.'

The train went into a tunnel, and the line broke.

Sickened, Mel switched off the mobile and put it in her bag. She had to do something. She knew what Philippa's book said, she knew what the helpline would say too: there was little she could do in this situation; whatever Clare did, it had to be Clare's decision. It couldn't be forced. Blah, blah, blah. But nor could Mel just sit there and hope that she was wrong. She had to see her mother, talk to her and find out what was really happening. Maybe it was nothing. Maybe she was being silly – one injury, and perhaps she'd jumped to the wrong conclusions – but she needed to know. If Clare couldn't come to London, then Mel would have to go north.

Ringing her back, Mel let her explain and apologise all over again, and then she suggested coming to visit.

'Oh darling!' said Clare. 'I'd love that. When?'

They went through their diaries.

'How about next week?' said Mel. 'I could come any day except Thursday.'

Clare hesitated.

'What's wrong?'

'Darling, you know I'd love to see you, but your father, he –'

'He doesn't want to see me?'

'No, sweetheart. It's not that. But it might not be very tactful for you to come midweek. You know, when you could be working.'

'OK,' said Mel, not wanting to rock the boat. 'I'll come at the weekend.'

There was a pause as Clare turned the pages of her diary.

'It's the first weekend in October, Mum. Found it?'

'Yes,' said Clare, sighing. 'Yes, darling, I have but ... well, it's maddening. We've got bridge with the Campbells this coming weekend and then it's Paul and Angela ...'

Every year, Mel's parents went fishing with Greg's sister Angela and her husband Paul. They went to Ireland, to exactly the same river, year after year. Greg and Paul adored it. They spent all day on the river and all night in the pub. Angela didn't mind it – if she wasn't painting watercolours, she'd be sleeping. But Clare had nothing to do. Greg liked her to be with him, just so long as she didn't talk. So she'd take crossword books and magazines and sit in silence, thinking about what she'd have for lunch, or what Mel might be doing, or when the rain might stop.

'. . . so that takes us to the 28th–29th.'

'OK,' said Mel. 'There's a department jolly that weekend, but I can easily get out of –'

'Oh, hang on,' said Clare, 'I'm just wondering now if that's the weekend your father's going to his conference in Glasgow, or if it . . . no. No, that's right. It's been moved to November, so –'

'Dad's going away?' said Mel.

'Yes,' said Clare. 'A whole week in Glasgow at the beginning of November! Don't know what'll I'll do here all by myself.'

Mel hesitated. It wasn't as soon as she'd have liked, but the fact that Greg wouldn't be around was an opportunity she really couldn't pass up. At last – a real chance of getting her mother to talk. She might actually get to the truth.

'Then – then why don't I visit you then?' she said. 'I could take a few days off, come up and keep you company.'

Clare thought that was a wonderful idea.

*

The other person who was supposed to be there, inspecting venues that Saturday, was David.

'Ready?' Mel had said that morning, bag in hand and the wedding file under her arm.

David didn't move. He was sitting in the same place he'd occupied when Joss had told him about Laura getting pregnant, looking out at the rain.

'Oh shit,' said Mel, looking at it too. 'We're going to need an umbrella. Where's that one you got in Edinburgh? The big one with the nasty tartan pattern and the . . . Darling?'

David turned.

'What is it?'

David sighed.

Of course he'd come if she really wanted him to. He understood completely how important it was, and if they needed him, he'd be there like a shot. But . . . but would she mind very much if he didn't? There was just so much for him to do at the studio, what with the Savils expecting him now in November, and finding something half decent for the New Impressionists' Christmas exhibition – they wanted two pictures from him this year. And then there were his racks and his drawings, still a mess after the time he'd hurt his toe, and they were off to Nathan's tonight, weren't they? There was just too much – and, well, the last thing he felt like doing was wandering round some club or other, talking about the wedding.

'You don't really mind, do you?'

Mel stared at him. 'Of course I bloody mind,' she said. 'This –'

'It's only a room.'

'It's not *only a room*. It – it's the place where you and

259

I are going to get married, for God's sake. This is something we should do together. Don't you care where it takes place?'

David sighed. 'I'll come if it really matters to you, Mel. I just –'

'Forget it.'

Mel tugged the umbrella out of the stand by the door, and left.

So it was just the two of them – Mel and Virginia – greeting one another in the rain, on the steps of William Nicholson's old club.

'Where's David?' said Virginia, balancing herself to kiss Mel's cheek.

Mel gave an edited explanation.

'Oh, that boy is *useless*.'

Agreeing silently, Mel accompanied Virginia up the steps.

The club hall was quiet, cold, and empty except for the retired officer who'd been despatched to show them round. He was sitting on a sofa in the shadows with his legs crossed, reading the *Daily Telegraph*. They could see only his shoes, highly polished, one of them pointing nonchalantly into the air, and it was only when they got closer that he realised who they were.

The feet snapped to the floor, the broadsheet was flung aside. 'Ah!' he cried, voice echoing. 'Here you are! Hello! Hello! Francis Fewkes! How do you do? Now, let's see,' he checked a book on the desk by the door, 'that's right, it's a wedding, isn't it. And you're Mrs Nicholson and – and you, my dear, must be the blushing bride! Congratulations!'

Mel was still upset with David – upset, pale, cross,

and not remotely blushing – but she smiled as she shook the hand of Francis Fewkes, and the three of them climbed the staircase. It was carpeted in red, and hung with paintings of cavalry charges, sieges, and baroque scenes with serried ranks of uniformed officers.

'That was Krishnapur,' said Major Fewkes. 'And that – see? That's Wellington's army. And that one you're looking at, my dear, that's the Light Brigade.'

They went into a room on the first floor that was clearly used for parties. It, too, was covered with paintings. It had a high ceiling and a row of windows that gave on to the street. Rain trickled down the glass.

'Pouf!' said Major Fewkes. 'Bit gloomy in here. Let's see if the lights are . . . That's better!'

But it wasn't. The lights were modern. Bleak strips of white round the tops of the walls. And although they'd been concealed by boarding, they shone straight up to a peeling ceiling and only made it worse. Mel and Virginia looked at one another.

'Do you have any other rooms?'

Major Fewkes didn't.

'But this is a splendid room! Splendid! You need to imagine it full of people, of course. Full of all your lovely young friends! It's perfect for a wedding reception.' Major Fewkes leant close to Mel. 'And I should know,' he said. 'Got married here myself.'

Five minutes later, Mel and Virginia were back on Piccadilly, under the tartan umbrella, hailing an old black cab. It stopped beyond a puddle, and Mel opened the door. She took Virginia's stick and followed her in.

'Well?' said Virginia, turning to her as they pulled off. 'What did you think?'

Wondering how rude she could be without causing offence, Mel looked back – and Virginia laughed. 'Quite,' she said. 'I quite agree.'

Mel laughed too. She was glad that her parents weren't there, or even David. This way, she and Virginia could sort it all out between them with minimum fuss, and even have a bit of fun. Having David there – long-faced, dragging his heels – would have ruined it. She was still thinking of how lucky she was, thinking of the women she knew who had really terrible mothers-in-law, when Virginia stopped laughing and asked how Edmund was.

'Fine,' said Mel, surprised. 'I think he's fine. He . . . Well, he must be working quite hard because we don't really see that much of him. He's out at the crack of dawn and seems to have a fairly hectic social life.'

'Not still seeing that girl, is he?'

Mel hesitated. She knew that Ned had taken Alice to the Savils' party last night. In spite of everything, Alice was still on the scene. Mel didn't know – didn't want to know – what was really going on between them. She and David had talked about it and, while David had been dismissive, Mel wasn't convinced. Her own guess was that Ned still wanted it to work, but she wasn't sure he'd thank her for telling Virginia this.

Virginia, however, didn't seem to be expecting a reply. She sighed, looked out at the rain and went on musing. 'Poor Edmund,' she said. 'To look at him, you'd think he'd have no trouble at all. He's tall, nice-looking, clever, amusing, successful . . .'

'Perhaps he's just picky.'

'Can't be that picky if he's still wasting his time on schoolgirls. It's bizarre. David was always the one we'd worry about! He's supposed to be the one who needs looking after, needs more – more guidance, I suppose.' She smiled and squeezed Mel's hand. 'But now he's found you. And after all that worrying, it turns out that it's Ned with all the problems – and I haven't got the first idea how to help him.'

'Maybe you can't,' said Mel.

'Maybe,' said Virginia sadly. 'Maybe he doesn't want me to.'

That night, still smarting from their earlier row, David and Mel went down the steps that led to Nathan's flat. Neither of them had said much in the car, and they were both looking forward to the relief of other people. They rang the bell and waited. The geraniums had gone and, in their place, were rows of ornamental cabbages soaking up the rain.

Nathan opened the door. 'Hi, there,' he said.

Mel went in, kissing him, followed by David, who handed over a bottle of wine.

Inside, it was immaculate. A vast arrangement of flowers, or not so much flowers as spiky orange creatures and curly twigs, occupied the coffee table. And there were candles. Not ordinary candles, but ones that smelt of vanilla and cloves.

'Christ,' said David, sounding just like Ned for a moment as he took off his coat. 'What's happened in here?'

He was throwing it over the back of the sofa as

Fenella came in from the kitchen, plum hair bouncing, black clothes floating. She gave Nathan the bottle of champagne she was holding and turned to Mel, smiling. 'Hi, Mel.'

'Hi.'

They kissed.

'And you must be David.' Fenella picked up the coat and hung it on a peg by the door. 'It is such an honour to meet you,' she went on. 'Nathan's been showing me your work, which of course I've seen before, but I'd no idea you were so young!'

David could think of no response. Instead, he raised his champagne flute and said, 'So what's this? Have you two got something to celebrate?'

'Don't need an excuse for champagne,' said Mel, taking a good slug.

David pulled the bottle towards himself. 'But this is vintage.'

Mel looked from Fenella to Nathan – and then found herself staring somewhere deep into the twiggy arrangement, with vintage aftertaste in her mouth.

'Well?' said David.

Nathan put his glass on the table. He smiled at Fenella, and then he looked at Mel. 'Well,' he said. 'Well, yes. We do have something to celebrate. We . . .'

He was struggling, and in the end Fenella said it for him. 'We're getting married.'

Nathan didn't have a dining room in his flat, but Fenella had altered the kitchen so comprehensively that it did almost as well. She'd lit it with candles so that only the table was visible, and had laid up the table – an old wooden slab that Mel had done all her law exams revision on – with elaborate care, covering it with damask and silver, and napkins rolled in ribbons of silk. They ate cheese soufflé to start with – in individual ramekins – followed by *boeuf en croute*, *pommes dauphinois*, *haricots verts*, caramelised carrots; and ended up with deep dark chocolate mousse. Nathan and Fenella were euphoric. Unlike David and Mel, they'd found a wedding date within days of getting engaged. Nathan wanted it to be as soon as possible, so they'd agreed on the weekend between Christmas and New Year and were already discussing renovation plans for his flat.

'It's not perfect, of course,' said Fenella, 'but there's a lot we can do with the space. I – No, do have some more, David. Please. Help yourself . . . I was just saying to Nathan the other day that if we knocked through into Mel's room then we'd get light all the way from the garden. Mel needs some more wine, darling . . . No, red . . . What was I saying? Oh yes. We could put a door in the outside wall, maybe turn Mel's room into the kitchen, and then just imagine what an effect that would have in the living area! So much better! We'd still eat in this section, of course.'

Nathan put a final spoonful of mousse into his mouth. 'She's brilliant with space,' he said to David. 'Half a mind to get her on to the gallery.'

'Oh, Nathan, no. No, I'm just a –'

'And modest.'

'No, really.' Smiling, Fenella leant towards him. 'But don't you think it would be good, darling? All opened up?' She fell along his arm, rested her chin on it and gazed back up at him. 'We'd even have room for that sky scene I know you want.'

Nathan twisted round and kissed her in the

candlelight. They rubbed noses and kissed again. 'Let's do it tomorrow,' he murmured.

Fenella laughed. 'Well, perhaps tomorrow's a little soon.'

'What's wrong with tomorrow?'

'Well, apart from anything else, my love, where would Mel go?'

For a second, no one said anything. Mel sat opposite, unable to look at them, and unable to look at David. What could she say? The obvious answer was that she should move into the studio, but David had never suggested it. Even after they'd got engaged, she'd continued to live, officially, with Nathan. It was important to her that the offer came from David, but David still said nothing. For one reason or another, he wasn't ready and she was much too proud to ask.

'I'll move out,' she said, standing up and stacking their plates to take to the sink. 'I'll move out right away.'

'There!' said Nathan. 'See?'

Fenella looked at Mel. 'But where would you go?'

'She'd move in with David, silly.'

It was raining again when, half an hour later, Mel and David climbed the steps to the street.

'Mind you don't slip,' said Nathan, switching on the light. He stood behind Fenella, arms encircling her waist while Fenella leant back on him and waved. 'Bye!'

'Bye,' said Mel, closing the gate at the top of the steps and looking at them, standing down there together.

She sat in the passenger seat while David drove to

266

Battersea – both thinking the same thing, both knowing it.

'I don't have to move in,' she said, wanting to put a hand on his leg but somehow not able.

'I think you should.'

'You sure?'

'Of course I am,' he said, looking at the road. 'It's mad for you to stay on there.'

'Yes, but –'

'Must be costing you a fortune.'

Mel gave an empty nod.

David felt uncomfortable. He knew he should have suggested it months ago, when they first got engaged. But Nathan had seemed so sad about losing Mel, and Mel had felt so sorry for him all alone, it had suited all of them for her to remain officially where she was. But it seemed that David hadn't been entirely honest with himself about it. It wasn't simply about Mel and Nathan. It had suited David, too. He'd rather liked the space, the sense that his studio was still all his, and now he felt that things were closing in, fast. His life was no longer his own. There were more and more things he should have done, should be doing – like choosing venues this morning – when all he really wanted was more time to himself.

Mel couldn't understand it. David had asked her to move in with him. He'd said exactly what she longed for months to hear, yet she felt acutely sad.

'You OK?' said David.

Mel couldn't reply for a moment.

'Oh, darling,' David stopped the car at a bus stop. 'What is it?'

'Nothing. Nothing.' Mel smiled hard. 'I'm fine. Tired, a bit. Worried about Fenella.'

David raised his eyes to the roof of the car and smiled. 'What *does* he see in her?'

'It's what she sees in him that's worrying me.'

'You think you should say something?'

'What can I say, David? He's –'

'Besotted.'

They got back to the sight of Ned on the sofa, alone, with a curry, watching a late-night movie. The curry smelt bad, the takeaway wrappings lay on the floor.

'Hi,' said Ned, still watching the screen. 'Have fun?'

'Great.'

'What's the film?'

Ned smiled. 'Not sure,' he said, chewing at another mouthful of curry. 'Think it might be Czech – the girls are out of this world.'

As David got into bed that night, he reached for Mel and pulled her close.

'I'm sorry about today,' he said. 'The venue thing.'

'It doesn't matter.'

'I wasn't thinking.'

'Yes,' she said. 'I know.'

They lay together for a while, and then – like most nights – quietly moved apart.

20

As with almost all his pictures, David held on to the portrait of Alice so that he could get it framed. He tended to know far more about frames than his clients and usually they trusted his judgement. But it was clear, in this case, that Alice's father didn't and David decided it was safer to take him along too. He didn't want Enderby upsetting the framer as well as everybody else. So Roger and Camilla had accompanied David to a framer he knew in Putney – they'd chosen one themselves – and the fully framed portrait was now back at David's studio, awaiting collection.

The following Tuesday, Roger and Camilla collected Alice from school and went with her to pick the painting up, give David a cheque and have a celebratory drink. David was pleased with the picture. It wasn't his best, but it was very like Alice and it had strength. He was considering entering it for the Royal Society of Portrait Painters' Exhibition next year.

'Really?' said Camilla, taking a glass of champagne.

David nodded. 'It's strong. Alice is very striking. I think it would look good, don't you?'

Camilla beamed. 'Darling? Darling, did you hear that?'

Roger was sitting some distance away. He was sprawled next to Alice on one of the sofas, listening to Mel explain the regulatory aspects of a business acquisition. Mel, who was still in work mode, was giving him a comprehensive answer and Roger was rather regretting having asked about it at all. He was much more interested in Mel's dark eyes than he was in what she was saying. And instead of pulling the subject back to something less dry, he found himself driven – by a joint desire to impress Mel and not look foolish in front of his daughter – into asking 'intelligent questions' that sent him firmly in the opposite direction. Camilla's interruption could not have come at a better time.

'Hear what?' he said, jumping up.

Camilla pointed at the portrait. 'David says he thinks it's good enough for the Portrait Painters' Exhibition!'

'Only now that he's finished the wretched thing,' said Roger, laughing, walking towards it.

Only Mel could see the irritation in David's smile.

Still laughing, Roger felt for his inner pocket. He pulled out his chequebook. 'Now then, what's the damage? Two grand?'

'Plus VAT,' said David. 'I did tell you about that when we talked prices, remember? You said you might be able to find a way to avoid it.'

'Yes, yes, I know. I just . . . darling, have you got a calculator?'

'It's one thousand four hundred,' said Mel.

'God, what a brain. OK. So it's eight grand, plus

270

one four, plus –'

'Plus three fifty for the frame,' said David, handing him an invoice. 'It's all here.'

Glancing at the invoice, Roger scribbled out the figure, tore off the cheque and handed it to David. 'There!' he said. 'One daughter down. One more to go.'

'One more?'

'Oh yes,' said Camilla, as if they'd already discussed it. 'When *do* you think you'll be able to do Isobel? We were rather hoping some time in January.'

David's smile lit up with sudden sincerity. There was no compliment greater than a follow-up commission and, sitting them down on the sofa, pulling out his diary, he began to talk about dates for Isobel.

'She's back in January for Nathan's wedding,' said Camilla, 'but only for a few days, and then –'

'Nathan's wedding?' said David, smiling nicely as he slipped into social charm. 'You're going?'

Camilla laughed. 'Well, I certainly hope so,' she replied. 'Roger's his godfather. That's why we patronise his gallery so much.'

Alice wasn't interested in Nathan's wedding. She lay back on the sofa, looked at the ceiling and yawned. It was over a week since her lunch with Joss and she could think of little else. He'd rung her the next day. He'd left a message on her mobile, followed that up with more 'anonymous' flowers and then another call. And although Alice hadn't responded, she was tempted. She wasn't used to being pursued so rigorously, or in such apparent contradiction to the things he'd been saying, and her curiosity was starting to outweigh her concerns about his wife.

Mel watched her, thinking how easy it was at that age. Men came and went. It didn't really matter. Girls like Alice didn't get hurt. Not for long, at any rate.

'If someone sends you flowers,' said Alice, sitting up suddenly, 'that means they fancy you, right?'

Mel smiled. 'Depends who it is,' she said, thinking instantly of Ned.

She wondered what, if anything, was happening. She knew that he'd taken Alice to the Savils' party – David had told her, and he'd told her how he'd left them together on the side of the road, laughing and singing – but since then they'd heard nothing. Had Ned spoken to her? Had he confronted Alice regarding her designs on David? Or had he feigned ignorance? Mel rather suspected the latter. Ned had Alice's body, but only because she already had designs on his – and that, Mel guessed, wasn't good enough for a man like Ned. He wanted more. He wanted the heart and mind, the bits that mattered. And that needed a different strategy: something gentler . . . more restrained.

'A man,' said Alice. 'If a man sends you flowers, masses and masses of them. Orchids and lilies, Mel. So many, you can't begin to carry them.'

'Well,' said Mel, amused. Not that restrained, then! 'Unless the man's your godfather –'

'He's not.'

'Or an uncle or something, and of course if you're in hospital, or if you become a musician and it's a first night.'

'Yes, yes.'

'Well, if it's none of those things, and if there are – as you say – masses and masses, then I think you can safely assume that whoever sent them fancies you.'

'Even if he denies it?'

Mel frowned. 'Well, what did the note say?'

'There was no note.'

'Then how do you know who sent them?'

'I just do,' said Alice. 'No one else could have done it. But why would he send me flowers, and then deny that he fancies me? He even denied sending them!'

'Then maybe he didn't send them.'

'Oh, he did,' said Alice. She seemed very certain.

'Then you must have scared him off in some way,' said Mel gently. 'Maybe he's just waiting for a little more encouragement. It sounds to me like the ball is in your court. It's entirely up to you. If you don't respond, he'll probably look elsewhere. But maybe that's what you want.'

Alice hated the idea of Joss looking elsewhere. He'd tossed a ball – a brilliant ball – high in the air, kicking and spinning with just the right degree of deviation. And the instinct to stick out her arm, to catch it plum in her palm, was just too strong.

Anyway, she was doing nothing wrong. Joss had said, very clearly, that he didn't fancy her. So what, if she didn't believe him? Why shouldn't she simply take him at his word? He'd expressed an interest in her career, and a man like Joss could be very helpful. Very helpful indeed. She wasn't going to *do* anything.

So when he rang her mobile the following day, Alice answered.

'I was worried about you,' he said.

'Were you?'

'Thought something had happened.'

'Well, it didn't,' said Alice, her voice clean and clear. 'I'm fine.'

'I – do you – I mean, would you consider meeting me again – for a drink, perhaps? – to, er, reassure me of that fact?'

Alice hesitated, conscience jarring with her boredom threshold.

'I've spoken to my friend,' said Joss. 'The one at the Tsar Bar I was telling you about, remember? Not the bit we were in the other day, but the upstairs room, where there's a rather exclusive restaurant, and they're looking for someone exactly like you to play the piano there, add a bit of style. He'd be so disappointed if you –'

'I'll see him,' said Alice.

Joss was going to Scotland, but was due back in a month. Why didn't she come direct to Cheyne Lane that Monday? Monday the sixth, that would be. Six o'clock? Great. He'd definitely be back by then. They could have a quick drink, and then he'd take her on to Tsar's . . .

Part Two

21

With Mel asleep in the back and Edmund asleep in the passenger seat, David crossed the border. Cutting his speed, he drove over a stone bridge past signs that welcomed them to Scotland, and followed the road through a small stone town. It was late and still.

Edmund opened his eyes. A terrace of strong grey walls shot by, dotted with deep-set windows and sturdy doors that opened straight on to the pavement. The roofs were slated – sloping, northern.

'Where are we?'

'Almost there,' said David. 'That was the Tweed. Have you got the directions?'

Edmund switched on the light, took out his wallet and pulled from it a folded bit of paper.

'OK,' he said. 'We stay on this road for another eight miles. We go through another small town, Hedlawburn – pronounced Heddleburn, according to Joss – and there's a sign to the right to Merwick. And then after about a mile, he says, just before we get to Merwick, there's a row of farm cottages on the left and then a turning, which we ignore. But we take the next one, which isn't signed, and the gates are a couple of hundred yards on the right.'

Mel woke to the sound of tyres on gravel, barking dogs, and Edmund's voice saying, 'Mel? Mel, we're here.'

She'd been lying along the back seat. Opening her eyes into the road atlas in the black net at the back of the driver's seat, she listened to the others getting out, doors slamming.

Behind her, the boot opened.

'You want your easel out?' said Edmund's voice, close and loud.

'No.' David's, further away. 'No, thanks.'

There was a bit of shuffling and a thud as Edmund pulled a suitcase out from under the easel, and then she heard David.

'Oh my God –' his voice evaporating – 'look at the stars.'

Mel sat upright, opened her door and got out. It was cold, much colder than London. Hugging herself, she walked towards David. They stood with their backs to the house, looking up into moonless infinity – visible, glowing. A ring of cedars fringed the sky. Great low branches swept at the lawns, high tips brushed at the stars. To the north, the land fell to the river – they could hear the water tumbling. Beyond that lay a barren arc of moor.

Mel turned to what she could see of the house. There was no moon, but the sky-glow gave bluish form to a building that, with its steep balanced roofs, elongated doors and windows, its willowy symmetry, looked more French than Scottish. There were panes of curtained light at the windows, mainly the ones upstairs. But at one corner of the lower level, a group of longer ones shone softly. Not everyone had gone to bed.

Edmund lifted out his gun case and put it flat on the gravel, with care, next to their suitcases. Checking he hadn't missed anything, that the only things left in there were David's painting materials, he put up his hand and threw down the door to the boot. There was a rustle in the bushes nearby, and then silence. Picking up the cases, Edmund walked with them towards the house.

He was tired. The journey hadn't been bad. Last time he'd come to Merwick, it had taken nine hours. But even seven hours was too much. Especially when it was only for the weekend. And with all that fast heavy traffic, and David's hesitant driving . . . why hadn't he flown up, or got the train? It was all right for Mel, who'd slept the entire journey. And David, who hadn't had to get up at crack of dawn. But it was now two o'clock. Apart from the half-hour of neck-wrenching sleep he'd had between Newcastle and the border, Edmund had been up for twenty hours.

There was a time, once, when Edmund would have found weekends like this exciting. He'd have enjoyed the social side – the parties and the drinking – every bit as much as the shooting. But that no longer satisfied him. The time he'd spent in New York had given Ned a fresh perspective and ever since his return, he found that good shooting wasn't enough. Sure, it was great to have high birds, stunning land-scapes, and challenging conditions, but he wanted conversation to match it.

The trouble was that shooting invitations, like business dinners, were based less on real friendship than on a system of reciprocity. Very few people were invited who couldn't then invite you back. It was all about what your guests could give you in return and, until now, that had seemed to Ned to be an effective, if somewhat cynical, approach. He himself belonged to a syndicate shoot in Hampshire, a syndicate that had once included his father. William Nicholson had adored shooting, and had introduced both his sons to the sport at an early age. But while Edmund was a natural – and had a robust attitude to killing game – David had been reluctant, and when William died it was Edmund who'd inherited his guns and his slot on the syndicate. The syndicate didn't own the land, and they weren't responsible for the upkeep of the shoot. They'd simply pay their money and come down from London once a week – with the result that Edmund's knowledge of game crops and breeding pheasants was limited, but he knew how to handle a shotgun. The birds flew well, the lunch was good, and it was only an hour out of London.

Every year, he'd invite Joss as one of his guests. Every year, Joss would invite him back to Merwick. But it had less to do with whether they liked each other, and more to do with shared interests and a common code of conduct. Arriving at Merwick for yet another weekend, Edmund thought of what he'd seen of Joss in recent weeks and wondered suddenly why he bothered slogging the distance to spend time with a man he only quite liked.

He was at the foot of the steps when an outside light went on and the door opened. A pair of spaniels ran out barking and sniffing, tails lashing at his legs, before bounding on to the others. They were followed by Joss.

'Shut *up*, you horrible hounds! Let me take those, Ned. Here.'

And Annabel Glass.

Edmund was so surprised, he didn't try to stop Joss from taking the cases. He stood there stupidly, wondering if he'd made a mistake. Annabel stood at the top of the steps, smiling down.

'Hello, Ned.'

Joss, halfway up, turned back and grinned. 'You know Annabel?'

'Of course I do.' Edmund came up the steps and gave her a dutiful kiss. 'How nice to see you.'

He thought of her book, sitting at the bottom of his tray of things to do when other more important things were done. Weeks gone by and it was still there. He hadn't even read the first chapter.

'I've been meaning to ring,' he said. 'Your book . . .'

'Ned, darling,' Annabel took his arm. 'Stop it. You've driven seven whole hours to get away from your office and I'm quite sure the last thing you want right now is to talk about that stupid book of mine! You look like you need a good strong drink.'

'Do I?'

'What'll it be?'

As Joss went back outside to greet David and Mel, and bring in his spaniels, Annabel led Edmund down a short passage, into a sitting room. It was warm and scruffy in there, full of newspapers, ashtrays, dog-beds, and chewed up cuddly toys that squeaked as he trod on them. A fire – unguarded – blazed in the grate. In the corner, a tray of drinks had been pushed on to a table of photograph frames.

Ned sat in a chair by the fire and let Annabel pour him a glass of whisky. Back down the passage he could hear the great door closing, Mel's voice, followed by Joss's, and the scattering of dog paws on stone, getting louder, until they were in the room and sniffing at his ankles. One of them leapt up and lay, possessively, over his lap – a toy in its mouth. Ned felt the weight. He'd have preferred the chair to himself but he was just too tired, even to push it off.

Joss came in. 'Oi, Flunky. Get off. I said, *off*!'

Flunky slid to the floor.

'Sorry about that, Ned. Now,' Joss looked around the room and back at Edmund with a grin. 'Well, I see Annabel's sorting you out,' he said. 'Need anything else? Sure? And you know where to leave your gun, don't you? Back down the passage, room at the far end. That's right. Great. Well if it's OK with you, I might turn in.'

Edmund stood up. 'I should really do the same. Early start and . . . ah.' He took the glass that Annabel was holding. It was heavy, dark and full. 'Thanks, Annabel.'

'I've shown David and Mel up,' Joss went on. 'So it's just you two. You need to put the grate back on the fire and turn out the lights when you go to bed. The alarm goes on automatically at three thirty, I'm afraid, so you do have to be upstairs before then. Really boring, I know, but that shouldn't be a problem for you, Ned.' Joss looked at his watch. 'Got at least an hour to get properly reacquainted, and . . . No, I'm *joking*! Annabel, you know where he's sleeping: the room two on from yours. There's a bathroom in between. And I've left your suitcase at the foot of the stairs. Well, good night then. Come on, Badger darling. Time for bed. And you, Flunky.

Flunky?' Joss walked out. They heard his footsteps on the stone. 'Flun-kee!'

Mel woke automatically at six the following morning. The room was dim and large. She lay in bed, gazing round at the furniture, the hangings, the great old prints, and listening to the rain. In addition to the usual bedroom furniture – cupboards, chests and dressing tables – there was a slim round table covered with lace and Victorian photographs. It sat between the windows with a pair of fragile chairs either side: one for her clothes, one for David's. A chandelier hung above them, grey light glimmering in its crystals. Without the bed, it might have been a drawing room.

Tiredness dragged at her. She could feel the want of sleep in the pockets of her eyes, the way the skin caught at her cheekbones. The prospect of another two hours in bed would usually bring a smile to her lips and easy surrender to sleep. Mel tried. She turned the other way and felt, in the turn, the soft weight of eiderdowns lined by fine cotton sheets that had long lost any starchiness, that seemed if anything to have been improved by decades of washing and ironing, a worn softness that couldn't be bought. She pulled the covers up, closed her eyes and waited. But her mind wouldn't rest.

David slept on, his back to her. Mel looked at it, at how smooth it was. She could see the bones and muscles, the movement with each breath. There was a time when she'd have touched it. He'd have turned, still half asleep, and taken her in his arms. But Mel no longer did that. Instead, she clasped her hands around her arms and looked at the pale back.

Nothing had happened. They hadn't had another row. The wedding was still on. It was set for the first weekend in April. They'd booked the church and the Bishop's Park venue. She'd been for her first wedding-dress fitting – standing virtually naked while the dressmaker ran a tape all over her body, calling out measurements to a girl in glasses, who'd taken them down with a serious expression. And there were countless other things she'd started: service sheets and invitations, caterers, florists, bridesmaids, music, drink . . . She had a special file.

She was winding up her job, passing clients on to colleagues. Telling them she was leaving 'to get married' was somehow the tidiest explanation. It wasn't great, but the truth – that she simply didn't know, hadn't thought of what she'd do instead – still sounded irresponsible and weak. She knew it wasn't. She knew that this was all about getting a grip on her life, making the choice *for herself*, but it was hard not to give the impression that she was running away. Mel wondered for a moment: if it was so hard to explain to other people, if she had to avoid the truth, then perhaps there were inconsistencies after all. Perhaps she should have thought it through more thoroughly . . . but there wasn't much she could do about it now. She'd think about it later, after the wedding, when she and David got back from wherever they were going for their honeymoon.

Mel still didn't know where that was.

'It's a secret,' he'd said, but she felt no excitement from him. Something wasn't right. And lying there watching his back swell, subside, and swell again, Mel realised that this was no fresh discovery. She'd known it for weeks. But instead of confronting it, instead of telling David about her fears and asking what he thought, she'd chosen – like her mother – to pretend. Everything was fine. And so long as it (whatever *it* was that wasn't right) was never mentioned, then it wasn't really there.

Except that, now, it was. It occupied her mind. And try as she might, Mel couldn't ignore it, couldn't sleep. Nor could she raise it, didn't dare. So she hung in limbo, staring at his back. And when at eight the alarm went, Mel heard it with relief. Reaching round to switch it off, she got out of bed.

David watched her: a slim white body-space, rubbed away in the charcoal light. She walked away from him across the room, pulling a towel from the rail in a weary gesture. For a moment, he felt the tension – wondered idly what was eating her – and then, as she went into the bathroom, he closed his eyes and returned, comfortably, to his half-remembered dream.

Mel hadn't planned to go out with the guns. She knew that David would be painting Laura that day, knew that they'd need solitude. She knew that everybody else would be out, that there wouldn't be much for her to do inside beyond reading the papers. But that wasn't such a bad way to spend the day, and she didn't like the idea of shooting.

Mel had never been shooting before. While her parents had moved to Yorkshire, she was still a Londoner, and had a Londoner's attitude to the countryside. She thought it was healthy, and beautiful to look at. She felt sorry for farmers, with the various disasters to their livestock and livelihoods that she'd read about in the newspapers. But she also felt detached. She didn't bother to read more than the headlines and the opening paragraphs – and why should she? It didn't affect her.

The one countryside issue she did feel more able to voice an opinion on, however, was blood sports. And while she wasn't passionate on the subject, while she knew no more than the next person, and wouldn't be going on any anti-blood sports march, it was still absolutely plain to Mel that killing *for fun* was wrong.

If other people wanted to do it, well, she wasn't going to fight them. There were bigger political issues for her to shout about than the deaths of a few odd foxes – or pheasants. But nor did she approve. She could see that slaughtering animals was necessary – whether for culling purposes, or for meat to eat. And it wasn't half as bad as battery farms (and if she herself ate meat, she was hardly in a position to complain about animals being killed). But to Mel it was important that these things were done soberly, with an air of regret. To kill because it was smart and expensive, because your grandfather had built up one of the best shoots in the country, because there was a certain skill to it, was – to her – distasteful.

But as she went down to breakfast that morning, Mel was having second thoughts. Not so much about the morality of shooting parties, but about how bad it would really be just to go and watch. She wasn't sure she could face all day alone with her thoughts. She needed the distraction.

Joss – with a long pair of socks in his hand, and the air of someone who'd been up for hours – met her on the stairs.

'Hello!' he said, standing aside for her to go down first. 'You're up early.'

'Am I?'

'Not expecting to see any of you girls until lunch – and now all of you are up! Does this mean you're coming out with the men?'

Mel wasn't used to being spoken to like that. Clocking the blend of chivalry and sexism, she didn't hesitate in her reply. She was, most certainly, coming too.

'Splendid! Good for you. We're in here.'

Joss opened the door to the dining room. She followed him up to a sideboard of coffee cups, hotplates, jugs of milk, orange juice, incongruous Kelloggs' cereal packets, and a large vat of porridge. He picked up a plate and lifted the lid on a tray of bacon.

'Want some?'

Pushing the dog's nose aside, Mel took a plate as well and held it out. Joss put a couple of rashers on each of their plates and moved on to the eggs.

'David up?'

'Won't be long.'

'He does know we're off at nine, doesn't he? I know it's a bore, but we can't hang around, not when there are so many people involved.'

'It's OK,' said Mel, refusing the black pudding with her free hand. 'He knows you're off at nine, but I think he said he'd be painting Laura this morning.'

'Of course he is,' said Joss, smiling. 'How stupid of me. Now, sit anywhere you like – how about here next to me, and I can introduce you to this motley crew?'

They didn't look motley: smartly dressed in shades of sludge, woollen ties at pristine collars, soft tweed breeches (even the women) over bottle-green socks, the only flash of colour at their garters. Mel stood with her plate as Joss went round the table.

'OK, this is Harry Denham.'

Harry Denham gave Mel a shy smile and continued to tuck into his breakfast.

'And Harry's wife, Rachel.'

Rachel Denham had her back turned and was talking quietly but indignantly to the woman beyond her. 'The man hardly spoke any English at all. And then he gets out, goes round and – get this, Miranda – he takes out my brand-new suitcase and throws – literally *throws* – it on the pavement . . .'

Joss pulled out a chair for Mel. 'Next to Rachel,' he went on, as Mel sat down, 'is Miranda. Miranda Steele. Annabel's sister. You met Annabel last night, didn't you? Oh. Well, she's the one up there at the far end, talking to Ned. And that fat bastard over there, see? The one with no hair, feeding bacon rinds to my dog, that's Miranda's husband, Benjy. Oh Benjy, no. Don't. She'll be sick. Benjy?'

Benjy sat up laughing. His face was almost completely round.

'This is Mel.'

'Hello!'

Mel smiled back and then, with Benjy and Joss exchanging remarks across her about each other's dogs, she picked up her knife and fork, took a mouthful, and looked back up the table.

Edmund was at the end, dressed in shooting clothes. His body suited the old-fashioned style of the breeches, his calves were strong and curved. He was sitting next to Annabel, gently spinning the lazy susan in front of him so that she could help herself to butter and marmalade, and listening to her. His hair wasn't quite dry.

'I really wouldn't want to,' she was saying.

'You've never tried?'

Annabel spread the butter – thinly and thought-fully – over her toast. Her shirtsleeves were rolled back and a bracelet of silver links slipped up her wrist. 'I think,' she said, 'for a woman to shoot, she really has to be better than the men. She just can't get away with making mistakes. It's embarrassing. The other day, I –'

'It's uncomfortable for men as well, you know.'

'Oh, absolutely. The other day, I was staying with friends in Wiltshire, and there was this woman there, shooting badly. I mean, really *really* badly. Missed almost everything. And I thought, what *is* she trying to prove? And the men were, as you say, incredibly uncomfortable.'

Edmund laughed. 'No, I meant when men have off days,' he said. 'When we miss everything – it's just as bad, you know. Just as embarrassing.'

Annabel crunched at her toast and swallowed it down. 'I bet you don't miss much. And anyway,' she went on, reaching for her glass of orange juice, 'I prefer to stand and watch. There's no pressure to – er – perform.'

'Is that right?' said Edmund. He looked up, noticed Mel watching them, and gave her an unusual smile, it was almost as if he was pleading with her.

'Good morning, Ned.'

'Good morning,' he said. 'Where's David? Not still in bed, is he?'

'No he is not,' said David's voice. Dressed in jeans and a new red shirt, he came through the same door that Mel and Joss had used, and nodded to the room.

Joss finished his mouthful. 'Everyone, this is David. David, help yourself. There's cereal and whatnot over there, bacon and eggs, and porridge, if you'd like some of that.'

As he spoke, Laura came in through the other door, the one that led to the kitchen. She was looking hassled, holding a fresh pot of coffee in one hand, dragging Flunky in the other. 'Morning, everyone,' she said and put the coffee to one side. 'Darling . . .'

'Darling, what?'

'It mustn't come into the house. You know how much I –'

'It?' said Joss, taking Flunky and lifting him easily on to his lap. Flunky was clearly used to being there. He went completely passive, and sank his soft black head against Joss's chest like a sleepy child. 'Did you hear that, Flunky, darling? She called you *it*.'

Laura returned to the kitchen, a cool expression on her face.

The table was silent. Joss looked round with a contrite smile. Putting Flunky down – making him sit – he followed Laura into the kitchen. Still, no one spoke. Mel saw Harry and Rachel Denham look at one another. She saw Harry shake his head, and take up his cup of coffee.

Gradually, they left the table. Benjy wanted to check something in the newspapers before the party left. Rachel wanted to give her dog a sedative.

Miranda wanted to borrow a pair of gloves from Annabel. And Harry, finishing his coffee, said he supposed they should all get a move on. It was almost nine.

David poured himself another cup of coffee from the pot that Laura had brought in. 'Anyone else?' he said, holding out the pot.

'You're not coming?' said Harry.

'I can't. I'm painting Laura.' David looked out of the window at thick grey mist. 'But the light's not great, so I guess it'll only be planning at this stage . . . Mel, coffee?'

Mel put down her napkin and shook her head. 'I'm going out.'

'But you said –'

'I know,' she didn't look at him. 'I've changed my mind.'

Edmund, who with much tact and diplomacy had managed to avoid a night with Annabel Glass, had been wondering how he was going to avoid spending a morning with her as well. He knew it wasn't kind. He knew what was expected of him, but he couldn't bear it. The neatness of it, the *he's single, she's single, what are they waiting for?* made him feel that if he gave an inch, she'd take the rest of his life.

'Excellent!' he said to Mel. 'You can stand with me.'

Ten minutes later they were standing in groups at the front of the house. There must have been about twenty or thirty people – eight guns, three dog handlers, the keeper, underkeeper, beaters and other hangers-on – all milling around, talking in low voices, their breath visible in the morning air. Around them were dogs of various breeds – mainly spaniels, a couple of Labradors, and a terrier – some sitting calm, some hysterical. The mist was thick but bright, round a soft white circle of sun.

Mel stood on the steps that led up to the front door, winding one of Laura's scarves around her neck, and looking out at the collection of tweed caps, walking boots, waxed coats, tweed jackets, woollen gloves, or sharp fingerless leather ones for those with guns. And, as she watched, the beaters and keepers began to move off, in preparation for the first drive. The area cleared, leaving only the guns and their companions. Annabel Glass was dressed in a long waxed coat that came well below her knees and a smart hat with a broad brim. Her boots were made of leather, with fur on the inside. She was relacing one of them as she chatted to her sister.

Mel poked the ends of the scarf into her jacket while Edmund stood beside her – silently checking he had enough cartridges. Joss stood further off dressed in the same tweed as his keeper. In one hand, he held a box of metal slips with the numbers one to eight on them. In the other, his gun. He held out the metal pieces.

'Come on, Ned. We're picking.'

Ned followed him down the steps. Mel watched as Joss turned his back and arranged the metal pieces randomly in their slots so that the numbers were hidden. Then he offered the box to each of the eight guns, himself last. Each man picked a piece, and each looked happy – some rather more politely so than others – with his choice. Joss then re-collected the pieces. He spoke generally. Mel heard him say something about not shooting 'ground game', and then the group dispersed.

'What was all that about?'

Edmund was looking pleased. 'We pick for where we stand in the line,' he said. 'And then we move on round with each drive. The idea is that all of us get to the hot spot at some point, but we keep the same guns next to us all day. I'm between Harry and some bloke from up the road, so I'm all right,' and then he laughed. 'But poor Harry's got Benjy – who has a rather nasty habit of shooting your birds after you've already shot them, and then claiming them as his.' He stopped as Joss joined them.

'Got everything? Great. Now why don't you two come with me,' he indicated the row of parked Land Rovers, 'second from the end. I'll be with you when I've got the others sorted out.'

Mel and Edmund did as they were told. Mel sat in the passenger seat and Edmund got in behind. The dogs were already in the back. They watched Joss stride across the gravel – large, authoritative, with a gun over one arm, his loose curls blowing slightly as he lit another cigarette and ordered everyone into the cars. Sunlight was breaking through the mist: glinting metal on his gun, sharper shadows on the gravel.

He was about to rejoin them when Laura appeared at the door. She ran down the steps.

'Darling . . .'

'What is it?'

Laura took his free arm. She held it with both hands, the sun right in her eyes. Ned watched them together on the drive, through the rear-view mirror.

Joss had stopped. He was smiling back at Laura, smiling in the same distracted way that Ned himself was doing.

'I'm sorry,' she was saying. 'Darling, I'm so sorry. If I'd known you were expecting me to be out then I wouldn't have agreed to sit for David. We could postpone it. We –'

'Sweetheart,' Joss kissed her mouth still, 'it's not your fault. And anyway, I now have a gorgeous blonde to carry my cartridge bag,' he nodded in Annabel's direction, 'so you see you're quite superfluous.'

'Joss.'

'You go back to David, and sit very still for him, like a good girl.' Joss was laughing. He kissed her again – and again. 'I'll see you at lunch.'

Putting the cigarette back into his mouth, Joss opened the door and handed Mel his gun – she took it from him, awkwardly. Then he went round and got in himself, slamming the door. They waited quietly for him to take one last drag from the cigarette, toss it out on to the gravel and start the engine.

'Right,' he said, checking his rear-view mirror to make sure Harry Denham was following. 'Let's go.'

22

By the start of the first drive the mist had cleared completely. As she walked with Edmund to his peg – the third one along the edge of a field of kale that smelt of rot – Mel felt the sun on her face, a rim of warmth over her cheekbones, and was glad that she'd come too.

They stood together at the peg and she looked back up the line to where Harry and Rachel were standing, with Rachel's Labrador straining on a lead that she'd tied to the peg. The peg didn't look stable. Beyond them stood Benjy, with Miranda, talking in low voices.

And beyond Benjy stood Joss, with Annabel Glass. She was holding his cartridge bag and standing behind. Mel watched him toss down his cap, and load his gun with a flash of crimson cartridges: slotted in, clicked shut. She continued to watch as, in one movement – arching his great body right back – he swung the gun up over his head, finding his rhythm as he flung its barrels round at a series of imaginary birds following their flight right through. It reminded Mel of someone playing tennis, the service action in reverse.

He settled, Benjy and Miranda fell silent, and the row of guns stood waiting for birds to be driven out by a fearsome line of men at the far end of the field. Mel watched them advance – heavy strides, through the kale – sticks flying this way and that against the light. As they got closer, she could hear the tapping, into expectant air. But no birds.

'Where are they?' she whispered.

Edmund didn't hear her. He was fiddling with the electronic switch on his headphones. They were designed to block out close sounds – protect his ears from the deafening blast of his own gun or the chatter of his companion – while letting him 'hear someone pee in the next field', was how Joss had described it when he handed them over. They were supposed to help him hear when birds took flight.

Edmund continued looking straight ahead. The tapping grew louder. The sun grew brighter. The Denhams' dog pulled and strained at her peg, and then three birds got up.

They flew with the wind, away from Ned and Mel's position – out of shot for Harry and Benjy – probably in shot for Joss, who left them for the man on his other side to bring one down. Mel watched its curling fall, a ball of feathers in the light, spiralling russet, through to the heavy drop. The dog was yelping now, fighting Rachel's restraint, then silenced by a rough kick from Harry.

Those first three birds were followed by a flush of seven or eight, flying in the same direction, then another flush, more than before, and then another: a steady flow of feathery targets, out of the rotten kale.

*

David was in a room they called the saloon: a domed space that worked as an anteroom to the drawing room, with a round table in the middle, and the kind of chairs one didn't sit on back against the walls. The day's newspapers lay there, unread, on the table and he was deciding which of them he wanted to read – in the absence of the *Guardian* – when Laura came in, a cup of coffee in her hand.

He turned. Unable to stop himself, he looked at her differently, his eye diverting to an abdomen that, if anything, seemed more fragile than ever beneath the plum suede trousers she was wearing. The belt, a little loose, was on its tightest hole. Then he looked at her face. The skin had lost its tan and a crescent shadow lay at her eye, the curve of her nostril was more acute than ever.

Apart from her rushed appearance at breakfast, David hadn't seen Laura since that dinner party in London. He hadn't spoken to her at all. Joss was his point of contact. And while Joss had been increasingly enthusiastic about the portrait, while he'd insisted that Laura was equally keen, David still worried that he'd made the wrong decision. Seeing her there, frailer than ever, did nothing to relieve his anxiety.

'Hello, Laura,' he said quietly. 'I so hope you don't mind this. Me being here – the picture and everything. I very nearly didn't come, you know, and if it wasn't for Joss insisting . . .'

Laura smiled. 'He told me. But honestly, David, you shouldn't have worried.'

'You were upset.'

'I was shocked. Guess I thought I'd put those days

297

behind me, and then you turn up like some ghost from the past.'

'I know,' he said. 'I'm so sorry.'

'Don't be. It's fine. I'm glad you're here.'

David watched her at the table. She'd moved round and was leaning over, sifting through the papers, with the long dark line of her arm against sunlight from the drawing room beyond – through the open door. The plum of her trousers, those icy walls, that morning light on the polished floor, bouncing through the thin material of her shirt . . . he could paint her just like that.

'Laura?'

'Mm?'

'Shall we make a start?'

'Sure.'

'We could think about what you might want to wear. Those trousers are fantastic. That colour . . .'

'These?' said Laura. 'Oh Lord, no! Joss would never want me done in these.'

'Well then, what do you think he would like?'

Laura wasn't sure.

'Something more formal, perhaps?' he said. 'Or would it help, do you think, if we had a look at your wardrobe? I'm sure between us we could find something?'

Laura led him to the bedroom she shared with Joss at the south-west corner of the first floor, overlooking the gardens at the back. Someone had been in there already and any trace of mess, of intimacy, had been cleared away. It was entirely fresh. The windows were open, the bedspread drawn up. The walls were covered in silk of pale striped eau-de-Nil that had been stretched over a specially constructed frame-work. There was no hardness, nothing sharp: orchids on the dressing table, cotton wool in porcelain pots, small lace cushions on the window seats. Trying not to think too much about where they were, David followed her through: past the bed, into the bath-room, then on to a dressing room beyond.

'OK,' she said, opening the first of about six walk-in cupboards. And then the second and the third. The fourth was devoted entirely to her shoes. The others remained closed. 'Take your pick.'

David looked into the first, at row after row of perfectly laundered clothes in special bags. She had to open them for him so that he could see properly what was inside.

'Well, there's this,' she said. 'Or this, or this . . .' – and it wasn't long before the dressing room was awash with dry-cleaners' wrappings, with suits and dresses and shirts and trousers flung here and there on the narrow bed.

David stood at the window. He could hear gunfire in the distance and turned to look out. 'What are they shooting at?'

'Pheasants, mainly.' She was right inside the cupboard. He could hear the metal hooks of the hangers on the rails. 'Sometimes there are partridges, or someone gets a woodcock, or a hare.' Out came a tailored suit of cream grosgrain, followed by an identical one in navy. 'Hares make a terrible noise . . .'

David turned his back to the window and watched her throw the clothes before him with hard pride.

'I adore this. And I know he likes that, although he may not think it appropriate . . . Or there's this? A bit summery, maybe. What kind of colours were you thinking of?'

They made a crazy pattern – mustard silk, puce wool, pastel-striped cotton, roughly overlapped by the powder-blue netting of an evening dress with rustling skirts, followed by a tweed trouser suit that slipped on to the floor. On and on. A short red skirt flew out, followed by a matching sequin boob-tube top that raised his eyebrows.

'Not that he'd want me painted in that,' she said. 'But you might like the colour. Or there's *this*.' Laura held out a light coat, slightly flared, in immaculate silver-grey cashmere. It had a belt and matching slip-dress. She waved it on its hanger, dangled it there for David to see, then tossed it on to the pile.

'OK. Moving on.'

Emerald embroidery, lime-green crepe, orange chiffon, beige corduroy, pink satin lining to a midnight-navy shawl . . . Eventually she stopped, came out of the cupboard, and stood in the middle of the room.

'Is there nothing here that you like?'

David, mesmerised, stared at the pile. It was too much. And the more he saw, the more he felt that the only thing he could do – with any sincerity – was skin.

Mel stood with her hands over her ears and her head to the bright blue air – the smell of cordite in her nostrils. It was close to the end of the drive, and Edmund hadn't missed a single one.

Up the gun had gone, up and over, effortlessly, time after time. She'd looked at his profile – at the waiting expression, the firm mouth. Then he'd lift his eye with the flight of his target, eye and hand co-ordinating perfectly, up and round. Up and round. It always looked as if he wasn't going to be quick enough, he seemed so relaxed, and then the bird would stop in the air for a moment before falling plum to the ground. There was no satisfied smile, no looking around to see if anyone else had seen. Just single-minded concentration.

The beaters were nearly at the end of the crop now, and she watched the last remaining birds: wings beating up and out of the great floppy leaves, up and low over Edmund, who deliberately let them go. As the horn brought the shooting to an end – guns broken open, unused cartridges removed – Mel took her hands from her ears and turned to him.

'What about those last ones?' she said.

'Too low.'

'Not safe?'

He shut his gun. 'Not sporting.'

Mel watched him slot the unused cartridges into the belt around his hips, brassy ends hooked into leathery loops. She followed him over to where a cock pheasant lay: spiked feet in the air, one wing flung open, broken. She noticed the soft bottle-green neck and the hard, dead eyes. He picked it up and was about to squash it into the inside pocket of his jacket – a pocket designed especially for the purpose – when a dog handler came up with Labradors at his heels and a game bag that already contained three or four birds. He was wearing a hat pulled low over his brow but, underneath, there was no mistaking the approval in his eye and he held out the bag.

Edmund dropped in the bundle of brown-maroon

feathers. 'Thanks, Tom,' he said. 'How are you?'

'Oh, not bad. Not bad.'

'This is Mel.'

The handler gave Mel the briefest of nods, slung his game bag over his back, and turned to Edmund. They walked back to the Land Rovers and other farm vehicles that would take them to the next drive. And while Edmund and the dog handler discussed the conditions – did he think the weather would hold? And wasn't this wind a bonus! Those Michigan Blues were flying like bullets . . . And how had the grouse been after all that summer rain? – Mel listened quietly, and felt even less important than the dogs.

'Like this?'

David moved further back. He held out his hands – squared them against each other in a frame of fingers – and looked through them at Laura by the sideboard, shutting one eye for a clearer image. He liked the line of the sideboard: a good, hard horizontal, right across the picture. He liked the way her black silk dress would be almost a silhouette, with just that flounce at the bottom. But he needed her more side on.

'That's great, Laura. Could you turn a little further round to your left?'

Laura turned.

'And look back at me?'

Laura looked.

'So in the end,' she said, 'I decided it was simpler all round not to tell him. It's not that Joss is difficult, but he wouldn't understand. Not properly. Sure, the collection in New York is full of nudes. He adores them. But he also has a fixed idea of me as someone who wouldn't do that sort of thing, someone with a bit more class, I guess. It's not his fault. I mean, all men feel that way about their wives.'

Trying to get a balance between not being rude, and not listening – he didn't want the same embarrassing results he'd had that day in London, with the second sketch – David gave her a quick smile and sat on one of the chairs. He lifted his sketchbook and started marking out the pose. Perhaps it would be better off centre, he thought, sweeping out his pencil to show where the edge of the picture should be.

'What way?' he said – late.

'Don't act dumb, David. You know what I'm talking about.'

'Do I?' David held the pencil in his mouth and, with both hands, lifted the sketch. He glanced from it to Laura and back to it again and sighed. An evening dress in daylight? In the dining room? Would she just look silly?

'Sure you do,' said Laura. 'Male possessiveness. The part of you that minds like hell about what we wear, or who we talk to, or if we're flirting or whatever. The kind that . . . Oh come on, David!'

'Mm?'

'Don't tell me you don't get jealous of your fiancée! There must have been times when you wished she was wearing something less revealing.'

David smiled. 'I think Mel would have a fit if I started to control what she wore or who she spoke to.'

Laura was silent for a moment. David sketched on, to the ticking of a grandfather clock in the corner of the room. Resolute in his attempt to block out her words. He was just deciding that the evening dress was really too much – Joss didn't want her casual, but nor should she look as if she'd walked off the set of *Dynasty* – when Laura suddenly spoke again.

'You know, David, I like it when Joss gets jealous. I honestly think I do. That's when I know he loves me. Imagine if he didn't care what I wore, or who I was speaking to, or whether I was flirting. Imagine how sad that would be!'

David sighed. 'I'm sorry, Laura,' he said. 'I think perhaps the dress is wrong. Could you bear to go upstairs again?'

23

Merwick shooting lunches took place in a draughty barn at the Hedlawburn end of the estate. David and Laura were set to join the others at one o'clock. At five to, they left the house.

Laura insisted on driving.

'It's a dirty old farmyard,' she told him. 'You don't want to mess up your nice car with all this mud. We'll take the Jeep. It's out at the front – door's open. I'll join you in a second.'

David opened the door and got in. He sat in the passenger seat, waiting – watching for Laura through the gap in the great front door, and wondered what to do about the portrait. He still hadn't decided what she should wear, and it was starting to bother him. Usually, he had no trouble. Was it really because he'd done her nude? Was that so significant? Or was it just a tricky subject? Perhaps they needed Joss there as well, in case they got it wrong again. Or would that make it even more confusing?

The sun went in for a moment, and David stared at the grey of the house – grey steps, grey pillars – its stony beauty. He found it hard to imagine any-one choosing to live in a place like that. Hard monochrome. It didn't fit with Laura at all. Not yet at any rate. But her tan was fading and her hair would, he supposed, one day lose its shine – from pregnancy, perhaps, and days of sunless boredom. All too soon, she'd settle in.

The door opened, and she stepped out, slim and bright, wrapped in a brown suede coat, soft against the masonry. The brown was too much, and Joss would no doubt want the coat to be smarter, but David suddenly saw the portrait he would paint. He saw it so clearly that it was as if, in that moment, it was done already: Laura in the doorway, against pillars and steps and lines of stone. Didn't matter that there was no sun. Didn't really matter if it rained. Laura would be sheltered by the porch. And he . . . well, he'd manage. In fact, rain would make it better. And in amongst that pile of clothes in the dressing room was a silver-grey coat in cashmere, with a belt and matching slip-dress.

Laura ran down the steps towards him. She got in, put her bag on his lap and checked her watch.

'Is it far?'

'Couple of miles.'

She slammed the door, shook the gearbox into neutral, and turned on the car engine. Pulling the gearstick into reverse, she checked swiftly behind, and put her foot down. The car flew back and round with a jerk and, with another thrust of the gearstick, she set off down the drive – at speed – feeling round for her seat belt at the same time. Avoiding her hand, David took it from her and clipped it in.

Rows of dead birds had been tied together in pairs

with orange string and hung from a game cart that stood at the gates to the yard. The beaters had congregated around it, leant on it, tied their dogs to it and were eating their lunch in the sun: muddy fingers around red cans of McEwan's Export or buns in half-unwrapped Cellophane. Seeing Laura's Jeep, one of them opened the gate while the others stood aside. Some looked, some didn't, just went on talking to one another in accents incomprehensible to David.

The shooting party stood at the other end of the yard, boots planted in amongst the rotting hay and spots of manure that littered the rough concrete at the door to the barn. They were drinking bull-shot – clear fortified soup – from hot pottery beakers with no handles, and making a lot of noise.

'Hundred and fifty,' said Edmund, handing a ten-pound note to Benjy Steele. Benjy put it in his pocket, made a note of the figure on a pad of paper, and looked at Mel, who laughed.

'God, Benjy. I don't know. What are we on at the moment?'

'You can't ask him that!'

Benjy jerked his great round head in the direction of the pheasants on the cart. 'Take a guess,' he said. 'And then add whatever you think we'll get this afternoon.'

'Ninety?'

Edmund laughed through the steam from his beaker. 'That's not very polite.'

Grinning, Mel turned again to Benjy. 'Can I give you my money when we get back? I haven't got anything with me.'

Edmund took another note out of his pocket and

put it in Benjy's. 'I'll do it,' he said. 'Seems a bit mean to take advantage of the poor girl's ignorance.'

'What ignorance?' said Joss, approaching with the jug of bull-shot.

'Mel's.'

'I'm sure Mel's not ignorant.'

They held out their beakers and, as he poured it in, Mel laughed. 'I'm afraid I am,' she said, 'when it comes to shooting.'

'Only because you're a woman.'

'Watch it . . .'

Joss smiled. 'I'm only saying that, as women don't shoot, it's not surprising you know less about –'

'I'm sure some women do,' said Mel – slurping at her drink and thinking of what Annabel Glass had said at breakfast. Which century were these people in?

'Yes I know, but –'

Mel brought the mug down. 'But what, Joss?'

'Well – well, look at today: all the guns are men.'

Mel smiled. 'I imagine that's because you don't invite women to shoot.'

'They don't want to shoot.'

'How can you be sure?'

Edmund looked out across the yard, at Laura and David getting out of the car. They were picking their way carefully towards the barn, heads bent, avoiding the pats of manure and puddles from the night's rain. Joss followed his gaze for a moment, and then looked back at Mel.

'All right then. I'll lend you my gun, and you can try your hand this afternoon.'

Mel's smile vanished. 'Oh, Joss, I didn't mean –'

'Well, make up your mind,' said Joss, laughing. 'Either you want to shoot, or you don't. Which is it going to be?'

Mel flushed. And suddenly, telling herself that so long as she didn't enjoy it, so long as she wasn't doing it for fun – and anyway, these birds led healthy lives, they'd be eaten, it wasn't entirely wrong – she resolved to give it a try. The one thing she didn't want to happen was for Joss to think he could get away with saying things like that. Someone needed to make a stand, and something made her think that the likes of Rachel and Annabel wouldn't.

'I'll do it,' she said.

Edmund kicked some dry mud across the concrete and turned to her. 'Have you shot before?'

'No.'

He put a hand on her shoulder. 'Mel, listen. You can't just go out with a gun. Not without proper instructions. If you want to learn how to shoot, I'll teach you. But you can't just go out there without any lessons. You could kill someone.'

'Oh, Ned,' said Joss, 'don't be such a spoilsport.'

Edmund shook his head. 'It's not –'

'Mel wants to show us that women are every bit as good as men, and I say we should let her.'

'It's not safe.'

'Not safe to let a woman near a gun?' Grinning, Joss turned to Mel. 'What do you say to that?'

'Well, Joss. Let's just say I could get very unsafe indeed – in your direction – if you go on being so –'

'Don't look at me! It was Ned . . .'

Edmund took the mug of bull-shot from Mel's hands. 'All right,' he said. 'Have it your way. But I'm giving you a lesson. And, for God's sake, don't drink any more.'

Trestle tables with tablecloths had been set out, end to end, inside the barn. Salads, pâtés, breads and cheeses, grapes, apples, biscuits, decanters of claret, all sat along the length of the tables. With the exception of the large sunlit square of doorway – large enough to fit any kind of farm machinery through – the barn was dark. It was old, much older than the house, with rows of massive rafters in the ceiling. But they were hardly visible on sunny days when it took so long for the eyes to get accustomed.

David sat at the end of the table facing the doorway with Annabel on his right and Miranda on his left. They'd finished eating. He had a glass of port in his hand, and was enjoying the extremes of light, the shadows of the party stretching away from him against the day, sitting at the table, some leaning forward over their food, and some back, chatting. And always there was Laura.

David watched her peel an apple, showing Harry Denham that she could do it in one smooth go, without breaking the peel. He watched the apple in her hands – turning swiftly – the ribbon of peel dangling in an S to her lap. He smiled as she reached the end.

'Throw it!' said Harry. 'Go on Laura – over your shoulder!'

Laura stood up. She turned and tossed the peel high – up over the table, into the afternoon light. Then it fell to the floor and they all looked to see what shape it made.

'Well, it isn't a J,' said someone, laughing.

'Looks like an O. Who's an O?'

'Or a U?'

'But we haven't got an O – or a U.'

'Or a C?'

David went on staring at it – trying and failing, with stupid persistence, to find a D in its crisp green curl.

'Are you drunk?'

'No.'

'OK.' With an automatic check to see that it was free from cartridges, Edmund passed her his shotgun. 'Hold this.'

Mel held it, barrels in the air.

'Not too heavy?'

'No.'

'Right,' said Edmund, taking it back and heading round to the field beyond the barn. Mel followed. She stopped next to him, their backs to the barn, looking out to where the field curved away, into the autumn sky.

'Maybe you think that what I'm about to say is obvious,' he began, 'but it's amazing how stupid people can be with guns.'

Mel looked at the mud on her boots.

'*Never* point your gun at anybody,' Edmund went on, 'even if you know it isn't loaded. That means, Mel, that when you're not shooting, you must always hold it the way you're holding it now. Don't try and be clever. Don't sling it over your shoulder or anything. I know I do that, but you can't.'

Mel nodded.

'Never point it at anyone. Never even *risk* pointing it at anyone – not even in jest. And certainly never point it down a valley, or into a wood, or anywhere you can't see . . . Mel?'

Mel looked up.

'You still want to do this?'

'Yes.'

'OK. Now here's how you hold it.'

Flicking her fringe out of her eyes, Mel let Edmund put the gun in her arms. He nestled the stock firmly into her right shoulder, placed her left hand underneath the cold grey barrels, and arranged her fingers over the trigger. She could smell the special gun oil he used to clean it with.

'Don't grip too tightly. And don't drop it either!' he laughed as he caught it. 'These things aren't cheap. OK – got it? Good. Now the thing about moving targets is that you have to catch up with them, then move through them – fire a little ahead – to stand a hope in hell of connecting. And remember you just squeeze the trigger – a calm, controlled squeeze – don't pull at it . . .'

It was with a subdued expression that, ten minutes later, Mel followed him back into the yard.

'Are you really going to do it?' said David.

'Yes, she is,' said Edmund, taking the gun from her while she climbed over the gate.

'Aren't you nervous?'

'Bit.'

'Good.' Edmund reached over the gate to give back the gun and then swung over it himself. 'Now we need to get you some more cartridges, and we need to find out which peg we –'

312

'Hey!' yelled Joss across the yard. 'Yee-haa! It's Calamity Jane!'

They rattled over fields in a convoy of Land Rovers and Jeeps. November sun stretched at the landscape. It pulled tree shadows into ever-thinner strands, drew flat ovals from the wheels of the vehicles, and great long legs with pinball heads from everyone as they got out.

Edmund took Mel quickly away, up the field to their peg. He wanted to get her settled before the drive began. They were followed by Benjy and Miranda, and then Harry – whose wife, Rachel, had decided she'd had enough for one day, had left the dog with him and had gone back to the house. Harry looked round the group by the Land Rovers. 'Laura,' he said. 'Want to come and stand with me?'

Laura smiled, thanked him, and explained that she'd be with Joss.

'Oh, Joss doesn't need you! Come with me. Come on . . .'

Laura shook her head. 'Take Annabel,' she said, and went over to where Joss was talking to the keeper.

David watched her. He watched the gloved hand tuck round Joss's arm while Joss continued talking. He watched her pressing at her husband and then, unable to bear it, he looked away. He should, he knew, be thinking about Mel. Mel shooting. According to Laura, he should probably be getting possessive and angry about the fact that Mel was with his brother. Instead, he felt that way about Laura. More than ever, after all the things they'd done that morning, alone together in her bedroom, with all those clothes. And he was eaten up with misery that she belonged – yes, belonged – to someone else.

His eye wandered up the field to where Mel stood with Edmund. She was looking good. Her rough short hair suited the conditions. She reminded him of a resistance fighter with that sage-green jacket belted at the waist, the shotgun upright in her hands, mouth slightly open as she listened to Edmund. David couldn't hear what Ned was saying, but he imagined it would be similar to the things that their father had told them when he'd first put guns in their adolescent clasp. Safety, at all times. He remembered the childish rhymes – *All the pheasants ever bred, won't repay for one man dead* – and went on gazing at them, searching his heart for the natural jealousy that Laura had spoken about. But there was nothing. Nothing beyond a nagging sense of guilt at his own detachment, and at the effect Laura was having on him. He began to wonder what madness the coming week alone with her would bring him to.

'Now,' said Joss, walking back towards the cars, 'where's that gorgeous blonde loader of mine? Where's – Hey, Annabel! What are you doing?'

Annabel was halfway up the plough with Harry. She turned and stopped.

'Annabel!' Joss called again.

'I'll stand with you,' said Laura, still holding the arm. Still pressing it.

Joss kissed her. 'Not when I have lovely Annabel!'

'But I'd like to.'

'You must learn not to be such a little wife, my angel! We're not joined at the hip. You go and stand

314

with David. Go on – you'll get a great view from the gate. And we'll see you later. Annabel!' he yelled, detaching himself. 'Come on. We're over here.'

Annabel did as she was told. She liked standing with Joss. She liked his chatter, his compliments, his attention. She thought it was naughty of him to have spent all morning complaining about the way Laura ran his shooting weekends – poor Laura was new to it all. But Annabel also understood how important it was for a man like Joss to have a wife that knew how to do these things. And if he implied that she, Annabel, would be able to do it blindfold, well, she couldn't exactly stop him. Taking his cartridge bag, Annabel positioned herself behind Joss, and looked up the line of guns. She looked at Mel with Ned's loaded shotgun in her hands, his cartridge bag flung to the ground. Ned was reminding Mel how to stand – feet firm, left foot slightly in front, properly balanced.

Mel had the gun up. Waiting, her ears blocked with small rubber plugs. Her hands were cold, her shoulders stiff. Edmund moved behind her, to the left. The wind had dropped and the land, touched by the last of the sun, seemed to Mel to be more beautiful than ever. Absolutely still. What was she doing with a gun in her hands, her heart a battle drum? Beside her, Edmund was looking in the direction of the wood, at the beeches with their pewter branches, all in shadow now.

'About to start,' he said. She could only just hear. Pressing her cheek back to the smooth walnut stock of the gun, she waited there, looking up its barrels into an empty sky.

But her eye was back on the landscape when the

birds – pushed by the line of beaters – began to emerge from the wood. Edmund was the one to see them first: a fine flush of eight or nine, flying well. He touched Mel's shoulder and pointed.

'There!'

Too late.

'You must concentrate – There! There! To your left.'

Too late again. And as the bird flew between them and the Steeles, Mel brought her gun back.

'Good girl. *Any* doubt at all, then don't – There! Straight up! Over!'

Mel swung the gun up and squeezed the trigger.

Edmund laughed. 'You had your eyes shut. And again!'

Swing and squeeze.

'Too far behind. Reload.'

Mel pushed the barrels down, picked out the smoking cartridges while Edmund put two new ones in.

'To your right,' he said.

Swing and squeeze.

'Again?'

Squeeze.

'No, sweetheart. You're still much too far behind. Here,' he held out another pair of cartridges, and smiled. 'You're doing great . . . there. Now here's more. Fix on just one, if you can, and fire *ahead* . . . Never mind. It's bloody difficult. Here . . .'

By the time the horn went off, signifying the end of the drive and the end of the day, Mel had yet to bring a bird down. Smiling, she handed the gun back to Edmund.

'That's me put well and truly in my place.'

'You did fine.'

Mel said nothing.

Edmund zipped the gun into the long canvas slip he used, slung it over his arm, and picked up the cartridge bag. 'You were safe, Mel. You should be pleased. And anyway,' he grinned, 'fuck them. You'll win the sweepstake, if nothing else. Ninety, did you say?'

They walked back to the vehicles, to bland smiles from the other guns, and predictable remarks from Joss.

'Well, I think it was great of you to try,' said Laura. 'Just great!'

Joss laughed. 'Lord, what have we started? Next thing we'll be having ladies' days.'

Throwing his birds on the cart, he turned to Harry, approaching with birds hanging from his fingers. 'Want to do a bit of flighting? Don reckons there'll be some duck at the lower pool.'

'Great.'

'Anyone else? Benjy? Ned? . . . Mel?'

Edmund touched Mel's arm. 'You want another go?' he said. 'It's less frantic than driven birds. We just wait in the undergrowth for them to come in for the night. You'll like it.'

Mel raised her eyes to a sky that was clear – clear, except for a smoky streak of cloud, low on the horizon, lined in deep pink from a sun that had already set. Was it worth it? She'd only miss again and feel an even greater fool.

Edmund saw her thoughts. He saw, beyond her upturned face, the darker forms of David and Laura, against the gate. They weren't looking at each other.

Edmund held out the gun.

'I think you should,' he said, and she took it.

It felt much quieter, and darker, after the others left: headlights flashing towards the road. Four of them – Joss, Harry, Edmund and Mel – were left. With Joss in front, they walked in single file along the side of the field, cut through a thin copse at the bottom corner, over a gate, and down to the bank of the river.

Joss looked round for Ned and then pointed to a gnarled tree on his left, a tree that hung its twisted branches out over the silver swirl of water. 'I reckon you and Mel should take that position there, see? By the tree?' He spoke in a low voice, almost a whisper, and Edmund nodded. 'Harry'll be down there, by the bridge,' Joss went on. 'OK?'

'OK.'

'And I'll be fifty yards on from that – other side – round the bend.'

Edmund nodded again.

'Shouldn't have to wait too long now. They'll be coming from the west, which is there,' Joss pointed at the fading glow.

Mel followed Edmund towards the gnarled tree. He stood for her at the bank, took the gun from her and placed it against the tree as he offered her his hand. Mel leant on it as she clambered down to the muddy area of grass and rushes. She stood watching while Edmund turned to the canvas gun slip. He zipped it open, and took out the gun. With a series of subdued metallic noises, he took a pair of cartridges from his belt, dropped them into the barrels and clicked the gun shut. Further away, against what was left of the day, Joss's great big body and Harry's slimmer one, followed by swish-tailed dogs, crossed the wooden bridge and parted. Harry slipped down into the shadows on one side, and Joss – over the bank – on the other.

Mel took the gun from Edmund, and stood where he told her.

'You might be able to hear them before you see them . . . quacking, or beating wings – sort of whistling sound . . . over in a matter of seconds, so you must stay on the ball – and remember to fire ahead – further than last time.'

She was looking in the right direction – due west – when they appeared. Three of them in a lopsided V. They were higher than she'd expected, aiming for a pool further upstream.

'There!' breathed Edmund.

She nodded.

'Stand a bit further out – closer to the water – that's right, and don't forget Joss and Harry in front of you.'

There was a shattering blast as Joss fired: once, and then again. But the birds merely swerved to the right and flew on past Harry, who was out of shot.

'Go for it,' said Edmund. 'Go on – now!'

Mel swung the barrels round.

'Now!' said Edmund again, and she squeezed.

For a second, she thought she'd missed. Then another awful second, when she thought she'd just wounded it. And then a strange combination of feelings, wrapped in relief, when the one that faltered fell, hard into the water, and the other two continued on their path.

She could see it there in the middle of the river, the

water carrying it back towards the bridge. Then there was a quick low, '*Goo-on* then, girl,' from Harry, and his young yellow Labrador was in the water, paddling out of her depth, neck straining.

'*Good* girl. *Good* girl. *Goo-on.*'

They watched Harry's dog collect the duck, swim back against the stream with its heavy weight in her mouth. Her tail wagged in the half-light – sprays of silver, left and right – as she came out of the water.

The Steelcs' Land Rover was old and shaky. The windscreen had only one wiper, and was spattered with mud. The front seats were covered with torn fake leather, and hard metal benches faced each other in the back. Annabel sat on one of the benches as Benjy drove them home, with her sister in the passenger seat. She couldn't help thinking of how often it had been like that: Benjy and Miranda – husband and wife – comfortable in the front, while she, Annabel, spinster sister, bumped around in the back. And it was some bumping around: her slim bottom hit hard on the metal. For once, she wished it was more like Miranda's.

They were talking about the day.

'What I don't understand,' said Miranda, twisting round, 'is why you weren't standing with Ned.'

'Because he was with Mel.'

'Yes, but why? Wasn't it obvious that you were meant to be with him?'

Annabel felt for one of the metal bars on the roof to hold on to, as Benjy lurched into the road. 'He was teaching her to shoot,' she said.

'Teaching her to shoot? Fine time for that, don't you think? And what about the morning?'

'I was OK, Miranda. Really. Joss was lovely.'

'Fat lot of good Joss'll do you. I mean, it's all right for whatshername – Mel. She's got her man. She's engaged. But you're still out there. It's staggeringly selfish of her to hog the only spare one all day, don't you think?'

Annabel shrugged.

'It's so *rude*,' Miranda went on. 'I mean, you've obviously been invited up for Ned: to partner him, and entertain him, and – and he's just ignoring you.'

Annabel listened. She hated her sister's pity. Hated sitting there, bumping up and down, while Miranda pointed out – again and again – that yet another man was ignoring *poor* Annabel. She hated Edmund, for putting her through this humiliation, again. And Mel. She hated Benjy, for driving insensitively. She hated all of them.

All of them except Joss who, one hour later, when the duck flighting party returned, came to find her in the little sitting room; who opened a bottle of champagne and poured her a nice big glass; who clinked it against his own glass of whisky and thanked her for being with him all day.

Annabel smiled, and drank. 'It was a pleasure.'

Joss sat down next to her on the sofa. He was still in his shooting clothes, but he'd kicked off his boots and was just in his socks. His body took up most of the sofa, but Annabel didn't mind. Still smiling, she played with the links on her silver bracelet. Loosened by champagne, her thoughts began to flow more freely.

Joss clinked the glasses again. 'We make a great team,' he said.

24

Mel stood in the boot room – a cave-like place with a stone floor and stone walls and about four great boilers at the far end – laughing into warm-wet air. Scarves, hats, gloves and gumboot socks had been hung to dry in rows on the great old pipes that lined the walls. The floor was littered with lumps of drying mud, dirty towelling dog bags, and discarded rubber boots: some black, some green, some in pairs against the wall, but most lay scattered where their occupants had stepped out of them. Edmund sat on a rickety wooden chair. He kicked off his own gumboots in two swift movements and began taking off his coat.

They were talking about the sweepstake. The bag had totalled a hundred and ten, which meant that Mel had won. Her bet had been the closest. But if Edmund had been shooting that last drive they'd have got another twenty, and Benjy would have won.

She stood on a wooden boot-pull with one foot, put the other into the 'V' and yanked up her leg.

'I'd no idea it was so much money,' she said, still laughing. 'Will they think I did it deliberately?'

Edmund threw the coat on to one of the boilers and wondered whether to wind her up. He was beginning to get the measure of her and knew now that he could – easily. But something held him back.

'They'll just be jealous. I'm jealous. Over a hundred pounds . . . We'll be sucking up to you like mad. You can take us all out to lunch tomorrow.'

'Joss said I should give it to the Countryside Alliance.'

'Give them half.'

Smiling, Mel picked up her shoes. 'Not sure David would approve.'

'None of David's business.'

It wasn't until later, cleaning his gun – spraying oil down its barrels, and then forcing small screwed up bits of loo paper from one end to the other with a special rod – that Edmund turned his thoughts to David, and Mel. Poking in the ball of paper, jabbing it down with a rising bup-bop-bip noise that resonated round the gunroom, he sighed.

Even as early as that lunch at Virginia's flat – with all that talk of churches and tiaras, and David quiet in the background – Edmund had harboured doubts. But because of what had happened with Alice, because of his work, and Annabel Glass, and flat hunting, he'd let it slip from the forefront of his mind. Now, however, in different surroundings, and with Laura Savil's beauty so absolutely present . . . Ned knew his brother too well. The sight of him that afternoon beside Laura, against the gate, thoughtful in the half-light, it was enough. David hadn't changed. His passion for Lauras was strong as ever. And Mel . . . Mel, it seemed, was just a front.

The oily wad of paper flew out of the end of his barrel with a pop, and Edmund began on the next.

You idiot, he thought, forcing the paper through. You prat. Where do you think this is going to end? Do you honestly think a woman like Laura Savil is going to kick in a lifestyle like this for your piddling studio in Battersea? Forget it. Any woman who looks like that and marries a man like Joss is bound to have ulterior motives. And what about the others involved here? Joss was all right – he'd be able to keep Laura to heel. But Mel?

Edmund thought of her: flushed and grinning in the boot room, shoeless feet in misshapen socks, padding off with a 'Thanks, Ned. Thanks for a lovely day', off upstairs for a bath, off to find David and tell him about her duck. He put the rod down, held up the gun barrels and peered along the length of the one he'd just cleaned. The tunnel of silver-grey concentric rings shone bright, and stretched his eye towards the light like an inverted telescope.

Mel's none of your business, he told himself, and turned to the other barrel.

David had had his bath. He was dressed in the same dinner jacket he'd worn at Mel's office party, and was putting on his shoes with a shoehorn when she came in: grubby, red in the face, and smiling.

'How was it?'

'Good!' she said, putting her things on the bed and going to the mirror. Oh Lord, look at the colour in her cheeks. Almost as bad as Benjy's. 'I shot a duck!'

David slipped on the other shoe. 'I thought you disapproved of blood sports,' he said.

Mel went into the bathroom and closed the door. The room was tall and lit with low-wattage lamps that would make it impossible for her to put her make-up on properly. An ancient boiler hung from the ceiling.

Next door she heard the sounds of David leaving the room. She heard him walk down the passage towards the stairs. He was right, of course. She did disapprove. What's more, she couldn't even justify what she'd done by saying that it wasn't any fun. Because it was. Great fun. Thrilling, in fact – and wrong. But couldn't he have said, 'Well done'? Couldn't he have been pleased for her, instead of this distant treatment? It was almost as if she'd done something terrible to offend him.

Bending over the cavernous bath, Mel turned on the taps, put in the plug and thought again of what it might be. It crossed her mind that perhaps he was annoyed about Edmund. Today was the first day that she and Edmund had really got on well, so maybe David was jealous. Maybe that was it. Throwing in far too many drops of Laura's bath oil – suffocating the room with the smell of stephanotis – Mel smiled sadly at the unlikeliness of it being as simple as that. She remembered too well the way she'd felt in bed that morning. She remembered the way she'd felt when David hadn't wanted to look at wedding venues. She remembered the night with Nathan and Fenella, and the way she'd felt afterwards.

Sure, she couldn't expect rosy happiness all the time. Sure, there'd be bad patches. But was it normal, she wondered, to feel so sad so soon?

Mel pulled off her clothes. Leaving them in a pile on the floor, she stood – tall and naked – over the bath, swilling the water round until it was the right temperature for her to get in.

David reached the end of the passage and turned towards the staircase, passing a bedroom with the door ajar.

'It's not really her fault,' said Harry Denham's voice. 'The girl's American. How can she know everything?'

'She should try a bit harder, or ask for help. I'd happily show her the ropes.'

'Maybe she wants to do it her way.'

'Bit late for that,' said Rachel, 'don't you think? If Laura wanted to do things her way, she shouldn't have married Joss. And now that she has, she should knuckle down and get on with doing the job properly, so that the poor man isn't –'

'Joss? Poor?'

'Oh, *Harry*!' Rachel was laughing. 'Stop day-dreaming about the way that girl looks. Breakfast was awful – I've never seen Flunky look so miserable. And then, as if that wasn't enough, she announces that she's not even bothering to come out with us. Goes off instead with that rather wet artist who's clearly never held a gun in his life.'

David stopped in his tracks.

'. . . she's not even trying.'

'Hang on there,' said Harry. 'Joss did tell her to go back inside, you know. He said –'

'He was just being *nice*,' said Rachel, coming up to the door. 'Or gooey-eyed, like the rest of you.'

The door closed.

David walked on to the top of the stairs and, thinking of what he'd heard, of the life that Laura had chosen, and of how that differed from where she belonged, he began to go down. He walked slowly, looking at the paintings on the walls – mostly landscapes, early nineteenth century, with heavy gilt frames. He was still looking at them when he heard a door open, this time below. It was the swing door that led straight into the kitchen and it squeaked back and forth on its hinge.

'Don't put that in just yet,' said Laura's voice. 'We won't be eating until nine at the soonest, and I don't want it overdone. . . . Really? Well, hang in there, will you? I'll be back in one moment, once I've put this damn thing down somewhere.'

David bent over the banisters to see Laura directly from above. She was barefoot, dressed in loose black chiffon trousers and a strappy spangly top, carrying a long silver platter – piled high with oysters and ice – in her arms.

'Oysters!' said Joss, appearing from the hall, still dressed in his shooting clothes. Laura stopped for him to take one. Joss squirted lemon on to it and knocked it back down his throat. 'Fantastic.'

She smiled. 'Helen got them from that market down by Lindisfarne – you know, the one George was telling us about.'

'Helen?'

'Mrs Samuels. Oh, and, darling, she and Denise *can* stay on. She said that was fine – until midnight, if you need them.'

'Sweetheart,' Joss took another oyster, 'you must *not* start calling her Helen.'

Laura shifted the plate so that it sat more evenly between her arms.

'If you call her Helen, what will I call Samuels?'

'Jim?'

Joss swallowed the oyster and laughed. 'I can't call him Jim! And I definitely can't call her Helen. No, Laura. Don't walk away from me when I'm talking to you.'

'I just need to put these down, honey.'

'Come back here.'

'They're heavy, Joss, and there's no room to –'

'Come *here* when I tell you.' He pulled at her arm, and the plate fell.

It was solid silver and didn't break, but the contents splashed to the ground. Oysters and ice cubes shot out in all directions, pearly shells scattering through the milky puddle, pulling dribbles of white with them, out over rugs, under chairs and cupboards, and over Laura's bare feet.

'Mrs Samuels?' Joss called out. 'Mrs Samuels?'

A young woman with shiny dark hair appeared at the door to the kitchen.

'Mrs Savil has had an accident. Would you be so good as to clear it up for her? And find something else for us to pick at before dinner, would you? Some crisps, perhaps. And, Laura, darling, you must get some shoes. No wonder you tripped! We're not at the beach . . .'

He went upstairs for his bath, passing David on the landing.

'Hello,' he said cheerfully. 'Got everything you need? There's champagne in the drawing room – just help yourself. I'm afraid you'll have to ignore poor Laura's little accident. Yes, I know,' he smiled and looked back over the banisters to where both Laura and Helen were wiping up. 'Poor darling. Still

328

finding her feet – and what lovely little feet they are! Oh, and if you prefer whisky, there's a drinks cupboard under the stairs. All right? Great! Well – can't hang around . . .'

Three hours later, Laura was sitting at the head of an extended dining-room table, watching the candles burn. It was bonfire night, and the twenty or thirty guests – more people had been invited down from Edinburgh for dinner, to see the fireworks display that Joss had orchestrated – were just finishing their cheese.

The mood around the table was wild. Some of the Edinburgh crowd had brought cocaine. Others had brought babies and put them to sleep upstairs. Some had brought both. An air of recklessness ran through the room, in the way people were drinking, the careless way they filled their glasses, spilling wine on the damask. Chairs were now in disarray – pushed round, or shifted back. One woman was sitting on another's lap.

A game of forfeits had begun at Joss's end. Couples started to swap clothes: Rachel Denham's velvet skirt found its way on to her husband's hips, stretching over his hairy legs, with her small appliquéd top splitting at his chest as he chatted to Benjy about foot-and-mouth disease. A giggling Miranda Steele crawled under the table to tickle the feet – or whatever she liked – of whomsoever she liked. David felt her jewelled fingers crawling up his trouser leg and shot back to see her gazing up at him, her head fringed by the tablecloth, laughing uncontrollably.

'I'm sorry, darling.' She clambered out, pressing

hard on one of his thighs to raise herself up. 'But you really shouldn't have been wearing loafers.'

'Forfeit!' yelled someone.

With Benjy insisting he fill it up first, David was made to finish the wine in his glass and the game moved on.

Things were rather more dignified at Laura's end, but eyes were brightening, port and joints were moving up in their direction. It wouldn't take long. David pulled his chair back in, lit a cigarette, and observed what was happening at the surface of the table – in amongst the candles, the silver and the fruit. He saw hands everywhere: reaching for grapes, fingering half-eaten biscuits, playing with spills of wax – the drops that had hardened mid-fall; hands that swilled red wine around the mass of precious glass, or knocked cigarette ash tumbling from the trays. And beyond all that was Laura. He hadn't been able to speak to her, but he'd been watching. He saw how quiet and still she was, how absolutely detached.

Edmund, meanwhile, was sitting next to Annabel, irritated to find himself, yet again, thrown next to her. Knowing that someone somewhere was trying to set them up, and suspecting that Annabel herself had something to do with it, Ned spent most of dinner with his back to her, talking to the woman on his other side. He knew it was rude, he knew he shouldn't be doing it and eventually, over pudding, his conscience won through.

Annabel had been drinking. He knew this not because she appeared drunk (if anything, she seemed rather quiet) but because he'd been filling her glass.

He'd been doing it instinctively all evening: reaching round to the right to top it up, before continuing with the conversation on his left. She must have drunk a bottle by now, and again the glass was empty. Filling it, and staying with her this time, he asked how she'd enjoyed the day.

'It was fine,' said Annabel, not looking at him.

'Nice to be out, in this weather . . .'

Annabel drank, and said nothing.

'. . . and weren't we lucky with the sun!'

'Yes,' up went the glass, and up again. 'Yes, I suppose so.'

'Must be nice for you,' said Edmund, smiling. 'Everything you do, everywhere you go – all new material for your writing.'

Annabel stared at the empty glass.

'I should think a shooting party like this would –'

'It's already been done.'

'Oh.'

Searching for some new subject, Ned looked out across the table, to where Mel was sitting. She was flushed and listening to Benjy with good-natured concentration as he told her about a gun he had with one barrel on top of the other as opposed to side by side. Nodding carefully, she glanced round. And, catching Ned looking at her, she smiled.

'. . . of course, the real advantage is timing,' said Benjy's voice. 'See . . .'

Ned smiled back. He'd never seen Mel look so well, so healthy. She was usually rather pale. But tonight she was warm: warm in the candlelight, warm towards Benjy, and warm towards him. Her hair was washed now. Not rough, as it had been in the boot room, but black and sleek and parted at the side with a broken fringe. She looked French.

Next to him, Annabel stretched for the bottle.

'Let me.'

Silently, Annabel let him take it and watched as he filled her glass.

'So,' he smiled, socially, 'how's the book coming on?'

Annabel looked at him. She must have been very drunk, but all he could see was pain – pain out of all proportion – and Ned couldn't rid himself of the notion that she was simply feeling sorry for herself.

'You haven't even read it, have you?'

He almost said, 'Read what?'

'You've had it for weeks and you haven't read a word.'

'It's not because I don't want to read it, Annabel. It's because I've had –'

'More important things to do. I understand.'

'It's not like that. I'll read it this week. I promise. And then I'll –'

'Forget it,' she snapped.

'But, Annabel, I –'

'Just forget it.'

Ned was still looking for the right thing to say when Joss stood up, glass in his hand, and a cigarette between his fingers.

'Right!' he bellowed. 'Fireworks! Get your boots on. We'll be starting in about five minutes, out on the west terrace, and you can have coffee when we get back.'

There was a general shifting of chairs and draining of glasses as people started to stand up. Edmund turned to an empty chair. He wondered for a moment if he should try to find her, and decided not to bother. If Annabel didn't want to be with him, he should leave her alone. And if she did want to be with him – if she wanted him to follow her to some place more discreet – then all the more reason to stick with the others.

They went back through the hall, Edmund with them, searching for gumboots, and coats that they could pull on over little lacy dresses and velvet smoking jackets. Joss was at the door, distributing umbrellas.

'You all right there, Ned?'

Edmund nodded.

'Great! Great! Hennie, you'll need a thicker coat than that – take one from the boot room if you . . . Anyone else for an umbrella? Umbrella, anyone? Annabel! My little blonde loader, where've you been hiding? Have an umbrella . . . here. No, I insist. Or – OK, why don't we share it?'

Edmund followed them out. He saw Annabel lean in close to Joss, hugging his arm, and suspected it was more for his benefit. She knew Ned was behind them. She knew he'd be worried about her. But instead of making Ned feel jealous, he simply felt relieved. And, reaching the terrace, he slipped round to the right and joined Mel, Benjy and Miranda sitting on the wall under a golfing umbrella, with their feet dangling down, drinking brandy from the bottle.

'*Oh*, I'm so excited,' said Miranda, shifting up to make room for him. 'Last year, we had almost half an hour of the most incredible – I mean really incredible, mind-blowing – rockets. Don't know where he gets them from –'

'Some friend in Hong Kong,' said Benjy.

'– but don't they go! We even had the policeman out from Hedlawburn. Or maybe that was the year before.'

Edmund sat on the far side of the wall, next to Mel, who was wrapped in a coat, swinging her legs and smiling. She didn't fit under the golfing umbrella, but she didn't seem to mind. Her eyelashes glistened in the floodlights.

'How are you?'

'Wet,' she said, laughing, wiping them. 'Wet and drunk.'

He passed her the bottle. 'Well, have some more, then.'

Mel drank, passed the bottle on to Miranda, and turned back to Ned.

'How was dinner?' she said, with a particular look in her eye.

Ned raised his eyes to the rain.

'That bad?'

He glanced at Miranda, who was still chatting to her husband about last year's fireworks, and lowered his voice. 'It's not really Annabel I object to, it's the whole set-up thing. I hate it. Absolutely can't bear to be thrown together with –'

'Especially when your interest lies elsewhere,' said Mel, smiling.

'What?'

'Alice told me.'

'Told you what?'

'About the flowers! Oh, you old romantic. Honestly

334

. . . No, don't pretend you don't know what I'm talking about! I *know*. Orchids – wasn't it? And lilies, I heard. Masses and masses of them – so many, she couldn't even carry them home! But if I were you, I'd be straight with Annabel, and –'

'Ssh . . .'

'Sorry.' Mel lowered her voice. 'Just tell her you're keen on someone else. I'm sure she'd understand.'

'But, Mel, I'm not interested in Alice. Not any more. I –'

'Ned . . .'

'I'm not.'

'Then why on earth did you send her all those flowers?'

'I didn't,' he said, but his words were drowned out by an explosion so massive, it shook the terrace wall.

Mel lip-read his response.

'Rubbish,' she mouthed back.

'It's true!'

Shaking her head and laughing, she turned to the display.

David, meanwhile, was still inside. He had his coat on, and was waiting for Laura. He waited in the hall with an umbrella, heard the first explosions, but still she didn't come. Going back inside, he crossed the hall and checked the dining room, then the drawing room, and then the kitchen. Two women were in there: one washing up, one drying and feeding titbits to Flunky and Badger.

'Seen Laura anywhere?' he said.

The women shook their heads.

He went back, still holding the umbrella, and out

to the west terrace, where Joss's pyrotechnics thundered into the rain. The party stood under dark umbrellas, heads raised at the same angle, with the pulse of flashes reflected in their eyes. Behind them, in the windows, bursts of flame repeated themselves all over the front of the house.

And upstairs – at the corner – a bedroom light went on inside, and a curtain closed.

After that, the party disintegrated. Some of the newcomers – the ones with children – collected their offspring and left. Others decided to stay the night. The party lost its centre. It sprawled into the billiard room, the drawing room, Joss's little sitting room, and back into the dining room. Someone ran out to a car to collect a couple of CDs and put them on Joss's system: acid jazz, cutting through conversation, drowning out order, and easing them on to a more anarchic rhythm.

The washers-up finished quickly. They hung up their cloths and left, shutting the dogs in the boot room with their water bowls and toys. David saw them leave, and wondered what they thought. Turning from the window, he walked back through the hall to where Miranda Steele and Rachel Denham were dancing on the stairs. One fat, one thin. They danced down, laughing, and offered him their cigarettes.

'No thanks, Rachel. Really . . .'

They weren't listening. Rachel's nose, Miranda's chin – all exaggerated by drink – circling for a moment in ridiculous mock seduction, tugging at the coat he was still wearing, and then stumbling on. Half impressed, David watched them go. He hadn't expected them to get so crazy, hadn't thought they had it in them.

He decided to go to bed. Still torn up by Laura, he probably wouldn't be able to sleep, but the peace of his bed was surely better than this bedlam. Taking off his coat, he went to leave it in the boot room where Flunky and Badger appealed to him through the thick glass door. David decided not to go in – he wasn't sure quite what he'd do if those dogs ran out – and he went on to the gunroom at the end.

The passage was long, dark and lined by strips of light from doors that opened into more civilised parts of the house. David walked on, muted acid jazz thudding through the walls. He was nearly halfway up its length when he noticed a couple in one of the doorways, silent against the light. The man was backed against the wall in complete darkness. As David watched, the woman undid her top. It was heavy crocheted silk, and fell easily from her back.

Oh God, thought David wearily, and stopped with the coat in his hands. How often was he going to have to stumble across things he shouldn't be seeing? Were country houses deliberately designed with this in mind? He looked again: at the limbs and clothes and long pale hair; at straps slipping, skirts shifting; at the man's hands pressing to undo more, and the woman pulling away. Pulling and turning . . .

It was Annabel Glass.

'Little loader . . .'

'Not here,' she said, with a low laugh. 'We really can't do it here. Someone might –'

'Then come upstairs.'

'But what about the others? Won't they notice?'

Joss moved into the light, his shirt crumpled, and bent to pick up the crocheted top. 'No one will notice.' He hooked the top clumsily over her shoulders. 'Not if we go now. Your room's not far, and if we go up the back stairs, past the nursery, no one will see us at all.'

David stood in darkness, watching them leave through a door at the end – voices fading.

Edmund sat on a sofa, smoking, with the rest of the party spinning, dancing, laughing, falling, twirling on around him.

The second Mel had mentioned Alice's flowers, he'd known who they were from. He knew Joss too well. This was the old Joss, the pre-Laura Joss, the man who got crushes on impossible women, and then made extravagant gestures. And now he was doing it again. But why? Why – when he had Laura?

Ned ran through the options. Perhaps it was to do with Laura being pregnant – some people were strange about that sort of thing. Maybe Joss was bored. Or maybe he was finding Laura's beauty difficult to live with. All that attention she got . . . maybe he felt competitive towards her. Maybe he needed to undermine it in some way.

There were hundreds of possible reasons. The point was: Joss had sent Alice flowers. And Alice was just too curious, too naughty, too ignorant of what this could do to her, not to respond. She'd go for it. Of course she would. Married man. High society. Fast lane. She'd have the affair, just to see what it was like, and find herself embroiled in secrecy and dirt.

And what if the press found out? Joss would be all right. So would Laura, probably. They'd rise above it in the supposed sanctity of their marriage. But Alice was vulnerable, much more vulnerable than she realised.

25

All over London, intermittent explosions hit the sky. Alice sat on the high flat roof of her parents' house, watching them and drinking. The night was clear and she could see for miles: the lights of Chelsea Harbour to the south and, behind her, the gentle rise of Notting Hill. She listened to the noise – to the mere phut-phuts in the distance while, closer to, came hard bright blasts from the annual firework party in the square gardens below.

Around her – some sitting on the low wall that ran round the perimeter of the roof, some standing in groups in the middle, smouldering cigarette ends dangling from their fingers – a small party of her school friends had started to gather momentum. Roger and Camilla were away visiting friends in Cambridge this weekend and, encouraged by Emily, Alice had decided to take advantage of it. If she couldn't be with Joss, she thought, then a wild party of her own would be the next best thing. But she was starting to wonder, now, if she'd been right.

She'd made an effort with her clothes. She looked, she thought, fabulous. She was geared up for a big night, but something was lacking. The others might have been excited by the bangs, the darkness, and each other, but Alice couldn't find the spark. Bored by the company, and vaguely restless, she decided that the only way she was getting through this evening was if she got drunk.

So she filled her glass from the bottle of warm white wine that Steve and Tim had brought, knocked it back and then refilled it while observing the scene with a critical, if blurry, eye. The roof was dirty and neglected, and covered in grey asphalt that came off on their clothes. It was dominated by covered water tanks, pipes, and disused chimneypots. It had a certain charm. But Alice – still thinking of Joss and Laura's party, the pretty nightlights, the hurricane lamps, the elegant garden – was blind to it. The candles she'd brought up had gone out and the party moved in darkness, startled by occasional bursts of white light that revealed the state of the roof and a sea of self-conscious teenage faces.

Without asking, Alice borrowed Emily's lighter and lit another cigarette. 'Where's Sam?' she said.

Emily didn't know. 'Might have said something about meeting her brother, but I –'

'Johnny?'

'No,' said Emily. 'No, the other one. You remember. The one at Oxford, with the motorbike and the –'

Alice grabbed her arm. 'Not the good-looking one? Not the one you told me about, the one you *fancy*!'

'I don't fancy him. I just –'

'You do! You do!'

'OK,' said Emily, smiling. 'OK. But it's no big deal. I mean, everyone fancies Bruno Mason.'

'Including Bruno Mason?'

Emily laughed. 'Yeah, probably. But . . . well, in any case, he's not interested in me.'

'How do you know?'

'He only likes blondes.'

'What – he *told* you that?'

'Sam did.'

Alice digested this. 'Bummer.'

'Mm.' Emily nodded and ruffled her friend's hair. 'Still. Maybe you'll be in with a chance.'

'Me?'

'Why not? You look great at the moment.'

She was right. Alice had put on a few pounds, but instead of making her bulky it merely made her glow. And underneath the bohemian-looking sheepskin coat that Camilla had worn in the sixties, Alice was wearing her clothes differently. Of the sloppy look that Emily knew – the loose and careless street-cred uniform – Alice had kept only the street-cred. She was wearing a tight black silk shirt, a black leather miniskirt, and sheer black tights. Her feet were in pointed black leather ankle-boots that would have made any but the most perfect legs look awful. Alice's looked gorgeous.

'He'd be in for a bit of a shock,' said Alice, giggling. 'I'm not really blonde.'

'Don't think that'll fuss him.'

Alice shook her head. 'And I'm not interested in undergraduates – however good-looking they think they might be.'

The fireworks in the square were ending when Sam arrived. She rang on the doorbell and, getting no reply, went back down the steps for a better angle.

She waited for a break in the finale of blasts, and shouted up.

'Alice!'

Alice's head appeared over the edge of the rail. The sudden movement, distorted by alcohol, caused her to sway for a second. There was a rushing in her brain. She had to grip the rail to recover her balance, and then the moment passed. She looked down. Far below, she could just about see the bikes in the road, and Sam's distinctive curls. Beside her was a man dressed in leathers, taking off his crash helmet. Alice felt in her coat pocket for the set of keys.

'Catch!' she yelled, tossing them down as another rocket flew into the sky.

Sam caught them, and the sky went berserk with thunderous light. Strobe-like flashes covered the street as she and her brother locked their bikes and approached the door. Alice turned back to the party on the roof. It was hard to see in the blitzed lighting, especially with what the drink was doing to her brain. She could just about make out the forms of Steve and Tim, leaning over one of the water tanks. It wasn't hard to guess what they'd be doing. And, sure enough, as the thunderflashes ceased, Alice's suspicions were confirmed. They were rolling the most enormous joint.

'Hey!' Steve licked it up and waved it at her. 'Hey, Alice. Check this out! It's massive!'

Alice grinned. She went over, trying not to trip on the pipes in her new boots, trying not to look quite as drunk as she felt, while Steve lit the joint. They were smoking it when she got there, passing it between them. But when Tim offered it to Alice, she hesitated.

'Oh, go on.'

'Having enough problems with the alcohol,' she said. 'Not sure it's wise to –'

'Don't be wet.'

Alice took the joint and put it to her lips. It was strong, and she had to swallow her splutter. 'Jesus Christ, Steve,' she said, coughing. 'Where'd you get this shit?'

Steve took it from her. 'Can't remember.'

'He got it from me,' said Tim, and, for no reason, the pair of them convulsed in giggles.

Alice watched them: gawky in their soft-soled shoes, their too-short hair, their designer jackets, giggling helplessly . . . None of it appealed. Whatever that stuff was doing for them, it didn't work for her. She needed better company. But who else was there? Looking round, she assessed the alternative: Hari and Karen could talk only about work. Graham Jones was a hanger-on who hadn't even been invited. Andy, Mike and Seth didn't understand girls at all. They'd be talking about the football, or the latest PlayStation game. As for that group of girls at the far end, they'd only want to talk about the boys, and how dull was that? Apart from Emily, who was now helping Sam up through the hatch, there was no one.

Alice watched as first the crash helmets, and a bottle of wine, then Sam, and finally the brother, emerged. One final firework hit the heavens, and the party on the roof returned to peace and darkness: only a square of yellow light rising from the hatch, and a dim, ever-present city glow. Detaching herself from the hash-fuelled philosophical rubbish that Tim and Steve were spouting, Alice leant over the covered tank and turned her attention to the group by the hatch.

Emily was holding Sam's crash helmet while Sam took off her jacket to reveal an identical top to the one Emily had on. They were pointing at one another's chests and laughing while, beside them, Sam's brother wrapped his leather arms round the smooth curve of his crash helmet and smiled directly at Alice.

Alice smiled back briefly, and looked away, unsure what Emily had meant. How could 'everybody' fancy that? The guy was pretty average. The only immediately noticeable thing about him was his skin – which, like Sam's, was dotted with acne scars. In spite of all the leather, he wasn't really cool. That smile was too nice, too friendly, too safe. He had the intellectual air of a top-grade student. Not tough, in other words. Not challenging. Not a patch on Josslyn Savil's authoritative glamour.

With the fireworks finishing in the square and the night chill working through their clothes, the party moved down to the warmth of the Enderbys' drawing room. Alice discarded her sheepskin coat – left it on the floor – and lit a few candles. She turned off the lights, turned up the music, and helped herself to another glass of wine. Around her, the party was starting to see some action. Outer layers were falling away, leaving skimpy tops, linen shirts and the odd bare midriff. The group of girls that had stuck together on the roof were now operating solo, and the boys hadn't hung around. Hari and Karen – well, that was obvious. Anna and Tim. Sam and . . . oh God, she must be drunk – drunk or mad – Sam and Graham Jones! The guy would be in seventh heaven.

And Emily was engrossed in conversation with Steve.

All good for gossip on Monday and Alice would usually have been in there, in the thick of it: flirting, sparkling, hoping for Tim – or whoever it was – to pay her some attention, while pretending not to care. Now, it left her cold. She needed bigger game and higher stakes. She wanted more sophisticated players. These boys were just too easy to work. Take Sam's brother. He might have interested her once, but now there was no effort. He'd yet to speak to her, but he really didn't need to. She could tell he fancied her from the second he'd smiled across the roof. So predictable. Yes, see – here he was now. Coming over to join her.

'Hi,' he said – he had to shout over the music – and sat beside her on the sofa.

Alice gave him a cool smile. 'Hi,' she replied, and took another sip of wine. 'Who are you?'

'I'm Bruno. You?'

Alice smiled, and waved her glass at David's portrait above the fireplace. 'I'm your hostess.'

Bruno looked at the picture, appeared shocked for a moment, and then he laughed. 'Oh God,' he said, not looking remotely contrite. 'I'm sorry. Sam said it would be OK to come, but she's –'

'Forget it,' said Alice who, with a warmer smile, swung her legs round and landed her spiky boots on his leather lap. Occupied in the crazy liquid lurches of her brain, she was starting to enjoy herself, 'and have a drink.'

Bruno shook his head. 'Not when I've got the bike.'

'No drink at all?'

'Nothing.'

'Jesus. How do you survive?'

Bruno smiled. 'Actually,' he said. 'I like it. I like being in control. I like thinking clearly.'

'You don't get bored?'

He felt along the heel of her boot, up into her instep. 'No,' he replied, starting to undo the zip. 'I don't get bored. And I certainly don't get bored when I . . .'

Wearily, Alice removed her leg.

And, to her surprise, Bruno laughed. 'Yeah,' he said. 'Certainly don't get bored when I get that kind of rejection.'

Alice bit her lip. 'I'm sorry,' she said. 'But I'm . . .'

'A lesbian.'

She gave him a long stare. 'No, Bruno. Rejecting you does not automatically make me lesbian. I'm just not interested in you.'

Bruno didn't seem nearly as put out as he should have been. He grinned at her remark. 'You find me unattractive?'

'No.'

'Dull, then?'

Alice sighed. 'You're not old enough.'

Bruno shuffled closer. 'Not old enough?' he said. 'But I'm at university. I must be at least two years older than you. Surely that counts as someth –'

'You're wasting your time. I like men –'

'Ouch.'

'– in their thirties,' said Alice, smiling. But her head was spinning again. She squeezed her eyes shut, waited for the moment to pass. 'Men with jobs,' she battled on, trying to keep to the conversation while

347

her brain flipped and wriggled like a fish on a slab. 'Jobs, and houses, and cars, and –'

'And wives?' said Bruno.

Alice raised both her eyebrows. She gave him her most enigmatic smile, and then – with sudden horror – realised that she was about to be sick.

'Oh my God . . .' Covering her mouth with her hand as she barged past her guests, she ran through the door, up to the loo on the landing and knelt at it.

Bruno followed her. 'Alice?' he called out. 'Alice, are you –'

The door slammed.

'Alice, are you OK?'

'I'm fine,' she said, but she wasn't. He could hear she wasn't and, trying the door, he found she hadn't locked it and peered in.

Alice didn't look round. Keeping her head well over the porcelain bowl, she knew that there was more to come. 'Go away,' she said quietly. 'Please, Bruno. Please just go away and leave me in pea . . .' but she couldn't finish the sentence.

Bruno came in, shut the door and locked it. He sat beside her on the floor, stroking her, holding back her hair, until the retching stopped. Then he told her to go to bed.

'But –'

'Just go.'

'I can't abandon my own party,' she protested, climbing the stairs with limp feet. 'What about my guests, and all the drink and stuff? I can't just leave it there –'

'I'll sort it out.'

Alice stopped and looked at him through the

348

banisters. 'But how will you –'

'I'll tell them you're not well. Now, brush your teeth and get into bed. I'll send Sam up with a glass of water and a bucket.'

Alice smiled. 'Don't need a bucket,' she said sadly, her hands on her stomach. 'Nothing more to come out.'

She came down the next morning to a room that reeked of stale smoke and drink – but glasses had been stacked to one side, ashtrays had been emptied, and some attempt had been made to dispose of the empty bottles and cans of beer. And there was a note.

'Call me,' it said, simply – followed by a number.

Alice looked at it for a while. It was nice of him to go to so much trouble. But it was also clear that, in spite of the banter, he was much too interested. It wouldn't be right to encourage him. Not with the things that Emily had said. She'd send her thanks via Sam, and throw the note away.

But, later in the day, Emily rang for a post-mortem. She teased Alice: said she'd noticed Bruno moving in on her, said how serious he'd been as he got everyone to leave, how concerned he was. It was sweet. Sam said she'd never seen her brother so infatuated with anyone in his whole life. He'd pestered them for Alice's number. He was keen.

Alice said nothing.

'You're not being like this because of me, are you?' said Emily. 'Because of what I said about fancying him?'

'Well, don't you?'

Emily smiled. 'If you hadn't got so rat-arsed last

349

night, Alice, you wouldn't have even needed to ask that question.'

'Oh my God. What did I miss?'

'Hang on a second and I'll put him on.'

There was a rustle as the telephone was passed over, and a man's voice said, 'Hey!'

Alice raised her eyes to the heavens. 'Hello, Steve.'

'Hey, Alice!'

'Get lucky last night, then, did you?'

Steve laughed. 'Well, Alice, I think in the circumstances you have to agree I did rather better than you.'

But Alice still wasn't going to call Bruno. She'd meant it when she said she wasn't interested. How could she ever be interested in a guy like him, when there was Joss – coming back from Scotland in his Ferrari, to take her to the Tsar Bar.

26

Open windows everywhere, a drop in temperature, a chilly air that blew through the house and sent the doors banging . . . but apart from these things, no evidence of the previous night remained when David came down for breakfast. The whole place had been cleared, cleaned, swept. Cushions on the sofas had been replumped, ashtrays dealt with, and glasses returned – still a little hot – to the cupboards. There was even the slight smell of polish. David walked through the house, noticing these things.

He also noticed how very quiet it was, and empty. Nobody in the dining room. No sign of breakfast. He walked to the kitchen, through a pantry – where abandoned clothes, lost earrings, a cigarette lighter, and a host of other random possessions had been heaped on a table – and on towards voices and a smell of toast.

'You could get the train with Ned and Mel.'

'Mm.'

'Or Joss is driving down tomorrow – I'm sure he could give you a lift. Joss, honey? You could give Annabel a lift, couldn't you? There's room in the car.'

Joss finished his mouthful. 'Bad idea, darling. I

mean, I'd love to take you, Annabel, of course. But there's a meeting at Newcastle,' he turned to Laura, 'that educational charity George has been pestering me about – I've no idea when it'll finish. He's got lawyers there as well . . . Good morning, David! How are you? Coffee? Toast?'

Laura got to her feet, poured David a cup of coffee from the pot in the middle of the table, and went to make his toast.

'It doesn't matter,' Annabel went on to Joss. 'And I really should get back tonight. Benjy and Miranda can take me.'

And at four o'clock – with Annabel in the back, surrounded by suitcases and coats, Benjy's gun case, and a brace of pheasants tied together and dangling from one of the metal bars – they left, tooting noisily down the drive. David stood on the steps with Laura and Joss, waving.

'Well, thank God they've gone,' said Joss, putting an arm around his wife and turning in.

Laura smiled. 'I thought you liked them.'

'I did. I do. But, darling, you've got to admit she is an awful bore.'

'Who?'

'Annabel. Didn't you hear what she was saying? I suppose that book's all she's got now, but when you think of how she was ten years ago: prettiest girl I knew, and *so* feminine.' Joss stood aside for Laura to go in. 'Now all she can do is tell you how important it is for a woman to have a career. It's sad, really. If she continues like that, maybe a career is all she will have. I mean, no offence, David, but not even Ned's interested in her any more.'

David followed, wondering what Joss would say about him when he left.

They had tea in the small sitting room. David and Laura read the papers while Joss sat on the floor by the fire and combed his spaniels, throwing their burr-filled fur – the lumps of it that collected between the teeth of the comb – into the flames. Helen Samuels was in the next room, wiping and polishing again, emptying ashtrays, picking up glasses, and taking them to the kitchen. The shutters cranked as she closed them.

David was reading an article about marital infidelity, illustrated with a large 1950s-style commercial drawing of a woman walking in on her husband with another woman. It said nothing new, but he read it intently, breaking off every so often to look at the drawing, or over the edge of his paper at Joss on the floor, at the foot of Laura's chair. He was leaning against her leg. Looking at them there, David found it hard to believe that the things he'd seen last night had really happened.

'All set for tomorrow?' said Joss.

David put the article down, and picked up his cup of tea. 'Yes,' he said. 'Yes, I'm quite excited. I thought I'd get Laura to stand in the –'

'Don't tell me!'

Laura looked up from her crossword. 'But, honey,' she said, bending round to see Joss's face, 'honey, I thought you –'

'I've changed my mind. I want a surprise.'

'Don't you want to know what I'll be wearing?'

Joss pulled hard at a knotted bit on Flunky's stomach, and shook his head. 'No. I'm going to leave the whole thing entirely with David,' he said, 'if that's OK?'

'Of course it is,' said David. 'It's great. And I'm sure we'll find something suitable in one of those cupboards of hers.'

Joss stopped combing. 'You took him up there?'

'Yes, honey. But I –'

Thinking the session was over, Flunky tried to stand, but was firmly pushed down again by Joss's great big hand. He turned to Laura. 'What – up to your dressing room? Through the bedroom?'

'David needed to see my clothes.'

'I'm afraid I do have to do this with all my sitters. Often have to go through their clothes. For me, it's as important as the setting and the pose. But if you'd rather I didn't . . .'

'No, no,' said Joss; it was hard to tell his mood. 'It's fine. You go ahead. You do whatever you need to do. That's fine by me.' Returning to Flunky's coat, Joss rolled the dog on to his other side and began work on the feathery bits at his ankles. 'Whatever it takes – eh, Flunky? Whatever it takes.'

All evening, Joss remained at Laura's side. He held her hand when she was sitting, held it even when he was on the telephone. He touched her back when they walked to the kitchen, spoke for her when David asked a question. And marked his territory with unambiguous resolve.

Because they'd driven up in David's car, and because David was staying behind to paint Laura, Edmund and Mel took the train back to London. They found seats opposite one another – next to a sleeping couple

354

– and it started to build up speed. It rattled over the
Tweed, and on south, past Northumbrian beaches,
Holy Island, and a long line of sea – a cool blue –
flashing in and out between sand-dunes, sea grasses
and sudden grey rocks.

Ned sat back and watched while Mel found the
papers and turned to the business section.

'Why are you bothering?' he said.

Mel smiled. 'I find it interesting,' she replied. 'And
anyway, I'm still working. I've got at least another
month.'

He leant forward, over the table. 'And then what?'

Mel looked away.

And then what? Marry David? Live happily ever
after? She thought of him – his pale back turned to
her yesterday morning. She thought of his hard
remarks, his silences, his obstinate indifference, and
tried to remember how it had once been. She tried to
think of what it was that had drawn them together.
She remembered laughing with him at Nathan's
gallery. She remembered marvelling at his talent.
She remembered loving Virginia, thinking what an
excellent mother-in-law she'd be – long before she
should have done. She remembered coming back
from work, desperate for him. Missing supper,
hurriedly undressing, clothes falling to the studio
floor, not caring that people could see in.

She remembered him asking – at last – to marry
her, not minding at all that it was done casually. Flash
locations, fancy restaurants: not her style. It was
better that he did it his way. Taking her hand on the
sofa, telling her he'd fallen in love with her, telling
her how right they were for each other, how good it

was going to be. And because he'd taken so long to say it, because she thought he never would, because she doubted that he really loved her, those words had seemed like a miracle. Of course she would, she'd told him, wiping her eyes and laughing.

And she remembered the other things. David criticising her clothes, her cooking. Sitting beside him on the same sofa, scrambled eggs on their laps, watching television for the fifth night in a row. And then – because she'd complained – going to an art house film with him and waiting almost an hour for the night bus because a taxi was too much, even though she had a meeting first thing in the morning. And then there was the way he'd looked at her the day she cut her hair.

Edmund was sleeping when the train pulled into York, and Mel looked out at the bustle on the platform. She found it strange not to be getting out – just passing through – and her thoughts turned to her parents.

Ever since the time they'd cancelled their trip to London, Mel had been worrying. She hoped she'd made the right decision. Back at the beginning of October, it had seemed absolutely the right thing to do – to wait until her father was away. But now, a month later, she wondered if she'd got it wrong. Should she have insisted on coming up there and then? Should she have been more forceful? Or would that only have caused more problems? Mel feared that, if pushed, her mother might clam up altogether.

She'd called every day, but it was clear from the way Clare spoke – from the firm wall of bonhomie – that he was always there, in the background. Clare was scared of him, and Mel knew in her heart that nothing would be achieved in his presence. Clare would simply say whatever he wanted to hear. Mel had no choice but to wait. But it was agonising, and she longed for next weekend, when she could go up, be with her mother, and gently prise open the truth.

Mel continued to look out of the window. The platform was emptying now: just a determined old woman with an earnest younger couple. They were heaving her luggage on to trolleys, trying to stop her from doing it herself, and looking for the exit signs. At last they set off, followed by the old woman, pointing vigorously in the direction she wished to go. Still thinking of her parents, Mel watched the white coiffure weaving round the groups of other passengers and their bags. On it went, on and round a corner, out of view. Mel's eye drifted up, taking in the masonry, the iron bridges, the great glass ceiling, and then back round to Edmund. He was awake, looking at her.

'Want a drink?'

Ten minutes later he was back with a bottle of red and a packet of crisps, righting his balance as the train lurched forward out of the station. Clearing the newspapers off the table, he threw the crisp packet down, put the bottle between them – plastic beakers on either side – and began pulling out the cork.

'So tell me a bit more about you and David,' he said casually. 'Of course, I've heard it all from him. Got the director's cut from my mother – but why don't *you* tell me?'

'You want the story *in my own words*, Counsel?'

Ned grinned.

She told him about the exhibition at Nathan's gallery, and their very first date. She told him how refreshing it was to spend time with someone who wasn't a lawyer, someone talented, someone different. She told him about the little things that David had done – the cards he'd drawn for her, the books he'd given her, and the funny pair of earrings he'd found for her in Camden Market.

'Reckless spendthrift . . .'

Mel laughed. 'Strange as it may sound,' she said, 'I happen to like little cards and earrings. And I certainly prefer them to – say – vast arrangements of orchids and lilies.'

'So do I,' said Edmund, laughing too. 'And, for the record, I did not send Alice those flowers.'

They looked at each other, over the table, both very still, with the scenery flying.

'Really and truly, I didn't.'

'Then who did?' she said.

Edmund was tempted to tell her. That would shut her up. But he was also aware that this involved rather more than a bunch of flowers. It was about a marriage. And although he suspected that the Savils' marriage was already in trouble, Ned knew it was better and kinder – for everyone involved – to keep Joss's indiscretions discreet.

It felt a little strange, arriving back together at David's empty studio. Edmund was still living there. It had taken longer than expected for him to find a flat of his own – he was still negotiating an acceptable price on the one in Notting Hill – and, in the meantime, David was glad of the extra money he paid in rent. It was a little cramped for the three of them, but with David away painting, Ned and Mel had the place to themselves.

With Ned carrying the suitcases and Mel finding the keys, both of them were conscious of behaving like a couple.

'So, my angel,' said Ned, dropping the cases and stretching broadly. 'What's for supper?'

Mel crossed her arms, lowered her chin, and – to Ned's amusement – managed to pull off a surprisingly impressive pout. 'Sweetikins. Surely you know by now that we always go out for dinner on Sunday nights.'

Half an hour later, they were sitting at the bar of Ned's favourite brasserie, tucking into steak frites and laughing.

'Used to know a girl who did that to me for real,' said Ned. 'And the worst thing was: I fell for it. Every time. Her eyelids would flutter – no, I promise you it's true! – out would go her bottom lip, and I was putty.'

'I must remember to tell Alice.'

'God, don't. She's bad enough already.'

They talked on, discussing the weekend, the charm and the drawbacks of shooting parties, and the merits of shooting itself: how tricky it was, how rarefied –

'So when did you get started?' said Mel.

Ned smiled at his plate. 'My father taught me,' he told her. 'Must have been about fourteen.'

He explained about the syndicate in Hampshire, the way his father had loved it, the journeys they'd shared, there and back, just the two of them, season after season . . . and then his eyes lit up. 'Perhaps I'll take you with me next time.'

'Really?'

'Why not?' He grinned at her. 'Or are you scared you'll draw another blank?'

Mel laughed. 'Actually, Ned, I think I did rather well.'

'Yes, but –'

'If anyone's scared I'll miss, I think perhaps it's you. Teaching skills not quite up to your father's . . .'

Edmund filled her glass. 'Give me a chance!' he said. 'Dad started me by firing at paper bags and clays. You went straight in at the deep end with live targets and not so much as a –'

'So, in fact, I *was* quite good!'

Ned grinned again. 'You were excellent,' he said. 'And your timing was exquisite. I'd have given anything to see Joss's face when you brought that duck down . . .'

Mel smiled and reached for her glass. They weren't drinking. It was Sunday night, Monday morning loomed, and after a weekend of Edwardian luxury it was important to them both to return to a more professional rhythm. Yet she still felt irresponsible. Even slightly drunk. For her, there was still something illicit about dining out on a Sunday night, even if she wasn't drinking. Sunday nights involved television, sofas and quick light food. Maybe a bit of ironing. Instead, she was perched on a high stool in a busy bar, a great half-finished steak before her, running with juices and garlic, and waitresses calling out in French as, hurriedly, they reset tables.

There was something illicit, too, about dining out *à*

deux with an attractive man. Since meeting David, Mel hadn't looked at another man in this way. She'd expected it to happen at some point – she wouldn't suddenly stop noticing good looks or sex appeal, nor would David, the important thing was not to act on it – and in many ways she was surprised it had taken so long for her to be remotely affected.

And in any case, this wasn't really 'another man'. It was only because Ned had a look of David about his eyes, and the way he spoke, that she felt like this. It was still about David. David at his best. Funny and charming and . . . Realising sadly how much she missed the old David, Mel hoped this bad patch wouldn't last too long. The laughter left her mouth and Ned noticed.

'What's up?' he said.

Mel's smile was dim. 'Oh – nothing. I was just . . .'

'You're tired,' he said. 'Let's get the bill.'

Mel reached for her bag. She opened it and as Ned spoke to the waitress she pulled out her purse. Not cheap, she thought, looking at the menu prices and calculating her share, but definitely worth it. Indulgent, without being excessive, it eased the transition back to the real world and reminded her that a city life had plenty of charms as well. It wasn't all cut and thrust. It had its own oases – ones that were really more comfortable than formal parties in Scotland, ones she even preferred.

She was just wondering whether to pay by card or cash when she felt a hand on her arm.

'What are you doing?'

Mel looked up: bag open on her lap, purse in one hand, menu in the other. 'I'm –'

'Please don't.'

'But –'

Saying nothing, Ned took the purse from her and put it away himself – back into the bag with a snap of the catch. Then he sprang from his stool and, ushering Mel towards the door, gave the waitress a couple of notes and left.

He got it right. He managed to do it without a trace of the patronising sexism she'd felt from Joss – and Mel loved it. It didn't control her so much as make her feel looked after, and she realised with some surprise how restful, and unfamiliar, such gestures really were.

27

Edmund was in the office at eight o'clock the following morning. It was a busy week for him. His offer on the flat in Notting Hill had been accepted and completion was due on Friday. He needed to pack up all his things, ready to move out, and arrange for the furniture he'd left in storage to be released. And he had his regular workload to contend with. But there was something he had to do first.

Picking up the telephone, he dialled Alice's mobile. She had to be warned away from Joss. She had to understand the risks that she was taking. He caught her while she was walking to school.

'Are you free tonight?'

'No, Ned, I'm not,' said Alice, smiling as she strode along the pavement. She was seeing Joss tonight – Joss, and the man from the Tsar Bar. No way was she free.

'Can you make yourself free?'

'Why?'

'I want to speak to you . . .'

Alice went on walking.

'. . . about Joss.'

Alice stopped. 'Whatever you've got to say to me, Edmund, say it now.'

'It really would be better face to face, you know. It's not exactly –'

'Just say it.'

Edmund hesitated. He'd have preferred to speak to her about it in person, make sure she was listening, but it was vital to catch her before Joss did and he was scared that if he left it any longer, it might be too late.

'OK,' he said. 'I've heard that Joss Savil has been sending you flowers, and I'm worried.'

'Worried about me, or him?'

'You, Alice. You're completely out of your depth.'

'Actually, Ned, I'm not,' she said, picking up her bag and walking on. 'I'm not out of my depth. I'm not a child. I'm – Who are you to tell me what I can and can't do? You're sounding more and more like your brother.'

'I just want you to *think*,' said Ned. 'Use that considerable intelligence of yours and *think*, for a moment, where this might lead. I'm not trying to tell you what to do –'

'Then don't.'

'But do you really want to embark on the kind of affair that might end up in the papers? With God knows what degrading things written about you for everyone to read, and –'

'Thanks for the concern,' said Alice. 'But I don't think that the national press will have quite the same interest in my love life that you seem to be expressing. It's none of your business and . . . and, I'm sorry, Ned, but I'm going to do what I think best.'

'Fine,' he replied. 'So will I, and I'm sure your

parents will have rather more forceful ways of preventing you from pursuing this little matter, should the need arise.'

'*What?*'

'Your parents.'

'Ned, you can't. You –'

'I can.'

'But what will you tell them?'

'I'll tell them the truth. I'll tell them that Joss Savil has been sending you flowers, and that they might want to watch out for you, protect your reputation, that sort of thing.'

'Just because a man sends me flowers, that doesn't mean we're having an affair.'

'Absolutely. I agree. And I'm making sure that you don't.'

Later, over lunch, Alice sat on a bench in the schoolyard, thinking about what Ned had said and listening to a message that Joss had left for her – 'On my way. Can't wait to see you. Back around four, so come over the second they let you out of there, and we can get straight down to business. Mark's expecting us at Tsar's around six' – over and over again. She had one music lesson that afternoon, and then two free periods to the end of the day. She'd set aside that time to go to the library and finish her essay on Charlemagne, but she couldn't do it, not with Joss's and Edmund's voices ringing in her ears. Her main thought was that Ned would never know about it – not unless Joss told him, which wasn't likely to happen. On the other hand, Ned was sharp. He'd keep his eyes open, he'd figure it out. Add to that the rather strange situation with Joss, the fact that he'd told Alice quite specifically he *didn't* fancy her . . .

It was tricky. But the thing that swung it for her was Edmund's tone.

'You're completely out of your depth . . .'

Well, she wasn't. She'd show him that she wasn't. All she was doing today was pursuing a real chance to further her music career. And why should she let Ned Nicholson spoil her fun?

Alice went to her locker. Ringing her parents, she told them she had to stay with Emily that night. She and Emily often stayed at one another's homes, but it was usually at the weekends, and it took a bit of pleading.

'Mum, we've got a timed essay tomorrow. That's kind of like a test. It's on Charlemagne – *all the work we've done this term* – and Emmy's lost her notes. I've promised her she can use mine, Mum. I can't just let her down. It really matters, you know, how we do in this.'

'But what about you, darling? Won't it affect your result?'

'Not if I go round to hers. Then we can share the file.'

'Can't she come here?'

'Mum.'

Camilla let her go. Amused at her mother's ignorance of technology (their notes were on computer – all she'd have needed to do, if she'd been telling the truth, was put them on to a floppy disc and give that to Emily), Alice pulled on her coat, slung her school bag over her shoulder and walked out of the gates.

It was a cold afternoon. The sky – pale yellow – was

streaked with feather-grey cloud, the sun was close to setting, and Alice walked on quiet pavements, sunk in bluish shadow. Everything was muted: no loud colour, no loud noises, just the swish of the street sweepers, taking advantage of the dry weather to clear the streets of leaves.

It took her almost an hour to get to Cheyne Lane, and even then she was early. Not expecting Joss to be there, Alice rang the bell anyway – just in case – and to her embarrassment was let in by Grace.

'You want to wait upstairs? Mr Savil will not be long now, I think.'

Alice went up to the drawing room. She was at the piano, playing a Bach fugue, when Joss got back.

Joss didn't care what Grace thought – not after the cash sums she got from him on top of her regular salary. Grace wanted enough money to be able to go home permanently to her family in Thailand. That was all. Once she'd seen her children through school, through whatever courses they needed to get jobs – proper office jobs with suits – then Grace would go home and, in turn, be looked after by them. Joss and Grace understood one another very well. He was helping her achieve her aim. She, in turn, did not need to be told what to do to help him achieve his.

Driving in London traffic after five hours of motorway speeding made Joss aggressive. Aggression made him randy. Hearing Alice at the piano – the dense complexity of notes – he pictured her as she was at the party, in that see-through shirt, done up to the neck, and ran upstairs, two at a time. He walked in, saw her there in the fading light, her hair falling out of a ponytail, and got an instant rush.

Alice heard him enter. Heart beating, she continued to play, but her concentration was off, she was missing notes, her timing was hopeless. Joss was beyond noticing. He walked towards her, slowly. By the time he reached her, all she could think was that they were alone. They were alone together and, for someone about to receive career advice, this was not the way it should be. He stood directly behind her. She could feel his eyes on the back of her neck, and then she felt his fingers.

Alice stopped playing. 'I thought you said you didn't fancy me,' she said.

'I don't.' He yanked her from the piano stool.

'Then –'

'Shush.' He pushed her to the wall and, pinning her there, looked into her eyes. There was no way she could move. 'Don't fancy you at all,' he murmured, and bent to kiss her throat.

Alice struggled, and he strengthened his grasp. She could feel his teeth in the kisses, he dragged at her clothes with his hands. He was clumsy, inept – almost like he didn't know what he was doing. Alice felt nothing from him but raw determination. He couldn't work her belt, he struggled with her bra, pulling at the front.

You're completely out of your depth.

'Joss –'

'. . . I don't fancy you. I don't. I don't.'

'Joss. Stop it.'

He pulled back, grinning. 'Oh, you little tease. You've been asking for it since the day we met.' He fell on her again. 'And now you're going to get it.'

Alice froze.

Later, she realised that if it hadn't been for her mobile ringing, she probably wouldn't have been able to stop him. But the nagging tone – its electronic lack of passion – threw Joss from his purpose.

'That thing yours?'

Alice nodded.

'Well, shut it up – can't you?' He pulled away, so that she could get to her bag, and Alice grabbed her chance. She ducked beneath his arm and, bag in hand, made a dash for the door.

'A –?'

But she was halfway down the stairs.

'Hey, Alice! Alice, come back!'

On she went, on and out through the front door. Out and down the path, through the gates, into the street, the telephone still ringing in her bag.

Getting to the safety of the King's Road, Alice slowed her step. She stopped by a shop window, pulled out her mobile and checked the display panel. No name came up, but the number was slightly familiar – the triple seven at the end. It wasn't any of her parents' numbers. It wasn't Emily's, or Ned's or David's. Alice racked her brains as the ringing continued. Why did she recognise it? And then she remembered. She remembered it written in his own free hand, discarded now in the wastepaper basket beneath her father's desk. And here it was again, converted into digital figures.

But she didn't want to talk to Bruno Mason, not now. And with a shaking hand, Alice switched the mobile off. Holding it, she wondered briefly if she should call anybody else, but no one sprang to mind. No one who'd understand. No one who'd think, for a second, that she hadn't brought it on herself.

Alice put the telephone away. Zipping shut the black nylon bag, she slung it over her shoulder and set off through the crowds of early-evening shoppers, a grey look in her eye.

It was after six o'clock, and Mel was still in the office. She'd had a busy day: meetings all morning, and an afternoon spent amending documents to send to the client that night. But instead of feeling overloaded, she had a simple sense of achievement. She was pleased with the amendments she'd negotiated. It was a good contract, and she'd fought it with a combination of personal and intellectual skills that, today, came easily. Using humour, she'd kept it light and elegant, virtually stress-free, and now the contract was ready to send out. With a spring in her step, Mel walked down the corridor, the contract in her hand. Finding a trainee to run it through the photocopier, she returned to her desk, cleared its surface, and made a quick list of things she needed to do tomorrow.

If only it could always be like this, she thought. Everything in order. Everything calm. After the chaos of her personal life, it felt good.

The trainee brought back the copied documents.

'Thanks, Chris.'

'Anything else?'

'No, that's it. Have a good evening.'

'And you,' he replied.

Mel thought of what her evening held – back at the studio with Ned, but no David – and decided that it wasn't so bad. Sad not to have David there, but Ned was good company. And maybe it was a good thing that David wasn't around. Perhaps a few days apart were exactly what she and David needed. Nothing like missing someone, to appreciate them again – know their true value – and in the meantime, she could get to know her future brother-in-law a bit better. Slipping on her coat, Mel put the copied contracts into packages to send out. Then she took the packages down to the post room to be couriered off that night, and left the office building.

When David painted portraits in the past, Mel had missed him. She'd felt uncomfortable alone in the studio, and had always gone back to Nathan's. But this time was different. While Mel was still officially living with Nathan (nothing more had been said about her moving out and she assumed that Fenella must have enough on her plate – organising the wedding at such short notice – without the added upheaval of renovating) she wasn't keen to take advantage of it. She felt she didn't belong there any more. She couldn't face that bedroom – with its chilly air, its narrow lack of soul – and she couldn't face Fenella.

'She's even put photographs of *her* sister's wedding on *his* desk,' she'd said to Ned the night before. 'There's Rimsky-Korsakov on the CD player, vanilla candles everywhere, and –'

'Sounds rather civilised.'

'Civilised? Nathan isn't even allowed to use his own bathroom any more. She says he makes it smell.

Ned had laughed. 'Makes you look positively mellow.'

Still thinking of the previous night, Mel walked up the stairs, smiling. The studio was empty, but Mel didn't mind. Nice to have a bit of space, she thought, turning on the lights. Nice to be able to ring her parents and David in peace, have a bath perhaps, and eat when Ned got in. Mel poured herself a drink, took the telephone over to the sofa, and dialled her parents' number.

Clare picked it up.

'. . . Oh, I'm well, darling. Really well. We've had such a lovely day, picking sloes – filled three whole cartons! And your father's been training Bess to fetch things. So clever of him, and you know how stubborn that dog can be. . . . We're so looking forward to seeing you. . . . Yes, darling, that's right. Both of us! Dad's decided to put off his trip to Glasgow until after you've gone, so you'll see him after all, isn't that wonderful? He's got various ideas about your job. Things he wants to run by you, things he thinks you should bear in mind. . . . Says it's worth sacrificing the conference for. Isn't that unselfish of him?'

Mel's heart sank. She'd waited for weeks to be with her mother alone and now, after all that, it wasn't going to happen. Her father would linger. He might leave them for half an hour – to walk the dog, or fetch the papers – but half an hour wasn't enough. She'd never get her mother to admit to a life of misery in that space of time.

Ending the call, Mel tugged at her hair and groaned out loud. All that time wasted. She should have gone that very first weekend. Then, at least, she'd have seen the damage. Now, there would be nothing: the bruises would have faded, the anger put under control. All the ghastly rubbish of their lives would be stuffed away in cupboards, under bedspreads, behind doors and smiles – and Mel, as always, would have to play along.

Because to do anything else was futile. How could she help her mother, when Clare so clearly didn't want to be helped? And if she got up and made a stand, if she tried to get either of them to admit that something wasn't right, Mel feared they'd close off altogether. She'd put her mother at even greater risk, and it just wasn't worth it. Better, surely, to remain a concerned presence, but how could she sit by and let it continue? There had – just *had* – to be something else.

Her head in her hands, Mel wondered with increasing desperation what else she could possibly do. Ring Philippa? But she knew already what Philippa would say: ring Women in Crisis. And Mel knew now, off by heart, what Women in Crisis would say.

And so, wishing that she'd confided in him when her suspicions had first arisen, Mel rang David. She didn't really expect David to have any practical advice, but nor could she handle this one alone. But David wasn't answering his mobile. She dialled the number again, and then again – hoping each time that he'd hear it, or that it would suddenly be switched on, or maybe she hadn't dialled it correctly?

And she was still dialling – this time with the redial button, that same pattern of beeps in her ear, over and over again like some elaborate oriental torture – when Ned got back from work.

'Hello, my little peach!' he said cheerfully resuming yesterday's joke. 'How was your day?' Then, coming further in, he noticed her expression. He noticed how stiff she was: completely overwound, the way she'd been that evening when the Savils had come to look at David's paintings. 'Are you OK?'

Mel shut her eyes.

'Is it work?'

She managed a smile. 'No. Work's fine. I – I just need to speak to David about something, and I can't get hold of him. He's not there. He . . .'

Quietly, Ned took the telephone from her hands. 'Can I help?'

Mel took a deep breath. Perhaps you can, she thought. But just as she was about to speak, the telephone rang. Thinking that it would be David, Ned smiled at Mel as he answered.

'Ned?'

'Alice?'

'Oh, Ned, Ned, thank God. Where've you been? I've been trying to get you for hours. I . . . Oh God . . .'

Edmund glanced at Mel for a second, and then he stood up. 'Alice, calm down. No. . . . No, sweetheart. I'm here now. It's fine. Just take a few deep breaths – that's right – and tell me what's wrong?'

He took the telephone up to his bedroom and shut the door.

Ten minutes later he reappeared, slamming the door behind him. His expression had changed into one of revulsion.

'What's happened?' said Mel.

Edmund came down the stairs. Part of him felt it was wrong to tell Mel about Alice, but he wasn't sure he could stay silent, so great was his outrage.

'I shouldn't really be telling you,' he began.

'That's OK.'

'But I will, Mel – because I trust you, and because I just can't *believe* what that *bastard* has just done to her.'

They went into the kitchen. And while Mel cooked pasta, Ned sat at the table and told her about what Joss had done to Alice. He told her about them flirting at that dinner party she'd missed, about the subsequent conversations he'd had with Alice, and the flowers.

'They weren't from you?'

'No,' he said. 'No they damn well weren't.'

He talked on, and she let him. It was good to hear about someone else's problems for a change. She needed the distraction. But as she listened to his rising indignation, and the protective tone in his voice, Mel realised how strongly Ned felt. OK, he hadn't sent the flowers. But what were flowers and frippery, next to concern like this?

Draining the tagliatelle, rinsing it, and adding olive oil, Mel struggled with a sudden wave of sadness. Not once, she thought, had David expressed anything like that for her. Nor would he ever – because it wasn't in his nature. It was always Mel who did the protecting; it was Mel who worried, fussed, and got concerned. David merely sapped it up. For a while, that had been fine. Mel had liked being the strong one; liked that role. Right now, however, she needed more support and she realised, with some shock, that David couldn't give it to her. Those adolescent looks reflected an adolescent lack of stamina and, for the first time, Mel longed for something more dependable. Even if his mobile had been on, he wouldn't have cared enough to involve himself emotionally, not like Ned was doing for Alice. He'd say the right thing but it would, Mel knew, be hollow. She remembered what Virginia had said that day they'd looked for venues – '. . . *David was always the one we'd worry about! He's supposed to be the one who needs looking after, needs more – more guidance, I suppose. But now he's found you . . .* – and felt the truth in it.

Throwing the pasta on to some plates, Mel put them on the table.

'Oh, wonderful,' said Ned, breaking off from Alice and Joss for a second. 'Wonderful . . .'

With his lighter, he lit the dusty candle in the middle of the table. It was a round candle, half hollowed-out, that had been there for as long as Mel had known David, but she'd never seen it lit. Refilling their glasses with wine, Mel put the bottle on the table and – half inclined to complete the mood by switching off the lights – she decided against it and sat down. Weakened by worry over her parents, by doubts about David and fears for her future, Mel's instinct told her it was dangerous to sit in candlelight with Ned right now.

She didn't feel she could quite trust herself. Right now, there were problems with David and, because of that – and perhaps because Ned was nearest to her at the moment – she was harbouring some strange feelings, feelings best left buried. Yet the more she knew of him, the more Ned seemed to Mel to have the best of David – his eyes, his charm, his voice – with none of the side effects. He seemed almost perfect. She was just a bit lonely at the moment, and falling back on David's brother was not the answer to her problems. It was best to keep the bright lights on.

And, anyway, Edmund was hung up about Alice. Mel listened to him agonising.

'. . . just can't believe I let it happen.'

'But you didn't,' said Mel, twisting the pasta round her fork. 'It wasn't your fault, and anyway "it" didn't happen. Alice had a lucky escape. She got out, remember.'

'But, Mel, I introduced them. I took Alice into a world that was completely unsuitable.'

'You didn't know that.'

'But I should have known. I should have taken more care. I – I can't bear the fact that he might have broken her. He might have –'

'Alice is young,' said Mel, smiling. 'And robust. This won't break her. In a few days, she'll probably forget it ever happened.'

But Ned wasn't listening. 'I guessed something wasn't right,' he said, thinking of the way Alice and Joss had been flirting at that dinner party. 'I should have acted, not just sat around waiting for disaster to happen.'

Mel looked down and thought of her parents. She couldn't sit around either. She needed to act. But how – when? Toying with the idea of talking to Edmund about her parents, she knew she couldn't. She shouldn't lean on him, not when she felt this way. It would only make matters worse.

She went to bed early that night, but she couldn't sleep. She lay there listening to him move around in the next room: drawers opening, curtains closing, and the click of a light going out. There was a loose floorboard in there, under the carpet by the door. She could hear when he stepped on it. In the darkness, it was safer to let her thoughts run free, and Mel's drifted back to the weekend. She thought of the way he'd taught her to shoot. She thought of him looking at her over dinner at Merwick. And again, on the train at York.

Hurriedly, Mel turned her thoughts to David. Her mind flew over the things they'd done, the places they'd gone to, the jokes they'd shared – searching for the spark, but forever returning to the cool pale back, turned to her, in the big old bed at Merwick. And then the floorboard in Edmund's room would gently creak again.

28

Edmund wasn't sure what to do about Joss. Tempting as it was to beat the shit out of him, he knew it wasn't wise. For a start, Edmund wouldn't necessarily win. A life spent fighting verbal battles had done nothing for his ability to fight the physical ones. Joss was significantly bigger. And in spite of his weight, the guy was probably fitter too; the number of days he spent walking over fields with a gun in his hand must have had some impact. And even if Ned did win, what exactly would that achieve? No, the days of duelling were (thank God) a thing of the past. Ned would have to rely on other means of showing his disapproval, and he did that by ringing Joss first thing the following morning.

'Hello, Ned!' said Joss, stretching. 'Bit early for a social call, isn't it?'

'This isn't a social call.'

Joss sat up. 'What's happened?'

'I think you know what's happened.'

'Oh Lord,' Joss sighed, and lay back in his sheets. 'It's that little trollop, isn't it? What's she gone and told you, now?'

'If by that you mean Alice, then you may as well

know that she's told me everything, and that you deserve to be torn apart and fed to your dogs.'

Joss gave a dry little swallow. 'What exactly did she say?'

'You really want to hear?'

'Of course I bloody well want to hear. The girl's slandering me, and I think I have a right to know what she –'

'Oh, Joss. Please.'

'I'm only –'

'Don't you think I've been working for long enough in this game to tell when someone's lying?'

'But she –'

'Actually, I don't care what you think. Take it from me: Alice isn't lying – which makes you pretty unpleasant. The question is: what does a man like me do about that? Do I encourage Alice to report you to the police for indecent assault? Do I inform your beautiful wife? Do we go to the press? Or – or what, Joss? What do you think I should do?'

Joss was silent.

'Well?'

'What do you want from me, Ned?'

'An apology.'

'Well, Ned, of course I'm sorry. I just had no idea you were still interested in –'

'Not to *me*, you idiot. To Alice. Unreservedly.'

Joss agreed to do it.

Ned was having a busy time. Sorting out Joss and Alice was really the least of his problems. Once he'd spoken to Alice – who, as Mel had predicted, was already bouncing back.

'Oh, *excellent*!' was her reaction to being told about

Ned's conversation with Joss. 'Ha! I *love* that, Ned. Just love it! You're so *cool*.' – and once he'd recovered from the pleasure of being called cool, he could draw a line under that business and turn back to his own affairs.

He had a couple of cases still active, when he'd expected the parties to settle within days. Both were now pushing for hearings, and Edmund knew that the next few weeks would be intensive. It was fine. He could cope. He'd been here before and, in any case, now that he was a partner, he could easily delegate the hard graft to one of his assistants. But he was still getting used to being back in the London office. He didn't know the assistants well. And while he didn't necessarily have to put in the long hours that he'd clocked up before he'd gone on sabbatical, the pressure was still there. It was still his responsibility to make sure things ran smoothly. If any of his assistants messed it up, it would be Edmund who'd take the rap.

On top of those cases, there were various bitty tasks – like the endless business development initiatives that Martin Teviot kept thrusting on to his desk – and, of course, there was his new flat. It was expensive, but he'd earned it, and he was looking forward to getting the keys later in the week.

He got back to the studio tired on Tuesday, cheered by the thought that Mel would be there. He'd love telling her about his success with Joss. He could say that she was right after all about Alice. And she'd be pleased to hear about his flat – he'd been too incensed about Joss to mention it yesterday evening – pleased and no doubt rather relieved to get the studio back to the way it had been before; just her and David, alone together. Ned felt a little guilty for intruding on their privacy at such a special time in their lives. Guilty, and grateful to them both for not objecting, for not making it difficult, for even – especially in the last few days – seeming to like him being there. There was no way Mel would have cooked for him last night, if she hadn't. Ned found his keys and opened the door – noticing that it wasn't double-locked. She was back. Great, he thought, hanging up his coat. Great. Maybe there'd be some more of that pasta again.

Walking in, however, Ned saw that his hopes were in vain. He'd have to cook his own supper. Mel was there, sure, but she was sleeping.

He approached quietly, and looked at her. She was curled on the sofa – curled away with her back to the edge, her face in the cushions and a book in her hands. She looked pale, and thin, and tired – much tireder than he. Ned realised with a shock that she'd looked like that for a while. He hadn't noticed before, because he only saw her with her eyes open, because he was always more interested in the energy there, the intelligence and humour. He hadn't really focused on the rest of her – not since Saturday night at Merwick, when she'd looked so lovely and French at the Savils' dining-room table. But that was different. That had been in mellow light, after a day outside.

But now . . . Ned gazed at the sleeping face.

How could he have expected her to cook for him? How could he have banged on about Alice when she . . . when . . . Ned remembered that same face as he'd come in last night, he remembered her frustration with the telephone. She'd looked unhappy. She looked unhappy now, and he prayed it wasn't David. Had she, too, noticed the way he looked at Laura? Edmund hoped not. He couldn't really imagine what slow torture it would be to leave the person one loved in the hands of someone they couldn't take their eyes off.

He decided not to wake her. Instead, he went upstairs and brought her bedding down. Taking the book from her hands, Ned put it to one side and covered her in clouds of duvet. Then he turned off the lights in the studio, went into the kitchen, and quietly shut the door.

Mel woke, slightly stiff, in the middle of the night. The studio blinds had not been lowered, and the place was awash with lunar light. She sat up, still dressed in office clothes, and an outer-wrap of duvet. For a moment she didn't move. Just sat there – with one thought, one person in her mind. Then, bundling the duvet in her arms, she picked up Philippa's book and took herself to bed.

Mel's briefcase had a leather strap. Slinging it over her back on Friday night, she picked up a basket at her local supermarket and considered the fruit on offer. Ned, she'd noticed, liked apples. And they both liked seedless grapes. Then those green beans from Kenya . . . Mel moved up the aisle . . . the ones they did in those packets, already topped and tailed. Excellent. She threw them in.

Standing at the checkout, she loaded up her bags to the beeping from the till, handed over her card, and looked at her watch. She wasn't good in super-markets. She never wrote lists, and spent hours making up her mind. It had taken even longer this time because Ned was such a connoisseur. He wouldn't be palmed off with pasta indefinitely. He needed something better than that.

But when she got back to the studio, Mel found that he was there already – dressed in casual clothes – in a state of high excitement, dangling a set of keys on the end of his finger.

'Hello.'

Mel let the door slam, and put her bags down. 'Why are you back so soon?' she said, smiling. 'I was going to cook you dinner. I had special mushrooms – see? And look – that bottle of champagne I told you about. The one I got from United Bathrooms . . .'

Ned took the bottle. 'You can forget about dinner,' he said, examining the label. 'But this is perfect. Get a couple of glasses, will you? And let's go.'

'Go where?'

'To see my gorgeous, brand-new, hideously expensive flat.'

An hour later, they were there; sitting on Ned's terrace in their winter coats, drinking Mel's cham-pagne. Ned was wishing he'd put the bottle in the freezer for half an hour. He was wishing that the freezer was working, but the flat had no power. They'd crept around in the darkness with him blathering on, 'I'm going to have a cupboard – a fitted one, I think – here, and maybe here as well. And the bed'll go there. And this bathroom . . . well, you can't see it properly of course but it doesn't need a thing doing. Apart from lights that is, and –'

384

laughing, he'd felt for the taps. 'Yes, I thought so. No lights, no water. How embarrassing.'

'Ned, it's great,' she'd said, following him back down the stairs, both creeping like old people, making sure they held on to the rail. 'I love it.'

'What you can see of it. There's supposed to be a gas fire right here in this pillar, but . . . well . . .' He stood up from the fireplace, laughed again, and scratched at his left eyebrow.

Beyond him, through the sliding glass, Mel could see the terrace, the varied shapes of plants that lined the perimeter. She saw bits of twisting bark, overlaid with the broad flat leaves of camellia bushes and the sharper spikes of yukka plants, caught here and there by marks of brilliant green where the spotlight from a neighbouring flat worked its way through the trellis.

'Shall we just open the bottle and get drinking?'

They'd gone out on to the slats that Alice had stood on, back in September, in Indian summer heat. Now it was nearly winter. Edmund and Mel sat on the bench seats – the ones that had been covered in canvas cushions, cushions that were now in some cupboard inside. They drank the champagne and talked about his plans for the flat, about how easy it would be for him to get to work now – straight up the Central Line.

'And back again,' said Mel, 'that's even more important!'

Edmund nodded. 'I'll be back in time for dinner.'

'Ah, but no one to cook it for you any more! Poor Ned. No more of my delicious pasta and salad waiting for you when you get in.'

'How will I survive?' said Ned, laughing.

Mel gave him a suspicious glance.

'No – no, Mel. I love your pasta. I will miss it, I promise. I'd beg you to cook it for me now, again, if only my cooker was working . . .'

'Guess you will have to take me out to dinner, then,' she said, smiling.

Ned laughed. 'Guess I will . . . what would you like?' He emptied the bottle into her glass. 'There's my friend's place in Westbourne Grove. There's Dakota, The Cow, Zucca . . .'

'Just so long as it's not pasta,' said Mel.

Still smiling, she stood up and peered over the edge, as Alice had done, down into the Portobello Road. The stalls had all been cleared away. Just marks on the road, marks and numbers, where they should be. Edmund sat back and looked at her there in semi-darkness, her coat buttoned up to the neck, hair gone crazy in the cold dry air, and drained his glass.

'OK,' he said, 'what about that new place on Ledbury Road? The one we passed in the car just now?'

But her telephone was ringing. It was in her bag, beyond him on the bench seat. Passing the bag over, he watched her open its flap and pull out the mobile.

'Yes?'

Ned waited. She was silent for what seemed like hours, her hand over her mouth, listening to the person at the other end of the line as her look of pleasure vanished.

'. . . On her face and *where*? . . . Oh my God. But – but she will be able to use her hand, eventually. Won't she?'

Ned stared at Mel, who sighed, turned, and pushed at her fringe. There were tears in her eyes.

'And how long will that take? . . . No, the *grafted* skin. I'm sorry, doctor. I can't believe what you're – I mean, she's not senile. Or clumsy. It must have – Well then, she must be talking under anaesthetic or something. It doesn't make sense, for God's sake. Can't you see? It isn't logical.'

Ned went on watching. She was pacing now, her voice was rising, she was about to start crying – and all he could do was sit there, staring.

' . . . no, I do see that. I'm sorry. I know. Thank you, doctor, I'll come tonight. . . . Oh. Oh, OK then. Yes, of course I understand . . . But tomorrow, then. Surely I can – great. Would you tell her that? No, tell it to her personally, will you? I'll be there, and I'll call first.'

She put the mobile back into her handbag and found herself incapable of telling him. But he was obviously waiting for her to say something.

'I'm sorry, Ned. What were you saying? A new place in Ledbury Road?'

'Sit down.'

Mel sat. Edmund sat beside her, waiting.

'It's my mother,' she said at last. 'She's in hospital with burns – terrible burns – and I . . . well, anyway, she's scalded. On her face and down one side of her body, and . . .'

'What happened?'

'An accident at home, with boiling water.'

'Shit,' said Ned.

'She's going to be fine, they say. She may need a skin graft operation for her face but they don't know yet whether she . . . well, anyway she'll be in hospital for some time and she hates hospitals, Ned. Really hates them.'

'But your father will be with her, won't he?'

Mel stared at him – and for Ned, who was good at making connections, it was enough. Everything slipped into place: the strain she'd been under, the things she'd said just now to the doctor, that book in her hands the other night . . .

'Oh God,' he said. 'You – you think it was him?'

Mel's hand went to her mouth again. 'I don't *know*,' she cried, into the muffle of her palm. 'I don't *know*. I don't *know*. I don't . . .'

'Come here.'

He pulled her towards him and held her – rubbing her back – until she could speak properly. And then it all tumbled out, as it had at that lunch with Philippa, while Ned listened with increasing disgust. The man made Joss Savil look a saint.

Annabel couldn't understand why Joss hadn't rung. All that week, she was supposed to be making final amendments to her novel. It was due back with the publishers the following Monday and it needed a lot of work, but Annabel couldn't concentrate. She sat in her dark Kensington flat and stared at the tree outside, its fungal bark-patterns, its last few leaves – dripping, decomposing – against a neutral sky.

It was vital not to be the first to ring. Annabel had read books on the subject and she knew that if she and Joss had any future, then the move had to come from him. Absolutely had to – especially if he was married. It wasn't her place to ring him. But when by

Saturday Joss still hadn't rung, and the page proofs of her book still sat untouched on her desk, Annabel decided to break her own rules.

Picking up the telephone, she told herself that these were exceptional circumstances – not least because, right now, she couldn't function. The book would suffer. Even if the news was bad, she wanted to know what it was. Annabel braced herself.

But Joss, still smarting from his encounter with Ned, was pleased to hear her voice. 'It's my little loader!' he said, with real warmth. 'Ah, little loader, how are you? No, more importantly, *where* are you?'

Annabel smiled. 'I'm in my flat,' she said. 'Working.'

'Working? Working? You can't be working. It's almost seven o'clock.'

'Got a lot to do, Joss. I'm a busy woman.'

'Too busy to see me?'

Annabel hesitated.

'Oh, go on,' he said. 'I'll get us a table at Blake's.'

'Well, I can't tonight,' she lied. 'And tomorrow's bad, so it'll have to be Monday.'

'Monday, Monday,' sang Joss, finding the page in his diary. 'Hm. Let's see . . . no, it's not looking good, sweetheart. That's when Laura gets back.' He sighed. 'You sure you can't do tonight?'

Annabel didn't know when they'd have another chance, not with Laura back in London.

He did take her to Blake's. They sat in the darkest corner. And when, over pudding, Joss asked about the hotel rooms, Annabel knew she wouldn't be able to say no. It was months, years even, since she'd been properly spoilt. The thought of all that money and all those pillows, the flat crisp sheets, the bath essence bottles – the careless extravagance of hotel paraphernalia – it was simply too much.

29

There were lots of things David didn't like about commissioned portraits. He didn't like the lack of autonomy, the way his clients interfered. He didn't like the pressure to get the likeness absolutely right. If it was difficult (and some people were definitely harder to capture than others) then he'd have to sacrifice brushwork on the face, which would then look as if it belonged to a different picture altogether. And he didn't like struggling with other people's drawing rooms, staircases, studies. Each time, he'd tell himself it was the last portrait he'd do on location – not in his studio – and each time something, usually money, drew him back. Once he'd found his spot, he hated having to clear his stuff away every evening, so that the family could put the room back to its proper use. He'd have to stick masking tape all over the floor to mark out exactly where the chair should be – or the sitter's foot, or hand, or whatever else it was.

And there were other things, like the way he was treated. Some people behaved as if they had a brand-new friend to stay: pouring him drinks, inviting people round to meet him, having dinner with him, taking him with them when they went to parties, never letting him rest. With others, it was as if they had an extra servant in the house. He'd eat in his room, or find himself helping heave the dining-room table out to its fullest length for a dinner party he certainly wouldn't be attending. He'd have to avoid calling them anything – a Christian name would certainly cause offence – and end up, maddeningly, with a better picture.

Usually it was people who lacked confidence socially who treated him like staff. He'd done the ex-Harrods perfumery assistant wife of some ageing aristocrat in Cumbria last year and it was the wife who'd created the problems. Gerald had been charming – had insisted David join them for dinner, had poured him far too many glasses of whisky and quizzed him about life in London. But Gerald had left to go fishing while David was still halfway through the picture. Suddenly it was baked beans in the pantry with the cook, while Lady Pennine dined alone, a Pekingese on her feet.

With Joss and Laura, it was the other way round. Laura was easy. Joss was the one with the complications, the snobbery, the latent fear. David wasn't sure what Joss, who had everything, was scared of – except, perhaps, losing it – but the one thing he did know was that his week at Merwick, painting Laura, would be infinitely improved by Joss's absence.

From his bedroom window that Monday morning, David watched Joss leave – the sleek Ferrari gliding through the gates. He smiled, pulled on his paint-spattered jeans, and began to think of how he'd deal with the rain. He liked it. He wanted it. Laura would be protected by the great protruding porch. But David would be out there, on the gravel, in the wet. He could turn the car round and sit in the back with the boot open, but the canvas would still be exposed.

'What about a horsebox?' said Laura, over breakfast. 'Jim can bring that old one up from the stables. I'm sure you and your easel would fit, if you don't mind the smell, and all that straw.'

They backed it up to the steps, opened it, and pulled down the ramp.

'Perfect.'

There was a problem with getting enough light on to the canvas, under that great metal arch – David had to rig up one of his spotlights – but the horsebox would do.

He slotted the canvas on to the easel and rubbed in a burnt base colour. The base colour was thinned by turps so that it wouldn't dominate, so that it was still canvas he was working on, not paint. But he needed that russet warmth to bring out all the blues and greys and silvers, the slates and stones, and watery light. He needed the contrast. The hair and skin would glow.

The brown canvas – the scraped swirl-marks from where his cloth had rubbed – waited for its first real mark. David didn't hang around. He picked his biggest brush, poised its sable end over the palette for a moment. Then, eye dancing, he flicked the brush rapidly into the snaky piles of colour that sat like toothpaste on the edge of his palette. Chalk white first, with a good dose of turps from the wells he'd clipped to the edge, then tinting it with alarizin crimson, veridian, and . . . He looked again at the stone – really looked this time. Next to the North Sea-grey of Laura's coat, it was more heathery. Warmer. His brush was in the yellow ochre – the smallest bit – whisking it into the mix and . . . There. Straight down with the first pillar. Wet and shiny, like a watercolour. A few dribbly horizontal steps. Then more veridian, more crimson, thickening for a smoother stroke round the gap in the door behind her head. Stopping perfectly where the hair began, and using the stone – flat, behind her – to get the line at her shoulder, her arm, the broad sweep of her coat.

'Could you bring your foot forward a bit, Laura? The left one – just a fraction . . .' He had to call across the gravel. '. . . and get your shoulders back. Look at me. Chin's too high . . . that's better. Don't smile.'

Down the steps again, wiping out the dribbles, angling his brush for a wider line with each stripe. More white for those thin silver puddles . . . getting closer, faintly exaggerating the perspective, right forward and out of the bottom of the canvas. Then back, and back again, to the woman at the centre.

Adrenalin flooded his system. He worked on with the same big brush, drawing with it at this stage – placing and describing, as opposed to blocking out. But his eye shone with a million messages – relating, adjusting, thrilling – harnessing instinct to ingrained techniques.

Laura stood in her soft grey coat. The edge of the door dug into her shoulder. And although an electric fire was there out of sight, warming the backs of her legs, the rest of her froze in November rain. But while she wasn't used to the climate, Laura was used to the work. She had the stamina. She knew there was a point where you stopped getting uncomfortable, a point where you went numb. And she stayed there, completely still for a full two hours, watching David's face – the mania in his eye.

When the Savils weren't entertaining at Merwick, the house was all but shut up. David and Laura ate in the kitchen and spent the rest of their waking hours on the portrait, or in Joss's little sitting room.

The portrait would follow them around. David had never been so excited by a painting, and he wouldn't let it out of his sight. Having worried that it would be like all the other chocolate-box Lauras, he was thrilled to see that it wasn't – not yet, at any rate – and determined not to let it from his grasp. During supper, he'd prop it up against the larder door with one of his spare spotlights on it while they ate. Then he'd carry it through the hall, down the passage to the little sitting room. Taking care not to get wet paint on the covers, he'd put it on a sofa that had its back to the wall and sit in the armchair opposite, drinking coffee as he discussed it with Laura.

David had phenomenal concentration, but there were side effects. And the better the concentration, the less able he was to register anything but the object of his focus. Everything else fell away. He forgot about London, his mother, Ned. He forgot about the studio and the gallery. He even forgot about Mel and the wedding. He wiped his mind of everything but the portrait – and what it said about the emptiness of Laura's marriage.

He was now convinced. There were signs of it all around him: in those enormous cupboards of unworn clothes, in the hours Laura spent talking to friends in America, in the time that she and Joss (not six months married) were prepared to spend apart, their different interests, their lack of communication. Joss hardly rang at all. When he did, it always seemed to be for some practical reason. Had she remembered that Flunky had only two scoops of biscuits? What had she done about getting the car serviced? Where did she keep the Cheyne Lane writing paper? Oh, and would she order some more in any case – this time without the international dialling code?

David knew about these calls because Laura would tell him. She'd come into the sitting room, pour herself a drink, and ask David outright if he thought it was a wife's responsibility to get a car serviced. She'd laugh about how bossy Joss could be.

'What's happened to all the romance?' she'd moan cheerfully. 'Where are my flowers, my dinners out, my sweet-nothings?'

David knew that she was joking, but it jarred. Joss was neglecting her openly. He was quite ready to insult her. Sometimes she suffered it, like she'd suffered on Saturday night. And sometimes, like now, she laughed – but it wasn't happy laughter. She was merely coping according to her mood.

And she never stood up to him. It never seemed to cross her mind that she didn't have to put up with that kind of treatment. She could leave him. She just didn't want to do that: either because she loved him in spite of it, or because of the child she was carrying, or because she liked the benefits of being a trophy wife. David could just about understand the sacrifice if it was to do with the child – he wasn't sure he'd be able to make that kind of sacrifice himself, but he accepted the fact that many people did. No, it was the other reasons that bothered him. How could Laura love a man who treated her like that? How could she put up with so much degradation, for a few pretty dresses and a few smart homes. Where was her pride?

As the week wore on, as he got to know her better, David became increasingly troubled by these thoughts, and by what he'd seen Joss doing that weekend, with Annabel, in the corridor by the gunroom. His instinct was to stay out of it. However tempting it was to feed Laura the kind of information that might well split them up, that kind of interference was fundamentally wrong. On the other hand perhaps it was equally wrong to let Laura build a marriage, raise a child, on quicksand.

Caught between these arguments, David said nothing. And if it hadn't been for a particularly strange call from Joss on Saturday night, he might never have broached the subject.

This call was not like the others. It went on for some time, causing Laura to miss supper altogether. She joined David afterwards in the sitting room, with a radiant smile on her face.

'That was Joss!' she said.

'Oh?'

'He – this is so adorable, David – he rang to tell me how much he loved me, and that he was missing me. Can you believe it? All that nonsense about fading romance . . . I take it back! I'm married to the best man in world! I'll get his car serviced any day he likes, I'll arrange for his trash to be collected, I'll fix his stationery, I'll . . . I'll put up with anything for calls like the one I've just had!'

David smiled. 'So it doesn't really bother you, then?'

'What?' said Laura, settling in her chair. 'What doesn't bother me?'

'You know – the way Joss talks to you, the things he expects you to do for him, the way he . . .' flirts with other women, David was going to say, but stopped himself in time.

It was late. Laura was drinking warm milk from a mug. She brought it close to her chest, curled up her legs, and smiled. 'Oh, David,' she said, with a low chuckle, 'he doesn't mean them. It's just the way he is.'

'And you don't mind it?'

'Oh, sure I mind. But I'm not so dumb as to think I can change him now. And anyway,' she said, 'I don't want to change him. I love him. He loves me, and –'

'But, Laura,' said David, with rising passion, 'he's horrible to you. I saw what happened with those oysters. I saw the way he lied, the way he put the blame on you. I noticed your face on Saturday night. I noticed you went to bed early –'

'I'm pregnant.'

'All the more reason for Joss to treat you with a bit of respect.'

'But he does respect me. He loves me.'

David clutched his head. 'How can he love you, Laura, when he speaks to you the way he did that time at your party in London? When he insults you, plays around and gives you nothing in –'

'Plays around?' said Laura. 'What – what are you . . . ?'

David said nothing.

'Are you saying that Joss is having an affair?'

David released his head and looked at her. The room was very quiet – just low hissing from the fire in the grate – and she seemed very small in that chair, cradling the mug in her hands. Small, and scared, and . . . suddenly, he felt awful.

'Who is it?' she said.

'Oh God, Laura. I never meant to –'

'Who is it?'

David couldn't look at her. 'It was Annabel,' he said to the grate. 'On Saturday. After you'd gone up.'

Laura put her mug down with a laugh of disbelief. 'Annabel Glass? But, David, that's ridiculous! Joss doesn't even like her! He said so – remember? He said so as she left! He said –'

'That doesn't mean he wouldn't –'

'Wouldn't what?'

'You know what I mean.'

'No, David. No, I don't know what you mean. How do you know he did this? What exactly did you see that night?'

'I saw them together in the corridor, Laura. I saw them kissing. I saw him – you want me to go on? OK, I saw Joss take off her top, and I saw them go upstairs together. I heard them –'

Laura stood up. 'I'm not listening to this. Joss? And Annabel Glass? It's absurd. It's not true, and I –'

'Laura, please don't walk away. Please. It's only because I care so much that I'm telling you. It's only because I –'

Laura stopped at the door. 'Joss is my husband,' she said. 'He may not be perfect, but I love him and I won't listen to you say these terrible things. I'm going to bed.'

David lay awake that night – impotent, appalled. How *could* he? Rolling his head in the pillows, covering it with his arms, David cursed himself. He should never have brought up the subject. It was none of his business. He should have gone with his instinct and said nothing.

His mind raced on and it was four o'clock when, longing for calm, the image of Mel's face came suddenly into his thoughts. Mel – his future wife, eclipsed absolutely by his love for Laura Savil . . .

Guiltily, he felt for the light. The mobile was there, switched off, on the bedside table. David picked it up, pressed in his pin number, and waited. He hadn't checked for messages since Thursday.

'Welcome to the Orange answerphone. You have four new messages . . .'

Mel. Mel again. Nathan. And then Mel, slightly cool.

'Just calling to say I'm off to York tomorrow. Saturday. Mum's in hospital. Not critical, but . . . well, I'll tell you about it when we speak.'

30

'It's the Dawson wing,' said the receptionist, looking up from her list. 'Third floor.'

Mel went up. It was a smart hospital, a private one, with carpets and wallpaper and flowers. If it wasn't for the smell, it might have been a hotel. Her mother was in a warm room with a view of York Minster. It had a television attached to the ceiling, at an angle. She and Greg were watching the football when Mel came in.

'Hello, darling.'

Mel hadn't prepared herself visually. She tried not to look too shocked, but the sight of her mother in great white bandages – over her face and down her far arm – made it hard for her to speak.

'Looks worse than it is,' said Clare. 'In a couple of weeks, I can take them off.'

'That's great.'

There was a loud cheer from the television. Greg grabbed the remote from the bed, turned up the volume and stood forward – gazing at the replay.

'It's the semi-finals,' said Clare. 'Leeds were winning but now it looks as if Chelsea – at least I think it's Chelsea . . .'

Mel sat on the edge of the bed. 'Mum,' she said, 'tell me what happened' – and then realised what a stupid question it was. She already knew what her mother would say.

Same old lie. Same old *clumsy me* story that people always bought, because it was easier to hear: one she'd heard now not only from her mother, but from all those women she'd never even met – only read about, or heard about from Philippa. Mel thought of all those accounts of what they'd say to cover up the truth: so many accounts, so many women, but always the same tale. A tale as old as the ones they'd read to their little girls before they went to sleep.

'Amazing it hasn't happened before, really. I was carrying the pan to the sink when I tripped on Bess's lead, of all the silly things, and fell forward, and the next thing I know, I'm flat on my face with boiling water everywhere.'

It was bad enough without him around, but with Greg actually there, what else could her mother say? Wondering why it was she'd bothered to ask, Mel looked at her father and noticed he was listening. He'd switched off the television and returned to his seat by the bed.

Mel watched him take her hand. 'She was in a bad way . . .'

'But how did the water get to your face?'

'It just did,' said Greg.

'The pan fell against the edge of the sink, darling, so the water came out in a jerk – straight up – and I was falling. It hit me on the side of my head as I –'

'The pan hit you?'

'Your mother was unconscious for nearly five

minutes. I had to clear it all up. There was rice everywhere. That water was agony. Got burnt in a few places, myself. The whole place was full of steam. And then, of course, I rang for the ambulance – and that took for ever,' he sighed. 'We've had quite a dramatic couple of days.'

Clare's bandages shifted with her smile. 'He's been marvellous, Mel. He came with me in the ambulance and he stayed with me all night – and then got me into this fantastic place. He's been talking to the doctors about my options – getting second opinions. Really, I don't know what I'd have done without him . . .'

Mel disengaged. It wasn't so much for her ears as for her father's – and she simply couldn't listen any more to what she knew were lies. Her only option was to sit it out: wait, and wait, and wait, until he went home. And while she sat there, she thought of what she was going to say to her mother. Nothing overly direct, to begin with. She'd just point out how 'accident prone' Clare was, and how strange it was that she, Mel, had never seen any of these 'accidents' occur. She'd talk about Greg's 'moods', maybe even comment on his current 'good mood' so that it didn't seem too critical, and see if she could lure Clare into admitting something (that was Ned's idea). And then, very gently, she'd tell her the things she suspected. Clare would deny it. She'd say that the suspicions were completely wrong. But – as Ned said – at least Clare would know how worried Mel was. At least there'd be the sense that, at some time in the future, she'd have a willing listener in her daughter.

Ned had been full of good advice. He'd pointed

out that perhaps one of the reasons Clare was so keen to hide what Greg was doing was because she might be worried that Mel would reject the idea of her father as someone capable of such things. Mel shouldn't expect a 'result' today, he'd said. Just a start.

Greg, however, had other plans – and it wasn't until the nurse came in with their tea that Mel realised what he'd done.

'There you are,' said the nurse, putting the tray on Clare's lap and turning to Greg. 'Oh, and your room's ready, Mr Ashton. Whenever you like. It's the one at the far end, I'm afraid. Opposite the bathroom. We couldn't get you one right next door because old Mrs Elwes really can't move these days, but you can pop in and see your wife whenever you like.' She smiled at Clare. 'Aren't you lucky? Most men would pay for a few nights *away* from their wives.'

Clare gave a tired smile.

Mel couldn't believe it. She looked away. Even if Greg did leave them for a few minutes, it wouldn't be enough. He'd still be there, padding up and down the corridor in his slippers, coming in to borrow toothpaste.

She waited for the nurse to leave, and then stood up. 'I'd better be off, too,' she said to her mother.

'Oh, darling . . .'

'Got a long drive south.' There was no room on her mother's face, so she kissed the good hand instead. 'Take care of yourself, Mum. I'll call – OK?'

Then she glanced at Greg. 'Bye, Dad,' she said, and left.

She walked back along the corridor, towards the lift, with tears in her eyes. Passing the same nurse who'd come in with their tea, she averted her face, but the nurse stopped.

'Are you OK?'

Mel hesitated, new thoughts streaming through her mind. The nurse could keep an eye on Clare – and, more importantly, let Mel know when she was discharged. Clare was safe in the hospital – that wasn't the problem – the trouble would only start when she got home and it was important to know when that would be. It was important, too, to put the nurses in the picture. Stop them from saying how lucky Clare was, if nothing else.

'Is there somewhere we can speak in private?'

The nurse was appalled she hadn't spotted it. She understood completely – her sister had put up with the same treatment for years. She'd do everything she could to make sure Mrs Ashton was properly observed, and of course Mel would be told Clare was discharged. Could she do anything else?

'What else is there?' said Mel miserably. 'What can I do?'

The nurse met her eye. 'Just be there for her.'

'But I can't be there. I live in London. I –'

'I mean in spirit.'

'What good is my spirit when she's knocked unconscious? I – I want to *do* something. I want to grab him and punch him and pull out his hair. I want to pin him to the floor and yell at him until he admits to what he's done. I – I can't *bear* the fact that he's getting away with it.'

The nurse sighed. 'He'll get away with it,' she said,

'for as long as your mum denies it. And you can't confront a violent man on your own. You mustn't. You'll put yourself in danger, and it will almost certainly make things worse for her. Believe me, love. I'm speaking from experience. You have to start by talking to her.'

'How can I, when he won't let me near?'

'You could write a letter,' said the nurse.

'He'll open it first.'

'Not if I handed it to her . . .'

Darling Mum, Mel wrote.

You won't like what I'm going to say, but please read it. I'm writing because I care about you, because I can't speak to you alone any more – and there's just so much that needs to be said.

She stopped and stared at the blank page of hospital paper – searching for the right words.

I know about Dad. I know what he's doing, and I can't sit by and watch him destroy you – because he is. He could kill you. And the longer you stay, the greater the danger. I've been speaking to professional people. I've been reading about it and – oh, Mum, I know how *difficult it is to leave someone you love. You may not be ready to do that yet. You may not even be ready to talk about it. But please know that – when you are ready – you have my total support.*

I love you.

Ned was waiting in the car outside.

'Was he there?'

Mel got in, shut the door and put her face in her hands.

'Oh, Mel . . .' He threw his newspaper into the back and turned to her, unsure what to do. He couldn't hold her very well, not over the gearbox, so he put a hand on her shoulder and waited.

When Mel was ready, Ned drove, very fast, back to London – foot on the accelerator, flying down the outside lane – as she told him what had happened. He listened attentively, asking questions and nodding, making sure he understood everything. And the more she talked to him about it, the more grateful Mel was that she didn't have to do this by herself. She wondered what plans he'd had to cancel to come with her today and felt, again, those uneasy feelings that had prompted her to keep the lights on in the kitchen the other night.

It was a quick journey and they got back in time for supper – to a cold studio and the message light flashing on the telephone. Still thinking about her parents, Mel went into the kitchen while Edmund pressed 'Play'.

'Ned?'

It was Alice.

'Ned, it's me. Where've you been? Would you call when you get in?'

Edmund disappeared into his bedroom to make the call and Mel, standing in the kitchen, heard the door close. No wonder he'd been rushing back. She felt completely, suddenly, achingly empty. Still wearing her coat, she sank heavily on to one of the chairs and closed her eyes. Part of her, she realised, must have been hoping that Alice was no longer around. Part of her had been wishing that Ned's manner towards her today was more than friendly; that it wasn't simply affection or concern. Worst of all, part of her was minding. How could she marry David, if she felt this way about his brother?

She had to get away from him – go back to Nathan's. Go now. She should never have stayed at the studio this week. She should never have relied on Ned today. She should never have let it get to this. She'd known it was dangerous, and now look at her. She was a mess. Not because David still hadn't rung, but because Edmund was still in love with Alice after all.

She left before Ned finished the call. Packing her bags, she scribbled a friendly, slightly superficial, note – thanking him for giving up his Saturday – and left it for him on the kitchen table.

Alice was ringing to let Ned know that, contrary to what Joss had told Ned, five days had gone by and she'd had no apology.

'He hasn't even *tried* to call you?'

'No, Ned – I'm sure. I've left my mobile on deliberately so that I wouldn't miss it. Do you think he has the right number?'

'Of course he has the right number! He just can't bring himself to dial it. Clearly needs a bit more "persuading". Leave it with me, sweetheart.'

Ned rang Joss straight away, but there was no reply, so he left a curt message instead.

'It's Ned,' he said. 'About that matter we discussed earlier this week. I understand that you've yet to perform your part of the deal, and . . . well, let's put it like this, Joss. You've already had five days. As it's the weekend, I'll give you another two. But if you still haven't been able to – er – perform your obligations by Monday night then I'm afraid the deal's off. And I think you know what that means.'

Then he rang Alice back. He told her about the message he'd left for Joss. 'And listen, Alice. If you find that – on second thoughts – you don't actually want to speak to him after all; if you find you'd really rather keep your mobile switched off and make the bastard sweat . . .'

Alice giggled.

'. . . then I can't exactly stop you, now. Can I?'

He was surprised to find Mel gone when he came back down to the studio, and surprised by the breezy note. He'd been expecting to have dinner with her – maybe even take her to that brasserie again. Cheer her up a bit. And now, suddenly, she'd upped and left. Holding the note in his hands, Ned supposed that the things she'd been through today must have been too much. Maybe an old friend like Nathan was exactly the sort of person she needed at a time like this. Yet, for all that, Ned was disappointed. He was hurt by what her departure implied: that he wasn't quite enough for her; that there were other better people for Mel to turn to in trouble.

Clare waited until Greg had gone to bed, until the nurse had put her head round the door to say that his light was out, before opening Mel's note. As the door closed, she reached under her pillow and found the letter. And in the bright hospital bedside light, she unfolded the piece of paper, laid it flat, and read.

Half an hour later, she rang for the nurse and asked for pen and paper to write a reply . . . if the nurse wouldn't mind posting it for her?

The nurse gave Clare a soft look. 'Of course I can post it,' she said. 'And if there's anything else I can do, I –'

'I'm fine,' said Clare, smiling.

'You don't want me to throw that one away for you?'

Clare looked at her daughter's letter in her hands. She wanted to keep it. She wanted to keep it for ever. But the chance of Greg finding it was just too great a risk, and she handed the letter to the nurse with a quiet nod.

'Thank you,' she said.

It didn't really matter. In any case, she already knew it by heart.

Alice was bored. She'd done all her work. She couldn't even turn her mobile on – in case Joss rang – and a long Sunday afternoon stretched ahead. She prowled around the kitchen, picking at grapes, looking at odd bits of paper, and getting in the way.

'Why don't you give Emily a ring?' said Camilla, closing the dishwasher and switching it on.

'Emily's with Steve.'

'Or what about Anna? Or Rachel . . . or what about Sam?'

Alice rang Sam, and they arranged to meet in Hyde Park, in the little wooden gazebo by the Round Pond.

'Hyde Park?' said Camilla, laughing. 'But you're mad! It's raining.'

'I like the rain.'

Alice set off under her mother's umbrella in the direction of Hyde Park, just glad to be out of the house. The streets were virtually empty, so was the park, and she liked it like that. There was no wind and the rain fell heavy, around her small circle of shelter. Rivulets formed in the gutters. Only people with dogs to walk were out as well, and most of them were hurrying. Alice, however, walked at a slower pace. And by the time she climbed the broad path that led towards the gazebo, her feet were sodden.

She looked out through lines of rain, unable to see if Sam was there under the little wooden roof. And it was only when she was really quite close that she realised Sam had not come alone. Bruno was there as well, standing in the shadows, a long-suffering look in his eye.

'What the hell are we doing out here?' he said, laughing, as Alice drew close. 'You're mad.'

'Don't you mean – what the hell are *you* doing out here?'

'I think we should go to the pub,' said Sam quickly. 'What about that one near you?'

'The Scarsdale?'

'Why not?'

'You think we should march half an hour back in the other direction?'

'Bruno can take you on his bike,' said Sam, keeping a straight face. 'We've just left them down there – see? On the other side of the road. And yes, he has got a spare crash helmet.'

They walked back down the path, out of the park gates, to where the bikes had been left. They waited for a break in traffic, and crossed – Alice under her umbrella, Sam and Bruno encased like spacemen in their helmets.

Alice had never been on a bike before. She waited for Bruno to get his spare helmet, and stood in the rain, very still, not meeting his eye, while he put it over her head and did up the strap.

'How does that feel?' he asked in a muffled voice.

Alice put her hands up to the helmet and shook it.

'A bit wobbly? Here.' Smiling, he tightened the strap. 'Now try.'

It was fine.

She stood to one side while he started the bike and then, nodding at her, he shifted forward and patted the back seat. 'Come on, then.'

Alice got on.

'You have to hold on to me, I'm afraid.'

Alice put her hands on his waist.

'No – properly.' He released the handlebars and pulled her hands forward so that she was hugging him, her whole body pressed against his back. Bruno turned. She could just see him smiling behind the visor. 'That's better. I promise you it's only for safety.'

And then he set off, following Sam through the slippery traffic, accelerating suddenly, and slanting the bike as they took the corners. Alice held on very tight indeed, and he was laughing when they got to the other end.

'I'd no idea you were feeling so friendly towards me, Alice.'

'You said hold on tight.'

'Not so that I couldn't breathe!'

'Serves you right for driving recklessly.'

'So you liked it, then?'

Alice grinned.

They followed Sam into the pub and settled by the open fire, chatting and laughing. Alice drank beer, the others drank Coke – and they stayed there all afternoon, with the blue at the windows growing ever darker, and with Alice's mobile, neglected in her nylon bag, collecting message after message from an increasingly frantic Joss.

31

When David came down for breakfast the following morning, Laura was already there, dressed in the grey wool coat, with a newspaper spread before her on the kitchen table. She remained bent over it as David poured himself a cup of coffee and sat beside her.

Laura stared at the text.

'I'm sorry,' he said. 'I feel awful. I should never have said those things about your marriage, and about Annabel. I only did it because I care about you and because I . . . But it got out of control. It's not my place to speak to you like that. I should never have interfered, and I'm just so sorry that I –'

She closed the newspaper and looked at him with tired eyes. 'It's OK,' she said.

'No, it's not OK. It's terrible. I – I've just ruined your –'

'You haven't ruined anything, David. I'd have found out at some point.'

'Not necessarily. And even if you did, that doesn't excuse my –'

'Actually,' she said, undoing the bracelet at her wrist. 'Actually, I would have found out. You see, there have been other things.' Laying the bracelet on the table, Laura toyed with the links, bending them, making a little silver zigzag.

'Other things?' said David. 'What other things?'

Laura went on with the zigzags.

'I – I'm sorry, Laura. I don't understand what you mean.'

Laura held up the bracelet. 'I found this the other day,' she said.

David looked at it, at the vertical line of silver links.

'. . . in our room. I was wondering whose it was,' she went on. 'Wondering why it was there, thinking that maybe Helen had made some mistake. And then last night, I thought over what you said, and I realised. It belongs to Annabel.'

'Are you sure?'

'I remember her wearing it.'

'But – but she might have just, you know, just gone in there looking for you, Laura. It might have just fallen off or something.'

'When I say I found it in our room, David, I don't mean under the bed, or on the floor, or even in the sheets. I found it in the drawer where I keep my lingerie.'

David looked down.

'She left it there deliberately, and I need to know exactly what you saw them doing that night.'

An hour later, David stood in the horsebox – brushes in hand. It was the last painting day. Tomorrow, they'd be driving back to London and this was his last chance to make it perfect, but David couldn't concentrate. Over breakfast, he'd done as Laura had asked and confirmed exactly what he'd seen Joss and Annabel doing. Laura had listened, nodded, thanked him, and put the little bracelet away as if some quiet business had been concluded. In place of the emotions he'd witnessed last night, there was calm – and her tidy manner made it impossible for him to get close. It was obvious she didn't want to talk about it. So they'd returned to the portrait and behaved as though nothing had happened, except, of course, that wasn't true. A great deal had happened, and Laura now had a choice to make. Would she confront Joss? Would she leave him? Or would she turn a blind eye and stay – for the sake her child and her lifestyle.

With these thoughts in mind, David observed Laura standing in the doorway to that great cold house – standing as she'd stood all week, only now with all that knowledge in her eyes. It was even worse for her, he supposed, to be scrutinised by him when she must be longing to escape upstairs with her troubles and lock the door. Unlike him, she didn't have to think, or create anything. All she had to do was stand there and look lovely. But it was still an ordeal, and only the sense of 'business as usual' kept them there. That and the knowledge that at least after today it would be over.

In fact, thought David, standing back from the portrait, perhaps they could stop sooner than that. Perhaps it was already finished.

He often had trouble recognising the point when his pictures were finished – when it was time to stop fiddling with details and leave the canvas alone – and he stood there, deliberating. He wanted to stop. Sure, there were things he knew could be improved, but sometimes it was better to live with mistakes in the detail for the sake of the balance of the whole. He'd put every last drop of energy into this portrait, he was very tired, and it didn't help matters that the day was quite so glorious. Sunshine threw the scene awry. Instead of the damp air and grey gloom of the picture, the real world shone. The stone had warmth. The light was fabulous – that rare, sparkling, vapoury variety – and he wasn't sure it was helpful to stand there all day, trying to recapture the sodden tones of what had been there before. He was terrified of spoiling what he'd done.

So, at twelve o'clock, he told Laura it was finished – she could change out of the coat and dress – and started packing up his materials. Laura came down the steps towards him to see the final result. He stood aside as she climbed the ramp, so that she could get round the easel, and the two of them stood under the arched roof of the horsebox looking at the painting. For a long time she said nothing. She looked at it very carefully, noticing every detail. Then she peered round the canvas at the real scene – empty there without her – and finally turned her attention back to the painting again, to what David had made of it all in oils.

'It's beautiful.'

David scraped lumps of paint from his palette on to paper he could throw away. He sloshed the remains of his turps over what remained and began to wipe the palette clean.

'Well,' he said, smiling at the paint-smeared surface, 'well, I guess you could say that's got rather more to do with the subject than my interpretation of it, but –'

Laura laughed. 'Honestly, David! When will you stop being so British, and just accept a compliment?'

'When will you?' he replied, smiling at her this time.

And, much to his surprise, she held his eye. Thinking of the damage Joss had done, David wanted to drop his palette there and then and hold her. Instead, all he could do was look down and concentrate very hard on wiping away every last speck of paint.

For a moment, Laura simply went on looking at him. Then she picked up one of his dirty brushes and, laughing suddenly, dabbled some smoky grey on to the end of his nose.

'Oh, come on, David!' she said. 'Cheer up. I'm going to take you out for lunch. I'm going to take you somewhere real nice. We'll drink champagne, we'll celebrate this beautiful painting of yours, we'll enjoy this wonderful sunshine and – and forget about the real world for a bit. How does that sound?'

It sounded good. She took him to a place the other side of Hedlawburn – a quiet restaurant with only one other couple dining there – and they sat in the window, in the warmth of the sun, drinking champagne while they ploughed their way through two dozen local oysters.

Laura slipped another one into her mouth. 'So what do you think, David? You glad I ordered for you?'

'Yes,' he said, shaking Tabasco on to the one in his left hand while, in his right, he held a fork.

'You know, they're much better without that stuff. Here . . .' She picked another one from the plate, loosened it from its shell, and held it up. David's mouth opened automatically. 'When they're this fresh,' she said, shaking it slightly, 'you want them just as they are.'

The oyster fell in.

David swallowed it whole. It tasted, he thought, of little more than brine – but he nodded, agreed, and took a gulp of champagne. 'How come you know so much about oysters?'

'How come you don't?' she replied, and then she smiled. 'It's only because I love them so much and I'm not supposed to be eating them in my condition: shell fish and pregnancy, not allowed. Not supposed to be drinking either.' She leant forward, glass in hand. 'Are you shocked?'

David shook his head. 'I think you should do whatever you want,' he said, refilling her glass. 'Right now, you need it.'

'I'm not usually like this, you know. It's kinda naughty, and . . . well, Joss would have a fit!'

'Exactly.'

Grinning, they raised their glasses.

Because David wasn't insured to drive the Jeep, Laura had to drive it home. She drove very badly along the empty roads. Badly, recklessly, giggling. Ordinarily, David would have been shocked. But this was Laura. This was the country. The road was dry, benign and empty. The light was glorious. He'd just had the most perfect lunch of his life and nothing – nothing – was going to spoil it for him now. If anything, the wayward steering, dodgy gear changes and sudden stalling only added to the thrill.

Everything had swung. All hardness, all reality, was confined to the severe picture that waited in the hall. And David and Laura – isolated in the car, weaving around on that empty winter road – they played in a different world.

That evening they sat together, as they'd done for the last six nights, in the small sitting room. Without the picture this time, but other than that it was exactly the same routine. They sat opposite one another, both in their usual chairs. Laura kicked off her shoes. As with previous nights, she pulled on a thick pair of socks and curled up into her chair, the mug of hot milk in her hands. Flunky and Badger were, as usual, sprawled before the fire. It hissed, as it had hissed every night, and Laura and David talked around the same subjects.

But in spite of those things, there was nothing usual in the subtext. The pleasure-world of their afternoon had stayed with them. The sun hadn't really set. They were still drinking champagne, still tossing oysters to the back of their throats, still a little crazy. Laura carried a new air about her. She seemed to David to be absolutely open to him – to anything he said – and little by little he crept forward. He crept with agitated joy; wondering when he'd bump against the boundary, astonished when he didn't. And the more they talked, the more he began to wonder if the only boundary that lay between him and Laura was his own fading sense of duty towards Mel.

And so, for the first time that week, it was David who ended the conversation. It was David, not Laura, who said it was time to go to bed.

'I have to get my things together. It's a long drive we've got ahead of us tomorrow.'

Laura stood up with him, smiling, the mug of hot milk clasped in both her hands. He loved her in her great big socks. 'It's been a good day, hasn't it?'

David smiled. He didn't trust himself to speak.

'Thank you.' She kissed him with sudden fervour. 'Thank you for making it that.'

He dreamt of her all night.

And he dreamt of her all day as, heading down that Monday – foot hard on the floor of his old estate car – they travelled south to London. It might not have been a Ferrari, but at least it was big. And it needed to be. The boot was full, the back seat down, and there were things on the roof as well. Laura had three suitcases and a birch tree she wanted to plant in the London garden.

David had stood on the gravel, pointing at it. 'You're not expecting me to fit that in, are you?'

'Let me try then,' she'd said.

David hadn't let her. But the birch tree had none the less gone in, its twigs now tickled his ear.

And then there was the portrait, all seven feet of it. There was the travelling easel that, thankfully, folded away to nothing. There were spotlights, paintboxes, sketchpads, that basket from the Philippines. And David's own suitcase.

David liked driving, especially in conditions like this: another clear dry day – pale sky, grey trees, a wide stretch of road – and Laura sleeping beside him. Her neck flopped a little, her knees touched the gear-box. David had not stopped thinking of last night, of where it might have gone, where they might have ended up. He thought of what he might have turned away, and asked himself, again and again, how could he have been so stupid.

He didn't like stopping on long journeys. Filling the tank at a petrol station in Hedlawburn, he'd bought sandwiches for their lunch, and had planned to drive on through. But when it got to four o'clock, when he'd been on the road for six solid hours, he decided he needed a break. He was shattered. With Laura still asleep, he pulled off the motorway into a service station near Luton. He put his seat right back, set the alarm on his watch, and closed his eyes.

He was deeply asleep when the alarm went. So deeply asleep that Laura had to reach over, find his wrist, and switch it off herself. She had to undo her seat belt. David woke to her bending over him, hair shading her face from the sun. There were birch twigs everywhere. Smiling at her, David inhaled that same sweet scent he'd smelt before. And Laura was smiling back at him, leaning on him – warm and soft and sleepy – and then she started kissing him.

It was late – late and dark – when they drove back in to London.

32

After the weekend she'd just had, Mel did not feel like going in to work on Monday morning. Troubled about Ned, and troubled about her parents – as yet, there had been no response from her mother to the letter she'd left with the nurse – Mel found it harder than usual to focus on the list of things she had to do that day, particularly as most of those things involved the difficult task of extracting herself from the various projects in which she was now thoroughly immersed.

She had a meeting with Len Purves, the finance director of one of her long-standing clients, and Len was not going to like her news. She'd put off telling him about her departure precisely because of this, because she knew he'd panic. But Len had rung on Friday to say that he wanted a meeting. He wanted to bring the other directors and he wanted Mel to bring partners from the tax department, trusts department, EC, banking . . . He'd sounded on a high. It was clearly some kind of major restructuring and Mel knew she couldn't leave it any longer.

'Len, listen. I won't be able to get our tax specialist,' she'd said, 'not at such short notice. And Guy

Fedora's in Brussels next week. But that doesn't mean that you and I can't meet. There are a few things I need to discuss with you in any case.'

The meeting had been set for eleven, but Mel and Len were still in the conference room at four o'clock that afternoon. They'd been joined at lunchtime by Philippa, who was doing her best to reassure Len. He didn't need to worry. She would take personal responsibility for the file. And Len – who'd heard about the state of Philippa's office, and who did not like the idea of his spreadsheets and his Heads of Agreement swimming with banana skins and theatre programmes on her desk – was saying, for the fifth or sixth time, that the working relationship he had with Mel was vital to this restructuring. Couldn't she stay until it was finished?

'But when do you think that would be?' said Philippa. 'Come on, Len. This isn't some quick acquisition. You're not selling off dead wood. You're as good as creating a new business, and you're aiming to get it done before the end of the tax year – right?'

Len undid his top button and looked at them both. Philippa was right, and Len knew that Mel wouldn't hang around until April. Probably be pregnant by then. But he couldn't actually say the word 'yes', couldn't even bring himself to nod, so badly did he want her on board. They were still waiting for him to respond when the telephone rang.

Mel picked it up.

'There's a Ned Nicholson on the line for you.'

Mel hesitated. After the way she'd felt about him on Saturday, after her abrupt departure while he made the call to Alice, she'd been trying – not without success – to put Ned from her mind. Now here he was, calling her in a meeting. She didn't need this. She really didn't.

'Says it's urgent.'

'OK, Gail. Put him on.'

'Mel. Excellent. Worried for a moment there that –'

'What is it, Ned?'

'There's been a flood at the studio,' he said. 'Water everywhere, according to the man in the basement. Right through the ceiling. Someone needs to get over there now and let in his plumber so that they can stop the flow, and I was hoping that you –'

'You've got a set of keys, haven't you?'

'Yes, Mel, but I'm tied up now until at least six.'

'So am I.'

Edmund took a breath. 'You're saying you can't go?'

'I'm sorry, Ned. I would if I could, but –'

'Mel, please. Please go. I know it's a bore, but I'm counting on you here. I . . .'

Mel took the telephone out of the room, into the corridor. She felt muddled, and irrationally upset. She also felt weak, and her instinct in such situations was to protect herself by being contrary.

'You seem to think that because I'm due to leave my job at the end of the year, I'm free to jump to whatever domestic tasks need doing. But I'm not. I'm still working. I'm with a client right now, and I do not like you thinking that this kind of stuff's my problem. The man in the basement rang you. You sort it out.'

'But, Mel, I can't.'

'Just do whatever you'd do if I hadn't been there.'

'Fine,' he said. 'I'm moving out next week. So I guess I don't care that much. The water will just have to go on gushing.'

'Fine,' she echoed. 'You can do the explaining to David when he gets back tonight,' and put down the receiver.

But within an hour she was at the studio. Cursing Edmund, she unlocked the door for the plumber to get in. It wasn't David's plumber but one that Gopal, the man in the basement, had found. For a moment, the three of them – Mel, Gopal and Gopal's plumber – stood in the doorway and stared at the carnage. Water was, as Edmund rightly said, gushing from the bathroom. It was spilling from the gallery upstairs, pouring through gaps in the banisters, and out over rack upon rack of David's work, all over the sofas and on to the floor. A great pool of it lay in the middle, washing over rugs, soaking into sofa valances. The floorboards had not yet collapsed, but it was only a matter of time.

'Right, miss. Where's the supply?'

Mel had no idea. She and Gopal stood there, while the plumber searched. He opened the cupboard by the door, and one under the stairs and then, anxious not to add weight to the pool in the middle, crept round the edge of the room and into the kitchen.

'Ah . . .'

Mel and Gopal followed, treading softly.

There, in the corner, water was falling through the ceiling, and straight on through to the flat below. The plumber squatted at a cupboard, reaching in for the lever that would switch off the water supply from the mains. The flow eased.

'There. Now get me buckets,' he said, finding one in another cupboard and throwing the contents – the yellow plastic bottles, transparent spray-pumps, various scrubbing brushes, cloths and rubber gloves that David used to do his cleaning – into the sink. 'Buckets and saucepans, anything that'll contain it. And I want something to cover up that hole. Don't care what it is. Rug'll do for a bit, or some of that canvas.'

The plumber left at six. He and Mel had managed to get rid of the worst of the water, but the studio was sodden, the sofas stank, and wood that had once gleamed was clammy now with damp. Mel turned to the racks of drawings, racks of work that was now, she suspected, ruined. But maybe not all of it was spoilt. She began to pull the sheets of paper out – quiet pencil drawings, followed by great bold charcoal studies, pastel landscapes, pencil nudes – pulled them out, held them up, and looked for places to lay them out to dry.

She was still sorting drawings when Edmund returned. He opened the door to the sight of her with her back to him, in office clothes, balancing on a chair in stockinged feet, Blu-Tack in one hand, sketch in the other as she reached up to stick it to the window.

'Knew you'd cave in,' he said, his laughter more hopeful than careless.

Still standing on the chair with her arms outstretched, pinning the sketch to the glass, Mel turned her head. She wasn't smiling. 'I can't believe you,' she said. 'If this isn't enough for you to feel an ounce of shame, why don't you check out the kitchen? And the floor here, and over there, and look at the sofas – and

427

all these drawings ruined, or nearly ruined. And I don't even want to think about what would have happened if I hadn't "caved in", as you put it. That area there was covered in a pool of water that took us an hour to drain. If I hadn't caved in, I strongly suspect that the floor would have done so in due course.'

Ned grinned. 'Good thing you came back then.'

'Yes, it was,' she snapped – clambering, unsmiling, off the chair to pick up another sketch.

'I'm sure David will be very grateful.'

'I'm sure he will,' said Mel, balancing herself back on the chair.

Edmund watched her sticking up the sketch. He watched the tall body stretching, and the tense way she thumped the edge of her hand on to the corner of a page so that it stuck against the Blu-Tack.

'I expect he'd also be grateful,' she went on, 'if you stopped staring at my bottom and started helping.'

'But I like staring at your bottom,' said Ned, taking off his coat. He put down his briefcase and, rolling up his sleeves, knelt beside her chair so that he could help by passing the sketches up. So shall I pass a couple of these things up to you then, or what?'

Mel glanced down at him there on the floor, and brightly met his eye. 'Don't think you're getting away with this,' she said.

'Oh, I don't.'

'I'm still cross with you.'

'Furious. I can tell. But look, Mel, look how contrite I am, kneeling at your feet.'

Mel grinned. 'Yes,' she said. 'Yes, and I think you

should stay there, Edmund, until you have learnt the error of your ways.'

Laughing, Edmund did just that. He stayed on the floor, taking up each one of David's pictures, shaking off any excess water before handing them up to Mel on the chair. And they worked on, getting closer and closer to the ones of Laura – the ones that David had never quite got round to throwing away.

Edmund hadn't seen them since the night he'd first met Mel – the night when, woken by the crashing from David's racks, she'd emerged half asleep on the balcony. He'd certainly never recognised Mrs Laura Savil in the sweeping curves of David's charcoal, the studied hands, the small suggested belly button. Ned's only anxiety was that they were nudes, and he hesitated with the first of them in his hand. Naked breasts? And . . . oh dear. In the mood she was in, he wasn't sure what Mel would make of –

'Stop ogling, Ned, and pass it over. Never seen a nude before?'

She whisked it from him, stuck the Blu-Tack on, and the nudes began to go up. And because neither Mel nor Edmund wanted to be caught looking too closely, it was only when they were done, when Mel got down from her chair and they both stood back to see the results of their efforts – the sight of the windows covered, floor to ceiling, with David's work – that they realised who it was.

And then the doorbell rang.

Glad of the distraction, Edmund answered it while Mel stood staring at the patchwork – the varying angles and materials, the line studies, the hurried two-minute suggestions next to more considered, fuller pieces, all blending to a single impression of one woman's body. And the first thing that struck Mel was just how beautiful it was. Sure, Laura's beauty was a given, undisputed. But, until now, Mel had linked it more to her sense of style and the way she dressed. Seeing her there through David's eye – and without the distraction of expensive clothes – Mel experienced a moment of pure admiration before the inevitable mob of implications, suspicions and fears dragged her mind elsewhere.

Ned picked up the entry phone.

'Hello?'

'What the fuck is going on?' said the voice downstairs. 'I've been trying to call Alice all damned day. I've been trying to call you, and just getting that awful secretary of yours. And – Jesus, Ned – what is this? I'm happy to apologise, for God's sake. I really am, if only you and Alice would bloody well let me. God knows how many messages I must have left on that little trollo – on that girl's voicemail. Laura gets back any minute and – and I – Ned, please. It would destroy me – destroy Laura, too – if this ever got into the wrong hands. It . . . Ned? Are you still there?'

Ned swallowed. 'Yes,' he said. 'Yes, Joss. I'm still here.'

'Well, let me up, man! I . . .' then Joss's voice changed, and Ned heard another voice and a key in the door. 'Oh, oh, thank you – yes, that's right. The studio. Oh, thanks a lot – yes, of course . . . Ned, this man – some neighbour of yours I think – he . . . there's a bucket he thinks you might want back . . . here. Why don't you give it to me? I can take it – save you the climb . . .'

Edmund spun round, hand over the intercom receiver. 'Take them down,' he hissed to Mel. 'For God's sake, get them down. It's Joss.'

Mel pulled hurriedly at the nearest two, but they were wet and tore from the Blu-Tack.

Ned turned back. 'Joss?'

But there was no reply. And from the other side of the door, he could hear Joss's step, heavy on the stairs, and the clank of the metal bucket.

Mel was on the chair now, pulling at the paper, not caring that it ripped. She didn't know when or why David had done so many pictures of Laura. She didn't know if they were from his head or whether Laura had actually ... No, they must have been from his head, unless something had happened that day he'd sketched her in London. But how likely was that? Mel remembered how David had been that night. She remembered the sketch on the easel: Laura snaked on the stool in a dark denim skirt ...

Mel wondered at her own reaction. This was David, her fiancé, caught with a collection of fascinating nudes of another woman, a woman they all knew, a woman he was – right now – alone with. Yet all she could feel, after initial shock and curiosity, was detachment. She felt so detached, she thought she might have been numb. Perhaps she was numb. Perhaps the pain would come later.

She pulled, and the sketches fell to the floor, but there wasn't time to pick them up. And there wasn't time for Ned to help her. Joss was knocking at the door.

'Hey, Ned. Come on. For God's sake, man, don't

do this to me.' He rattled the bucket against the door. 'Let me in!'

Ned glanced round to where Mel was still pulling. She'd got about half of them down.

'Ned?'

Thinking that if he could stall Joss outside somehow, then it might give her enough time, Edmund went out, closing the door behind him, and found Joss in the corridor.

'Thanks.' Ned held out his arm for the bucket, but Joss didn't give it to him. He held it back with a welcome, if somewhat limited, sense of power.

'Well?'

Ned sighed. 'Well what?'

'Have you told anyone?'

'Of course I haven't, Joss.'

'What – no one at all? Believe me, Ned, I'll –'

'I promise you, Joss. No one knows. I'll tell Alice that you've tried to apologise – I'm sure your message will have been sufficient – so I think we can call it quits. Just give me the bucket, and –'

But Joss slung the bucket over his arm and, grinning at Ned, held his ground. 'Well, go on then,' he said. 'Are you going to show me what you've got in there? Or am I going to have to force my way in?'

Edmund looked puzzled.

Joss laughed at his expression. 'What are you hiding?'

'Nothing, Joss. I just –'

'Come on, Ned. I wasn't born yesterday.'

'It's nothing.'

'I don't believe you.' Joss shoved past him and

pushed at the door, but it had locked itself shut. 'Is it a woman?'

Edmund hesitated, wondering how Mel was getting on with tearing the sketches down. Surely she'd be done by now.

'And why the secrecy? Is she married or something? Do I know her?'

Edmund found the keys in his pocket and opened the door with a sigh. 'Yes, Joss, you do know her, but it's not what you think. Not all of us are quite as unscrupulous as . . .'

Joss walked in, not listening. Inside, Mel had managed to get the offending sketches down. She was picking them up from the floor as the door opened. 'Hello, Joss,' she said in a normal voice.

'Mel.' He looked at her, momentarily disappointed.

'We've had a flood.'

'So I see.' Joss took in the dripping studio, the water lines on the upholstery, and the mass of ruined work that dominated the centre of the room – wondering, still, about the origin of Edmund's secretive manner. It couldn't just be this flood. Half wondering if Alice was there in the studio, Joss walked forward with the bucket in his hands. Ned and Mel both prayed that the other would find a distraction . . .

But neither of them did, and Joss was over by the windows, picking up a sketch, before they could think of a subtle way to stop him. Mel tried to take it from his hands without snatching. But Joss, sensing trouble, held fast.

'A-ha!' he said, turning the drawing the right way up.

Edmund and Mel stood breathless, watching him hold it out, watching his great lopsided face as he realised what – and who – it was. He released the bucket and pulled at another sketch, and another.

And then, without saying a word, and still holding on to the sketches, Joss got up and made for the door.

Edmund tried to block his path. 'Joss, wait.'

With one jerk of his arm, fuelled by fury, Joss thrust him aside.

'Joss!' Edmund picked himself up and followed Joss out, down the stairs. 'It's not what you think . . .'

And Mel stood among the pictures on the floor, listening to the hurried steps, the urgent shouts, trying to understand what Edmund meant.

It's not what you think.

What else could it possibly be?

She was still in the same position when, minutes later, Ned returned. 'Lost him. There was no way I'd keep up with that car of his. Did you hear it go?'

He looked at her, but she'd bent forward. She was sweeping the sketches into her arms, and her face was hidden.

'Mel . . .'

Mel stood up, arms full, unable to look back. 'Would you ring David?' she said, dumping the sketches on to the desk, past caring that they crumpled. 'Warn him? He's driving south with Laura today – dropping her at Cheyne Lane. Probably there now. With Joss in the mood he's in, I don't think it would be good for them to –'

She bent forward again, sweeping up more, but Edmund's hand was at her arm. He was taking the paper from her hands, putting it to one side, finding a chair that wasn't wet.

'These pictures were done at art school,' he said. 'They were done years ago.'

Mel shook her head. 'They're of Laura, Ned. They can't possibly –'

'I agree. I don't understand it either. But these sketches aren't recent, Mel. I know them. He did them years and years ago. Either this girl looks very like Laura, or – or Laura herself posed for David back then. But this isn't a betrayal of you, Mel. It's . . .' Edmund broke off.

'It's what?'

He could tell Mel with complete honesty that the sketches were no threat to her. They were old. They proved nothing. But that did not mean that nothing had happened. With his suspicions about David stronger than ever, Edmund could not bring himself to mislead Mel. Nor could he betray his brother.

'It's what?' she said again. And then she closed her eyes. 'Actually, Ned. I'm not sure I care. I'm exhausted, and I think it's best if I get my things and –'

'Just wait,' said Edmund. 'Please, Mel. Wait until David gets back. He'll have an explanation.'

'That's if Joss doesn't beat him to a pulp first.'

33

When Edmund rang, David was unloading the car at Cheyne Lane, his head light with ecstasy. Somewhere in the back of his mind there were questions, hard moral questions. But his joy was too wild, too charged, to give them his attention. All that mattered now was Laura. Kissing her had given David a hit of absolute clarity. After years of questions and murky hesitation, years of struggle – searching for ways to control his desire – he was through. It was piercingly simple.

There were no questions. He had no choice. All choice had been with Laura. And after what had happened today David understood at last that it, this connection they had, was beyond his control. He remembered the first time he'd seen Laura. He remembered walking home after that very first class, portfolio under his arm, struck even then by the importance of what had happened. In one moment, his brain fired by creative purpose, David had raised his eye to the new model's head. He'd intended to use it to position her weight correctly, above the left foot. Instead, she'd returned his gaze and thrown David's concentration to an entirely different level. He no longer saw her head, or even the ring of her eye, he saw far more deeply than that.

I've met you before.

I know you, intimately . . .

He'd felt as if everything before had been working towards that point. Here was the very centre of his life. Here was its driving force. Paralysed by these feelings, David had not been able to finish the sketch. Nor had he been able to finish the moment.

Instead, it had been bottled away. And now, after years of waiting, it was out. This was what his life was supposed to be about. This was the most important thing. It wasn't some mad obsession. It was a deep conviction that this woman was everything in his life. He'd known. He'd always known. And now – at last – his instincts had been proved right.

There would be difficult weeks ahead. He was going to have to break off his engagement to Mel. He was then going to have to face his mother, and his brother, and Nathan – and the idea of upsetting all four of them made him feel slightly sick. But what else could he do? They all loved Mel, they all wanted it to work, but he couldn't go ahead. Not now. Not when another woman could have this effect on him. However sanctimonious it might sound, it wasn't fair on Mel. The mistake had been made months ago, when he'd asked her to marry him. He should have known then that something was missing. He should have understood that passion isn't something you grow out of. It's there for ever. All he was doing now was facing up to that truth. However awful it was, however much pain it caused, the alternative was surely worse.

He was carrying the birch tree into the garden at the back when his mobile rang. Resting the root-bag on the balustrade, holding the slim silver trunk in one hand, David felt in his pocket with the other.

'Where are you?' said Ned's voice.

'Just dropping Laura off.' David looked at his watch. 'Should be with you in . . . oh, I don't know –'

'Listen, David. Joss has been round. We've had a flood, and . . . and he's seen the sketches, David – the nudes – and he's not happy. He's on his way back now. That Ferrari got from nought to seventy at least by the end of the street.'

Still holding the birch tree, David stood listening to his brother. And as he listened, another noise cut through the voice: the sound of tyres on tarmac, burning it black. Shoving the mobile into his pocket, dropping the birch, David ran back into the house – past the luggage in the hall, the tall painting propped against the stairs. He caught Laura at the door. 'Joss is here. That was Ned, my darling – on the phone. He –'

'What?'

'He's here. He –'

'*Who*?'

'Joss. He's just been at the studio. He – he's seen the sketches – there were ones I kept from the life class – and he –'

Outside, they heard the car door slam.

'Get out of here,' she said, white-faced.

'Laura – no. No. We must face him. Now is the time to –'

'Get out,' she said again.

The iron gates sighed and clanged.

'But I –'

Laura pushed him, her slight weight forcing him through the door to the small sitting room on the other side. 'David. Please. We haven't got time.'

The door shut in his face.

David stood at the crack, listening like a dog. He heard the thud of the great front door – right back against the wall – and Joss's tread on the stone.

'Hello darling,' he spat. 'Had a good week?'

'I –'

'No, don't tell me. I'm sure you did. You and that – that man. I'd no idea that you and he were such – er – such very good friends.'

'Joss, please. Let me explain.'

'Explain?' said Joss. 'What's there to explain? Those sketches of his were way too accurate for you to pretend that –'

'It was at college. David did them at college, honey. Years ago. I didn't know him then. I was . . . I was just the model, and there were lots of students there in the class with us. Honey? Oh, honey, please listen. It wasn't intimate or –'

'*Honey*,' Joss mimicked, his voice a chipmunk squeak. '*Oh – honey – please listen. Please let me tell you how I pulled down my knickers for those nice young boys . . . honey, honey – please let me explain how much I enjoyed opening my legs for them so that they could –*'

'It wasn't like that, Joss.'

'You're disagreeing with me?'

'. . . No.'

For a moment, all David could hear was what sounded like Joss kicking the suitcases over the old stone floor. 'You let those greasy students all over your body, and – and then you . . . come here when I speak to you.'

Slight gasp.

David's hand was on the door handle.

'I'm so sorry, Joss. I –'

'Don't tell me. You needed the money.'

'I was poor.'

'You were poor. And how much did they pay poor little Laura for her poor little peepshow?'

'It wasn't –'

'Don't answer back,' he said. And then, 'So what were you worth? Was it by the hour? Yes, of course it fucking was. Fifty pounds? A hundred?'

'Ten.'

'Ten pounds?' He was laughing now. 'Ten pounds? Well! No wonder you had to marry me – you gold-digging bitch.'

'Oh, darling, I –' There was a scuffle. 'Darling . . .'

'Oh – and yes. Look here. Here we have the slut herself. Lady of the fucking Manor, and who would have guessed? I think perhaps that denim skirt might have been better, after all. Don't you? Don't you? Or . . . I know. Better still, Laura, my dear, tell me, did you manage to get a few nudes in as well, for old times' sake? Did you twist and thrust your way to another tenner before the week was out? Or has your price – that beauty's rather soiled by pregnancy, you know – gone down?'

There was a sudden crack, a low tearing noise – ripping, ripping . . .

'Joss, don't. Please don't . . .'

David burst back through the door. To his relief it was only the picture. Joss was yanking it apart,

440

splintering the stretchers. He saw a great gash right through the middle of the canvas – through Laura's face, and on down through the steps. The paint had not yet dried in parts. Joss had smudged the sensitive work on her hands – and his own hands, his shirt, his chin were stained with murky grey.

'What?' Joss spluttered, throwing the picture down. 'What the hell are *you* –'

Grabbing Laura by the arm, David rushed her through the door. Through the door, down the path, under the old gas lamp, and out into the street where his car – still with the doors open, keys in the ignition – waited to take them home.

Joss ran after. They heard him thundering up the path, heard the superior Ferrari engine as they sped away. It caught up with them at the King's Road junction, nudging and bumping their rear while Joss leant out of the window, shouting, startling the flow of shoppers.

The cars slid through the traffic with the Ferrari gaining on them, then losing ground and then, just when they thought he'd given up, it would be there again in the rear-view mirror, flashing, honking, revving. They crossed the bridge: jumping lights, overtaking on the inside, bumping up and round on the pavement for a second, with passers-by leaping aside for them, while other cars pulled up, some drivers thumping at their horns, others shaking their heads.

On David drove, with Laura beside him, silent. He was too busy at the wheel to think about much else. There'd be time enough for talking later, and the important thing was to get her home before Joss got there. He was glad she was quiet. It meant he could concentrate and, somewhere in the back of his mind, he knew it meant that she'd acquiesced. If she was doing nothing to stop him, then she must want it as well. He was doing the right thing.

Getting closer to the studio, David thought of a quick way round, a sudden left turn the wrong way up an empty one-way street that Joss would certainly miss. It would give them enough time to get into the building, and then they'd be safe. He double-parked with a jolt and they rushed into the building, caught in the headlights of Joss's car.

Inside, David was dismayed by the state of his studio. He'd wanted to take Laura somewhere safe and quiet. Instead there was carnage. And there, sitting on a pair of wooden chairs at the far end of the room because the sofas weren't yet dry, were Ned and Mel.

'Laura's in shock,' he said. 'Mel, could you . . . Ned, would you make her a cup of tea or something? I'll just take her up and get her settled. And is the room dry? Or . . .'

'The room's fine,' said Mel, slipping a foot into one of her shoes and reaching for the other.

And then the doorbell began to buzz. On and on. Buzzing. Joss's great fat finger, hard on the button.

'Don't answer it,' said David.

'I'm sorry,' said Laura to the others, as he led her upstairs. 'I'm so sorry. I –'

'Shush,' said David. 'Now mind the steps – they're quite narrow.'

With the doorbell still buzzing, Edmund got up, but delayed going into the kitchen until David and

Laura were in the bedroom. He was aware that Mel was putting her shoes on for a reason, and felt her reaction as if it had been his own.

'Don't go.'

'Edmund, please.' Mel stood up. 'I'm tired, and I don't need you telling me what I should or shouldn't do. I have to go. I should have gone before.'

She caught sight of her reflection in the windows that had been covered with the drawings. She saw the hair, the dirt, the exhaustion on her face and – comparing herself to Laura – felt the sharper edge of David's rejection. Her own rejectability. Who could blame him?

'But it's not safe. Not with that –' as Ned spoke, the buzzing went from a long continuous noise to a series of insistent bursts '– that demented prat down there.'

'I'll use the back entrance.'

'No,' he persisted. 'No, Mel, wait. We'll get David to tell us the truth and then you can make up your mind. But please don't just assume –'

'Assume what?' said David, coming back down the stairs. 'Come on, Ned, get a move on with that tea.'

Edmund felt a flash of rage. 'Since you ask,' he said, shouting over the buzzes, 'I was just telling Mel – your fiancée, remember? – that she shouldn't assume the worst from these nudes. I was trying to convince her that there's nothing to worry about, that you're sure to have an explanation. But I have to tell you, David, I'm having difficulties. It's hard, you know, when the woman in question happens to have that name, when you're the one she runs to the second Joss erupts, and when you seem quite happy to put her in your bed.'

The buzzing stopped. The room was thrown into silence.

David reached the bottom step. 'Just get the tea, will you?' he said. 'And let me talk to Mel.'

When Edmund came back with Laura's tea, Mel had gone. David was standing at his desk, sifting through the drawings.

'Where did she go?'

'Home. There's a flat she shares with Nathan – you remember Nathan? Nathan Hunt, the gallery man?'

But Edmund wasn't interested in Nathan Hunt. 'What did you say to her, David?' he said. 'What happened?'

David looked up. 'It's over. No more engagement, no more wedding. It wasn't working for either of us. Mel said she'd known for some time that something wasn't right – wasn't right for her, every bit as much as me.'

'You're telling me that this has nothing to do with Laura?'

David hesitated. 'It wasn't just me, Ned. I promise you. Mel was clear. She wanted it too.'

'Of course she bloody well did. Would you stick around if you found out that the person you loved was obsessed with somebody else?'

Mel opened the door to Nathan's flat to find him and Fenella on the floor, at the low coffee table in the middle, looking through their guest lists, trying to get the numbers down before sending the invitations out. Smiling, Nathan got to his feet.

'Mel . . .' he said, kissing her.

Mel smiled at him, and turned into the room. 'Hi, Fenella.'

'Hello.' Fenella turned back to the list and pointed at it with the end of her pen. 'Look, darling, can't we scrap Helen and Caspar Dreyfus? He's OK, but we're not going to stay in touch with them as a couple, are we? I find her so uninteresting.'

Mel put down her briefcase, and came over.

'We're trying to decide who *not* to ask,' said Nathan, sitting back down – making sure there was enough room for her beside him at the table. 'It's agonising . . .' He smiled and shook his head. 'How are you and David handling it?'

Mel sat next to Nathan. Curling her legs back round, getting comfortable, she then reached out for his hand.

'We're not getting married,' she said, squeezing it – almost as if Nathan was the one that needed the support.

'What?'

Mel shook her head, unable to find the words again.

Fenella looked across the table to see Nathan with Mel in his arms, rocking her.

'Hey . . . hey, it'll be all right. Oh no, no, darling, you have a good cry. Artists are ghastly and selfish. Didn't like to tell you at the time, but . . . Well, I know Fen's one, but that's different. I know what I'm letting myself in for! Fen, darling, get her a glass of wine while you're in there, will you? And that box of tissues?

'. . . can be an odd fish at times. Did I tell you about the nightmare we had with the catalogue for the last exhibition? Jesus . . . that's a story and a half! Here, take one of these – and another – go on. Blow, we don't mind. Blow hard. And another, and another – let's see if we can get the whole packet strewn across the . . . OK, Fen. Thanks – Look, love. Here's a bin.

'. . . it will get better. And one day you'll thank God – you really will – that it happened now and not after you made all those promises . . .'

Fenella stood there, appalled. She hadn't particularly liked Mel – mainly because, with her career and her fiancé, Mel seemed to be so exasperatingly sorted out; and because Mel and Mel's life seemed to be for Nathan a kind of ideal. But the sight of her there, wrecked and sobbing – her lovely life in tatters – changed all that instantly. And instead of feeling competitive, Fenella was filled with pity and concern. She stood, plum hair flopped about her anxious face, and tried to think what Mel might like . . . but she didn't know Mel well enough. So Fenella did for Mel what she knew that she, Fenella, would want in the circumstances and ran Mel a hot bath, filling it with bubbles.

She poured Mel a large glass of wine, found her a fresh towel and told her there'd be supper waiting, whenever she was done. Mel went into the bathroom, and was touched to see vanilla candles dotted along the windowsill and other ledges. The room was full of flickering and steam. She took off her clothes, got into the bath, and was just taking her first sip of wine when she heard the doorbell, followed by Edmund's voice.

'. . . So sorry to trouble you, Nathan. I was just . . . Is she there? . . . Oh, I see. Yes. Oh well . . . yes, of course I understand. I'll come another time when she . . .'

Still holding the glass of wine, Mel clambered out of the bath, grabbed a towel and, wrapping it round her body, opened the bathroom door. Ned took in the clouds of vanilla steam, the bright red feet and the large glass of wine.

'Mel.' He stepped forward. 'Oh, Mel – I was worried about you, disappearing like that. I thought you might have . . . Are you OK?'

Mel nodded.

'Really?'

She nodded again and hitched the towel so that it sat more securely.

Edmund noticed. He felt the awkwardness in the gesture and looked round to where Nathan and Fenella stood, transfixed, in the doorway to the kitchen. 'But this is a bad time,' he said, turning back to Mel. 'You get back to your bath, and I'll find a better evening.' He was smiling at her. 'We've got a lot to talk about, but – no, nothing that can't wait until tomorrow night. Are you free then?'

They agreed that she would come to his new flat for dinner. He'd cook. Ned sat on a sofa, wrote out the address on one of Fenella's brand-new envelopes in case she didn't remember where he'd taken her, and handed it to Mel. Then he kissed her goodbye and left.

Mel returned to her bath with a smile on her face that Nathan had not seen before. He'd expected to scrap Edmund from the guest list. Fenella didn't know him and, while Nathan liked him, he only knew him through meeting him at David's exhibitions. But seeing Edmund that night – his concern, and Mel's reaction – Nathan decided to invite him after all.

Unless they were specifically marked 'private and confidential', all letters addressed to people who worked under Philippa Stone were opened, first, by her. She wasn't nosy. She didn't want to know the ins and outs of their private lives. It was just the most efficient way of keeping abreast of what was happening on all her files – and everybody accepted it.

Mel's mother, however, knew nothing of this rule. She wasn't used to office etiquette, to doing things like marking letters 'private and confidential', and consequently it was Philippa – and not Mel – who opened her letter on Tuesday morning.

'I am so sorry,' said Philippa, barging into Mel's office at ten o'clock with the note in her hands. 'I – I'd read it almost before I knew what I was doing. I . . . Here.'

Mel recognised the blue of the hospital paper instantly. Taking it from Philippa, she unfolded it and began to read.

My darling, wrote Clare in her disjointed hand.
Your letter. . .
So many things to say to you – and this is not the time. So much of what you say is right, but there are still things you don't understand – and at some stage, I promise you, we will talk about this properly.

But in the meantime, you mustn't worry. Will you promise me that? Nothing will happen until I get strong again, which won't be for weeks. The doctor

doesn't think I'll be properly well again until
Christmas – and that's over a month away! So you
see, I'm fine at the moment.

I know it's hard, darling, but you just have to be
patient – be patient, and know that it is enough for
me that I have your support.

I love you too,

M

PS – please don't try to reply to this, it really isn't
a good idea – not with your father staying here too.

Mel looked up to see Philippa still standing there.
'. . . She's right, you know.'

'Oh God.' Mel tossed the letter aside, and laughed
bitterly. 'Not you too. How long am I expected to
hang around like this, waiting for him to do it again?'

'It's her decision, Mel. And I'm sure it'll be easier
for her to make it, knowing that she has you to help
her when she's ready.'

'When she's ready, when she's ready . . . What's she
waiting *for*?'

Philippa shrugged. 'I don't know,' she said. 'But
after this, you may find it happens sooner than you
think.'

*

Joss Savil's houses had excellent security systems. He
paid a fortune for an ex-secret service man to come
privately, each year, to discuss new methods and
ensure that each system was impenetrable. Joss was
obsessive about it. He had a strong sense of territory
and possession. It was bad enough when they had
trespassers at Merwick, but the idea of being burgled
– some stranger rifling through his things – filled him

449

with particular horror. He'd sleep with a knife, or sometimes even a gun, to hand – should an intruder make the mistake of entering the house while he was there (Laura got quite a shock the first time her affectionate hand slipped under Joss's pillow and made contact with the hard steel sheath of a nine-inch blade). And, if he was away, the electrical systems were connected not only to the police, but also to his mobile telephone so that he'd know exactly what was happening in which house, all across the world. But the one thing he hadn't considered – the one possession he was unable to wire up – was his wife.

Taking his hand off the buzzer-button that night, conceding temporary defeat, Joss had driven back over the river in a kind of trance. His rage shifted from noisy fury to cooling vengeance and as he drove, he planned.

Joss knew that Laura loved him. He'd seen her expression the day they married, he knew how much he could give her, how fully she'd adopted his lifestyle. Laura enjoyed luxuries. She enjoyed dressing well and being noticed. It meant a lot to her to have the financial weight that would allow her sense of style full sway.

And she didn't just love his money. Joss still couldn't quite understand it, but Laura really did seem to love him too: his body, his voice, his smell, his laugh. She noticed his quirks – like having lime not lemon in his gin and tonic, always having a window open, an extra pillow on his side of the bed – and loved them too. She never minded when he put her down, always understood when he was tired, or bored, or when he felt like sex. And always delivered.

And then there was the baby. Laura's parents had separated when she was little, and Joss knew that she'd do everything in her power to give her child a better home – unbroken, secure. It would take more than some measly middle-class artist to wreck this marriage, and Joss was certain she'd come back. Probably come tomorrow.

He wouldn't forgive her right away. There would be punishments, but only mild ones – just enough to ensure she didn't do it again.

And in the meantime . . .

Two can play at this game, he thought, as if he was talking to Laura directly. And if you're considering alternatives, then why the hell can't I? It's not as if I'm short of them.

There was Annabel Glass – too easy, really. And there was Alice.

Alice running out on Joss the day he'd got back from Merwick was not, Joss knew, because she'd gone off him. It was because he'd frightened her and, of course, because he was married. Alice, quite rightly, had expressed doubts on that subject. Joss respected her for it. What's more, he found fear – fear in someone so feisty – extremely sexy. If Alice knew that Laura had left him – perhaps if he were to hint that the split was directly as a result of what had happened with Alice – then maybe, just maybe, she'd feel differently. It was worth a shot.

He'd call her about it tomorrow. He'd reiterate his apology, and then give it a little twist.

34

Ned was cooking dinner for Mel. He'd cleared all his boxes into the spare room. He'd laid the table very carefully, trying to get the right balance: not overly intimate, but not cold either. He'd decided against a tablecloth, and not to have any flowers there, but he thought he could get away with a couple of candles, and there was a good bottle of wine open on the table. He'd use the big glasses.

Wondering for a moment if flowers were too much even for the sitting room, he stood there with the vase in his hands, and felt a wave of apprehension. All the confidence he'd had in the supermarket – happily buying organic food, vintage wine, extravagant flowers . . . that confidence had left him. What if she didn't feel the same way? What if she was still in love with David? Such feelings didn't vanish overnight.

Ned threw the flowers away. He didn't want to risk it. Stuffing the lily buds into the bin bag along with the food wrappings, the wine-cork, and ash from the three cigarettes he'd just smoked without realising, he felt calmer. He'd tied up the bin bag and had turned to his next task – peeling potatoes – when the telephone rang. Ned wondered whether to answer it.

He had only half an hour to finish cooking, have a shower and find a fresh shirt in one of the many suitcases laid out on the floor of his bedroom. He let it ring on to the answerphone, and listened.

'Ned,' said Alice's voice. It sounded surprisingly flat. 'Ned, it's me. Again. I'm sorry to keep doing this to you, but I – I've just had another call from Joss, and I . . . Oh God, Ned. I can't believe what I've done. You were right all along and I've only got myself to blame, but . . .'

Ned stopped peeling mid-potato and ran to the telephone. He picked it up.

'Alice? Alice, sweetheart, it's me. I'm here. There's nothing for you to – Hang on while I switch off the machine – there. Now. Tell me exactly what Joss said. He has apologised, hasn't he?'

'Oh yes, he's apologised. That's all fine.'

'But . . .?'

Alice relayed the things that Joss had said: about separating from Laura, and how it was all because of Alice. She wasn't going to let Joss down now, was she? She couldn't turn her back on him. Not now that he'd left his wife – sacrificed his marriage – all for her.

And Alice had felt so awful, so guilty, she'd agreed to see him. But she was scared. She didn't want to see him. She didn't want –

'You're seeing him tonight?' said Ned.

'What else could I do? He sounded so upset. He – he'll be here in ten minutes, Ned, and I'm –'

'Alice sweetheart, where are you?' She was in a bar in Mayfair.

'. . . OK. Now listen carefully – got a pen? I'm giving you my new address . . . That's right, the place

453

I took you to, and you're to get a cab and come straight here. You understand? Don't speak to him again. No – just stand him up. He's . . . . Well, I'll explain it all when I see you.'

Alice didn't spend long at Ned's flat. She sat on the newly carpeted floor of his sitting room, drinking from the bottle of wine that Ned had intended for Mel, listening to him explain the truth about Joss and Laura – and why it had nothing to do with Alice at all. As they talked, the soft smell of roasting chicken wafted through from the kitchen.

Alice lifted her nose and, sniffing appreciatively, caught Ned's eye.

'No.'

'Oh, go on, Ned. I'm starving.'

'Then go home to your parents and eat with them.'

'Just a little mouthful . . .'

'No,' he said, laughing. 'No, Alice. There won't be enough to go round.'

'Go round?' Alice got to her feet and went into the kitchen, where a table had been laid for two. 'Oh God!' she wailed, running back in. 'Why didn't you *tell* me? Right. Where's my coat? I'm out . . .'

He tried to make her wait for him to call a cab, but she was determined. 'No, Ned,' she said, marching down the stairs. 'Absolutely not. I'm not playing gooseberry to your date. I'm a big girl now. I can find one by myself.'

Back down on the street, however, Alice's spirits drooped. It had been warm and comforting up there with Ned. Now, out here, she was thrown back on her own company and the anxiety of the last few hours – back to the horrible things that Joss had said to her, and the guilt that she'd felt. It wasn't good. She needed company and, hailing a cab on Westbourne Grove, Alice went home to her parents.

They had finished eating when she got in, and were sitting at the table in the kitchen, looking at photographs and laughing.

'Oh, darling, do come and have a look at these! It's Izzy – see? And is that the new boyfriend, do you think?'

Alice put her bag on one of the chairs, took the photograph, and laughed. 'Yes. Definitely. Look where his hand is.'

'Where?' said Roger, grabbing it.

Camilla took a plate of food from the oven and handed it to Alice with a grin. 'He's been like this all evening. First there was that call for you –'

'What call?'

'Darling . . .' Camilla turned to her husband, reproach in her eye.

Roger looked up, innocently, from the photograph of Izzy. 'What?'

'Darling, you did write out Alice's message, didn't you?'

'What message?'

Camilla sighed and smiled, simultaneously. 'The one from that young man you took an instant dislike to. The one that left you huffing and puffing like some over-protective –'

'I did not huff and puff. And as it happens, Alice, I didn't take a dislike to him. He was very polite. But if your friends will persist in ringing when we're just sitting down to dinner, then you can't expect me to engage them in conversation. We might cook for you,

455

and ferry you around, and accommodate you, and fork out thousands for your education, but I really do draw the line at being your social secretary. Just get them to call you on your mobile, can't you? That's why we gave you the damn thing in the first place.'

Alice looked at her mother. 'Any idea who it was?'

'Bruno – wasn't it, darling? Something like that. And . . . Oh, and look!' Camilla tore the corner off Roger's newspaper. 'Not so useless after all.'

Smiling, Alice took the shred of paper with Bruno's number on it – the triple seven at the end – and put it in her pocket.

This time she would, most certainly, call him back.

It wasn't far from Nathan's flat to Ned's, and Mel decided to walk.

She wasn't happy about her mother's letter, but it was – she supposed – a breakthrough. Like an addict, it had taken a long time for Clare to admit that there was a problem at all, and Mel couldn't help hoping that perhaps this would be a turning point. Of course it was still worrying, and her father was still every bit as dangerous, but at least the stalemate was over.

Mel wasn't sure whether to believe what Clare had said about Greg not hurting her while she appeared vulnerable. But she did believe that while Clare remained in hospital, she'd be safe. She could also take comfort from the fact that, when Clare was let out of hospital, the nurse would let Mel know. When that time came, Mel would have to think very carefully about what action she could take. In the meantime, all she could do was take Philippa's advice, follow her mother's instructions, and wait.

There was, in any case, more than enough for her to be thinking about here in London – cancelling the wedding venue, the florist, the caterers, and the humiliating call to the dressmaker. They'd all sounded so sorry for her. And, of course, she'd had to tell her parents. It hadn't been easy reassuring her mother that it was the right thing for both of them, and then calming her father's rage.

'. . . when I think of everything I did for that young man! All that money spent on –'

'It's okay, Dad. You'll get it back.'

'So I should hope . . .'

But nor had it been as distressing as she'd expected. Maybe she was still numb. Maybe, in contrast to what was happening with her mother, it wasn't so bad. Or maybe it was because of Edmund.

The way he'd spoken to her at Nathan's, the fact he'd come at all, the way he'd kissed her goodbye, and the things he'd said – *We've got a lot to talk about* – set her mind racing.

Three months ago, David was everything she'd wanted in a husband: beautiful, romantic, and slightly intriguing. She'd liked the lack of predictability about him. She'd loved the fact that he was an artist. She'd loved Virginia. And she'd adored the combination of healthy family *and* romantic career, stability *and* excitement. It was very seductive to someone like Mel, with her safe career, and bruised family.

But she wondered now if David had ever really made her happy. Sure, she was happy when they'd started going out. She was overjoyed when they'd got engaged. But that happiness had been more about

457

realising a dream, a personal goal, than anything shared with David. She'd admired him. She'd wanted him – badly. But when she thought about their daily lives, the way he'd keep things from her, the way he always seemed to need more space than she did, his reluctance to sacrifice any kind of independence . . . she realised that the lack of warmth had hurt her. He was kind, but he managed to be kind without really engaging his heart. He was intense, moral, sensitive – all things that should have made him warm – and yet he wasn't really warm at all. Not to Mel, at any rate. Or Virginia, or Ned. He treated them all with the cool watchfulness that an adolescent would show towards an overloving parent. And after months of trying, something had quietly snapped. Mel wasn't interested any more in winning the heart of a man she no longer respected. David was a wonderful 'acquisition'. But he was no match for her, no real companion in the rough business of living.

The fact that it had been David who'd blown the whistle on their engagement was simply a relief to her. And once Mel had recovered from the sting of being rejected, she was grateful. Not only had David removed any guilt she might have felt if she'd been the one to do it (especially if she'd done it with his brother in mind), he'd also caught it in time. Mel hoped she'd have had the sense to call the wedding off. But she was glad that, in the end, she hadn't had to. David had done it for her. She'd had a lucky escape.

All of which meant that she could, at last, turn to Ned. She could indulge her mind with thoughts previously forbidden. She could mull over all the little things he'd said to her, and done – waking up that night, wrapped in the duvet he'd brought down, was her favourite at the moment – without the usual interruptions from her conscience. She could walk to his flat with a spring in her step, her head held high with guiltless anticipation.

Ned was built of stronger material than his brother. He was less refined, less graceful, less boyishly beautiful. With Ned, things didn't need to be perfect. He had views, and he aired them – happy if someone were to disagree, happy to debate. If he cared what people thought of him, it was clear that he'd long given up believing he could make them change their minds. He was flawed and inconsistent, but that only seemed to make him more tolerant of flaws in other people – in fact, he seemed to prefer it. Mel smiled into the air as she thought of the way he'd handled her bad mood on the night of the flood at David's studio he hadn't confronted her, or ignored her. He'd just laughed, laughed with affection, and waited for her to get over it.

Mel was aware that there might be a very simple explanation for this sudden change of heart: overexposure to one kind of person, and of course she'd be attracted to the opposite. And perhaps Ned's very differences from David were what drew her to him now. Only . . . only Mel didn't think it was that. There was more to her feelings for Ned than the mere fact that he wasn't David.

For a start, there were definite similarities. Certain aspects of Ned's appearance – the set of his eyes, and the way he walked – echoed David's. The two of them sounded identical. And, like David, Ned was never predictable. He was always surprising Mel, always throwing their conversations around so that she never knew which angle he'd come from next. But he did it for fun – to see her reaction, to make her laugh. It was his way of communicating, of forging a bond. Not because he wanted to keep her at arm's length; not because he had preoccupations he'd really rather not share with her.

Mel had never been with someone who gave so much so effortlessly. She knew now that this was what she wanted. This was the kind of happiness that would stay with her, in one form or another, for the rest of her life – because it was happiness that came not so much from owning him, or admiring him (although of course she'd get joy from doing those things as well) as simply being in his company. And when she thought of Ned like that . . . well, David was irrelevant.

It was hard for Mel to control her excitement as she got close. Walking in the darkness that November night, in and out of streetlighting – past the boutiques and antique shops of Notting Hill, the bars and gardens, the delis and the bakeries – she did try to tell herself she could be wrong. She tried to listen to the voice of caution, reminding her that Ned had not been specific. All he'd said was that they had a lot to talk about, and Mel had to prepare herself for the unlikely eventuality that this wasn't a date. It was possible – unlikely, but still possible – that Mel might have misinterpreted the invitation. He could just be being nice. He could be worried about what had happened with David, and making sure she was OK. She mustn't expect too much. Mustn't set herself up for another disappointment.

But the kick in her stride and the light in her eye, the way her mouth wasn't quite closed – they told of different expectations. Men looked at her as they passed her on the street and when, at a crossing, she caught sight of her reflection in the shop glass on the other side of the road, she walked towards it, and realised why they were looking at her. Gone was that drained look from the other night. Gone was the practical businesslike professional. This was simply a girl on a date – and she looked good.

Turning into Ned's street, however, Mel stopped short. There by his door was Alice Enderby, climbing out of a cab, miniskirt riding up her long dark legs, and falling into Edmund's arms. Mel watched him pay the cab driver. She watched him hold Alice – stroke her hair – and take her into the flat.

Mel leant against a wall, and let the sight sink in.

Then she turned and walked in the other direction, back to Nathan's flat.

At nine, he rang her mobile.

Again, at nine thirty.

At ten, he rang Nathan's number – but Nathan and Fenella were out, and Mel didn't answer that either.

Before she went to bed, she listened to his messages. Nice and friendly, almost apologetic for ringing at all, then sympathetic 'Oh well, maybe you've forgotten – but don't worry. We can always do another night. Or perhaps you're stuck in some meeting?'

And then a little deflated.

'Oh well. Guess you're not coming. I'm going to bed now, but let's speak tomorrow – OK?'

Next day, he rang her in the office.

'Ned, hi – yes, I'm sorry. I know . . . No. It wasn't that. I'm afraid I just forgot. I'm sorry. I just . . . Yes it would, but . . . but Ned, the truth is I'm really busy right now. Got a lot on. Can I call you when it's less manic?'

Ned got the message.

It took Joss an hour to realise that Alice wasn't coming – sitting in an empty corner of that Mayfair bar, drinking, and thinking miserably of Laura. He missed her. He didn't want some precocious schoolgirl. Not really. He wanted his Laura, his lovely wife with her lovely face and her lovely, lovely body.

Joss was drunk. He didn't want anyone else – but nor did he want to be alone. And when Alice didn't appear, he found himself searching for Annabel's number in his mobile telephone directory.

That evening at Blake's had given him a kick because it was naughty, but he hadn't been that impressed by Annabel. After Laura's fabulous figure and well-groomed skin, Annabel could hardly compare. He didn't like her bottom, or her scent, or her underwear. Underneath the trim neat clothes was a neglected woman with an old grey baggy bra. She'd discarded it pretty quickly, but he'd noticed. It had made him realise how lucky he was to have Laura. Lovely Laura. So next morning he'd paid the Blake's bill and left Annabel there in bed – a big shaggy sex-mess with little piggy eyes – and hadn't followed it up. And when Annabel had rung him, he'd told her he felt guilty. He simply couldn't do it to Laura.

But that was before he knew about David. Just one

more visit couldn't hurt anyone. Annabel had obviously enjoyed it, and while she had her limitations, it was better than being alone. He couldn't be alone tonight. He just couldn't bear it.

Annabel had just got in from a photo-shoot to accompany an article she'd agreed to appear in, to promote her book. She was happy and excited, and keen to celebrate. Why didn't she join him in the bar? Or – she was giggling slightly – why didn't they go back to Blake's?

'I'll come to you,' he said.

Annabel still hadn't taken off the make-up from the shoot when, ten minutes later, she opened the door. Because the book was about glamorous people, they'd gone for a heavy high-gloss look – with exaggerated lips and eyes. In the orange streetlight, she looked like a prostitute. Back inside, in the lamplight of her small sitting room, she looked more like a clown. Joss turned off the lights and came towards her, pulling off his shirt. Muttering the usual rubbish, the usual passwords: *beautiful, darling, love, for ever* – they always worked – Joss undid his zip.

'What about Laura?' said Annabel, arching sexily. 'I thought you said you couldn't do it to her. I thought you –'

Joss tried not to listen. He pressed himself to Annabel with added strength – grabbing at her hair, her breasts, her arse . . . but something wasn't right. Something was missing.

He pulled back. 'I'm so sorry,' he said, suddenly exhausted, suddenly sober. 'I'm sorry, Annabel. I – You're right. I can't.'

'What do you mean, you can't?'

Joss did up his zip. He couldn't even look at her.

'You mean you're . . . Joss.' She was smiling. 'Joss, darling – it doesn't matter. I don't mind. It could happen to –'

'It does matter,' he said, picking up his wallet and walking to the door.

'But it happens to everyone. It's –'

'I don't want to talk about it.'

'But, darling –'

She reached out to him, but he shook her off. 'I just want to go home – all right?'

'Is it me? Is it the make-up? I can wash it off, Joss. I can –'

He shook his head. 'I'll call you,' he said, opening the door, barely looking back.

But they both knew he wouldn't.

Joss walked towards the car in tears. It wasn't just Laura's body he missed. It was the way she'd made him feel about himself, the way she'd given his life some kind of purpose. With no career to focus on, Joss had needed other projects – and no project had thrilled him more than the one he'd embarked upon with Laura. Not only had their marriage grounded him and added gentle structure to his days, Laura had brought his riches to life. With Laura beside him, the Ferrari flew and the dinner parties glowed. He could taste the champagne.

The idea that he was back to the Joss he'd been before he'd met her – the aimless, insecure man who'd take up offers indiscriminately – emptied him of energy. He didn't want to be like that any more. He didn't want those lonely freedoms. He didn't want Annabel, or Alice, or anyone like that. He just wanted Laura.

So he went home to wait for her. And when, by Friday, she still hadn't appeared, Joss decided to act. He knew that Laura was due for a scan that morning. He knew which hospital it was, which ward, which doctor – and decided to go along too.

35

Virginia couldn't believe it. How had it happened?
How could David do that to Mel? And how could she
just walk away? Didn't she have any fight in her?

'She wanted the break-up as much as me,' said
David.

Virginia didn't believe that, either. It was clear
from the wall of silence at her end of the line.

David sighed. 'She did, Mum. She really did. I
promise you, it's for the best.'

After they spoke, she sat down and wrote a long
tear-spattered letter to Mel. Then she tore it up in
disgust and rang Ned at the office. Ned would know
what to do. And if anyone could stop this dreadful
thing from happening, it was him.

Ned, however, had better things to do than talk at
length about David and Mel, and ways to get them
back together.

'Darling, please.'

'I'm really not the person to talk to about this,
Mum. There's nothing I can do. And anyway, I'm
late for a meeting.'

'Couldn't I see you later?'

'I'm out later.' Ned sighed. 'I'm sorry, Mum, but

it's really David's problem.'

'And Mel's problem,' said Virginia, close to tears again, 'and mine . . .'

Ned agreed to meet her for lunch. 'Get a cab to my offices. You have the address, don't you? Fenwick & Moore, City Square – that's right. North side. Go into the lobby and ask for me.'

Virginia had never been to Edmund's offices. She was dropped at the doors of a marble building with a vast façade, and 'Fenwick & Moore' etched above the door. Virginia paid the driver and put her gloves back on. It was a bright day. Winter-bright and cold. But inside the building, it was dim and quiet. Virginia's feet tapped across the floor. They echoed, as if she was in a cathedral, into an air of hushed respect.

'Edmund Nicholson?' said the man at the desk. He seemed to whisper slightly. 'Ah – Mr Nicholson's on the top floor, ma'am.'

'Thank you,' said Virginia, heading for the lift.

'But you'll need . . . ma'am? Ma'am, I'm sorry, ma'am, but you do need to sign in. Thank you, ma'am.'

Virginia took the pen, wrote her name in the book, and was given a plastic pass.

'Just clip it to your handbag, ma'am. That's right. And it's the first lift on the right. Takes you straight up.'

Edmund was there, waiting for her, at the top. His suit was dark, discreet, worn with unselfconscious ease, and the tired expression on his face only made him more impressive.

'Right,' he said, kissing her. 'Let's go.'

'But can't I just have a quick look at your office? I want to see where you sit, darling, and what your view is. Must be amazing, all the way up here. And –'

'No, Mum. You can't.'

'Oh, go on . . .'

He shook his head, and held the lift doors open. 'It would be a breach of client confidentiality, now come back in here. Let's go down and find something to eat.'

'I can't get over how smart it is,' she said, as the lift fell – floor after floor. 'And you're at the very top.'

'Only literally.'

'What?'

'Well, I may have offices up there, and I may be a partner,' he said, smiling, 'but there's some way to go before it's Fenwick, Moore & Nicholson.'

Virginia wasn't listening. 'It's amazing,' she said, as the lift reached the bottom and the doors slid open. 'I – I can't tell you how proud your father would have been, darling. So proud of what you've done . . .'

'You mean that?' he said, slowing his step.

For some reason, Virginia couldn't look at him. 'Of course I mean it,' she said briskly. 'Now – where are we going? Left or right?'

He'd planned to take her to a wine bar round the corner, but after the things she'd just said he felt entirely different. They went to the Hungry Trader. It was filling up, and tables had been reserved, but there was still enough room. They were ushered to a table in one of the booths and given a couple of menus.

They talked intensely, and at length, about David and Mel. After his reluctance to speak about it on the

468

telephone earlier, Virginia had not expected Ned to be particularly forthcoming. Instead, he had all kinds of views on the subject. He was opening up to her, more than she'd ever thought possible.

'I think David was looking for another mother,' he said to her, smiling. 'He adores you, Mum. He loves the way you spoil him.'

Virginia looked down at her empty plate. 'Oh, darling,' she said. 'It's only because –'

'It's because he needs it,' said Ned, for her. 'Or seems to need it. I understand. I understand because –' He touched her arm. 'Mum? Look at me. You mustn't worry. I know what it's like, because I spoil him myself. So does Mel. We all do it, but I don't think it's actually what he wants. There are all kinds of difficulties with Laura – like how he's going to afford her, for starters – but she is someone who needs looking after herself. She's someone he wants to take care of, not the other way round, and maybe that's not such a bad thing.'

'But what about Mel?'

Edmund sighed. What about Mel, indeed? Mel: who'd coolly failed to turn up for dinner, who'd given ground to his fears that she wasn't interested – not like that – and who was now was out of their lives altogether. Mel: whose blind attempts to find happiness and fulfilment seemed to lead her in precisely the opposite direction. And it wasn't just her career. It was men, too. Why couldn't she see how ill-advised it was for her to hold a candle for a man like David? Wasn't it obvious that she needed someone with a healthier outlook and a stronger mind?

'I love David, Mum, I do. But would you really

wish that bundle of neuroses and obsessions on Mel? Don't you think she deserves someone with a bit more – strength? More maturity?'

Virginia stared at him.

'She's better off without him turning her into a nanny, holding her back. She needs to find herself an equal. Someone who'll –'

'Someone like you?' said Virginia, and then wished she hadn't. She was feeling closer to Edmund than she'd done in years, but this was pushing it.

Ned leant back for the waiter to take his plate, and gave a bitter smile. 'Oh, Mel's not interested in me,' he said, reaching for his cigarettes.

'How do you know?'

He didn't reply, merely shook his head, and asked the waiter to bring them the bill.

'Well, I'll just go and tidy up,' said Virginia, awkwardly, shuffling along to the edge of her booth, bag and stick in her hand. 'Won't be too long.'

Edmund sat alone, waiting for the bill. He looked out over the restaurant. It was emptying now. Time to be back in the office. Time to get on with the afternoon. Business, business . . . and then he heard her voice – clear, quiet, calm – coming out of the next booth.

'It's no good, Philippa. I can't. You know I can't. It's a personal decision, and I feel very strongly about it.'

A shiver went down his back.

'Even if I say that we can offer you double what you're making at the moment?'

'But that's –'

'That's what?' said the other voice, laughing.

470

'That's more than a partner's starting salary! You can't . . .'

'We can, if we make you a partner.'

Philippa Stone was worried. She knew about Mel's mother going into hospital. She knew that the engagement was off. And she knew that Mel was looking for somewhere new to live (in spite of Nathan's and Fenella's protestations, Mel was still determined to move out). She saw the hours that Mel was spending in the office – the standard of her work was higher than ever – and dreaded what would happen when she left. That girl was heading for a breakdown. She couldn't see it – they never did – but the one thing holding it all together was her job.

Checking the number in the internal telephone directory, she'd dialled the secretary of Ian Oliphant, the senior partner, and asked when would be a good time for her to come up and see him.

'Hang on, Philippa,' said the secretary, twisting to see through the glass. 'I think he . . . yes, he's in there now. Shall I put you through?'

'No. No – I'll come straight up.'

The following day, she took Mel out to lunch. She told Mel's secretary not to expect them back for at least three hours, and took her to a new restaurant she'd been told about on Bishopsgate. Ian Oliphant thought it was marvellous.

'How exciting!' said Mel, holding the cab door for Philippa to get in. 'What's it called?'

'Hungry Trader – something like that. You probably know it already.'

Mel didn't know it. She followed Philippa into the

warmth – they were ushered into one of the booths – and was handed an extensive menu. Putting it to one side for a second, she looked out at the mass of suits and wondered if she'd miss City life: the affluence, the competition, the energy . . .

'Now, let's get something seriously good to drink,' said Philippa, grabbing the wine list and frowning at it.

. . . and the kindness, thought Mel with a smile. God only knew how she'd ended up with the kindest boss in town, but she'd definitely miss that.

'You see, Mel. You think I'm taking you out to lunch to say goodbye, or good luck, or to cheer you up, or something sentimental like that – but now that I have you here, I can get to the real reason.'

'Real reason?'

Still looking at the list, Philippa grinned. 'Come on, you know what they say about free lunches.'

'Oh God.'

'Right,' Philippa looked at the waiter. 'We'll have the Montrachet. No, not the Puligny. Not the Chassagne. The Le.'

'Le Montrachet it is, madam. And is madam ready to order food?'

'We most certainly are not.'

Philippa waited for him to go and then resumed her subject. 'Now, before we get completely pissed, here's my offer.'

'Your offer?'

'I spoke to Ian yesterday – told him about you, and about . . . well, about this madness of you leaving. And we discussed what more we could offer you to tempt you to stay.'

Mel shook her head and reached for the bread. 'It's no good, Philippa. I can't. You know I can't. It's a personal decision, and I feel very strongly about it.'

'Even if I say that we can offer you double what you're making at the moment?'

The bread fell from Mel's hand. 'But that's –'

'That's what?' said Philippa, smiling.

'That's more than a partner's starting salary! You can't . . .'

'We can, if we make you a partner.'

They sat in silence while the waiter stood beside them, opening the bottle. He wrapped a napkin round its neck and poured some for Philippa to approve. Pouring, wiping, swirling, sniffing, nodding . . . as the ritual went on around her, Mel thought about what this meant. There was a clunk as the bottle landed in the ice bucket.

'We're also offering you a lump-sum incentive – straight up – of a hundred thousand. Not huge I know, but you can expect much more of that sort of thing when you make equity partnership – which you will, Mel. In much less time than you realise.'

'It's not the money, Philippa. Or even the prospects. It's . . .'

'You may not care for money and prospects in themselves, but they show how much you're valued, and – I'm sorry, Mel – I know you too well. Those things matter to you. What's more, you're good at this job, not just competent. And –'

'I don't enjoy it.'

'Rubbish!' said Philippa, laughing. 'Rubbish! It's perfectly obvious that you get a great deal of pleasure from this kind of work. Just look at the hours you do,

473

even when the pressure's non-existent. For God's sake, girl, you're leaving us next month and you're still in at ten o'clock!'

'Some of those documents bore me rigid.'

'Me too. But what about the clauses you actually negotiate – do they bore you as well?'

'No, but –'

'Well then.' Philippa refilled both their glasses. 'That deals with that one. What else? What else don't you like?'

Mel picked up her glass. 'The truth is, Philippa, I was pushed into this job. I didn't choose it. It was entirely my . . .'

'Your father?'

Mel nodded.

'So what would you have chosen, Mel, if things had been different? What would you have done?'

Mel didn't know. She put her head in her hands. 'I – I'm sorry, Philippa. I . . .'

Mel couldn't help it. The sweet concern, and that extraordinary offer – from the one person who was expected to treat her like dirt – while her father couldn't even bring himself to listen. Philippa reached over the table, held Mel's wrist, and waited for her to calm down.

'I'm so sorry,' said Mel. 'I guess I –'

'It's OK, love. You've had a rough time.'

Wiping her eyes with her napkin, Mel smiled and swallowed. 'I don't know why you think I'm worth so much to the firm,' she said laughing. 'Look at me!'

Philippa did not return to the subject of Mel staying on. The offer was on the table, she'd just have to wait and see what Mel chose to do. They ordered their food, drank their wine, and began to talk about other things – Mel's flat hunting, Philippa's children, the firm's Christmas party.

Virginia hated restaurant loos. They were never easy to get to, and it always took for ever to climb up and down the stairs. Ten minutes after she'd gone, she reappeared and – leaning heavily on her stick – made her way back to the booths. It was only when she got quite close that she thought she recognised Mel.

She had to come right up close to the booth Mel was sitting in to check that it was really her.

'Mel?'

Mel turned.

'My God, how extraordinary. How –'

'Virginia.' Mel clambered spontaneously out of the booth, 'Oh, Virginia . . .'

Virginia simply hugged her. Then, breaking off, she pulled back and called out, 'Ned? Ned, come out here.' She poked her head round the booth partition. 'It's Mel!'

Ned came out and round. He stood beside his mother and gave Mel a small nod.

Mel stared at him.

And Ned – expressionless – briefly met her gaze, before turning to the woman Mel was with.

'Oh,' said Mel automatically. 'Oh, of course. Ned. Virginia. This is my boss, Philippa Stone. Philippa, this is Virginia Nicholson and her son, Edmu –'

'I know Ned!' said Philippa, laughing and kissing his cheek. 'We were at law school together. And this is your mother?' The two women shook hands, and then Philippa turned back to Ned. 'Great article in

The Lawyer last week, by the way – that photograph made you look as if you were in your twenties.' She peered at Ned's hair. 'Did they airbrush out the grey, or did you dye it specially for the occasion?'

Ned felt his head and laughed. But his smile faded as he turned to Mel. 'How are you?'

'Fine.'

They fell silent.

'Well,' he went on, turning to Virginia. 'Well, I guess we'd better get a move on.' Extracting himself, he went to fetch their coats.

Outside, Virginia slipped her arm into Ned's and they walked up to the street, to find her a cab.

'Well?' she said briskly, when they got to the top of the steps. 'Are you going to tell me what all that was about? Or am I going to have to ask Mel myself?'

Guiding her on, slowing his step with hers, Ned told Virginia the things he'd overheard. He told her about the offer, the rejection, and the tears.

'How can she throw it all away?' he said. 'All because of that ghastly father. How can she?'

Virginia listened to the feeling in his voice, the passionate frustration. And as she listened she thought of Mel's face, just now in the restaurant, so pale, so visibly affected by Ned's sudden appearance. And it occurred to her that perhaps David had been right after all. Perhaps Mel had really wanted to break it off, every bit as much as David. Perhaps she, too, was in love with someone else.

Virginia stopped at the side of the road. 'I think you should go back,' she said.

'What? To the restaurant?'

'I think you should go there now. Go back and tell

her how you feel – no, don't look at me like that, Edmund. You know full well what I'm talking about.'

Ned shook his head. 'But I told you before, Mum, she's not interested in me. She –'

'How can you be sure?'

He told her how Mel had stood him up on Tuesday night.

'So you're just going to walk away, are you? Without even telling her how you feel?'

'But she's made it very clear that she –'

'Well,' said Virginia 'no wonder you've never had much luck with women. I'm sorry, Ned, I don't want to hurt you – but honestly! What do you expect when you shy away at the first sign of difficulty?'

Ned said nothing.

'Speak to her,' she urged. And, hailing a cab with her stick, Virginia got in and wound down the window. 'Go back,' she said again. 'Do it now. The longer you leave it, the harder it will be.'

Ned went back to the restaurant. They won't still be there, he told himself. They'll have gone.

But they hadn't. They had their coats on, and were just coming up the steps as he turned to go down.

'Mel,' he said quickly – running down to her. 'Mel – please. We must talk.'

Mel slung her bag over her arm and looked at him. The look was strained, as if she thought it was going to be an ordeal, listening to him, and Edmund started to lose his nerve.

'I'll see you back at the office,' said Philippa, hurrying up the steps. 'Bye, Ned.'

Mel waited until she was gone. 'Well, what is it?' she said. 'I do need to get back to the office as well, you know. There's a lot of stuff to do before I leave.'

They walked up the steps and stood at the top, face to face in the cool air. Ned looked for a crack, a small sign, something to tell him that she might care – but there was nothing.

'I want to talk to you about your job,' he said, instead.

'You overheard?'

'Yes, I did, and I think you're mad.'

Mel shook her head, and began walking towards the road.

'In a few weeks' time, you'll have nowhere to live, no one to look after you, no job, and no means of helping your mother if ever she decides she's had enough.'

Mel walked faster.

'I don't know how much money you have saved up, but, believe me, it runs out pretty quickly when there's nothing coming in. You'll be struggling, Mel. Struggling on all fronts – and none of it remotely necessary. Of course, I can help you out,' he went on, 'but that's not –'

'I don't want your help.'

'Then how are you going to do it? How will you survive? Are you expecting to win the lottery? Are you waiting for some white knight to come along and save you?'

Mel continued walking, indignant rage in every step.

'Oh, for God's sake . . .' His hand swung out to stop her. 'Think – will you? Just think for a second about what it'll be like.'

Mel turned to him. 'I have thought about it.'

'You're telling me you'd rather live on benefit, in council accommodation, getting your clothes from Oxfam, your food from bargain baskets? You'd rather travel on public transport when you're a shaky old woman with people barging into you, no pension, no security, relying on the NHS . . .'

'But I'm not going to do that. I'm going to get a job.'

'What job?'

'It doesn't matter what job,' she said. 'Just so long as it's not law. Just so long as it's my choice.'

'You'd rather clean loos or do telephone sales? You'd rather –'

'I won't have to do that, Edmund. I'm a qualified lawyer.'

'Who's about to become a temp.' Edmund took a pack of cigarettes from his inside pocket. He offered her one – which she refused – and lit up. 'I'm right, aren't I? Of course, you won't earn a fraction of the sum Philippa was offering you at lunch today – yes, I'm afraid I did overhear that as well – but you won't care. You'll say you prefer it like that because at least it's your choice, because it has nothing to do with your father – yes yes, I heard that too – and you'll probably do OK for a while. And then you'll start to realise that temp work is a pile of shit. Nobody notices you, nobody cares if you're happy. You'll have none of the long-term benefits: no health plan, no pension, no prospects. You'll get dispirited. Your heart will go out of it. And one day you'll take a job at a law firm, simply because legal temps get paid more. And someone – the person you might have been – will be interviewing you, discussing how much to pay you, asking you to stay late to type in yet more amendments to a document you might have drafted yourself if you . . . Mel,' he said, anger draining from his voice. 'Mel, please. Don't let your father ruin your life as well as your mother's. Don't let him do that to you.'

'But what do you think I'm doing?' she said, upset. 'Don't you see? That's precisely why I'm leaving.'

'If the only reason you're quitting your job is because your father forced you into it, then – I'm sorry, darling – but it's the other way around. It really is. You think it's your decision, but it's not. How can it be when, in the same breath, you admit that it's only because of him that you're quitting?'

'It's not –'

'Forget about him. Forget about me. Ask yourself what you want.'

'I want it to be my choice.'

'Yes, Mel – and what is that? What is your choice?'

Mel said nothing.

'Your choice, as I see it, is simply to do whatever it is your father doesn't want. And, of course, that isn't really your choice at all. It's still all about him.'

'You think I should do what he wants?'

'I think you should find the strength to choose the right job – the one you already have – for yourself, your own reasons.'

'He'd think he'd won.'

'So what?' cried Ned. 'So what if he crows and gloats? If you go ahead and do this – if you quit – you'll be letting your life be dictated by the one person you're trying to escape. Now tell me – be honest – is that really what you want?'

'Of course it's not.'

Ned's expression didn't change. 'Are you sure about that?' he said.

'What?'

'Well, I'm just wondering if, underneath it all, you don't secretly long for it to be someone else's problem. It's perfectly natural. People do it all the time. I mean, if you think about it – all that responsibility, all that independence – not everyone can handle it. Isn't it easier to put the focus on someone else? Isn't it less stressful, directly or indirectly, to base decisions around them, let them run your life and let them take the blame when things go wrong? Isn't it easier sometimes not to grow up, not to be free, and let someone else take charge?'

'If I agreed with that,' said Mel, turning, walking away from him again, 'if I was really that weak, then – according to what you've just said – I'd start doing what you wanted me to do. I'd let you take charge, blame you when it all went wrong. Either way, it seems I'll be accused of letting someone else dictate to me.'

'Don't get clever with me,' said Edmund, following her.

'I'm not. I just –'

'You know what the strong decision is.'

Hailing a cab, Mel shook her head. 'The point is, Ned, it's *my* decision. Not Dad's, or yours. And if you were my friend, you'd support me.'

She didn't have the strength to go back to the office. It was almost the end of the day, and she couldn't face the light-hearted teasing she'd no doubt get from Philippa, or yet more attempts to persuade her to stay. But when she got home, no one was there. The evening stretched ahead, with only the television between her and thoughts of the future, and everything Ned had said.

36

Mel woke, cold, the following morning, bang on six. She had a shower, soaping herself in steamy water, using up the entire tank – not caring. She stood at the sink and brushed her teeth, looking at herself in the mirror. Her eyes had a flat light to them, as if she'd spent all night in tears. Then she dressed. Black skirt, black jacket, black tights, black shoes. Black coat, grey scarf . . . and she was out.

It was foggy that morning, heavy vapour that made her wonder for a moment if there was something wrong with her eyesight. Cars were moving slowly as she walked back over the canal towards the under-ground station. She was nearly there when the orange light of a vacant cab came through the mist towards her and, hailing it suddenly, Mel got in. She sat there as it swung back round the way it had come, and headed east towards the City.

Shocked as she'd been at bumping into him yesterday, and disturbing as it was to hear what he'd said about her job, Mel knew that Ned was right. For a small second, the sight of him at the top of the steps to the restaurant had made her wonder if perhaps he was rushing back to tell her something else. Perhaps she'd been wrong about Alice. Perhaps . . . but the truth of it was that he hadn't come to tell her anything like that. He'd come to help her save her job.

Unromantic and disappointing as that was, she could now, in the dispassionate air of morning, see the sense of it. He was right. She didn't have the luxury of being able to turn down her job. She didn't have the luxury of rejecting what her father had chosen for her. It simply wasn't worth it. She had to look after herself, stand on her own two feet, and be grateful for the opportunity.

She was going to be rich. She was going to have a high-status job, more money than time to spend it, and – at some point – an apartment as flash as Ned's. She'd be able to leave Nathan and Fenella's flat this weekend, move straight into a fully furnished place of her own. She'd be big news on the in-house magazine. There'd be photographs and congratulations and bottles of champagne. There'd be respect. In a week's time, her bank account would shoot into the black, into the black and way, way up . . . She'd have to instruct a stockbroker to invest that kind of money for her, and there'd be more coming in each month.

But there was no pleasure. She felt calmer than she'd done in months. She knew now that she could, when the time came, look after her mother properly. She could look after herself. From now on, nobody but Mel would be in charge of Mel's life. It was adult, responsible, strong – and cold.

As the taxi headed down Marylebone Road, the visibility worsened. Looking out, Mel realised she couldn't even see the pavement, or the faces of the people in the other cars. She'd hoped that the cab would remind her of the luxury, the comfort of a healthy income. She'd hoped it would feel more civilised to travel to work that way – to know that, every so often, she could. She'd wanted some reminder of the perks. But as the driver stretched a ringed hand round to close the partition between them – muting the voice on his radio – she simply felt shut in. Shut in, shut out, shut down and alone in the shiny black shell of the cab.

Philippa was absolutely delighted. There and then, she rang Mel's major clients, starting with Len Purves.

'Lenny!'

'Don't call me that.'

'Come on, Len. Cheer up. It'll soon be Christmas.'

'I'm Jewish.'

Mel and Philippa both cringed and then looked at one another like naughty children.

'And take me off that vile speakerphone. You know I can't bear it when you –'

'Len, I've got Mel with me.'

'Mel?'

Mel picked up the receiver. 'Len? Len, hi – yes. Just thought you'd want know that Philippa has worn me down, and persuaded me to stay ... I know. Incredible persistence on her part. It's a fantastic offer, so ... that's right,' she laughed. 'You are indeed talking to the youngest partner at WJO ... and, of course, I'll be there at the meeting tomorrow, Len. It'll be a pleasure.'

Later, she rang her mother, but she could tell from Clare's tone of voice – the cautious way she said, 'Oh, hello, darling' – that Greg was there as well. So Mel didn't tell them about the offer, or the lump-sum incentive. She didn't tell them that she was going to be made a partner. She simply said that she had changed her mind about her job.

'Darling, how wonderful! I'm so pleased! And your father will be absolutely . . . Greg? Greg, darling, it's Mel. She's decided she's going to stay! She's not leaving work after all.'

There was a crackle as the receiver found its way into Greg's large hand.

'Is this true?'

'Yes, Dad. It is. I guess I just –'

'You came to your senses,' he said for her. 'And you're coming up for Christmas? Good! Good! They'll have let your mother out by then and we'll find you a nice welcoming home present! Oh, it's good to have my girl back where she belongs. Well, love, here's your mother. Don't let her gas on too long, will you?'

Laura slept badly that first night at the studio.

David, who'd insisted on doing what he thought was the decent thing, lay on dry sofa cushions on the floor by the bed and listened to her getting up repeatedly throughout the night to go to the bathroom. At first he worried that she'd changed her mind. He worried that she was leaving, and lay there – body tense – listening for her step on the spiral stairs. But it never came, and soon she was back in bed. When he woke the following morning, Laura was still there sleeping and Edmund had yet to move into his own flat, had already left for work. And while

David was glad – it meant that he and Laura had the place to themselves – he was also conscious that the place was a mess.

They hadn't finished unloading the car at Cheyne Lane and a few of Laura's things – enough for her to survive – had come back with them to the studio. It could have been worse. But David was worried about the studio. He was worried about the inevitable contrasts with Merwick and Cheyne Lane, and set about doing what he could to make it a little less uncivilised. He rang a special cleaning service to deal with the upholstery and the damp wood. He rang Nathan for the name of a builder who could mend the hole in the kitchen floor and ceiling – those bits of hardboard were useless – and a respectable plumber.

And then, just for the hell of it, he rang Jake. David wasn't quite sure what he wanted from Jake. He didn't want that man anywhere near his plumbing system again and, realistically, there was little chance of getting any money back – not when the cheque was already cashed. But an apology would be good, and an explanation. Jake would probably put the phone down on him, but there was no way that cowboy was going to get away with it, not without an earful from David and a good strong threat of legal proceedings. David had heard the way Edmund and Mel spoke in situations like this. He knew the language, and was confident that he could scare Jake into making some sort of conciliatory gesture.

But Jake's telephone number was no longer working. A disembodied voice – mockingly calm – told him that the number he'd dialled had not been recognised, '. . . please check, and try again.' David checked, tried again, and was in the act of throwing the receiver to the floor when Laura appeared at the top of the stairs, in his dressing gown.

'Everything all right?' she said, smiling as she tied the cord.

His heart still beating wildly, David looked up – felt like rushing up the stairs and tumbling into bed with her there and then.

'You look beautiful,' he said simply. 'You look –'

'I can't get the shower to work properly. Is there another bathroom?'

'Oh, darling, I'm sorry but we're just going to have to wait for the plumber. He's coming this morning.'

Laura nodded. 'Yes, honey. But I still need to wash.'

'If I get you a flannel, do you think you could make do with the basin?'

David had hoped to get the plumbing fixed that day, and the rest – the minor building work and furnishings – done by the end of the week. But it was clear by the end of that day that the work would take much longer than that. What made matters worse was that he had a joint exhibition coming up. Fortunately, the relevant paintings had been at the framers' workshop in Putney at the time of the flood. None of them was damaged. But he needed to take them to Nathan's gallery that day, supervise the hanging tomorrow, and attend the private view on Thursday.

David was desperate to be with Laura, desperate to give her the time, attention, and reassurance he felt she needed. Desperate to show her just how much she meant to him. Instead, he was fully occupied with his work, and it was Laura who stayed in the studio and let the contractors in. She was the one who had to block her ears to the drilling and the dust, and open windows to let out the fumes of the specialist cleaners. She did all of this without complaining, but it was clear to David that she wasn't happy.

He couldn't even hold her at night. For all her flirting, and that marvellous kiss in the car that day, in amongst the birch twigs, Laura had cooled off. By going to bed early and shutting the door, by turning from him when he kissed her, it was clear she didn't want to sleep with David. And while David told himself it was only understandable – she'd had a very traumatic time, she wasn't ready, she needed the space – he noticed the reluctance, and felt the rejection. When Edmund finally moved to his flat in Notting Hill, David had no choice but to move into the spare room, hang in there, and hope.

Every evening, he made a point of taking her out to dinner. It was good, he thought, for her to leave the studio behind. It meant they could concentrate on each other. But something wasn't right. Laura always seemed too special, too smart, too beautiful for the kind of places he took her to. She didn't look right in the pizza restaurant, or the wine bar that had opened opposite – even in jeans. He'd try to get her to relax a bit by filling her glass, but it was always full. He tried telling her how wonderful she was, but she never said it back to him. Didn't even smile, or blush. She just looked uncomfortable. The only thing they could talk about with any conviction was Joss, and why it was good that she'd left him. But even that had started to sound hollow.

He took her to the private view on Thursday, and she wandered round Nathan's gallery as if she was at a different party altogether. David watched her talking to Fenella, but not really listening. He saw Fenella's expression: simultaneously fascinated, jealous, and irritated. Laura was sad – that was only natural – but he felt she should be talking about it, letting it out, not bottling it up. David resolved to take her away somewhere that weekend and to get her to talk about it. Maybe she had things to tell him that he wouldn't really want to hear, but anything was better than this.

First, however, he had to take her to the hospital for her scan. The appointment was set for Friday. Eleven o'clock. And it was raining hard as – windscreen wipers fighting – they found a place to park.

'I'll wait here,' said David.

Laura nodded, opened the door, and made a dash for the steps.

David sat in the driving seat with water streaming down the sides of the car. He couldn't see out. Turning on the radio, he pushed the seat back, shut his eyes and – news washing over him – thought about where he'd take Laura. There was that hotel in Shropshire, the one he and Mel had liked. Of course, it would be better to go somewhere fresh – it was a little crass, he knew, to blur the lines – but there wasn't time to search for somewhere new. And surely it was better to go to a place he knew was good than to take a risk. They could leave after lunch, avoid the worst of the traffic, and be there in time for dinner.

It was strange, he thought, how quickly he'd stopped thinking about money – how quickly it had become irrelevant. The weekend would cost him three hundred pounds. He'd sold a couple of paintings last night, but he still couldn't really afford it. There was the gallery's cut, and the framer's bill, and there would be the massive expense (only partially covered by the insurance) of the plumbing overhaul that the studio needed. Three hundred was a lot to spend on two nights in a hotel. When he and Mel had gone before, they'd ended up splitting the cost, and even then it felt extravagant. Now, it was a necessity. Keeping Laura happy was the most important thing. It didn't matter what that cost. And, bizarrely, he liked it that way, liked the fact that this woman meant everything to him.

He lay there, daydreaming, while gusts of rain swept by.

Even if he'd had his eyes open, he wouldn't have been able to see out. And even if he'd been able to see out, he probably wouldn't have recognised the large but huddled figure, under the umbrella, striding grimly through the rain towards the revolving doors.

But by midday – the time Laura was due out – the rain had eased. David heard the news beeps on the radio and opened his eyes. It was still grey and windy, with pools of water spread across the tarmac. Intermittent spits pecked at the surface, and David watched them as the minutes ticked by. At quarter past, the specks returned to drizzle and the hospital doors swung round. Laura was coming through, a Polaroid scan in her hand. David strained his eyes to see her expression. And as he watched, she stopped – the doors revolving on round behind her. She examined the picture once more, before turning. A man was following her out, and David saw that it was Joss – grey as the day – opening his umbrella. The black web stretched over them both as, together, they descended the steps.

David switched off the radio. He opened the door, got out, and stood with the drizzle in his face. When they reached him, Laura was in tears and Joss – strained and dignified – explained that she would be coming home.

'With you?'

'Yes.'

David looked at Laura, but her head was bent. He couldn't see her eyes at all. 'Laura,' he touched her arm, 'Laura.'

She raised her eyes.

'Is this what you want?'

Joss squeezed her other hand. 'I'll wait for you in the car,' he said, and left her with the umbrella. Laura waited until he was out of earshot and then – Polaroid photograph in one hand, umbrella in the other – she started to explain.

'I love him,' she said. 'I know he gets angry, he says things he shouldn't, and he's even been unfaithful – but now so have I. He's had Annabel. I've had you.'

'But you haven't, Laura! You haven't had me at all. It was just one kiss and –'

'Joss doesn't know that.'

David stared at her.

'We've promised each other that nothing like this will ever happen again, and now we . . .'

Rain was running down David's neck. He felt it on his cheeks, his nose, and soaking through his hair – fringe clinging to his forehead.

'. . . I'm so sorry,' she said, tears starting again.

'Laura – don't.'

'It should never have happened. I should never have encouraged you to –'

'Don't.'

'And now with this . . .'

David looked down at the Polaroid image in her fingers – the unborn child with the monstrous head. Joss's child. Choking, he turned his back.

'Goodbye,' he said.

Laura stood under the black umbrella. She didn't move. Just stood there, in the middle of the parking lot, as the car reversed back round. Then it set off through the pools of water, past her, and past the other cars – the Ferrari and the doctors' slots – and out, south, over a grey river.

Part Three

37

It wasn't going to be a white Christmas. It was too warm, too wet and windy, for that. Driving north, alongside lorries that threw up jets of water and thundered along with wakes of dirty spray, Mel was glad she wasn't in her old car – glad to be overtaking them for once, glad not to be buffeted around. She was glad of the bigger engine, the decent heating system, the warm calm power.

She thought of how close she'd been to losing all that – not so much the luxury, but the ability to survive, protect, and hold her own. And then she thought of Edmund. Part of her (the part that had been his friend) still wanted to ring and thank him – kiss and make up, rebuild the friendship. He'd told her things she didn't want to hear, he'd been hard on her, but he'd been right. He'd been a good friend to her, and she missed him. She missed the laughs and the banter, the real sense of equality. She missed being understood so well; missed the natural way he'd read her mood, pick up the signals, make the connection.

He was her friend. But friendship wasn't enough any more. And right now Mel knew she couldn't handle the particular pain of being in love (because that, she realised now, was absolutely what it was) in love with a friend – not when he was in love with someone else.

The holiday traffic was bad, and it was late when she arrived. The place was dark. Her parents had gone to bed. Mel took her suitcase from the car, and the other case of presents, and carried them inside, bolting the door behind her.

The kitchen was immaculate – a note had been left on the table, in her father's hand, welcoming her home. The tree was in its usual place by the stairs. Mel could smell it. Walking through, still loaded with her bags, she saw that the mass of tiny lights had been left on. She looked at the glow – the pale mystery – and, stopping for a second, caught something of the way she'd felt about Christmas as a child.

But it was like trying to remember a dream, and, just as quickly, the moment passed. The lights were that cheap multi-coloured string they'd always had. Mel remembered now her mother's terror at the thought of breaking them, the cautious way they'd drape the green wires in amongst the pine needles, tree after tree, year after year – 'Watch where you tread . . .'

And although she was only home for a few days this year (Nathan and Fenella's wedding meant she had to be back in London at the weekend) it would still be exactly the same. She'd go through the rituals – open her stocking, say the right things, and attend morning service. She'd overload the plate, wear the paper crown, drink the special brandy. She'd find her pile of presents under the tree – one from each of her parents, something from her aunts and a persistently generous godparent, and a couple of cards. Nothing changed.

Mel went into her room and switched on the light, dim, single. Her mother had turned back the bed, the curtains were closed. A vase of holly sat on the dressing table. She hung up the clothes that would crumple and turned to the bag of presents, presents she'd yet to wrap.

Scissors and Sellotape. Shiny rolls of paper – determined not to lie flat – and strips of ribbon. Ribbon that sprang into curls and coils with a brisk run of the scissor-blade. Mel had quite enjoyed Christmas shopping now that she felt rich. She'd got her father a book on gardening. It looked dull but Clare had told her it was what he wanted, so that was what he was getting. She'd also got him a wallet like Ned's – smart, discreet – from a flash shop in Bond Street.

In the same shop, she found her mother's presents. The first was a purse – like her father's wallet, only the female version and in brown, not black. Her mother liked brown. And a matching handbag with the same good-quality thin brown leather for its handle and corners, and lightweight canvas sides. Mel wrapped them up and put them beside her father's presents, to take with her when she went to their room the following morning.

And the third present she'd got her mother – also from that shop – was a small weekend suitcase. It, too, had a thin brown leather handle, thin leather corners and lightweight canvas sides. Inside, it had a detachable washbag, a shoe compartment, and room enough for a few well-chosen clothes. She hadn't needed to get such a smart one. Glamour wasn't exactly the point and, at the time she'd bought it, Mel wondered if she was being a little silly. But as she opened up the case that night – pulled out the scrunched-up paper that the shop had put in to pad it out, sniffed the reassuring smell of leather – she was glad that she had. Glad of anything that might sweeten the pill.

Reaching round for another plastic bag, she turned it upside down. A mass of small packages fell out all over the floor: chemist things – toothpaste, toothbrush, flannel, her mother's favourite cleanser and moisturiser, a hairbrush, shampoo, deodorant – as well as a mini-dryer, a slim address book, set of keys, and a small mobile telephone. Mel put the chemist things into the detachable washbag. She spent some time on the address book – filling it in with her own hand. Then she turned to the mobile telephone. She charged it up, entered relevant numbers, and tested it by ringing her own mobile. Everything worked. Then she put it, the address book, the dryer, and the keys – along with an envelope containing two hundred pounds in cash – into the shoe compartment and clipped it shut.

But she didn't wrap the suitcase – just put it under her bed.

Later the following day – after lunch, when Greg was watching the telly – Mel took her mother upstairs. She watched as Clare felt under the bed and pulled it out, watched as her mother – not understanding – undid the catch. The case fell open.

'That's a detachable washbag . . .'

'How clever!' Clare turned to her daughter. 'But,

darling, it must have cost an absolute fortune – and . . . you know, sweetheart, we don't really go away at weekends.'

'That compartment there's supposed to be for your shoes.'

'Beautiful . . .' Clare stroked the lid.

'Except it hasn't got shoes in it, Mum. Not at the moment.'

'Well, of course! Darling, you've already been much too generous. I'm not expect –'

'Open it.'

Clare opened the shoe compartment. She saw the mobile, the keys and the address book. She looked in the envelope and, eyes swimming, saw the cash.

'Of course, most of that can go into your purse and handbag,' said Mel quietly. 'But it's probably better you leave it there for the time being, so that everything's in one place. But remember you'll probably have to charge up the telephone before you use it – I'll show you how in a minute. Get some clothes in there as well – OK? And if I were you I'd leave the whole lot under here until . . . until you're ready. Now,' Mel picked up the mobile. 'Here's how you switch it on, see? Easy. No, that's the recharger. But look. If you do this . . . yes, that's right. You do it.' She put the mobile into her mother's hands. 'Press that one – twice – see, there's the number of that cab service in Wheaton. You just press 'call' and then you wait. Here's my number at work – see. And my mobile number. And this one's the number of my new flat . . . only renting until I find somewhere to buy, but it's lovely, Mum. Hardly needs a thing doing to it. I'm moving in next week – the address is in that little book there, see? And this is your own set of keys, if I can't leave work for some reason – or if it's very late at night.'

38

Mel hated wedding clothes, hated the hats and the high heels. They made her taller than ever. Getting out of the cab, she paid the driver and waited for her change, watching the other women struggle up the path that led towards the church. It was covered in ice. Mel followed, wishing she'd trusted her instincts and stuck to flat shoes, silk trousers and the velvet burgundy coat she loved. Instead, she was in a tight bottle-green suit with a very short skirt. The hat was black – unremarkable. She'd take it off the second she got to the gallery. Probably kick off the shoes as well. They were new, narrow, slippery. Looking where she stepped – she didn't want to trip – Mel went through the church gates, and joined the line of wedding guests that waited on the flagstones.

She wasn't looking forward to this wedding. David would be there, alone (she'd heard from Nathan about what had happened with Laura, and felt more sorry for him than anything – but it would still be strange). And the Enderbys, of course – Mel remembered Roger saying that he was Nathan's godfather. And if the Enderbys were there, then that would include Alice, wouldn't it? And Edmund?

Would Alice bring him? And how was Mel going to cope with that?

Not very well – that was the truth. If Nathan wasn't such a good friend, Mel would have found some reason not to be there at all. As it was, she'd slip away at the earliest possible moment.

Taking a service sheet from one of the ushers, Mel was about to walk on when the usher said her name. Mel turned. It was David with a heap of sheets in his hand.

'How are you?'

'OK,' she said, standing aside for the group behind to go past. 'I'm OK.'

'You look great.'

Mel couldn't say the same to him. David was thin – really thin. His hair needed cutting and his skin was a mess. He took her up the aisle to a pew near the front that was already half full. It wasn't until Mel got there that she recognised Alice – Alice without Edmund – sitting between her parents, under a dark cloche hat.

'You remember Alice, don't you?'

Alice beamed at Mel.

'And Alice's father, Roger.'

'I know Mel!' said Roger, shuffling up. 'Met her at your studio, David. Back in September, I think it was. How are you, my dear?'

David pressed her shoulder. 'See you later,' he said.

Mel felt the touch through the material of her suit – forgotten, intimate. She found it upsetting. It was intrusive, unwanted, uninvited. She wondered where Edmund was. Perhaps he was still a secret from

Alice's parents. Perhaps he hadn't been invited. Perhaps he was coming later. Who knew?

Opening the service sheet, she read the words without taking them in, until the bride arrived.

The outside door was banging on its latch. The wind blew in the rain. It was getting wet, now, in that corner of the kitchen, but Clare didn't move. Around her, supper was still cooking – water was about to bubble over, and there was a smell of roasting lamb. And the crystal bowl – the fruit salad, much too cold for this time of year ... you stupid bitch, when will you learn ... the redcurrants, syrup, and slices of peach, the sprays of glittering glass, were there like an exclamation all over the kitchen floor. She was at the table, top-and-tailing beans, but the knife was gone. She sat at the pile of green, with nothing in her hands.

Beyond the bangs and rattles – the wind in the stones of the house – he was there still, outside. She heard him pacing the yard. Heard the clunk of Bess's chain, the barks, and scattered footsteps – fading out towards the gate.

The room grew cold around her and she thought of the little suitcase, upstairs, under the bed.

Nathan and Fenella had learnt their vows. They said them, without prompting, to a church of hushed vanity. Feathers rustled. Weight shifted in polished leather and waistcoat buttons strained. Fingers toyed at service sheets, handbag clasps, wedding rings and cufflinks. Some pairs of eyes were closed in prayer, some in weary lack of interest. Others darted down the pews, flew in and out of the flower arrangements, the bridesmaids' dresses, the lace in the train on the cold stone floor. Who else is here? Am I wearing the right clothes? Not bad. Interesting. Wrong season, really . . . and why is everyone choosing that awful reading this year?

There were some that longed to be married, and some that wished they weren't. Children and babies – results of other services in other churches – attached themselves to tired young couples. While others, yet unburdened, looked on with troubled relief. One couple, just back from honeymoon, clasped together their smooth brown hands and remembered a few weeks back. And in the pew behind were other hands – older, fleshier, liver-spotted – that had seen forty years of it. Not how they'd expected it to be – different joys, different struggles – but they'd survived, they'd dragged each other through and on, and sometimes down as well. Had to hold on tight. Not easy. Not easy at all. But the clasp was strong. Hard times had forged the bond.

But for some people in that church, every word was mocking. Every sentiment false. They'd made those vows themselves. They'd believed in them utterly. But these people now knew that they could promise nothing. Nothing was certain. Statistics backed them up. And while they wished no one harm – good luck to Nathan and Fenella – they didn't see how any person could make those kind of promises. Nobody knew themselves that well – far less, somebody else.

. . . For better, for worse
  for richer, for poorer,

in sickness, and in health . . .

A little bit worse was bearable. But what if it got bad? Really bad. How much 'worse' could they go? How much could they actually stand?

Dear Greg, she wrote – the Biro jumping on the page where the wood of the kitchen table wasn't even.

When you get back, I won't be here. Don't get out a search party, or call the police or ring round the hospitals. I'm not lost or injured. I haven't been abducted. I'm leaving you. Don't come for me. I'll write again when I'm settled, and explain more of this in full – there isn't much time now – but really, I think you know already. . .

There were tyres on the gravel outside, headlights on the far wall. The cab stopped with the engine running. The windows were shut, but she could still hear the tone of Radio York.

She put a sweeping C at the bottom – like so many notes before: *In the garden – C, Walking Bess. Back around five. C, Gone into Leeds to pick up your photographs – C* – notes that let him know exactly what she was doing, and kept him in control.

But still it felt too ordinary. Feeling for her set of keys to the house, Clare took them from her bag and put them on the note – together with the rings he'd given her. Her fingers felt a little strange. Rubbing them, she looked round the kitchen, until she noticed the digits on her oven clock. Quickly, she picked up the suitcase and took it to the door. Again she looked at the room. Then she turned off the lights, shut the door behind her, and walked towards the cab.

Mel stood next to Roger Enderby. She closed her eyes and listened to Nathan's vows, to the voice that rose and fell around those beautiful words – reciting them like a spell – and thanked God it wasn't her up there.

At least, not her and David. She wondered again what she'd seen in him. He was attractive, intelligent, talented. But flimsy. There was something missing, a lack of warmth that would have made the struggles empty, the compromises futile. Sure, she'd admired his talent and his looks. But had she actually loved him?

The priest turned to Fenella. Listening to the smaller voice, Mel's thoughts moved on. Was it really love, when the brother's opinion was always the one that carried more weight? Was it love, when the brother was the one that made her laugh, made her angry, surprised her, made her think – and could even make her change her mind? She'd never really loved David and yet – yet she was that close to marrying him, that close to the hell of having Edmund forever present in her life, and forever beyond her grasp.

Mel closed her eyes and thanked God that it wasn't her in the dress of billowing white. She thanked God, too, for Laura. Because of Laura, she'd never marry David. Because of Laura, it wasn't too late.

After the service, Mel walked down the street to the gallery with Alice and her parents. They were ushered in to trays of drinks and canapés, and bright bursts of flowers. Handing Mel a glass of champagne from one of the trays, Roger asked how her job was going. What was she working on these days?

Mel was still giving him her answer when David joined their circle – and they all stopped and smiled.

'So what did you think?' he said.

'I thought it was awful,' said Alice. 'Hideous dress. Hideous hymns. Hideous, hideous music. When I get married, it'll be in the middle of summer. I won't be in white, and I definitely won't have some organ droning on in the background.'

'That's if anyone asks you to marry them, darling.'

Alice laughed. 'Oh, they will,' she said, glancing merrily at David. 'Bruno's already asked – twice. And I'm sure David would too, if only to be polite . . . and, anyway, why do I have to hang around waiting for them to ask me?'

'I doubt very much that you will,' said her father.

Mel couldn't help herself. She turned to Alice. 'But what about Edmund?'

'What about him?'

'Who's Edmund?' said Roger.

'Just an ex of mine,' said Alice airily. 'Nothing for you to –'

Mel couldn't believe what she was hearing. 'You're not going out with Ned?'

Alice lowered her voice. 'I think Bruno's really more the right age for me,' she said, with a grin.

'And he's here?'

Alice shook her head. 'Nathan said there wasn't enough room for him, but I think that's rubbish. I mean, if we were married he'd have to include Bruno – right? And just because –'

'No, Alice, I'm talking about Ned. Is Ned here?'

'Not sure,' said Alice, looking round the room. And then, 'Oh yes – yes, he is. See? Over there on the far side.'

Mel followed the line of Alice's arm, through a gap in the flow of guests. He was standing by himself in the line-up, looking bored, with an untouched glass of champagne in his hand.

'Won't be long, Alice. Just got to . . .'

Mel didn't finish her sentence. Leaving Alice, she went towards him – weaving through the guests. And as she got closer, Edmund turned.

He'd known she'd be here. He wasn't surprised. As Nathan's ex-flatmate and lifelong friend, she'd hardly miss his wedding. And Edmund had been waiting for this moment, knowing he'd hate it yet somehow unable to stay away. He had to see her, whatever the cost. He'd cope. He was prepared – at least, he thought he was – and for a brief second everything was OK.

He smiled.

She smiled.

And then his heart seemed to slip right up into his throat, blocking the flow of air. Everything shut down: his ears, his sense of touch, his ability to move. Only his eyes were working, and even they seemed to be controlled far more by what Mel was doing than by his own internal instructions. He stood, in a state of real paralysis, as she approached.

He'd guessed that she would be looking lovely. She always did when she tried (she looked lovely even when she didn't try, sometimes even lovelier, but it required more discernment on the part of the observer). Tonight, however, she'd have caught anybody's eye. And while part of him was glad – it meant she was in good spirits, and perhaps her decision to leave the law was right if it had this effect on her – it also put her out of reach. She was happy. She didn't need him. There were lots of men she could have, lots of decisions she could make entirely independently. And why not? Why shouldn't she? What business was it of his?

He thought of all the advice he'd tried to give her, and all the times she'd refused (probably wisely) to listen to a word of it. She was doing things in her own way: she'd quit her job, she'd blown him out over dinner. She had her own agenda, and it didn't include him. She wasn't interested. He should have understood this by now, should have given up months ago. And yet . . . yet here he was, coming back for more.

Edmund looked away. Suddenly, he couldn't bear the thought of talking to her – and he'd have left the party altogether if that momentary paralysis had not rooted him to the spot.

Mel moved round, into his field of vision. 'Hello, Ned,' she said.

Edmund nodded.

'Is everything all right?'

He nodded again. 'Yes – yes, fine. Nice wedding.'

'Yes it is,' she said, still with that smile. Edmund wasn't sure how much of this he could take. It was bad enough that she was glowing and fabulous, but it was really too much to have all that loveliness thrust upon him when they both knew she wasn't serious. Was she doing this to him deliberately? Didn't she know the damage she was causing?

'It's good to see you,' she went on, touching his arm. 'It really is.'

Edmund swallowed. 'It's good to see you too, Mel.'

'How's work?'

'Work? Oh, work's fine. You?'

'Yeah – yeah, it's fine for me too,' she said, taking a sip of champagne.

'Good. Good . . .'

Edmund took a sip as well and the pair of them stood, silently drinking. He waited for her next question, but none came. And, looking at her expression – brimful of merriment – he had the strange sensation that he'd missed something, that she was expecting more from him than this, that . . .

'What did you just say?'

'You heard.'

'You – you mean you're still there? You never left?'

Mel laughed. 'So much for knowing my own mind,' she said. 'So much for –'

Ned couldn't stop himself. Putting aside his glass, he wrapped his arms round her and closed his eyes. 'Oh, Mel,' he said, holding tight, both arms round her waist. 'Of course you know your own mind. Of course you do . . . but it's not easy – when it pulls in different directions.' Letting her go, he stood back. 'And – and are you happy?'

Mel hesitated.

'Ladies and gentlemen!' said a man in livery. 'Pray silence for the father of the bride . . .'

'Well?'

'I'll tell you later,' she said, as the room fell quiet and Fenella's father touched the microphone with a shaking hand.

The cab took Clare to York railway station. She sat in the back with her bags, listening to the radio programme, while they bumped over the lanes and down to the motorway. She didn't look out. Instead, she bent her head and stared at the hands in her lap, the crossing fingers – ringless, unfamiliar – and waited for tears that wouldn't come. Perhaps she was just too stunned, and perhaps it was better that way. Better not to attract attention, better to keep it in.

It was busy at the station – busy with passengers returning to London, back to work, at the end of the holiday season. Clare queued at the ticket office with shouts and announcements echoing around her. She bought herself a ticket, and a magazine from the newspaper stand, and waited at the platform, still and quiet, while others rushed around her.

The train was on time. She saw her reflection in its windows as it slowed down, saw a middle-aged woman, hair in a tidy cut, face expressionless, in dark flashes that broke intermittently with the joins in the carriages. The train stopped, and beyond her reflection – inside the glass – were other faces, other travellers: reading, chatting, sleeping. The doors opened automatically, and Clare got on. It was full, and she had no reservation. Walking down the aisles, she searched for empty seats, but there were none. So she stood in the gangway with her bags until they got to Doncaster and somebody got out.

Mel couldn't listen to the speeches, and she couldn't look at Ned. She felt shy. Suddenly there were no obstacles. There was nothing to keep him from kissing her, except that old man at the microphone, praising his plum-haired daughter.

And after Fenella's father came Nathan.

And then it was Nathan's best man.

And after that came dinner.

'Well?' said Edmund, as they walked to the tables, laid up and sparkling with wedding silver.

Mel smiled at him. 'Well, what?'

'Are you happy?'

Mel looked away. Was she happy? She felt the balance – tipping in his hands.

'Why didn't you come that night?' he said.

They reached the table. Mel saw her name written in calligraphy on stiff card, in front of a place setting between two men with unfamiliar names, and picked it up.

'I thought you were with Alice.'

'Alice?'

'She was there,' Mel went on, folding the card, and folding it again. 'There – outside your flat. I saw her in your arms.'

Edmund closed his eyes. 'Oh God . . . Oh God, Mel – I'm not . . . There's nothing – we're only . . .'

'Yes, I know,' she said. She was smiling, bending the card in her fingers. 'I know that now. Alice just told me.'

His eyes opened. He saw her expression. He saw her smiling at the card, and, snatching it from her fingers, threw it aside. 'Let's get out of here.'

Sitting down at last, with the train rattling on its tracks – faster now, hurrying south – Clare took out the telephone that Mel had given her. She rang Mel's mobile and got the voicemail. She rang Mel's new home number, but, again, it was just an answerphone. Nor did the office number work. From a practical point of view, it didn't matter. She had the keys and the address. She had money. She'd be fine.

Leaving a brief message on Mel's mobile, just saying what time she'd arrive, Clare put the telephone back in her bag and pulled out the magazine she'd bought. On the cover was a photograph of a beautiful pregnant woman.

Laura Savil talks exclusively – for the first time – about life with millionaire husband, Joss . . . sets the record straight about the rumours of a split, and tells us about the baby they hope will make their perfect marriage complete . . .

They had to work against the flow of the other guests, moving in the opposite direction.

'Excuse me – I'm so sorry – thanks – thanks . . .'

With Mel behind him, her hand in his, Ned pushed on through the gallery and out to the privacy of the street. Cool and dark and quiet. With light from the gallery windows curving in their eyes, and the sounds of the party far behind, they closed on in. Lip to lip, nose to nose, eye to eye – into a kiss so natural, so full of possibilities, it might have been her very first.

Drunk on each other, laughing, running, they went in search of a cab. Down the back street, on to the back seat –

'Where to?' said the driver.

Ned looked the question on to Mel, who leant

515

forward with her new address and the cab set off.

They were both still dressed when they arrived. Both dressed – but full of smiling disarray, fired with the same desire, and that glorious mix of expectation and relief. Each with the other in mind. Mel found the key, opened the door, and led him up – stopping on the landing for more – and then on up to her soft new flat.

They went straight to her room and fell on the bed – laughing, kissing, undressing – rolling along, gathering their own chaotic momentum, tumbling now, over and over – buttons and clips, silk and skin, sheets and murmurings, limb on limb. Closing on up: the flash of her eye, the curve of his lip, the rim of her nose, the line of his hip . . . and with the visual flashes came flashes from her memory. Ned leaning round with the menu in his hands – pointing out the steak – at that little brasserie; his fingers fitting hers around the gun; his eyes across the dining-room table; his voice beyond the bathroom door the time he'd come for her at Nathan's – . . . *Is she there?*

Afterwards, caught in the crook of his arm Mel felt physically retuned. After years of wrenching, every muscle was back in place. There was no strain. It was as if she was floating, and they lay there side by side: their temperatures, heartbeats, breathing – all identical.

And then, just as she was drifting into sleep, Ned sat up.

'What was that?'

Mel opened her eyes. 'Hm?'

'That noise,' he said, and from downstairs came the small metallic rattle of keys as the flat door opened.

516

They heard it shut, and the stairs creaking, and the click of a light switch.

'Oh my God,' said Mel, throwing back the covers. 'Oh my –'

'What? What is it?'

'It's Mum!'

'*What*?'

Laughing at his expression in the half-light from the passage, she got out of bed, pulled on a dressing gown and kissed him. 'Just stay there. I won't be long – I promise.'

Clare was really too shattered to say much. She stood in the doorway to the sitting room with tears in her eyes, and took in the sight of Mel, a new Mel – beautiful, messy, glowing.

'What happened?' said Mel.

'I've left him.'

'Oh, Mum . . .'

Clare stood there, the smart case in her hands, tears streaming down her cheeks while Mel held her.

'It's OK. You're OK . . .'

She took Clare into the sitting room and sat with her on the sofa, holding her hand and listening as Clare told her what had happened – what Greg had done with the crystal bowl, and the way he'd grabbed the knife from her hands. Clare was shaking.

'I really thought he was going to –'

'Don't think about it, Mum,' said Mel, putting a glass of whisky into her hands. 'Not tonight.'

Clare took a sip. 'Silly of me to have it there, really. To be chopping away like that while he . . .' She took another sip. 'But he's never used a knife, or anything like that before, and . . . and suddenly it was in his hands and I was just sitting there. He could have –'

'But he didn't, Mum.' Mel squeezed her hand. 'And now he never will.'

Later, while Clare was in the bath, she made up the bed in the spare room – hunting for the new set of sheets she'd bought, unwrapping them, finding the softer pillowcases, and a couple of books for her mother to read if she couldn't sleep.

'Thank you, darling,' said Clare, coming in smelling of Badedas, wrapped in the towelling dressing gown that Mel had hung on the back of the bathroom door, the smart new washbag in her hands. Already, she was looking better – warm, washed, cared for.

Mel smiled. 'And what about something to eat?' she said. 'I've got eggs in the fridge, and some bread – and I'm sure there's some bacon there as well if you –'

Clare shook her head. 'I'm fine.'

'You sure?'

'Really. If I do get hungry I can always help myself.'

'But it's no trouble, Mum. I –'

'Go back to bed, darling, to whoever it is in there who's making you so happy – and I'll see you both in the morning.'

Mel stared at her mother. And, laughing quietly, Clare pointed to a large polished shoe in the passage, and another one that had somehow skidded down towards the bathroom door, along with a mustard silk tie.

'I take it those aren't yours,' she said.

'Oh God.' Mel put her hand over her mouth and

looked, aghast, at Clare – who, still laughing, shooed her out of the room.

'Off you go!'

'All right! All right!'

Not wanting to wake him, Mel crept back into her room but Ned was still awake, lying in bed with his eyes open, smiling at her.

'We're busted,' she said, taking off the dressing gown and getting in.

'I heard.'

Laughing, Edmund pulled the bedding round over them both. It was warm in there with him. Mel closed her eyes as he held her.

Down the corridor, Clare was still pottering around – unpacking, settling, arranging her things, and then she switched off the light. Edmund and Mel lay in absolute darkness.

'So she's left him?'

Mel nodded. 'I know,' she said, in a hushed voice. 'I can't really believe it. No more nightmare, no more pretending, no more fear. She's really going to be OK.'

Edmund brushed her hair away from her face and kissed her. 'Yes,' he whispered. 'Yes – and so are we.'

David waited as long as he could. He wanted to speak to Nathan – wanted to wish him well – but Nathan was busy and, at eleven, David decided to leave. Unnoticed, he walked through the empty gallery, collected his coat from the rails by the door, and went out into the street. There were lots of cabs, but David wasn't ready for the empty studio. Not yet. It had stopped raining and he set off up the hill, by foot, dressed in wedding tails. He passed pubs that were closing, people leaving restaurants and bars, hailing cabs, and getting into cars. Crossing the road, he walked on, lost in his thoughts.

At the top, he stopped and waited at the lights. Further up the road, a group of people were standing by a cab. Some of them were getting in. They were drunk and talking loudly.

'No, you stay there,' said a man's voice. 'You stay there – and . . .'

'Come on,' said someone else from inside the cab. 'Come on, Laura. Come with us . . .'

David couldn't help himself. He turned, eyes sharp, and caught a glimpse of leg, ankle, shoe – nothing he recognised, nothing special – and then the cab door closed.

He stood there at the corner with the pedestrian lights going green – the beeping loud in his ears – watching the cab U-turn and head back up the street.